The Quest for Land & Fortune

ALSO BY ALFRED ALLAN SCHMID

Travels with Alice

Travels with Kay

Travels

Romantics Abroad

La Bomboa

The Passionate Pilgrim

Roots and Branches

Lovely, Just Lovely

Souvenirs

Schmid Farm

Memory and Desire

See America First

The Seekers

A Pilgrim's Passions

Collected Poems

Catching Up and Moving On

The Tao of Travel

The Quest for Land & Fortune

Alfred Allan Schmid

Chapbook Press

Grand Rapids MI

©2013

Chapbook Press

Chapbook Press
Schuler Books
2660 28th Street SE
Grand Rapids, MI 49512
(616) 942-7330
www.schulerbooks.com

Copyright © 2013 by Alfred Allan Schmid
All rights reserved
Printed in the United States of America
10 9 8 7 6 5 4 3 2 1

This book is printed on acid-free paper, and its binding materials have been chosen for strength and durability.

ISBN 13: 9781936243587
ISBN 10: 193624358X

Library of Congress Control Number: 2013943434

Schmid, Alfred Allan

The Quest for Land and Fortune
1. Historical novel 2. Family history 3. Westward migration 4. Narrative non-fiction.   I. Title.

Set in New Times Roman

To my family and all who came before

CONTENTS

Prologue, i

Family Time Line, iv

The Virginians, 1

On To Kentucky, 20

The Minuteman, 40

On To Michigan, 58

Missionary to the Indians—Michigan, 71

Missionary to the Indians—Kansas, 82

A Mission of His Own, 99

Civil War Soldiers—The Cavalryman, 125

Civil War Soldiers—The Surgeon, 140

Civil War Soldiers—The Confederates, 158

The Wagon Master, 164

The Telegraph King and the Deacon, 196

The Irish Immigrant, 225

The Banker and the Gilded Age, 252

Strong Women, 280

Epilogue, 314

Acknowledgments

Thanks to my fellow participants in the 2009 Nebraska Summer Writers' Conference led by Jonis Agee; and to Patricia Palmer-Mueller, John Mark Lambertson, Gretchen Carroll, Sally Bonnen, Jerry Pillow, Jo Ellen Keith, Doris Keith, Craig Jones, Dorothy Brooks, and Teri Allen Mulliken. Special thanks to my editor, Emily Kilby.

Archival materials sources include Atchison City Library, Atchison County Historical Society, Atchison County Probate Records, Pony Express Museum, St. Joseph; Kansas City Archival Museum, National Trails Museum, Independence; Kansas City Public Library; State of Michigan Library; Journals of Jotham Meeker, courtesy of the Kansas State Historical Society.

Among the published works providing background: David McCullough, *1776*; David Fischer, *Washington's Crossing*; Isaac McCoy, *History of the Baptist Indian Missions*; Douglas McMurtrie and Robert Allen, *Jotham Meeker, Pioneer Printer of Kansas*; Allan Eckert, *The Frontiersman*; Chris Harley, *Stoneman's Raid, 1865*; James Reid, *The Telegraph in America*; *Maysville (KY) Eagle*; Kenneth Lewis, *West To Far Michigan*; Denis Caraher, *The End of Forever, The Story of Mekinges and William Connor*; *Stafford County, Virginia*; *The Atchison Globe*; Sheffield Ingalls, *History of Atchison County*; William Cutler, *History of the State of Kansas*; William Connelley, *A Standard History of Kansas and Kansans*; *History of Atchison County, Kansas*; J. Morton & Watkins, *History of Nebraska*; Alfred Andreas, *History of Nebraska*; Richard Bonner, *History of Lenawee County, Michigan*; *Mollie: The Journal of Mollie Dorsey Sanford*; William Lass, *From the Missouri to the Great Salt Lake*; Raymond and Mary Settle, *War Drums and Wagon Wheels*; Russell Headley, *History of Orange County, New York*; E.M. Ruttenber & L.H. Clark, *History of Orange County, New York*; George Anderson, *The Widening Stream*; Garrett Clift, *History of Maysville, Kentucky*;
The resource provided by Wikipedia is gratefully acknowledged.

   A previous edition of this work was published as an e-book by Amazon entitled *The Seekers*.

Prologue

The Quest for Land and Fortune, a work of narrative nonfiction, is a saga of five generations stretching from soldiers of the American Revolutionary War to a banker of the Gilded Age. The main characters will become the common ancestors of a babe born in Atchison, Kansas, in the 1930s. The main characters are actual people and their actions are real and can be documented. Their thoughts and dialogue are fictional, the author was not there.

Family Time Line

End of Rev. War	**End of Civil War**	**Families Joined**
1782	1865	1926

1745-<u>Joseph Todd</u> and Catherine Knapp
  1782 -Samuel Todd and Hannah Whitney
    1805- <u>Ransom Todd</u> and Sally Ann Wade
      1811- <u>Jeptha Wade</u> (Sally Ann's brother)
        1845-<u>N. D. Todd</u> and Hulda Aldrich
          1874-Luther Anson Todd--------:
                1903-N. W. Todd---:

    1820-<u>John Miller</u> and Ruthanna Bennett
        1855-Lillie Miller-------------:
    1821 <u>William Hetherington</u> and Annie Strimphler
      1850-<u>Web Hetherington</u>----:
        1877-Ruthanna Hetherington--:

    1829-<u>J. P. Brown</u> and Sarah Wagner
        1879-Alice Brown----------------:
            1903-Florence Byram-----:
  1804-<u>Jotham Meeker</u> and Eleanor Richardson
      1839- Emeline Meeker-------------- :
        1878-Warren Peter Byram------:
    1824-<u>Peter Byram</u>----------------------:
  1786-Augustus Byram and Sally Toulson
1760-<u>Peter Byram</u> and 1758 Lucy Phillips

Underlined names are major characters in separate chapters with their birth years.

The Virginians

Like many Virginians, Peter Byram was stirred by the Declaration of Independence and the call to arms. Patrick Henry's cry, "Give me liberty or give me death," rang in his ears, and he could not ignore it. Mt. Vernon was north of the Byram plantation in Stafford County, and Washington had just been named commander in chief of the revolutionary forces. Come Sunday, many of the planter families assembled in Overwharton Parish Church had much to pray for as they sat in their pews. Support for the war was far from unanimous amongst the worshippers, and the minister was a bit ambivalent as he tried to keep his parishioners focused on the Lord, not on their differences. Peter's mind wandered as the sermon droned on, and his eyes retraced the high square pews, the rails and columns of the gallery at the west end of the sanctuary, the three-decker pulpit near the southeast reentrant angle of the cross and the chancel occupying the eastern arm of the cruciform church. The "Peace On Earth, Good Will To Man" carved above the altar struck Peter as a bit ironical in the midst of all the war talk. He could barely make out the marble tablet embedded in the wall that dedicated the building "To the Glory of God and the Memory of the Race of House of Moncure, 1757." In the distance Peter could hear horses on the highroad that linked the towns of Alexandria and Fredericksburg. The parish church, called Aquia after the nearby creek, stood north of Falmouth, so named for its location at the falls of the Rappahannock River.

The Byram's big house on Austin's Run buzzed with talk of the rebellion after news came of the battles of Bunker Hill and Concord in the north. Like many sixteen-year-old males, Peter's warrior blood surged within him. He wanted to enlist, but his mother, Sarah, was not enthusiastic. Peter's younger brother William and his second cousin had already sought out Captain Bailey Washington and enlisted in the Virginia Militia. "Life is good; why go and get shot?" Sarah asked her son in her usual blunt manner. "With your brother gone, we'll be shorthanded." She had seen this coming when she read in the *Virginia Gazette* about the Boston Tea Party two years before. Sarah was somewhat reassured when Peter said that William Washington, a cousin of George and a Byram family friend, was forming a company in Westmoreland.

Aquia Creek and Austin's Run in Stafford County, Virginia

Peter enlisted on February 26, 1776, for two years in Virginia's 3rd Regiment, 6th Company. A week later the regiment was taken over by Congress. After a summer of training, they marched north to join the Continental Army. At first, the war news had been encouraging. Washington's success in Boston had forced the British to withdraw, and he marched for New York where he expected the Redcoats to land. There, the rebel army suffered a humbling defeat, and Washington scurried west across New Jersey heading for the west bank of the Delaware River. The Virginians joined him there in another bitter winter. The Virginians hated the cold and found the fellows from New England uncouth and argumentative. Peter was not at all enthused that his first action was running from the enemy. Maybe Washington was not the general he was reputed to be. In any case, Washington was glad to receive any reinforcements, however small. Two thousand of his troops had walked away early in December when their enlistments were up. More just deserted. Who could blame them when so many were without shoes and warm clothing for winter? Looking at them, Peter was mighty glad that he had relatively new shoes. Small pleasure, he thought. I never imagined I could be so excited about shoes.

Sleet stung the faces of the forty young men huddled together like apples in a basket as their boat bumped and thumped into floating ice on the

Delaware River. Each man carried sixty rounds of ammunition and enough food for three days. The company had drilled at two o'clock in the afternoon, then marched down to the riverbank to await darkness and their turn to cross. The plan was to have the crossing completed by midnight, but by the time they got in the flat bottomed, high-sided Durham boats, the intended hour had passed. Progress was slow as the storm worsened and the current grew stronger, making it difficult for the boatmen with their oars and poles. By the time all twenty-four hundred troops were on the New Jersey shore, the morning light ruined any chance of darkness hiding their ten-mile approach to Trenton where fifteen-hundred Hessian mercenaries were dug in—and warm. On the shore, an imposing figure in a long cloak urged them on. Sixteen-year-old private Peter Byram pulled his cocked hat firmly down on his head. It fit poorly over the scarf that his mother had made. He had tied it around his head to cover his ears. He remarked to his friend, Jeremiah, "Mother told me there would be days like this, but not so many." When he signed up for the 3rd Virginia back in February, he had not envisioned they would still be fighting into another winter. It was Christmas Day, and he was a long way from home and a bit scared.

The password for the day was "Victory or Death." Sure, Peter thought to himself, for some it may be victory *and* death. He tried to put it out of his mind. Privates just did what they were told. Peter was with the men in the center as they approached the little town of Trenton from the north. He was aware that the troops had been divided and others were probably going to attack from the east and west. He could see Knox's artillery set up at the head of King Street. As the Hessians poured into the street, they were met with deadly fire and quickly scattered into the side streets. Peter's musket and powder were completely drenched from the cold rain and of little use. The order came to fix bayonets, and savage skirmishing surrounding the one hundred houses of the town commenced. Though nearly blinded by gunpowder smoke and swirling snow, Peter could see that the Hessians had rolled out a field gun into the middle of King Street. Peter's company commander, Captain William Washington, did not hesitate, and with fourteen of Peter's comrades they attacked the men at the cannon and captured it. Quickly, the cannon was turned around, ready to fire back at the enemy. "William, your hand is bleeding," shouted Peter. "It's nothing," Washington replied through gritted teeth. "Just tie my handkerchief around my hand. I can't get it out of my pocket." Miraculously, not one of the fourteen was killed.

In just forty-five minutes, the surrounded Hessians had surrendered. Later, Peter would learn that only four Americans had been killed in the battle compared to twenty-one Hessians. Nine hundred of the German mercenaries were captured along with considerable arms and powder that had been in short supply in the Continental Army. That evening, as General Washington effusively praised his troops, Peter was proud to be a part of the victory. It erased his feelings of depression that had set in after the army had suffered ignominious defeats at New York City and had fled with their tails between their legs across New Jersey to Pennsylvania. He knew that the Continental Congress, fearing for their lives, had left nearby Philadelphia.

Later, Peter admitted to Lieutenant James Monroe that he had been mightily scared, then relieved that none of his comrades had been killed. That night, Peter dreamt of avenging angels with swords drenched in blood riding black horses across the grey sky. One swooped down and plunged a sword into Peter's gut. He awoke in a cold sweat and could not get back to sleep.

Peter had little time to reflect as the troops set out for Princeton. Washington was beginning to realize that his forces could not prevail against a main body of British soldiers and that his best strategy was to keep moving and fight a hit-and-run campaign. A British force under General Cornwallis, whose rear guard was in Princeton, entered Trenton only to discover that Washington had departed. Scouts from both armies met by chance, and a hot battle commenced in an open farm field and orchard of Clarke farm just outside of the village of Princeton. The Brits were caught off guard to find so many Americans out so early in the bitter cold. Peter hated to be out in the open with bullets and cannonballs flying everywhere. The dead and bleeding were all around him. He was next to a company led by regimental commander General Hugh Mercer and watched Mercer fall when his horse was hit during a British bayonet charge. It looked as if Mercer was being bayoneted and Peter witnessed a Colonel fall from a gunshot through the head as he tried to rally the brigade. The Virginians and the Pennsylvania militia, heartened by the sight of General Washington on horseback urging them on, refused to yield. The battle lasted only fifteen minutes, but it was more than enough for Peter. Later he learned that the two hundred British garrisoned in Nassau Hall on the campus had surrendered when a few rounds of cannon were fired into the building. All told, twenty-three Americans died. Many more of the British army lost their lives, and three hundred were taken prisoner.

Back in Virginia, William Byram was reading the January 31, 1777, issue of the *Virginia Gazette*. "Sarah, the paper describes Washington's successes at Trenton and Princeton. I think our Peter is with his army."

"It's so frustrating that we have no specific news of Peter, nor of son William for that matter," she replied. "Both could be dead, and we wouldn't know it."

"There is a reference to the First Virginia Regiment, but nothing on the Third."

"Let me see the paper." Sarah read on and found the description of the death of General Mercer at Princeton. "I am angered by stories of innocent women being ravished by British troops. They are evil men. May they rot in hell."

"Such strong language for a lady."

"Sorry; it just popped out."

Washington apparently decided to let well enough alone and retreated to the nearby village of Morristown where his army spent the remainder of a miserable winter. The Brits thought likewise and stayed in New York City, much to Peter's relief. But Washington's army was dwindling. On March 6, Washington wrote, "When the time of General Lincoln's militia expires, I shall be left with the remains of five Virginia Regiments, not amounting to more than as many hundred men, and parts of two or three Continental Battalions."

Peter's regiment suffered heavy casualties in 1777. In the spring, Colonel Thomas Marshall reorganized the depleted 3rd. Following Washington's directions, he ordered the recruiting officer "to enlist only able-bodied men under the age of sixty and free from suspicious principles." Peter wondered what was meant by suspicious principles. Was it spies with Tory sympathies or bad morals or both? How was the recruiter to know anyway? Each new recruit enlisting for three years was given twenty dollars, a uniform and promise of one hundred acres of land. Knowing what he knew now, Peter determined it would take more than that to entice him to enlist. Prussian General von Stueben had taught the Americans to drill, but many of the Virginia riflemen from the hills did not take to the instructions readily. They were great marksmen, but discipline was not their long suit.

In August, General Howe left New York by sea and landed at Elk River in Maryland at the top of Chesapeake Bay to begin his march toward Philadelphia. Washington marched his troops through Philadelphia to meet him at Brandywine Creek. The British found a hole in the American line, but the Americans quickly converged on them. Hand-to-hand fighting lasted for hours and Washington was forced to withdraw and abandon Philadelphia. He had committed a serious error in leaving his right flank wide open, but Howe, lacking the killer instinct, waited too long to take advantage of it and thereby missed his chance to destroy Washington. Captains Chilton and Lee of the 3rd Regiment were killed during the Battle of Brandywine, but Peter was still alive, though badly shaken.

Howe's march on Philadelphia turned out to be a costly blunder. British General John Burgoyne had led a seven thousand man army from Canada down the Hudson to Saratoga expecting Howe to join him where a victory there would cut off New England from the other colonies. When Howe got carried away with the symbolism of capturing the Patriot's capital, Burgoyne's force was outnumbered and had to surrender on October, 1777. Many would call it the turning point of the war.

In December 1777, Washington established his winter camp at Valley Forge. Peter and twelve of his mates built a rude log hut for their occupancy. Just before Christmas, Washington wrote, "I am now convinced beyond a doubt, that, unless some great and capital change suddenly takes place in the line [the commissary's department], this army must inevitably be reduced to one or other of these three things; starve, dissolve, or disperse in order to obtain subsistence in the best manner they can." On Christmas day it snowed four inches. Peter remarked to one of his comrades, "We are out of the wind here in our hut, but my teeth are chattering, and we are all hungry, going three days without provisions." Washington was well aware of their plight and noted that there has been little less than a famine in the camp.

"I don't think I can take much more of this. It is especially hard knowing the Brits are warm in Philadelphia. I am considering desertion," said Private Peyton.

"I couldn't do that," Peter said as if trying hard to convince himself.

February, 1778, brought the end of Peter's two-year enlistment. He didn't think his luck could hold much longer as so many others were dying around him. Captain William Washington had been promoted, with Captain John Mercer assuming command. Peter missed his old captain, as he was someone Peter could confide in. In his last camp, Peter came across William's new unit and the former commander urged him to re-enlist with his own 4th Continental Light Dragoons. "I know you like to ride," Washington reminded him, "and I can offer you a promotion and transfer to my new company."

"I'm tempted," Peter replied. "I'm still devoted to sending the Brits packing."

"Then what are you waiting for? Come to my tent, and my adjutant will sign you up."

Peter's brow furrowed as he considered the possibility, but in the end he knew it was time to go home. "Yes, I like to ride, but riding straight into cannon fire is something else again. How much longer can I hope the leaden balls will pass me by?" he asked. "I've been away two years and my parents need me."

"Sorry to hear it; you have the makings of a fine soldier," Washington offered. "And you know the cause is worth the risk."

The young patriot knew this was true, but the arguing was over. "I'm going home," Peter declared.

Sarah cried with joy as Peter unexpectedly came through the door. "I have been praying every day for your safe return."

Peter hugged her with all his might. "I've survived and come back to you. And, I even have all my toes. The scarf you made for me was a lifesaver that first winter."

With both of their sons gone, the elder Byrams had struggled to manage the land that previous generations had built with their blood and sweat. The tobacco economy had gone to hell as the British had blocked exports, and now the quartering of prisoners from Burgoyne's troops after their defeat at Saratoga had depleted local food supplies. The surrender treaty provided that the British troops be returned to Europe after promising not to fight again, but the Americans broke the treaty, choosing to keep the captured British in Virginia instead. This advantageous military strategy put a drain on the planters who had to feed the troops interned in their area

Peter's return home seemed to engender a time of stocktaking in the Byram household. Peter's father began a kind of family soliloquy as if to lay the groundwork for the future. He recounted how Peter's grandfather, also named Peter, had received one hundred forty-eight acres of land on Austin's Run in 1726 when it was proven that the quit rent fees had been paid to the Proprietors and Surveyors of the Northern Neck of Virginia. Grandfather Peter had also purchased ninety-nine acres from his brother Cudbath, with recordation in the county deed book as follows:

"This indenture made the third day of May in the year of our Lord God one thousand seven hundred and twenty seven by and between Cudbath Byram of the County of Stafford of the one part and Peter Byram of the said County of the other part. Witnesseth that the said Cudbath Byram, for diverse good, causes him thereunto moveing but more especially for and in Consideration of the sume of two thousand five hundred Pounds of good tobacco."

The record indicated that Cudbath's wife, Sarah, had relinquished her dower rights to the property. By law, wives were given an interest in their husband's land and this had to be removed before it could be sold.

The area of Stafford county located between Chopawamsic Creek and the Rappahannock River running into the Potomac had been explored by Captain John Smith of Jamestown who discovered iron deposits near Accakeek Run. The Northern Neck of over five million acres was granted by King Charles to various English nobility in 1649, but the holdings were consolidated by Lord Culpeper and on down to his heir, Lord Thomas Fairfax. Fairfax collected the so-called quit rents paid by the Byrams and the other planters in the area. The Northern Neck Proprietary was separate from the colony at Jamestown. Fairfax, the sixth Lord and Baron of Cameron, was a friend and patron of George Washington, employing the teenage Washington as a surveyor of his lands lying west of the Blue Ridge. Later, George had escaped from the austerity of his mother's home at Ferry Farm in Stafford County to the pleasant plantation life of his half-brother's manor on the Potomac. While he was staying with Lawrence at Mount Vernon, George was a frequent visitor at Belvoir, the beautiful estate of William Fairfax some four miles distant. He soon became an intimate of the family and formed in particular a warm friendship with Colonel Fairfax's son, George William.

During the golden age of tobacco growing in Virginia when demand for the crop in England had created high prices, Peter's grandfather had prospered. Tobacco was currency in Virginia and the court established inspectors and a warehouse to maintain its quality. The warehouse at Aquia Landing was like a bank, and receipts for tobacco stored there served as payment for large purchases, including land. Every square foot was planted to tobacco, but oversupply soon threatened the market. Laws enacted in 1657 forbade the planting of tobacco after July 10th. Tobacco grew slowly and if planted after that date, it would be of inferior quality. Earlier, the House of Burgesses limited each person to tending only six thousand plants to maintain the quality that the export market demanded. Without the gift of tobacco from the Indians, early Virginia would have been a different place entirely.

Before the war, Peter had been an innocent, fun-loving young man who gave no thought to the future or the past. After returning home, he matured quickly and became interested in his family and community for the first time. Peter remembered family stories of his grandfather who had acquired another 450 acres on Pignut Ridge in 1730. He perused the records of Overwharton Parish and learned that his grandfather Peter was listed as a slave owner in 1742. Officials estimated that there were one hundred twenty thousand slaves in Virginia colony by 1756. Slaves were valuable property, and their owners were taxed accordingly. He learned that church and state were the same thing, and the parish vestrymen were also the local government with taxing power, not only for the support of the church but also for local government services, including care of the poor. Peter was not sure when his ancestors first came to Virginia, but he knew there was a Thomas Byram in the Overwharton records purchasing land on Austin's Run in 1708, land where Peter now lived.

  The passion of a young man for patriotism now competed with passion of a different kind. Peter, now eighteen, was looking for a wife. It was not easy to meet young women of quality when the plantations were physically distant from each other and there were no towns to speak of. The best opportunity for socializing was on Sundays at church. Peter cast his eyes over the assemblage with new interest. It was customary for families to linger on the church grounds after the service. Considerable business was conducted there as well as a bit of courtship. After his military service, Peter had let his hair grow down in soft curls to his shoulders with a lovelock tied at the end with a black string, and he caught the eye of one of the daughters of Moses Phillips, a vestryman prominent in church affairs. The attractive young lady demurely smiled back and Peter's blood ran faster. But, that glance was all that happened on that first contact. Peter knew that he was not exactly handsome, but hoped his style, wit and character could win her.

  Some Sundays later, Peter asked his father to introduce him to Moses and his daughters, Lucy and Susan. It was Lucy who had caught Peter's eye. Peter was a bit awkward and did not know what to say, but he managed a few words before the Phillips family departed. The Phillips's plantation was just to the south across the Rappahannock in Spotsylvania County, but the next Sunday Peter managed to intercept them at Aquia Creek on the way to church and ride along with them. His breakthrough with Lucy came when the Peytons gave a party. These affairs were less grand than before the war but marvelous nevertheless. There were fiddlers and dancing, and Peter worked up the courage to approach Lucy who wore her long hair parted and pushed back softly from her face. "May I have the next dance?" Peter asked. Lucy made a slight curtsey and offered her hand. Afterwards, he asked, "Would you like a punch." "Yes, that would be nice," came the reply. Now what, Peter thought to himself. He could talk about his war experience. Lucy had heard of Washington's courageous crossing of the Delaware. But Peter did not really want to talk only of war. What was this attractive young woman like? By questioning her, he learned she could play the piano and liked to read and ride horses. Peter could see from her tanned face that she enjoyed the outdoors and did not try to protect her skin with clumsy bonnets as was the fashion with many women. "My sister and I ride almost daily," she told him. "Father prohibits riding off the plantation, but at church we make appointments with other girls our age to meet at the boundaries of our properties. Otherwise, we are so lonely."

"Yes, I am very fond of riding myself. I had a chance to join a cavalry unit at the end of my enlistment, but I thought I'd better come home."

The conversation revealed a sharp intellect and independent spirit in the young woman. Peter and she lamented that books were scarce and promised to exchange those they had.

"My father has a copy of Swift's *Gulliver's Travels* that I can lend you," said Peter hoping to curry her favor.

"Do you like the theater?" she asked.

"I have had no opportunity to experience it," he had to admit.

"Before the war, my father took me to Williamsburg to see *The Beggars Opera*. It was very funny."

Lucy told him about the time General Washington had stopped overnight at their plantation on his way to attend the House of Burgesses in Williamsburg. They agreed that he was a striking man of great charm and poise, though Peter had seen him only from a distance.

When they danced, Peter linked Lucy's hand in his and drank in her perfume and femininity. Her lacy, long, flowered dress with hoop skirt suited her and showed just a suggestion of décolletage. He dreamt about her for the next week. Lucy was two years younger than Peter, but she seemed more mature compared to other girls who struck him as rather flighty and insubstantial.

Lucy was impressed with Peter as well. She confided in her sister, "Peter is very stylish with a lovelock in his hair tied with a bit of black ribbon, and did you see that earring hung from one ear? He's a fashionable dresser too with his doublet of velvet, slashed in front with large loose sleeves and a band of Vandyke lace."

"I think you are smitten, my girl," Susan observed.

"I hope he will continue to call on me. The few other young men I know are so drab and dull."

The joy of Peter's new love was dimmed by the illness of his mother. It was a time of mixed change, sadness, stress, and opportunity. Sarah, Peter's mother, died at age 54. The blow was softened by an inheritance of land from her. Toward the end of the war, many loyalists returned to England or migrated to Canada. Much of their land was confiscated by the Commonwealth:

Court of 1780: Escheators Inquest Commonwealth of Va., Stafford County, regarding Act Concerning Escheats and Forfeitures from British Subjects:
PETER BYRAM claims as heir at Law of SARAH BYRAM (his mother) one hundred acres of said (Accokeek) Mine Tract, under a deed of Intail (Deeds produced) from Alice Fritter to Sarah Byram, and a claim of Thomas Russel of the State of Maryland of one half of said Tract and that the lands -- became forfeit and vested in the Commonwealth subject to the claims above recited according to the Inquest
(s) Chs Carter, Eschs).

The Byram plantation was struggling, and all were mighty glad to hear that Washington had won a decisive victory over Cornwallis at Yorktown in 1781. Earlier, the Continental Army had worked its way south passing through Stafford County after a tide-turning win at Saratoga. The patriots were happy to provide food and supplies, but it was a drain.

Peter's brother, William, came home after the surrender of Cornwallis. Their father, the senior William was in poor health and had about given up ever seeing his second son. Brother William had stayed in the Army all this time. Their father suffered from fevers and dysentery. Peter admitted to his brother, "I feel very much alone. If father dies, we are left to manage the plantation. I don't know if we have enough experience to direct all the planting, harvesting, and marketing of the tobacco if the market revives. Will the slaves mind us if father is gone?"

"We will do what we have to do. He is in such pain that death will be a blessing."

It went on for weeks, but finally their father died. The doctor could do nothing. The brothers served punch and wine at the funeral, but had to forego the customary gifts of mourning rings as funds were short.

In the boy's father's will, William had divided his slaves between sons Peter and William. The official record of 1883 read:

The Court on motion made, do appoint John R. Peyton, Wm. Rout and William Robinson, or either two of them to divide slaves of WILLIAM BYRAM decd son of PETER BYRAM decd agreable to Will of said Peter, and report to Court. Division & Allottment made in Consequence of above order
To PETER BYRAM, 5 named Nan, Lucy, Will, Monday, and Shadrach;
To WILLIAM BYRAM, 6 named Jack, Ceasar, Hannah, Isaac, Barsha, and George.

William had to laugh at the pretensions of his father in adopting slave names from classical Rome. He knew something of Virginia history and was aware that the original settlers of Jamestown had slaves. It seemed quite natural to him, and he was pleased with his inheritance.

Peter was especially glad to have his brother home. William suggested to Peter that they take off for a few days to Williamsburg, maybe even Richmond for a bit of rum, women and song to celebrate.

Peter said, "No, I've left that behind. Rather, let's have a ball at the home of our Uncle Cuthbert next week to celebrate your return and Washington's victory, and we'll invite someone that you may like and take your mind off of easy women. My lovely lady Lucy has a sister."

William enthusiastically agreed. "It's time we settled down and made a real life of our own."

A hand-delivered invitation arrived at the Phillips's plantation. Mrs. Phillips eagerly opened the envelope with her daughters watching. "It's an invitation to a dance at Cuthbert Byram's. This is very exciting. There have been few dances during the war, and I'm glad for the opportunity to get dressed up again."

"Mother, can we get new dresses?" chimed Lucy and Susan together.

"I'm afraid not. There is not time to make them even if we had a pattern. Times are hard, and you'll have to make do with your old dresses."

"I understand, but I hope my old dress still fits," said Lucy. "We don't have girlish figures anymore."

"Put it out of your mind for now," Mrs. Phillips admonished, "and help me knit socks for the slaves, and then we must visit the slave quarters as one of them is sick." Time passed more quickly than usual as the sisters anticipated the dance.

It was the day of the dance, and all was a bustle at the Phillips's house. When the girls came downstairs, their mother noticed Lucy's hair immediately, asking, "Lucy, what have you done to your long hair?"

"I had Bessie cut it a bit."

"But what is that one long tress that hangs over your shoulder?"

"It's called a heartbreaker," the young woman explained.

"Are you going to break some hearts?"

"No, but I surely would like to capture one. I'm not getting any younger you know."

"Now behave yourself."

"Of course, I will, Mother.

"When we are at church, I have seen you making eyes at Cudbath's nephew. He seems like a nice fellow."

"Mother, I do not make eyes, and yes, he's pleasant fellow from an old planter family that has been in Stafford County for generations. He is just back from two years in the war, and he has a brother."

"That sounds promising," trilled Susan.

"Let's go. We have a long buggy ride ahead of us. We will stay at Garrard's Inn so we won't have to travel back at night."

At the ball, Peter introduced his brother to Susan, and they hit it off immediately and danced one minuet and reel after another until midnight. The two young men were soon constant visitors at the Phillips's plantation. Father Moses expressed his disapproval of the boys' frequent visits, but did not turn them away. He had always found it especially difficult to deny Lucy her wishes. Soon enough, he was convinced of the boys' sincerity. As long as Sarah and her house slave, Bessie, were in the next room with the door open, he was at ease.

Peter and William were passionately in love with Lucy and Susan. During their visits to the Phillips's home, the women entertained them by singing and reading aloud. They read Fielding's *Tom Jones*. Most women of their class would not admit to reading Fielding, but Lucy and Susan were different. They also read from Pope's poem based on the story of Abelard and Heloise. Lucy almost swooned when Peter read a passage describing Heloise's wish that the neutered Abelard forget her, lest his anguish overcome him:

No, fly me, fly me, far as pole from pole;
Rise Alps between us! And whole oceans roll!
Ah, come not, write not, think not once of me,
Nor share one pang of all I felt for thee.

"It is so sad, so sad," she said. Peter thought it a bit much, but he could see that Lucy was a romantic and passionate woman, and he liked her for it.

Abruptly, Lucy changed the subject. "You must write a formal letter to my father requesting his permission to marry."

Peter was taken aback, for he had never mentioned marriage before. Not that he had not thought about it, but he kept putting it off. He was glad when Lucy took the initiative. "Yes, of course, I'll do that. I want to spend my life with you."

When Moses received Peter's letter, he discussed it with Sarah. "These Byram boys are from a good family and are substantial landowners and slave holders. They have resources to provide a good life for our daughters. I will consent to the marriage."

"Agreed; a wise decision," responded his wife.

The brothers would have been content to live out their lives modestly on the land they had inherited, searching for a way to maintain its productivity. But, an unexpected bonus and opportunity came their way after the war. Moses Phillips was well connected politically. He was a vestryman of Overwharton Parish along with other powerful men in the parish including Thomas Mountjoy, John Peyton, William Garrard, Elijah Threlkeld, George Burroughs and James Withers. Mountjoy, for example, also served as appraiser, sheriff, court record inspector, road inspector and election superintendent. These vestrymen were the powers that be and a close-linked group. Colonel Garrard had served in the Revolution and owned a popular inn and twenty-three slaves. Moses's father, William, was also a vestryman. Vestrymen were appointed for life, serving as judges of the court along with their church duties. Their power to levy taxes did not always make them popular with their neighbors. In one well-known case some years before, George's brother Lawrence Washington, manager of the Accakeek Iron Works, had objected to an additional tax to pay for a new church. He petitioned the House of Burgesses to dissolve the vestry. The petition was rejected, not surprisingly since many of the Burgesses were part of the same self-perpetuating ruling class in their home parishes.

Baptist church members had been thrown in jail in Spotsylvania County for refusing to stop preaching when ordered to do so. The Baptists had gathered ten thousand signatures supporting abolition of the established church, but the Burgesses rejected the petition in 1775. Only one year later at the height of the rebellion, Virginia exempted religious dissenters from attending and paying taxes to the Anglican Church by adopting the Declaration of Rights of Virginia. The Byrams were disappointed when George Washington and Patrick Henry favored taxes to support churches of whatever denomination the worshiper preferred. While the Phillips family remained staunch supporters of the established Anglican Church, the Byrams began to waiver.

"I'm not a very religious man, but support of any church should be a matter of conscience, not a compulsory tax," said Peter hesitantly, as he was not sure how Lucy felt about it. "Maybe we should discuss our religious beliefs before we are married."

Lucy had read Pope's "Essay on Man," which shaped her response: "I agree that it is our duty to strive to be good regardless of the situation. We must accept our position between the beasts and the angels. We can't fully understand the universe and thus must rely on hope which leads to faith."

"I can see that you have thought more deeply about religion than I have and that it goes beyond Anglicanism," replied Peter.

Lucy was glad to get the issue out in the open. "Since my people have been leaders in the Anglican Church for generations, it will take me awhile to get used to another," she said, "but I see your point. This is a new age of choice rather than mere custom passed unthinkingly from one generation to another. I suspect my father never entertained any option to Anglican membership, since it was the only way to be a good citizen and participate in government. However, the fact that Father once entertained an itinerant Baptist preacher may mean that he is more receptive to alternative religious views than I have given him credit for."

"I understand your concern," said Peter, "and I respect your father immensely."

"I think I can adapt to the changing times. Still, I think we might keep our thoughts on religion to ourselves for now. Father has a lot on his mind." Lucy's countenance softened, and she smiled as she recounted the itinerant Baptist's visit. "I recall that he was quite a storyteller. He told a tall tale of his travels that brought him to the door of a cabin in Rhode Island in the midst of a blinding snowstorm. He rapped on the door, and a woman answered. He asked if he could spend the night. She said that her husband was away and it would not be proper. After much persuasion she let him in, and he immediately went to bed in another room with his clothes on. Later, the preacher saw another man admitted to the house, who clearly was not the woman's husband. The two embraced. Soon another rap was heard at the door, and a voice declared, 'I'm your husband; let me in.'" Lucy lowered her voice to imitate a demanding male speaker and continued. "She quickly hid her lover in a large barrel used for flax and opened the door. The husband seeing the preacher on the bed doubted if he actually was a preacher. 'So if you're a preacher, let me see you raise the devil.' The preacher reluctantly agreed to the test of his position and asked that the outside door be opened, for the devil would rise in flames. He then took a hot coal from the fireplace and dropped it in the barrel. Within minutes, the man hiding there rose and ran for the door trailing fire and smoke."

"You tell a good story yourself," laughed Peter.

Land speculation was at the core of British settlement in America. After the Atlantic coast was settled, the elite turned their eyes across the Alleghenies to the Ohio Valley as a source of potential wealth. The Ohio Company of Virginia was formed in 1747 by influential Virginians, including George Washington's two brothers. It received a grant of two hundred thousand acres near the forks of the Ohio. Virginia Governor Dinwiddie was a shareholder and sent a military unit under the command of George Washington to the valley in 1753. None of these people wanted to farm, only to get rich from renting or selling land to those who did. This British activity in Ohio country angered the French, who had made earlier claims to the area, and contributed to the French and Indian War. The Grand Ohio Company received a land grant from the Crown. Ben Franklin was a partner. Nothing came of it because of the outbreak of the Revolutionary War.

Now after the war, Virginia Governor Patrick Henry was eager to substantiate his state's claim to the western lands. He saw that settlement of Kentucky territory by Virginians was the best way to do this. To that end, generous land grants in Kentucky were made to those with good connections. Moses Phillips, a man with many connections, was granted over five thousand acres. Moses's vision was to take his family, including his prospective sons-in-law, to Kentucky to claim his land. As veterans of the recent war, the Byram boys were also eligible for land in Kentucky.

The years after the war were difficult for everyone on the Northern Neck. The land and tobacco that had been so good to them was beginning to play out, and prices had fallen. Tobacco drained the soil of its fertility, and constant row crops resulted in erosion. Crop yields were dropping, and there was no more land to clear. Streams and ports filled up with sediment from the eroding land. In spite of their relatively large acreage, neither the Byrams nor the Phillips had enough productive acreage to keep their slaves busy.

It was in this context that the two families made the decision to seek new land. All of their energies were put into preparation for the move to Kentucky. Moses Phillips planned the move carefully, including discussions with his son Edmund, the Byram brothers and neighbor William Rout who was married to Peter's cousin, Winifred Byram.

When Moses asked the men, "Shall we take the Wilderness Road from Richmond through Cumberland Gap or float down the Ohio River from Fort Pitt?" it was Sarah who held the deciding opinion: "I'm not going to set up housekeeping in a new land without some of my household goods," she insisted. "And I am not going to live on squirrels for a year while the land is cleared and planted." Susan and Lucy heartily agreed with their mother.

"Mother, you exaggerate," said son Edmund, "but I get your point." The men knew that the overland route was fine for individuals on horseback, but it was far from adequate for wagon travel. The Wilderness Road, as it had been called since Daniel Boone had opened it in 1775 for the Transylvania Company, was the work of thirty-five axmen, following the old Indian trail through the Cumberland Gap in the Appalachian chain. No small factor in the families' decision was news that one hundred men, women and children had been killed on the Wilderness Road by the Chickamauga under the leadership of Dragging Canoe in the previous year.

So the Ohio River route was chosen. Still, considerable tortuous travel for the party lay ahead, taking them from northern Virginia to near Fort Pitt in western Pennsylvania. The Potomac River was not navigable beyond

Cumberland, Maryland, where, a few years before, the Braddock expedition had opened a military road through Pennsylvania to the Redstone Old Ford just above the fork of the Ohio where the Monongahela and the Alleghany Rivers join. The party could take river passage from there to Fort Pitt and on to the Ohio.

There was no way that the Byram-Phillips families could all get to Kentucky in time to plant a crop to carry them through the first winter. In the face of this reality, Edmund proposed a sensible plan: "If Rout would go with me, along with one of our Negroes, we could go in time to arrive in Kentucky in February, clear a small amount of land, plant grain and have it ready to harvest when the rest of you come in the fall. It will be easier for us to get to Fort Pitt when the ground is frozen, then the roads will be drier for you in the fall." Moses Phillips agreed with his son's idea, and the planning proceeded from there.

Information had come back from early explorers of Kentucky that a military outpost had been built near a bend in the Ohio where Limestone Creek joined the Ohio. That would provide a protected home base from which to explore just where Moses would select his land. Explorer John Filson's map of the frontier was widely studied. Moses's brother, John, joined the conversation and expressed his interest in coming out to Kentucky, but only after Moses and his group had established themselves. "Yeah, John, you want to be sure people can settle and survive the Indians before you come."

"Well, yes," said John, I'm not as brave, or perhaps as foolhardy, as you." Uncertainty stopped some men, and others seemed to find it stimulating.

The slaves on the Byram plantation soon heard the talk of pulling up stakes for Kentucky, and could talk of nothing else, mostly with great trepidation and fear of the unknown. In the closing days of the war, many slaves from across Virginia had tried to run away. And some had succeeded in escaping their bondage. During the British forays into Virginia, Thomas Jefferson's Monticello had been raided and crops destroyed by the Brits and many of his slaves captured and taken off. The British garrison had hardly been a safe haven for the slaves, as many had subsequently died from smallpox endemic on the post. On the Byram's plantation, Isaac had been sorely tempted to try escaping, but in the end had decided to remain where he was. Besides, the young Byram masters were not so bad. Now with this talk of moving to the frontier, his wife Hannah was alarmed by news of settlers dying at the hands of the Indians.

"We're blown about as leaves in the wind, never able to plan for a betta day," she moaned.

"I knows, I knows," replied Isaac, "I feel so helpless, but, still we have got to try to get something good out of every day."

"Yes, Isaac, we've been more fortunate than some, and our child has always been with us. It's a joy to see him grow."

"However," Isaac noted, "I can see the anger rising in him. The younger generation seems less willing to accept things as they are."

William Byram volunteered his slave, Isaac, to go with Edmund and Rout. "He's "a strong buck and the best axman in the county." Edmund approached the Negro with the choice between staying on the Byram plantation or being part of the advance party to Kentucky. Isaac said yes, even with a bit of enthusiasm and a sense of adventure. To Hannah he later explained, "At least it'll break the monotony of life here. I always wanted to see somethin' of the country besides these same hills, and this is likely my only chance. This is the fust time in my life that I've been offered a choice, and I'm goin' to make the most of it."

It was a cold, frosty morning in February when the three men, two white, one colored, mounted their horses and headed to the King's Highway and turned north toward Alexandria. They had an extra horse and a mule in case of injury to one of their mounts and to carry their axes, a saw, seeds, ammunition, a fry pan, heavy hoes, blankets and other gear. Edmund and William Rout had pistols in their belts, their rifles strapped to their saddles and an extra one on the pack animal. At their departure, Moses wished them Godspeed and voiced what everyone was thinking: "Take care, for we will be following before we know if you have succeeded in planting a crop, but it's a risk we have to take."

Edmund's heart was in his throat, but he joked, "We will succeed so that Mother won't have to eat wild game for a year!" The ride to Alexandria was uneventful, and they settled in that night at the newly built Gadsby's Tavern on Royal Street, knowing it would probably be the last comfortable bed they would sleep in, probably for years. Years—the word sounded ominous.

From Alexandria they followed Braddock's route west across the Shenandoah and through Winchester, then north to Cumberland. They passed the abandoned Fort Cumberland high on the river bank. Braddock's military road did not look like much. Edmund remarked to William, "This is going to be tough going for wagons." They were glad for the sake of the women to follow that a few rough cabins along the way accepted travelers even if they were sure Sarah would have a fit when she saw the flea-infested accommodations. In the mountains of Pennsylvania, the February snow slowed their progress. "At least when our families come there will be no snow, but the steepness of the road will still be a challenge for the horses." Large stones obstructed the trail all along the way, and several broken wagons had been abandoned at the edge of the road.

The three men felt a sense of accomplishment when they completed the overland leg of the journey at Redstone Old Fort built on an old Indian mound on the Monongahela. There they made arrangements for two flatboats to be built in readiness for their families' fall arrival. The builder took half payment from the advance party and would receive the rest when the families arrived. After waiting for the river ice to clear, the Virginians joined two other small parties to hire a flatboat to float their horses and gear to the fork of the Monongahela and Allegheny Rivers. Soon they were on the Ohio a short distance from Fort Pitt where they waited for several boats to travel together for enhanced safety from Indian attacks.

After nine days and four hundred miles they arrived in Kentucky where Limestone Creek entered the Ohio. They first stayed nearby at Waring's Station, an outpost of log cabins constructed in a rectangle with an open space in the middle. It was being established by Colonel Thomas Waring two miles from Limestone, a short distance west of the Lexington road, an old buffalo trace that ran from the Ohio River south to the center of Kentucky. The natural track, called *Alanantowamiowee* the Indians, arose in the million-years-old collision of land masses that produced a minor fault wherein shale from the lower strata pierced the limestone and the topsoil. This fault line, barren from its infertility, provided a readymade treeless path that buffalo and other animals followed to reach the salt licks and canebrakes. The migrating animal herds compacted the soil, further discouraging vegetation, and the Native Americans for eons had burned the underbrush, replenishing the soils with the ash and cultivating lush meadows to further entice the animals. To the Indians and now the encroaching white men, this part of the frontier was a kind of game preserve for hunting.

Waring brought settlers into the area and helped them find land. To the southwest was Washington Station, settled by Simon Kenton the previous year. General Henry Lee, Ned and John Waller of an old family in Stafford County were at the station. Rout and Edmond consulted them all, asking where they might find good land, and then headed for the North Fork of the Licking River to stake their claim. More settlers were arriving daily, and there was no time to waste. Their task was daunting. First, they built a log lean-to for shelter while they cleared some of the land. The sound of their axes reverberated through the woods from sunup to sundown. Every ten days they returned to the Station for supplies and a peaceful, warm night's sleep.

When spring came, it brought Indian hunting parties from Ohio. Edmund and Rout left their horses at the station, hoping that the absence of horses would make their expanding clearing less attractive to the Indians. One night in early spring, Isaac woke from a fitful sleep to hear low birdcalls from the stumps around their lean-to. He nudged the other men awake, and they listened nervously together. The calls did not seem right for this time of night.

Edmund and William primed the pistols they always had at their sides and waited, hearts pounding.

Meanwhile back in Virginia, the Byram and Phillips households hectically prepared for the move west. They sold some land and slaves to finance the trip, while older slaves were given a bit of money and their freedom. Items to take to Kentucky were selected and then the pile was further evaluated, added to and reduced again. Clearly, plows were essential equipment, and their great weight ruled out a lot of household items that the women wanted to take. Nevertheless, Sarah hid four Queensware plates in a flour barrel when the men were not looking. As mistress of the house, Sarah was responsible for organizing many of the supplies. She packed only the fittings of her spinning wheel, knowing that the wooden parts could be fashioned again in Kentucky. Also essential were an adze and auger for building a cabin, the chains, axes and iron wedges for splitting logs. There was a crate of chickens, some piglets, two lambs and two milk cows to haul and herd to eventually populate the new land.

During the packing, the slave woman, Hannah, suggested some fishhooks. "If we's goin' down a big river, there'll be fish to catch." Blankets, gunpowder, lead, flints, two kettles, frying pans were added to the pile. Peter and William taught Lucy and Susan to load and shoot a pistol. Lucy was enthusiastic and pleased that Peter had such confidence in her, but Susan would just as soon have passed on the honor.

The Byram and Phillips families were joined in September, 1785, in a double wedding at Aquia Church. It was a subdued affair, as preparations for the Kentucky move were consuming most of their energy, and money. Peter and William wore dark wool trousers, waistcoats and jackets with knee length white socks and black buckled shoes. Their white, linen shirts had ruffed collars and cuffs with black string ties at the throat. Peter had pulled back his hair in a neat queue. The brothers looked much alike, with the medium build and round, boyish faces typical of the Byrams.

The brides wore matching ruffled dresses that showed off their figures. It was almost as if they were saying to old suitors, "Hey, look what you missed by being too slow." Afterwards, family and a few friends assembled for a reception at the Phillips's house. After the guests departed, Peter and William put their new brides in a borrowed phaeton and raced to their ancestral home. Though they arrived after dark, their house and field slaves were assembled to greet them. After a quick tour of their new home, it was time to end an exhausting day, and the brothers escorted their brides upstairs. Soon all was quiet, or nearly so. The house slaves listened at the bottom of the stair. Low moans and creaking beds in each room seemed to be in harmony. In the morning at a late breakfast, the satisfied grins on Peter's and William's faces told the story. The new brides winked knowingly to each other. The next generation could be on its way.

Nothing had come of the night of bird calls in Kentucky. In the morning, Edmund's hand was shaking and he looked forward to a cup of coffee.

"Sorry, master, the coffee we brought be gone," Isaac reported, which elicited a muttered, "Damn!" from Edmund.

The three men never had a peaceful night after that, with one of them always keeping watch in case of a sneak attack. They kept their rifles close at hand as they worked in the clearings. They had only heavy hoes to dig in some corn and loosen the earth for a bit of barley to carry the horses through the next winter. Fortunately none of the passing Indian hunting parties attacked them while they were exposed and isolated on their new land. Isaac proved invaluable, as he was exceptionally strong and willing. The three men made it a contest every day to see who could fell and strip branches from the most trees. Living and working in close proximity, Rout and Edmund got to know a Negro as they never had before. And it was a new experience for Isaac to work alongside his masters, sharing the same meager food and spare living quarters. While game was abundant and readily at hand, hunting and butchering took time, and the diet quickly became monotonous. The little party needed all the firepower they could get, so as the two men's confidence in the Negro grew, they decided to teach him how to use a rifle. Isaac was overcome with emotion when he was handed the gun. He had never known a slave to be entrusted with a firearm. For the first time, he felt like a real man. Maybe Kentucky was going to be a better place after all.

~2~

On To Kentucky

All was in readiness, with four wagons packed and the four-horse teams hitched for the long journey to Kentucky. Patriarch Moses Phillips, his wife Sarah and their sons, John, Gabriel and Moses, Junior, took the lead. The Byram brothers and their new brides, William Rout's wife, Winifred, Edmund Phillip's wife, Milly, slave Isaac's wife, Hannah, and two other slave families completed the party of seventeen. With wagons to contend with, they followed a somewhat different route than had the three-man advance party. At Aquia landing on the Potomac, they put aboard a freighter headed for Alexandria. From there, they traveled overland across northern Virginia, fording the Shenandoah, to reach Winchester, then northward to Cumberland, Maryland. Continuing westward from Cumberland, they traveled two more days in Maryland before crossing into Pennsylvania northwest of Grantsville. They labored on through the Pennsylvania villages of Farmington, Laurel Hill and Uniontown to their destination of Redstone, high on the banks of the Monongahela. Sarah and her daughters slept in the wagons even when occasional roadside cabins were available. The men usually slept on the ground when it was dry enough. The Conestoga wagons they met on the way carried supplies to the western settlements and were driven by a crude class of fellows who usually smoked cigars, which everyone called stogies. When these crude drivers stopped alongside the Byram-Phillips caravan, their cigars did not endear them to the women.

Along Redstone's Front Street several overturned wagons bore silent witness to the danger of the steep slope leading down to the Monogehela's edge. Everyone in the party was enlisted to help prevent similar accidents with their own rigs. Grabbing hold of the ropes attached to the back of each wagon and digging their heels into the soft earth, they used their combined weight to slow the descent of one laden vehicle after another.

The two flat-bottomed "Kentucky boats" that Edmund had had built for them at the cost of thirty-five dollars each were ready and waiting at the wharf. They were fifty feet long and eighteen feet wide with a covered section at the rear. Blankets were hung to provide a bit of privacy for the families and to conceal the chamber pots when in use. A long oar stuck out the back of the vessel for steerage and two smaller oars were on the sides at the front. They hired a captain who claimed to know the river, based on his one previous passage, and two crewmen for each boat and set off for Fort Pitt. The crewmen had hired on looking for a free ride to settle in Kentucky. Each boat carried two

wagons side by side in the front, and in back of them were tethered the eight horses and other livestock. Behind the animals was a pile of fodder purchased in Redstone to feed them during the trip, then barrels of flour, meal and bacon, all purchased locally. The cargo was divided between the two boats so that if one boat should sink, they would still have some essentials.

On the first day out, one of the boats got stuck on a sandbar, and it took all the men pushing on the oars to get her off. They made only fifty miles or so every twenty-four hours, all the while on a northwesterly course opposite the direction of their final destination. Once the Monongahela merged with the Allegheny to produce the Ohio, they would be turning southward and on the homestretch to their new land. During the day the men rowed, and at night they drifted with the two boats tied together. In the dark it was impossible to detect submerged tree limbs, and they were frequently snagged. The men would work for hours to disengage the trapped vessel. With each snag they prayed that the boat would not be damaged and take on water. The utility of Hannah's suggestion to bring fishhooks proved prescient. Catfish, sturgeon and pike made fine soup. Peter shot a turtle, and Lucy asked the captain how to cook it. Their cooking could be done with great care on a small fire built on a bed of clay in the boat.

The banks of the Ohio River were beautiful with fall colors beginning to show scarlet, yellow and rust. They passed Wheeling situated nicely on a hill. In the dark they drifted past the mouths of Grave Creek, Cappatana Creek and Fishing Creek. Next, they passed the mouth of the muddy Muskingum where Fort Harmar was under construction and there was much cleared land. The reassuring sounds of drums and fife could be heard from the fort. By evening, they reached the Little Kanawha River. Opposite Flyn's Old Station there were cornfields and a dozen little cabins.

"We're now two hundred twenty miles from Fort Pitt, about halfway," said the captain. "Look," exclaimed Moses, Jr., "there are twelve deer feeding in the bottomland on the right bank. You couldn't see that in Stafford County."

The boatmen would sing to relieve the monotony of their rowing:

Oh, it's meeting is a pleasure,
Parting is a grief;
But an onconstant lovyer
Is worse nor a thief!
A thief and a robber
Your purse he will haave;
But an onconstant lovyer,
He will bring you to the grave!

Peter squeezed Lucy's hand and assured her that the melancholy lyrics did not apply to them.

The morning after passing the Little Kanawha, Indians appeared on the north bank, whooping loudly, no doubt to intimidate the travelers. A ball splintered the top board of the leading flatboat in which the Byrams and Phillips were riding. The captain immediately steered for the other bank, shouting, "All hands on the oars. Don't take time to raise your rifles. All women and children get down." More balls hit the gunnels, and one hit a horse, but by the time the Indians could reload, the lead boat was out of range.

Upon hearing the shots ahead, the men in the second boat immediately steered closer to the opposite shore and opened fire on the Indians. Their balls fell short of the attackers, but they were enough to discourage the Indians from launching their canoes. The captain explained that in places where the river narrowed, there was a tradeoff between gaining speed by following the strongest current and the greater safety afforded by sticking close to the left bank, which was more likely to be free of Indian hunting parties. The settlers feared what would happen if the Indians were to board the flatboats. "I bet we could outrace them," boasted young Moses, but everyone else knew better. To Peter, running the river felt like an infantry charge, with the outcome more a matter of fate than anything: Some would make it and others would not, through no cunning or fault of their own.

The horse that was hit during the Indian barrage was Lucy's riding horse, the only one on the boat. She prayed for its recovery, but in a few days it died, and the men struggled to push it overboard. Lucy choked back her tears and said to Peter, "I'm a frontier woman now, and I am not going to act like a silly girl."

The day they passed Point Pleasant above the Kanawha River where Fort Randolph and a dozen or more houses had been built on a few of the ten thousand acres George Washington had claimed for himself, they had made eighty-five miles. When they passed Big Sandy Creek, they were finally within sight of Kentucky there on the left. The day after passing mouth of the Scioto on the Ohio side, they made one hundred miles. Nearing Limestone, young Moses exclaimed, "Captain, what are those big, wooly wild cattle with humps feeding on the bottomland of that creek?"

"Son, those are bison," he explained. "I'm glad you saw them, as they are becoming increasingly rare in these parts."

The landing at the mouth of Limestone Creek was busy. It was becoming a major point of entry for the settlement of Kentucky because a curve in the river allowed flatboats to escape the river's current to pull ashore. That was the good news. The bad was the high bluff behind the little settlement. Watching others try to pull their wagons up the incline soon made it clear that three teams would have to be hitched to pull each wagon up from the river, and even at that, some of their gear had to be unloaded to lighten the burden on the horses. It would take two trips and a lot of cursing to raise some of the heavier items such as the plows to the top of the bluff. Still, the Virginians were in high spirits after completing their river journey successfully. It was great to be on solid ground once more. They spent several days dismantling their flatboats and hauling the lumber to the top of the bluff. The wood would be used to construct their house.

They proceeded first to Lee's Station being built by General Henry Lee between Limestone and Kenton's Station. They would build two cabins there for the women and children of the party to occupy for some time while the men erected cabins on their new land and cleared more acres. The station provided protection against marauding Indians from Ohio. The cabins were arranged in a rectangle with an open space in the center. The structures were built either abutting each other or with the spaces between blocked by a log palisade. At the corners blockhouses rose higher than the cabins with the top parts jutting out slightly so that rifles could be fired straight down on anyone attempting to set fire to the structures.

General Lee knew where Edmund and William Rout had claimed their land and sent word to them of their families' arrival. When they came in, after hugs of rejoicing, the first question was, "Do we have corn for winter?" The new arrivals breathed a sigh of relief when the answer was positive. The next day all the men went out and quickly harvested their crop. Edmund was eager to show the others the character of the land they had selected. He dug a deep hole. "See, Dad," he pointed out, "the soil rests on limestone and appears to be deep, rich and highly productive." Edmund was no chemist and could not know that limestone is porous and permeable, acting to filter and retain underground water that in turn pushes phosphate into the surrounding top soil.

"I like the gently rolling hills, so different from Tidewater Virginia," said Moses, "I wonder if the watercourses will hold up in the summer?"

"They appear constant, Dad. Let's name this one Phillips Creek. See those patches of cane over there? General Lee says that cane was the favorite food of the bison, and it suggests rich bottomland."

"I suspect cattle will like it too," remarked Moses, thinking ahead.

"During the summer it has leaves somewhat like a willow on a stout stem. Looks like the stems would make good fishing poles, though we've had no time to fish."

Lee's Station was one of more than one hundred similar frontier forts built between 1774 and 1782. The Shawnees were particularly enraged that the whites killed the bison for sport and left the carcasses rotting. Just a few years before the Phillips and Byrams arrived, an Indian force of five hundred had attacked one hundred eighty settlers living in Bryan's Station north of Lexington. Finally repulsed after two days of siege, the Indians retreated north to Blue Licks, where blue-gray limestone surrounded a natural salt spring that attracted bison and deer. A force led by Daniel Boone followed them, and after heavy fighting and loss of the lives of sixty Kentuckians including Boone's son, Israel, the Indians fled back to Ohio.

Left with few protectors, the brave women of Bryan's Station fooled the remaining Indians into thinking that the men of the station were still there and unaware of their presence, allowing time for help to be summoned from nearby settlements. The women, risking capture and killing, went about their usual business of fetching water from a nearby spring. Otherwise, the Indians would know that they had been discovered and would attack immediately. Despite the danger, they filled their wooden piggins with their dipping gourds and nonchalantly walked back to the station.

These early settlers demanded more military protection from Virginia's House of Burgesses and Governor Patrick Henry, under whose authority they were claiming their western land. At that time, north-central Kentucky was one huge county named Fayette. Even after the original county was subdivided to create Bourbon County, the Limestone-area settlers had to risk a long and dangerous forty-mile journey to reach their county courthouse. By the time the Phillips-Byram party had settled in Kentucky, their countrymen were petitioning the Burgesses to create yet another county and court. The signatures of Moses and Peter appeared along with that of Simon Kenton, one of the more notable frontiersmen, on the 1786 petition. That petition was refused, but only three years later, the Burgesses relented and carved another county from the larger division, naming it Mason after George Mason, the distinguished statesman from Virginia.

As the land was converted from forest to farmland, the staple crops became corn, hemp and tobacco. Wheat, barley and rye were also grown to feed horses, hogs, sheep and beef cattle. Settlers found that making whiskey from the corn produced a highly valued product that could be shipped economically even over the poorest road. The Phillips and Byram men were immediately caught up in the relentless labor of bringing their claim under cultivation and providing permanent shelters for their families. When the trees were cleared, attention was given to building cabins for each family on their own land. Chestnut was the wood of choice. It split easily to make shingles. The bark was used to make tannic acid for tanning leather.

Phillips Creek, Tributary of North Fork of Licking River, Kentucky

The families worked together. Logs of the same size were notched at the ends and stacked in an interlocked rectangle. A door was cut in one side only, making the cabin dark but safer than it would have been with windows. Moss and clay were stuffed in the chinks between the logs of the first one they built. But on the second cabin, they took a neighbor's advice and squared the logs with an adze to make them fit closely together and thus less likely to be penetrated by a rifle ball. It was a lot of extra work, but the structure was safer and sounder, which was particularly appealing to the women. An auger was used to make holes for wooden pegs securing the crossbeams. Sarah insisted on a puncheon floor made of split logs with the flat side up. "I'm not going to live on dirt," she declared. "We would never be clean." She saw a distinction between a log *cabin* and a log *house*. Her house would have a wooden floor and a shingled roof like those of civilized people back home. At the same time, the slaves' cabin would have a dirt floor and a roof of slabs put on without nails. As the families outgrew their original houses, another would be built ten feet to one side and the old and new buildings connected by a roof to link the living quarters and provide a sheltered open-air space for many household activities.

The Byram-Phillips families barely survived their first winter in Kentucky. Squirrel and other wild game had stretched their provisions enough to save them from starvation. Only the wild turkey bagged by the men satisfied Sarah's tastes, and she never let her oldest son forget her objections to the rest of the fare. In two years, the men had cleared considerable acreage and established fields of corn that allowed them the confidence of having food and fodder to winter themselves and their livestock over to the next season.

When the Phillips and Byrams landed at Limestone, later to be named Maysville, the town was composed of about a dozen permanent households and wharves. Daniel Boone and his family were living there and ran a tavern and store where Peter bought some supplies. On an early visit, Peter joined a small group of men in the tavern to hear Boone's tales of his many adventures. Sipping a drink served by Loos, one of Boone's slave girls, Peter had to laugh at Boone's response to a question about his ever being lost during his wilderness travels. "I have never been lost," he seemed to boast, "but I will admit to being confused for several weeks." Boone, like his fellow frontiersmen, Waring, May, Kenton and Lee, speculated in land and helped settlers with their claims, but he was embittered by the loss of many of his own claims. "Over and over I've been robbed of my lands here," Boone told his listeners. "I'm constantly being called on to give depositions in land-claim cases and told to sign papers, only to find out later that I've signed away the rights to my own land. These lawyers are always trying to make me falsify my oath." Boone was barely literate, Peter realized, which must have limited his understanding of the legal papers and proceedings his land speculation involved.

When Kenton joined the tavern gatherings, he'd share his stories of being captured by the Indians and taken to Detroit and of his escape in 1779. Kenton was a huge, bear of a man with auburn hair. He had to be superhuman to have survived running the gauntlet eight times while in captivity. Peter was mightily impressed.

Sometimes Boone would sing, "I been livin' here all my life. All I got is a Barlow knife; Buckhorn handle and a Barlow blade, Best dang knife that ever was made." And sometimes Peter and Daniel traded war stories. While Peter had been fighting the Brits in the east as a soldier in the Continental Army, Daniel had been in Kentucky fighting Indians incited by the British to attack settlers arriving from the insurgent colonies. The Indians were being paid for white scalps delivered to Detroit. Peter learned of the capture of British forts at Kaskaskia, Cahokia and Vincennes by fellow Virginian George Rogers Clark in 1778 and '79. Clark wanted to raise an army to attack Fort Detroit, but Kentuckians were more interested in protecting their own homes than any distant campaign of national importance. Peter and the others sympathized with that. Boone reminisced about the spring of '77 when the Shawnee under Black Fish attacked Boonesboro, the little settlement bearing his name. When two men went out of the fort to gather firewood and were attacked, Boone and ten other men had charged out to help them. Boone, shot in the leg, was seconds away from death from a tomahawk blow when Simon shot the attacking Indian in the chest, then picked up his wounded comrade and ran back toward the fort with two braves in hot pursuit. They got within ten feet of the gate with the Indians closing in when Simon turned and threw Boone at his pursuers, knocking both down and dazing the hardest hit. Simon kicked one so hard that ribs were broken, and he tomahawked the other one. Under fire from the other Indians, Simon scooped up Boone's unconscious body and ran to the gate with bullets kicking up the dirt around them and splintering the logs of the fort."

Along with their tales of danger and near death the frontiersmen gathered in the growing town dispensed practical survival information to the newcomers. Boone showed Peter a root that the Indians called *pocoon* that the natives used to treat snakebite when the root was mashed and applied as a poultice and as a decoction to drink when the leaves were steeped in water. The pocoon's red roots were also used as face paint by the Indians. There was a remedy to relieve the swelling caused by rheumatism made of the bark of red willow that seemed likely to work, but the recipe for ridding children of worms struck Peter as preposterous. How would chopping up a mess of earthworms and putting them on the stomach of the patient for six hours do any good? Boone once offered Peter a fair price for all the ginseng root he and his family could dig in the forest. The medicinal and aphrodisiacal powers of this wild plant were widely valued, and Boone shipped the Kentucky roots up to Pittsburgh for a good price. Later, when Peter used this commercial exchange as an excuse to Lucy for his late return from Boone's tavern, she wondered how much of the promised cash was frontier bluster and whether any of it would actually get into Peter's pocket.

Before 1784, settlers in the region were small farmers from the backwoods of Virginia, Maryland, Pennsylvania and North Carolina. They were a crude and fiercely independent lot working largely as subsistence farmers whose only communal activity was an occasional Sunday frolic marked by contests of strength, much drinking, cursing, gambling, fighting and sometimes sexual looseness. Men would wrestle and try to thrust a thumb into the opponent's eyeball until he cried out, "Kings Cruces," as an admission that he'd had enough. The Byram-Phillips families were part of an increasing influx of Revolutionary War officers and people of class from Tidewater and Piedmont Virginia accustomed to fashionable refinement and genteel manners. Upon hearing of the earlier settlers' crudeness and cruelty, Sarah, as matriarch of the combined families, laid down the law. "None of you are to go anywhere near these barbaric frolics, and I expect all of you to attend church." Churches were slow in getting organized on the frontier, and open-air revival meetings were more popular among the backwoodsmen, but despised by Sarah. Her family would attend services that were conducted by itinerant ministers at various settler houses.

William took up his mother-in-law's enthusiasm for religion. He helped build the Stone Lick Church, a part of the network of the Bracken Association of

Baptist Churches in north-central Kentucky. Once out from under the monopoly of the Anglican Church, many of the displaced Virginians found the Baptist theology with its preaching of equality—only among whites to be sure—and its minimum of doctrinaire rules to their liking. William built upon his wartime leadership skills and became a deacon in the Stone Lick Church. In hard times to come, he would turn to his faith for reassurance and comfort, and generations of Byrams would follow him in the Baptist beliefs.

On a hot August day in 1788, the second summer of their Kentucky venture, the Phillips boys—fourteen-year-old John and Moses, Junior, just twelve—along with Isaac, Hannah and their one son Bob were out cutting fodder in the tall corn not far from the station. When finished for the day, young Moses challenged the others, "I'll race you all to the split-rail fence bordering the field." John reached the fence first and climbed up to declare his victory at the same moment Isaac spotted danger and shouted, "Watch out!" But it was too late. An Indian hiding in the corn jumped out and felled John with a single blow of his tomahawk. The others ran back into the corn to hide from the rest of the Indian party. Hannah flattened herself on the dirt and thought, "Please God, don't let them find us," as she listened to the Indians thrashing through the corn around her. She and the two uninjured boys were soon found and rounded up by the Indian hunting party. Hannah pleaded with her captors, "Please spare de boys," but right there before her, they killed and brutally scalped her master's youngest son. Hannah shuddered and couldn't understand it. What had the boy ever done to the Indians? And where was Isaac? They couldn't have gotten him too.

In the commotion, her husband had escaped across the cornfield and disappeared into the woods. When the Indians discovered that John had recovered from the blow on his head and was no doubt running to the station to secure help, they decided not to follow the big black man and instead moved as quickly as they could with Hannah and her boy in the direction of the river.

At the alarm raised upon John's return to the Phillips's compound, Kenton and other men from the station set off in pursuit. Not far along, they found the body of the boy Bob who had been tomahawked, apparently because he was slowing them down. The Indians still had Hannah and probably would spare her life for later trading for the release of Indians held prisoner by the whites. The search party followed the trail to the banks of the Ohio and surmised that the Indians had crossed at Logan's Gap six miles below Limestone. There they gave up the chase, afraid to venture into the Indian lands north of the Ohio.

In the meantime, Isaac eventually circled round and returned to the station. When the men returned and reported the death of Bob, Isaac was disconsolate. This new land had claimed the life of his beloved son and taken his wife from him, her fate unknown. "Why, oh why did I choose to come to Kentucky?" he groaned in his master's presence

Moses had no good answer. His own son and namesake had suffered a violent death. His wife was lost in deep grief, deaf to his apologies and admissions of his own culpability. Choices could have horrible consequences as well as good. When things happened that you had no control over, you could just curse the fates, but he had been the one to bring them all to this new place. No amount of land gained could compensate for the loss of a son. Yet Moses felt that he had no choice but to soldier on: "The sun still comes up, and life goes on," he told himself, but it was no longer the same. John recovered slowly from his physical wounds, but he was traumatized and pleaded with his father to take them back to Virginia. He never again ventured out from the station unless accompanied by men with rifles.

The agrarian cycle began in March with plowing and sowing of meadows. Corn, oats, hemp, wheat, flax and peas were planted by mid-April. During May and June, wagons were repaired and houses repaired or expanded. By July, farmers were very busy as they cut wheat and oats and reaped hemp, put up clover hay and dug potatoes. Cutting wheat and oats with a scythe and gathering it in shocks to dry was backbreaking work. Lucy rubbed Peter's back with liniment every night before bedtime. In the fall, some cornstalks were cut with a long knife and put in shocks for winter animal feed and the rest was shucked when time allowed. Orchards yielded fruits from late summer into the fall when cider time was everyone's favorite. Hogs, pastured in the forests where they could fend for themselves and fatten on fallen acorns, were slaughtered in December. Wood cutting for the fireplace was done all winter long. Sugar trees were tapped for their sweet syrup, starting with the spring thaw in March. The young boys were kept busy herding cattle, sheep and hogs in the meadows and forests. Both horses and cattle liked the wild pea vines. Cows were very valuable in this raw land, and Peter wished he had brought more, but, by borrowing a neighbor's bull, he had several calves born each year to slowly build up his herd. Peter also found a mate for his two lambs brought from Virginia. His growing herds paralleled his own growing family, as Lucy bore a child every two years or so from their first year onward.

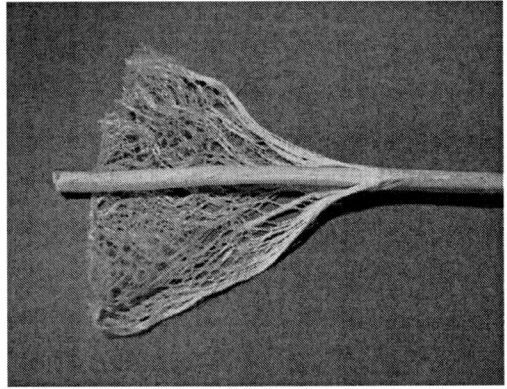

Hemp for making bags, oakum, and rope was one cash crop that could use their slave labor. The Byrams knew that Henry Clay at Ashland, his plantation near Lexington, grew hemp with a labor force of fifty slaves. Hemp, a plant with a pleasant aroma and attracted flocks of doves to feed on the seeds. grew higher than a man's head. It was cut, tied into bundles and conveyed to a deep pit of water, then covered so as to keep it submerged for a week when the fibrous material begins to separate from the reed or stem. Then it was carried to a pasture and spread out to dry. It needed turning it every few days. Then it was gathered up and stored, ready to be broken and beaten with a large wooden knife about two feet long with one thin edge called a swingle or scutcher. The growers established what they called rope walks that were long covered lanes where the lengthy strands of hemp could be laid out in overlapping swaths and twisted into rope.

The Byrams' flax field with its small light-blue flowers was a beautiful sight when in bloom, but Peter and Lucy never had time to admire it. The process for obtaining linen fibers from flax was quite similar to that for hemp, though the terminology for the process was not the same—retting, dressing, breaking, scutching and pulling the fibers through a comb called a heckle. It was tedious repetitive work, and both Lucy and the slaves sang to themselves:

> Niddy, noddy, niddy noddy
> Two heads, one body.
> T'is one, t'aint one,
> T'will be one by an by.
> T'is two, t'aint two,
> T'will be two by an by.

Having already endured the privations the war had forced on them in Virginia, Sarah and the women of her extended family were already practiced in some of the housekeeping skills required on the frontier. The purchased materials bought on their journey from Pittsburgh were very expensive, and Sarah taught Lucy to spin yarn from the wool of the homegrown sheep, using the reconstructed spinning wheel brought from Virginia. Wool was scarce because sheep were subject to much predation by marauding wolves and cats unless managed closely by the overworked settlers. Flax fibers were mixed with wool to produce linsey-woolsey to make the limited wool go further. Lucy was very pleased when she earned enough from cloth sales to buy a fine riding horse to replace the one killed on the trip down the Ohio. The Phillips women learned to bake good bread. Soon after their arrival they borrowed some starter from a distant neighbor. The evening before baking, a lump of starter about the size of their hand was mixed with three quarts of water. This stood to ferment and attract yeast spores until morning at which time the water was carefully poured off, leaving the sediment in the bottom of the bowl. Warm water was added and mixed with the flour and let stand while the oven heated. Then the loaves were formed and put in fiber baskets and let stand to rise before being put in the oven.

A year after they arrived, roads and commerce began a slow improvement when the Virginia legislature passed an act requiring three days of road maintenance per year from all males over sixteen in the community. However, the rule was more honored in principle than practice, as local politicians were loathe to enforce it in the face of opposition from those who did not want to take time from their farm work. The Maysville Road to Lexington remained in poor condition for years. Later, Congressmen favoring national planning and internal improvements voted federal money for the Maysville Road, eventually to connect it to the National Road to Natchez, but the bill was vetoed by President Andrew Jackson in 1832. Maysville merchants were buying linen, pork, lard, butter and ginseng and shipping them to New Orleans. The boatmen returned to Kentucky via the trace leading from Natchez on the Mississippi above New Orleans through Nashville, Tennessee, and on to Lexington. It was an extremely hazardous trip in both directions, but trade nevertheless expanded. If the trip was profitable, the boatmen could buy a horse for the return journey; if not, they walked back.

New Orleans was under the control of the Spanish, who had permitted use of the Mississippi during and after the Revolutionary War. But, suddenly, Spain ordered its agents to stop all American boats and confiscate their cargoes. Many Kentuckians recognized that the growth of their economy depended on trade and protested the blockade of river commerce. By 1793 they were ready to march on New Orleans and demand access. In a broadside published by the Lexington Democratic Society, Kentuckians proclaimed that "The free and undisturbed use and navigation of the river Mississippi is the NATURAL RIGHT of the inhabitants of the countries bordering on the waters communicating with the river." The Spanish governors had a different view of what rights Nature endowed, and the problem continued until Spain ceded its territory to the French in 1800. Then Jefferson's Louisiana Purchase of 1803 insured American access to New Orleans. However, it was a mixed blessing for Kentucky farmers, as competition from other western settlements stimulated by the territorial expansion kept prices low.

Peter was pleased when he heard that his old commander-in-chief was inaugurated as President in 1789. Now they lived in a real nation under a federal system and not just a collection of colonies. The dollar currency was introduced, though the Byrams saw little cash money at first. It would be a long time before pounds and shillings were supplanted on the frontier. Most commerce in the area proceeded without cash, anyway, with merchants in Maysville and Washington giving account-book credit or bartering for ginseng, yarn, beeswax and saltpeter.

Three years after the Indians had captured Hannah, a trader showed up at Moses' house with the Negro woman in tow. "I traded the Indians for her, and I offer her back to you for just a little profit." Isaac was overjoyed to hold his beloved wife again. He had given her up for dead. Hannah told the assembled families about her experiences with the Shawnee. "I was never mistreated, and the work assigned was no worse than what I did here," she said looking straight at Moses. She brought with her a tomahawk and a beaded bag as souvenirs. Moses' son, John, took them away from her. Hannah said nothing, but hatred and disappointment showed in her eyes. Even as a captive of the natives, she had been afforded more dignity and self-determination than she would ever know as a slave. Moses recognized her justifiable anger and knew that he should have stopped John. Yet, he couldn't put aside a lifetime of disregarding the humanity of the black people with whom he had always lived and worked. The world just couldn't function if he ever let the distinction between his people and theirs waver. However, something was different here on the frontier, he realized: Back in Virginia, he'd never given a moment's thought to intervening on the side of a slave.

The conflict between the settlers and the Indians seemed never ending. Many treaties were signed and all were ignored as the Indians were pushed out of whatever land white settlers wanted as their own. The treaties negotiated with the Ohio Indians assured them of their lands, while at the same time Thomas Jefferson's Report of Government for Western Lands conceived of five new states in the very lands where the Indians lived. Even as the Northwest Ordinance of 1787 included many exemplary provisions, such as prohibition of slavery north of the Ohio, freedom of religious worship, the right of *habeas corpus*, trial by jury and public use of streams and lakes, and nullified any claims the original colonial states might have on the western lands, the ordinance encouraged settlement and spelled the doom of the Indian way of life. The Indian leaders had to know it, and it must have weighed heavily on their hearts. It is no wonder that the Indians were embittered and violence increased.

Peter sensed that more intensive land use pushed out extensive use every time. The hunger for land always seemed to drive his countrymen past every negotiated line. Both settlers and natives were caught in a vicious circle of avenge and revenge, each atrocity justifying the next. Peter and his family lived daily with the consequences, remembering the past horrors and fearing future retaliations. He'd heard a remark supposedly made by Tecumseh, a Shawnee leader of some repute, that he couldn't help but agree with: "We gave them forest-clad mountains and valleys full of game, and in return what did they give our warriors and our women? Rum, trinkets and a grave." Peter didn't share such thoughts with other members of his extended family. They would not hear of any sympathy for the savages, who had killed his brother-in-law, and a young slave boy and spirited away the wife of his best man. The settlers could not see that the destruction of Indian villages and crops was also savage.

The Ohio Indians were themselves of different minds about how to respond to the influx of settlers taking over their ancestral lands. Blue Jacket was one who wanted to risk all to drive the white man from their lands, fighting to the death to the very last man. Other natives counseled accommodation and even adapting to, if not outright adopting, the white man's ways. Choosing to accommodate rather than fight, five septs, or clans, of the Shawnee nation numbering four thousand agreed to move to a place granted by the Spanish near Cape Girardeau, Missouri.

Even after six years in Kentucky, Lucy did not feel safe from Indian attacks. In the first three months of 1791, thirty-five settlers were killed in Mason County by the Shawnees. Maysville was in an uproar upon hearing of the death of their namesake, John May, killed by Indians on the Ohio at the mouth of the Scioto. When empty flatboats floated past Maysville, the residents knew that atrocities had occurred to their countrymen somewhere upstream. Two military expeditions against the Ohio Indians ended in disaster, with Little Turtle and Black Hoof triumphant. Upon hearing of the defeats Peter lamented, "Will we ever be safe from these Indians? Maybe we should have stayed in Virginia until this place becomes more civilized." But, he never spoke of his doubts to his father-in-law whose dream this all had been. The following spring, the young Tecumseh led a small band of warriors to Blue Licks, May's Lick, Washington and Maysville and stole forty-nine horses. "Perhaps it was to commemorate the new state," Peter said wryly. Simon Kenton organized a group of twenty men to pursue the Indians, but after a skirmish, the Indians escaped back to Ohio. When Kenton returned, Peter asked him, "Who is this Tecumseh anyway?" Kenton knew little other than that he was impressed with his enemy.

In spite of the dangers, settlers kept coming. Kentucky became a state in 1792 and by the 1800 Census, there were just over twelve thousand in the county, almost three times the population ten years before. The Kentucky constitution provided the right to vote to every white male over twenty-one regardless of property ownership. However, voters could directly elect only the members of the lower house. Following the same system codified in the federal constitution, Kentucky voters cast ballots for "electors" who then selected men to sit in the upper house. There was no requirement that these officials be educated, much to the chagrin of the Byram and Phillips women who valued education. To obtain income for the state treasury, the General Assembly levied two shillings on every one hundred acres of land and on every slave. Horses, mares, colts and mules were assessed eight pence each and cattle three pence each. Chariots, coaches and other carriages were assessed four to six shillings for each wheel. The highest assessment was for tavern keepers: three pounds for a license to operate a tavern and ten pounds to own a billiard table. When Peter heard of the tax rates, he opined, "I guess that tells you who has the ability to pay." Even at that, the assessments were poorly collected at first.

The years of toil and threats to his family's safety weighed on Peter's mind. In conversation with his brother William, Peter said, "You know that we are not even as well off as when we lived in Virginia. Our house is cruder and the furnishings more primitive. I'm working as hard as I can, but have little to show for it. I wanted much more for Lucy and the children."

"Don't be so hard on yourself," William counseled. "You can't compare now with what we had in Virginia because that life was doomed. The land was growing less and less productive. That's why we moved west."

"That all may be true," Peter admitted, "but I can't provide for my family the way I want, and it troubles me."

"Yes, I know," replied William. "But, the Good Book fills the hole for me. You might benefit if you attended church more often. The old hymns stir my soul." And William sang a verse of his favorite:

O God, our help in ages past,
Our hope for years to come,
Our shelter from the stormy blast
And our eternal home."

"I respect your devotion, but it does not work for me," Peter countered. "The promise of a better life in heaven does not satisfy here and now. Lucy does not complain, but I see the strain in her face. Those beautiful hands that I held when we first danced in Virginia are now permanently red and calloused."

Two events in 1794 brought some happiness to the Byram-Phillips families. Far up north, General "Mad Anthony" Wayne's victory over the Shawnee war chief Blue Jacket, and Buckongahelas' Delawares at the Battle of Fallen timbers on the Maumee River pushed the Shawnees first to the headwaters of the Auglaize River and later to Wapakoneta. Their attacks along the Ohio River and in Kentucky were then greatly reduced, and the defeated Indians ceded much of their land north of the Ohio to the United States. But, Tecumseh refused to sign the treaty.

That same year, John Phillips, Moses's brother who had promised to make the westward move once his older brother was established in Kentucky, arrived at Brook's Landing with his large family. Moses met him with his wagon and brought John and his family back to his home where John stayed until he could strike out on his own. "When I left Virginia, I was not sure I would ever see you again," said Moses as he embraced his brother, "I am glad to have more of my family here." Both men knew they were nearing the end of their lives and that they would value whatever time they had together..

Peter and William had gone out to the field that morning to hoe corn along with Isaac and three other slaves. Lucy, in the midst of preparing the noon meal with her eighth child, George, playing contentedly with his home-made blocks, felt like all was right with the world. Then suddenly her brother-in-law was driving the wagon wildly into the yard, his face ashen, and her husband was nowhere in sight. A paralyzing dread took hold of her even before he spoke. "Oh Lucy," he finally stammered, "Peter collapsed in the field. I felt for his pulse, but there was none. It must have been a stroke."

Lucy could not speak, nor could she move. Time seemed suspended. She could not bring herself to see if Peter's body were on the back of the wagon. She scooped up her youngest child so roughly that he began to cry and called for the other children to follow as she ran to her father's place not far across the pasture. "Peter is dead," she cried, trying to suppress the hysteria rising in her chest. "He died in the field while hoeing." Little Georgie was still wailing and the other children were in shock. Old Sarah gathered them up as Lucy mustered all of her strength to stay calm and deliberate.

"What will become of us?" she asked of her father. "Not a one of the boys is old enough to do the fieldwork, and I don't know enough to run the farm."

As soon as Moses could regain his own composure, he said, "Don't worry my child, I'll see that you are taken care of. I'll loan you some of my slaves, and Edmund and I will supervise them. Stay here tonight."

Lucy's sleep was fitful as she thought of her life with Peter. In the morning while feeding the children, she confided in her mother. "I remember our courtship in Virginia. Peter was so dashing and curious about the world. But, we never read poetry or discussed philosophy in Kentucky. There just wasn't time."

"I know the problem myself."

"There were times of intimacy that added to our family. I guess that's what life is really all about. We live on through our children, not through our accumulated treasures."

"That's what we women do."

"I never doubted Peter's love for me and the children. And the respect he showed for me never faltered. I know in talking to neighboring women that this is not always the case."

With the light of a new day, Lucy was a bit reassured, and with Georgie on her back papoose style, she started slowly back to her cabin, the other children trailing forlornly behind. But, as she marched along at the head of her troops, she kept repeating to herself—I can do this, I will do this; Peter did not marry a silly girl. Sarah, age nine, bringing up the rear, called out, "Wait Momma, we can't keep up."

In the dark days that followed, Lucy received the legal papers that contained an inventory of their possessions. It caused her to reflect on her life with Peter. She hated to admit it, but for all of their efforts, after fourteen years, they were still less well off than they had been back in Virginia.

Inventory and Appraisment of the Estate of Peter Byram. Deceased returned as follows (to wit):

	Pounds	S	D
4 Feather beds, 4 stocks and furniture	20	0	0
1 Wooling wheel	0	7	6
1 Flax wheel, 2 Ewes and 2 bulls £1.16	2	7	6
1 Hame, Saddle £ 2.02 1 Rifle gun £3. 15	5	17	0
1 Mare and colt	15	--	-
1 Table 7/6 and table furniture £5:8	5	15	6
5 Chairs 10/1 slate 2/6 Loom & tachlings	1	4	6
Potmottle £ 3:12 4 head of hogs £ 2:8	6	0	0
Farming utensils £ 3:15 2 cows & yearlings £8:10	12	12	1
1 case of razors, Sithe, 6 Lbs. wool 12/	1	3	0

We the appraisers agreeable to an order of Mason County after being sworn did appraise the said estate of Peter Byram.

Signed: Moses Bennett, Ephram Cole, Joseph Coryelle

At a court held for Mason County the 22 day of July 1799 this inventory and appraisment of Peter Byram deceased returned and ordered to be recorded.

Teste

(s) T. Marshall

Peter had died before the foundation they had built together in Kentucky could pay off. Still, Lucy was proud of her family and glad they had come west. She remembered the plaintive song of the Ohio boatman about the danger of an inconstant lover. Their love and commitment to each other stood in sharp contrast. It seemed to her that Peter had aged fast. One day he was a bold, young man eager to fight and love, and the next his dreams were fading into his grave.

Peter's premature death at the age of thirty-nine caused Moses to reflect on his own life. He felt himself aptly named, as he had led his people to the promised land, a kind of new Canaan. He admitted to Sarah, "The promise of great wealth temporarily blinded me and played a major part in our move to Kentucky. I had hoped not only to find land for myself and our sons and daughters, but also to sell much of my original five thousand acre grant." The first part of his dream had been accomplished with the patent in 1793 of eight hundred seventy-three acres on the North Fork of the Licking River added to his previous grants of four hundred fifty-three acres on Salt Spring and five hundred fifty-four on Licking Creek. The total of almost two thousand acres in landholdings was beyond his imagining. But his vision of great wealth never materialized. The difficulty of establishing negotiable title in the face of conflicting claims by other settlers and the machinations of speculators and their lawyers had whittled away his claims. "I am certainly not going to sell land to unsuspecting new settlers before titles are secure as some were doing," he told his wife. He consoled himself in the thought that more famous men had suffered a similar fate: Boone's fruitless defense of his claims had turned him into a debtor sought by the court and eventually driven him to Missouri; George Rogers Clark, also land poor, had died a debtor from financing some of his military campaigns with borrowed funds that Virginia never repaid. Even John May, who had amassed a fortune in land and had a town named after himself, was killed by Indians before he could enjoy his riches.

Moses Phillips lived to the age of eighty-nine, and as he lay dying with Sarah at his side and Lucy offering him what comfort she could, his mind spun with images of rich tobacco harvests and Revolutionary War hard times in Virginia, of the tortuous wagon trip to Redstone and the hazardous float down the Ohio, then the landing at Limestone, the clearing of land that would grow fine crops of corn and grain. Through all the memories were interwoven the smiles and laughter of his several dozen grandchildren who somehow survived the frontier hazards and diseases to grow into strong, honorable young folks. All the Phillips and Byrams in Kentucky gathered for their patriarch's burial on his land at Pea Ridge in 1811. There had been a special bond between the old man and Lucy, his first-born, and her father's death grieved her deeply. Lucy cried again when Moses' will was read: *In consideration of the natural love and affection Moses feels for his daughter Lucy and for five shillings, he grants her and all her children that she has by Peter Byram dec'd land in Mason part of my survey of eight hundred seventy-three acres patented to me 24 October 1787 located by McDermid's settlements to Coryells line."*

Indeed, he had provided for her as he had promised upon Peter's death. Land. His life had been about land, and his sons and sons-in-law together owned nearly all the land from the mouth of Stone Lick Creek to that of Phillips Creek.

It was now a year since Peter's death. Lucy tried to be patient and appear hopeful with her children, but the farm was not going well. Edmund helped her as much as he could, but the negroes' work was lackadaisical when their master was not working daily alongside them. She realized that the farm could not provide a living for all her boys when grown and that she must reduce the number of mouths she had to feed. To her youngest, only six years old, she said, "Georgie, my love, how'd you like to learn to be a carpenter? Your uncle Edmund told me that John Naylor in Maysville is looking for an apprentice." The boy's face turned to a frown and a tear ran down his cheek. "Will I ever see you again?"

Lucy's gut tightened and she replied, "Of course, my sweet darling, I'll come visit you."

The boy turned away and climbed to the cabin's loft and sobbed. That night Lucy cried herself to sleep; she had never felt so alone. She would miss tucking her littlest one, her baby, in bed at night. Nevertheless, the indenture was made as follows:

24 Feb 1800
Thomas Marshall Jr. clerk of Mason co And John Naylor of Mason co
*Transaction: Apprenticeship of **George Byram** for five years. Naylor to teach him the trade and mistery of a cabinet maker... and will cause him to be taught to read and write and common arithmetic including the rule of three. And during said term will provide him with good wholesome food, and cloathing fit for an apprentice. At expiration to pay apprentice three pounds 10 shillings and one decent new suit of clothes.*

A few months later she spoke to her oldest son. "Valentine my man, you are seventeen, and you need a trade to support yourself in the future. How would you like to be a hatter?

"Do you mean coonskin caps like Daniel Boone used to wear?

"No silly, fine hats for gentlemen and bonnets for ladies."

Valentine had always been an obedient child, and he understood there was no future for him on the farm. "I don't know anything about it, but I'll give it a try."

And so it was recorded:

28 July 1800 Thomas Marshall Jr. clerk of Mason co and Richard Soward of Mason co
*Transaction: Apprenticeship of **Valentine Byram** for three years.*
Soward to teach him art and mystery of a Hatter.

By 1810, when the census enumerator came, Lucy reported that she was head of the household with two males between 10 and 15, and one between 16 and 25; one additional female between 16 and 25, plus nine slaves. Valentine, working as a hatter, was in his own household next door with a wife and a boy and a girl under 10, plus five slaves.

In late winter of 1811, Lucy was awakened from her sleep by her bed moving under her. The house shook and she could smell dust. She tried to stand but fell to her knees and hit her head on the bed rail. She screamed for her children, but none could move for several minutes. "Come children; crawl outside."

The slaves were also crawling out of their cabins, and several were prostrate in the dust praying. "The devil has come!" one shouted. Another moaned, "It's the end of the world. Christ will come again!"

Lucy tried to calm them, saying "It is not the end of the world." She said it, but she was not sure. The temblors lasted on and off for two days. The slaves would not work and just sat around outside whimpering. Lucy and her boys went in search of their animals spooked by the shaking and roaring. Lucy wrote in her journal, "Earthquake, December 16, 1811. No one seriously hurt." About the time things were getting back to normal, the earth shook again in January and yet another time four days later. Lucy's reassurances fell on deaf ears, and in February, the biggest quake of all hit. The chimney cracked but did not collapse.

When she visited with her neighbors, some were planning had anticipated to move. But Lucy responded with, "It'll take more than a little shaking to make me give up the land I've worked so hard for and where my husband is buried." Later she learned that the town of New Madrid, Missouri, had been destroyed by the earthquake. "Can you imagine that the mighty Mississippi River ran backward for a time?" she posed an impossible but true thought to Benjamin.

"I don't doubt you, Momma, but it's hard to understand."

Children grow up and move on. By 1820, when the census enumerator came again, Lucy reported that she was head of household, and only her youngest, George, now twenty-five, was living with her. Of her three slaves, two worked in the fields and one was her servant and helper. Lucy's son Augustine, thirty-two, had married in Kentucky, then moved to Missouri. Westward, always pushing west, as had Daniel Boone and other early Kentucky settlers. Elizabeth married there at home, had five children, moved with them to Texas, where all but one child were killed by Indians. Lucy couldn't stop crying when she finally got the news in a letter from Elizabeth. Would this cycle of bloodshed never end? Sometimes it seemed as though Anna, her daughter who'd married Daniel Knapp and moved back to Virginia, was the only one with good sense.

Benjamin never married and moved back with his mother. Lucy tried her hand at raising horses, which she had liked since her youth in Virginia. When she had assembled a fine string, Benjamin wanted to sell them in New Orleans where, he assured her, the price would be much better than in Kentucky.

Lucy had heard stories of the lawlessness of that distant city and had grave misgivings, but finally she let him some friends go off with her sale stock. At the landing in Maysville, one of the horses shied and jumped when it was being led on board the boat, falling between the dock and the boat and breaking its leg. The friend called Thomas exclaimed, "This is not a good beginning to our trip."

Exuding confidence, Benjamin said, "Don't worry; one horse is nothing." They reached New Orleans without further mishap, unloaded the horses and sought a buyer. Immediately a dealer saw the fine-looking Kentucky horses and made what the boys considered a generous offer. Benjamin was ecstatic. "Mother will be pleased with me."

But, there were others who were watching the transaction as Benjamin stuffed the money inside his shirt. These rough characters followed when the boys checked into an inn. After a fine dinner, the boys were walking back to the inn when they were attacked by a half-dozen ruffians and dragged into an alley. Benjamin was knocked down and kicked unconscious. When he awoke, the roughs were gone and along with his money. Thomas was on the ground nearby.

When the boys recovered from their beating, they found jobs to earn enough money to buy passage back to Kentucky. Ben confessed to his buddy, "I'm so ashamed. I don't know how I can face mother. I think I'd better stay here."

"Nonsense. You can't leave your mother wondering whatever became of you."

When Benjamin returned home empty-handed, it broke Lucy's heart as well as her purse. After all her years of struggling to make ends meet on her land, she gave up, rented the farm and moved to Williamsburg, Kentucky, where she kept a tavern for a few years.

Late one night, a crude and boisterous group of men from out of town demanded another round of drinks. When Lucy brought them to the table, one of the men grabbed her and said, "How about a little kiss, dearie?" Lucy pushed him away and picked up one the glasses and poured it on the crotch of her assailant. She turned and ran back to behind the bar with the drunk staggering in pursuit. Lucy always kept a loaded pistol under the bar. She knew how to use it ever since Peter had taught her so long ago in Virginia. She found the pistol, pulled the hammer back and aimed for the drunk, stopping him in his tracks. He teetered, turned and fled with his buddies. "We're not going to drink where we're not welcome." The other patrons cheered.

Finally, Lucy decided she had had enough and moved back to Virginia to spend the last years of her life living with her daughter, Anna. "I don't regret marrying my dashing young soldier, Peter, nor moving to Kentucky," she'd told Anna. "Perhaps I've been seeking to escape from predictability all my life, but I don't have the strength anymore for living on the frontier." In 1836, Lucy Byram collapsed and died while walking in the formal garden of her daughter's home not far from the Phillips' ancestral lands. She had lived a full life of eighty-four years and had earned her rest.

~3~

The Minuteman

Joseph Todd was playing cards with some of his farmer neighbors at Baird's Tavern in Warwick, New York. His partner, Jake, kept criticizing his play. "That's a pretty weak lead. We'll never get ahead if you keep playing like that." Joseph's eyes flared, and he squared his big shoulders, sort of like a wild turkey to intimidate his rivals. On the next round he slapped the winning card hard on the table. "There, I guess my play is not so bad."

"You're cheating," accused Moses, one of the opponents at the table.

This was too much for Joseph. "I'm not going to take that from you, you little pipsqueak. Step outside," he said, rising abruptly from the table.

From behind the bar, Mr. Baird called out, "Calm down boys. We all need to be united as we face difficult days ahead. We can't be divided by petty quarrels."

Joseph sat back down and took a swig from his tankard. He steered the conversation around to the many complaints he had against the British crown.

Jake responded, "Quit badmouthing our motherland. We need the British army to protect us from the Indians."

Joseph frowned and said, "I'm tired of being ruled by some nitwit of a king far away. We can govern ourselves. Generations of Todds have put up with the king in England, but we made the perilous journey to America to be free and practice our religion as we please."

"You'll have a chance to be counted next week in Goshen when a petition will be circulated declaring support for the Continental Congress," replied Jake.

"I'll be there; will you?" Joseph received no reply.

Joseph walked home eager to tell his wife, Catherine, the news. "Next week I'm going to ride to Goshen and sign a revolutionary pledge."

"That will mean a whole day missed from fieldwork," his practical wife chided.

"I know, but we need to make a stand."

On the appointed day, Joseph rose with the sun and pointed his plow horse down the rutted road toward Goshen. When he arrived, he listened as the pledge was read: "On this eighth day of June, 1775, we the undersigned proclaim our support of the Continental Congress and resistance to British oppression."

Joseph emphatically added his X beside his name that had been printed out for him along with two hundred twenty-eight others from Orange County.

Joseph looked around the assemblage, but his card-playing antagonists, Jake and Moses, were nowhere to be seen. Damnable Tory loyalists, he thought.

The signers had known trouble was coming when the Orange County courthouse was built two years before and people argued about where to hang King George's coat of arms. In the words of the wags, it was a shield with three sleepy, yellow lions in a red field. A young hothead called out, "Give me the arms, and I will place them where no one will object." Abruptly, he grabbed the shield and held it up against the side of the building and broke it to bits with a carpenter's hammer. Those standing nearby went silent, but no one condemned him for the contempt he'd just shown of the emblems of royalty and distant authority.

The recent Boston Tea Party was on everyone's mind. Rebels dressed as Indians had dumped tea from three ships into Boston harbor. After the French and Indian War and Pontiac's uprising, the British knew they had to finance an effective army and colonial administration, and they did not want the colonial courts to be supported directly by the colonists and thus independent of the motherland. To serve these ends, they'd first imposed a tax on oil, wine, lead, paper, glass and tea. The colonists refused to pay, claiming that only their own assemblies could impose taxes. Colonel Washington proposed that Virginia not import any taxed goods. In response, the British retracted the new taxes except for a small duty remaining on tea. Parliament concocted a clever plan to establish an acknowledgement of their right to tax. The existing tea tax was reduced such that the total price of tea was less than it had been before. The British assumed the colonists would pay the tax rather than do without their favored drink, but they underestimated the colonists' resolve. Ships with tea were turned away in Philadelphia and New York. In Boston, seven thousand citizens came out to demonstrate on the wharf, demanding that the ships leave. When the British customs agent would not let the ships leave, about two hundred men boarded the tea-laden ships and threw the cargo overboard.

Catherine Todd, in her own small protest, made tea from the New Jersey tea plant. When she served the first cup, Joseph complained, "Cat, what's this weak tea we're drinking?"

"I made it from a wild plant because I'm not buying imported tea anymore. And, by the way, we're not using sugar imported from the Caribbean raised with the sweat of slaves."

"I agree, it tastes better with a little patriotism," said Joseph after taking his second sip, "but, I did like my tea sweetened a bit."

"We can get by with local honey," said Catherine proudly.

The Todd home in Orange County was in the Warwick Valley that was dominated by Mounts Adam and Eve on the edge of a swampy area referred to as the Drowned Lands. The story went that the area was once alive with rattlers and other snakes, thus explaining the Biblical names for the mountains. There were still snakes on the elevations, and the children were warned not to play there. Stories were told that young men sometimes went into the mountains in the spring and killed as many as one hundred snakes in a single day, solely as a test of their virility.

Mounts Adam and Eve

For all the wildness still surrounding them, the Todds were only thirty-five miles north of New York City. After Washington had suffered a humiliating defeat there and retreated across New Jersey in 1776, the British were firmly ensconced in the city. This emboldened the loyal Tories in the area, and they were making trouble. New Yorkers were divided, with the colony supplying five regiments each to both the Continental Army and the British Army. There was far from consensus that the rebellion was a good idea, and the debate was not always peaceful. The differences within the county led to an increasing number of harassments and mysterious burning of farm buildings. Ever since the Declaration of Independence and Washington's assumption of command of the Continental Army, there had been fighting on two fronts: the more or less organized battles with the British and a kind of civil war among neighbors.

In response to the arsons, a volunteer militia was organized, and Joseph told Catherine, "This afternoon I'm going to Warwick and join." Minutemen had to be ready to turn out on a moment's notice. Joseph wanted to join. Catharine objected, "You are thirty-one years old and responsible for our three children. I hate for you to join and be away from home for months on patrol. It's the middle of June; you haven't finished weeding yet. I don't have to tell you that without adequate cultivation, the harvest will be small and our winter survival in jeopardy." Her voice was calm but firm. "Let's discuss this more."

"But I signed the Revolutionary Pledge, and I feel obligated to follow through. Tonight a company's being organized."

"Why didn't you tell me before? I'm as committed to independence as you, but I wonder if this is the right time. We must think of our children."

"Freedom will be our children's inheritance. There's not going to be a good time. I know it's risky, but we can't hope to be free of the English without sacrifice. I can't in good conscience let other men risk their lives to protect our farm. I've been wrestling with my conscience and have just now made up my mind."

"Couldn't you just let the others man the patrols? The farm needs attention. Our children and I can do a lot, but it will be a struggle."

"Now, Cat, you know that many of our neighbors have risked their lives for us. Remember, when Burt, Ketchum, Whitney and the others chased the Tories that robbed the silversmith in Warwick? I wasn't along on that one. No, I can't just let others shoulder the burden. I will meet the company at the usual meeting point in Warwick tonight."

Catharine bit her lip to keep from crying. "The prospect of your getting killed is more than I can bear," she told him. "A lone woman with small children can't survive." Joseph did not reply, but stiffened and gathered his gear for the walk into town. He knew if he paused, he might lose his resolve.

"Wait, at least give me a kiss before you go. Don't go away angry with me." Catharine held her youngest to her bosom as she watched her man disappear down the road on foot with his musket and haversack on his shoulder.

Joseph left the house with his mind in turmoil. He met neighbor Ephraim as he walked along toward town and remarked to him, "There's something deep my soul that drives me to protect my family and land."

There were other thoughts that he kept to himself. He feared most of all being labeled a coward. In a rural community, where everyone knows everyone, a coward would stand out—the shame of it all. It might be hard to convince Catharine that he was thinking of his family, but he was aware that his children someday might want to marry into neighboring families who would be unlikely to welcome a groom or bride from the family of a coward. But, another thought also haunted him, and he confided to Ephraim, "I've never left Catharine alone with the farm and children."

As they trudged down the road, Joseph and Ephraim discussed their reasons for joining the militia. Joseph admitted he was obsessed with obtaining more land. He was not sure how to do it, but he was prepared to die trying. In 1763, King George had prohibited settlement and land purchases on the western frontier. The land hungry opposed the proclamation, taking it as further cause for growing anger against the crown and sentiment for rebellion. "I feel all cooped up here on the east coast when there are tens of thousands of acres to the west waiting for the plow."

Ephraim agreed. "My growing family could use more land, and there surely is none available here, but moving westward must be postponed for a while. I am concerned about the Indians, and there is no good way to move west over the mountains. What does your wife think?"

"She's in favor of getting free of rule by a distant, arbitrary king, but she's not enthusiastic about moving, and she wanted me to postpone joining 'til the corn is laid by."

Warwick in 1776 was little more than a wide spot in the road: a few houses, a tavern, tannery and a log meeting house. As he arrived at Baird's Tavern, Joseph could see the militia forming up under the direction of Captain Peter Butolf. The company was part of the 4th Regiment of the Orange County

Militia under the joint command of Colonel Henry Wisner and Colonel John Hathorn. Wisner was the hothead who'd smashed the Kings arms at the courthouse three years before, and he did nothing to conceal his part in that event. Militia captains achieved their rank by election, not appointment, and the congenial Butolf did not take his command too seriously, imposing minimal discipline on the company of thirty men. So as the last laggards were cajoled out of the tavern after finishing a rum for the road, they set off to patrol at random, not knowing where an enemy might be.

Catharine's house was as no-nonsense as was she. No decorations or pictures, though she had departed from the usual whitewashed walls and painted the kitchen a soft yellow by adding iron oxide to the paint. The circular braided cotton rugs on the kitchen/sitting-room and tiny bedroom floors were of her own creation. They were made of the family's old clothes once they got beyond patching, rather like ghosts of their former selves.

Every day after cleaning the house, washing and darning clothes and caring for the stock, the family donned their straw hats and set out to do the farm work Joseph had left in his wife's hands. Josh was eleven, Sarah nine, and Hannah five. The weather that summer was unusually hot and humid. Trying to keep ahead of the weeds in their corn was the most trying of their new duties. After a few rows of hoeing, sweat dripped from their foreheads and soaked their blouses. The girls' wet hair fell over their faces. They kept pushing it back, but to no avail.

Catharine had to laugh at them, "You girls look like dolls that have been left out in the rain." Little Hannah started to cry, "I can't help it, cornstalks keep swatting me in the face." Catherine left her row, bent down, held her daughter close and said, "I'm not making fun of you, just the way you look. You are doing a great job helping your sister, and I'm proud of you." Hannah wiped her eyes on her sleeve. When Catherine allowed the children a rest, she poured water on her kerchief and wiped the brows of her girls. Even as Josh struggled to keep ahead of the girls, he pretended he was not tired and would not stand to have his brow dried.

With more than a little bitterness Catharine watched the neighboring men who hadn't joined the militia work their fields. But she believed that a person made do with what she had and tried to keep complaints to herself, though she sometimes failed in the latter. She wanted much more than a life of field labor and housework for her girls. Each evening, Catharine and the children were exhausted and went to bed soon after supper.

One night, Catharine awoke to strange sounds outside in the barnyard. Were the Tories coming to burn their barn while her man was away? Joseph had their only gun. The girls awoke and climbed down from the loft trembling. "I'm frightened, Mommy," cried the littlest. Catharine in her most authoritative and sure voice said, "It's nothing. A wild animal must have spooked the cow." She gave them both a hug and led them back up the ladder. She kissed and patted them until they were asleep again. Nothing was amiss the next morning, but whenever she heard noises on subsequent nights, Catharine's heart raced, and she wondered when Joseph would come home.

The next morning, Josh was already at breakfast when Catharine called up to her girls still asleep in the loft. "Elizabeth, Hannah, the cock has crowed. There's work to be done if you want to eat this winter. Today, we will slice apples to dry in the sun." Groans sounded from the loft, but soon the girls were dressed, had their breakfast of cornmeal mush with a bit of molasses and were hard at work. They did not like it, but the girls understood that their work was critical while their father was gone.

When the barrel of cornmeal was almost empty, they hitched the horses to the wagon and took some corn from last year's harvest to be ground at the mill owned by the Burts on Longhouse Creek. Josh proudly took the reins as he had seen his father do, but in his enthusiasm his mother had to chide him, "Slow down Josh. If you hit a rock, our load will spill." Bellvale was a small settlement three miles east of Warwick village and the same distance from the Todd farm. Daniel Burt had been one of the first settlers in the county in 1760, having come earlier to establish a claim but soon after abandoning that isolated farm and returning to Connecticut for a time. Coming back to Orange County, he established his mill on the creek named after the Indian longhouse that once stood on its bank. "Funny how we name places after things that are gone," Catherine had remarked to the miller. The girls were impressed by the big overshot wheel that drove the gears. But, they complained as they took turns shoveling the ears into the chute to be shelled and then watched the kernels drop into the stone grinding wheels. "Hush," said Catharine. "In my youth, we pounded it by hand using a mortar. You don't know what hard work is."

Mr. Burt explained how his early settlement was an advantage in his business. "Some who want to build a dam and mill don't have enough land for the flowage behind the dam and can't persuade adjoining landowners to sell the necessary flowage rights at a reasonable price. I was here first and fortunate to own enough acreage."

"Where do the millstones come from?" Catherine asked. "I don't think there are rocks like that around here, even up on Mount Adam."

"The millstones must be imported from Europe," replied Mr. Burt as he continued with a bit of local history. "We have iron deposits here, and Bellvale was the site of Scrauley's iron forge, the only one in the colony, but it was burned by the British."

"Why'd they do that?" asked Josh.

"The durned Brits prohibited iron manufacture to force us to buy high-priced iron from them. Scrauley defied the law, but it cost him his forge." These past insults were now fueling the rebellion. The ironworkers later got even when they built the Sterling Iron Works in the southeast corner of Warwick that made bullets for Washington's army and forged the five hundred-yard, one hundred eighty-six-ton chain placed across the Hudson at West Point to prevent British ships from sailing upriver. When the family returned home with their cornmeal, Catharine remarked, "Mr. Burt surely is a talkative fellow." But she enjoyed conversation with anyone with information and opinions that might provide some news about the condition and whereabouts of the militia and her husband.

When Joseph returned home in September he and Josh worked frantically to harvest their corn. The yield was less than usual and might not be enough to get them through to the next harvest. Nevertheless, Joseph praised his family for their good work in his absence. They had done the best they could. The following spring, Joseph and Josh planted more potatoes than usual, hoping an excess in that crop would carry them through any shortage in cornmeal.

"It'll be scalloped potatoes for breakfast, boiled potatoes for dinner and baked potatoes for supper," Josh had laughed. "Good thing we have a cow."

Later in the spring, Joseph announced, "It's time to plant corn now. My father learned from the Indians to plant when white oak leaves are the size of a mouse ear." Joseph came from a line of ancestors who joined their colonial neighbors in local militias Indians attacked the settlements. The children of more than one of the Connecticut ancestors of Catherine had been killed or captured. Just as soon as the Indians were subdued and accepted their presence, the colonists pushed further west, and the conflicts began again. Only in Joseph's time, the picture was muddied with the war against the king.

The colonials weren't the only parties wrestling with questions inherent in the choice to accommodate or stand up to perceived injustice. The Indian's leader, Joseph Brant, had also struggled with the pros and cons of violent resistance against encroaching white settlements. Brant argued with himself about what to do. He was born of Mohawk Indian parents who gave him the name Hayendanegea, meaning "he places two bets." He had been selected to attend Moore's Charity School for Indians at Lebanon, Connecticut. He quickly became the favorite of Sir William Johnson, the British superintendent of the northern Indians of America. After the death of his European wife, Johnson married his former Indian mistress, who happened to be Brant's sister Molly. Brant became Johnson's assistant and helped him run the Indian Department headquartered in Quebec. Brant married a daughter of an Oneida chief, and they began farming near Canajoharie, New York. Two of his wives were to die of tuberculosis, an imported gift, so to speak, of the Europeans.

Brant thought that the future of his people depended on adopting the practices and culture of the whites. He joined the Anglican Church and translated the Prayer Book and Gospel of Mark into Mohawk. Many of the Iroquois were living much as the colonists, often in better homes than the frontier whites. They farmed and sent hunters to Ohio to bring back wild game. But, that was the problem: Not only were the Indians losing land to the settlers, the newcomers were destroying their hunting grounds. Still, Brant thought that the Indians were better off with the English than they'd be if the colonies became independent. He favored the Brits because they did not support the western expansion that seemed to drive the colonials, but rather wanted to maintain the fur trade with the natives on their ancestral lands. But, the King's law was ignored, and settlers spread into the Mohawk Valley. "What strange manner of men are these who would defy the orders of their King, risk Indian attacks and live under primitive conditions on the frontier, far from the benefits of civilization?" Brant had asked his mentor. Johnson replied, "They are seekers of land, pure and simple. Your lands." Johnson, himself in possession of much land, was also a slaveholder and passed on the practice to his protégé. Keeping slaves was not new to the Indians who enslaved members of defeated tribes.

In the same year that George Washington took command of the Continental Army, Brant had become the principle war chief of the Indian confederacy and received a captain's commission in the British Army. He sailed to England and was admitted into the best society, including visiting with the diarist, Boswell and having his portrait painted by the eminent artists Joshua Reynolds and George Romney. Reynolds saw a handsome face, not at all wild and fierce. Brant was duly impressed with the power and grandeur of the British, and he was more determined than ever to cast his people's fate with them.

For all of his civilized accoutrements, Brant could be a fierce warrior as captured in the words of Gen. John Burgoyne, the British commander in Canada, who launched attacks in the Mohawk Valley.

I will let loose the dogs of hell,
Ten thousand Indians, who shall yell
And foam and tear, and grin and roar,
And drench their moccasins in gore:
To those I'll give full scope and play
From Ticonderoga to the Delaware ....

In July 1779, another call to arms was issued in the colony. Word had quickly spread from one farmhouse to another in the valley surrounding the village of Warwick. Right in the middle of the war against the British, a force of three hundred Mohawk Indians, British loyalists and officers from Fort Niagara had attacked settlements near Minisink on the Delaware River, eighty miles northwest of New York City. Minisink was an Indian word meaning people of the strong country. A local company of volunteer militia was being organized to intercept the Indians before they did more killing and burning.

The Fourth Orange County Regiment under the command of Colonel John Hathorn had orders from General Washington to join together with a unit from Goshen commanded by Lieutenant Colonel Benjamin Tusten, who knew the strength of the Mohawk warriors led by war chief Joseph Brant. Tusten strongly suggested waiting for help from the Continental Army before pursuing the marauders. But emotions in the community were running high. Major Samuel Meeker mounted his horse, flourished his sword and yelled, "Let brave men follow me. The cowards stay behind." Any talk of delay was over; no one could risk being labeled a coward.

The next day after marching an exhausting seventeen miles, the men from Warwick joined those from Goshen. Hathorn split his force of one hundred twenty minutemen in two and moved to surprise and ambush the Indians as they crossed the river with their booty looted from farms they'd attacked. Because they were short of ammunition, Hathorn ordered the men not to fire until they were sure that every shot would count, but, just then, Bezaleel Tyler thought he saw the Indians leading one of his stolen horses and fired upon the culprit.

Alerted by the shot, Brandt quickly outflanked the two groups and many colonials fled for their lives. Joseph, with the group cut off from the main action, hunkered down behind a rock with several of his neighbors and fired while keeping his head down as much as possible. Acrid smoke seared his lungs, and to his right, he heard the cries of the men cut down by musket fire. In his report to General Washington, Hathorn described the horrors of the battle: "The cruel yelling of those bloody monsters, the seed of Anak in size, exceed thought or description. The people by this time was so scattered I found myself unequal to rally them again, consequently every man made choice of his own way." Forty-five militia men were killed, including Tusten who in warning of the debacle had been right, now dead right. The Indians lost only three men.

Several weeks later, a Continental Army of three thousand led by General Sullivan destroyed every Iroquois Confederation village in their path, some fifty in total. The Indians narrowly escaped with their lives, but their will to fight was lost in spite of Brant's strident urging to regroup and continue. Sullivan's expedition marched on without further opposition as far west as the Seneca village of Chenussio near the Genesee River. The army destroyed a red-painted, two-story longhouse with gabled roof and one hundred twenty-eight houses with substantial furniture. Twenty thousand bushels of the Indian's stored corn was burned along with acres of bearing fruit trees and vegetable crops, including pumpkins, squash, watermelons, potatoes, beans and turnips, produce of high quality, carefully tended and even irrigated by hand. It would be years before white settlers had anything its equal. Sullivan would eventually parlay his successful expedition against the Iroquois into a seat in Congress.

Joseph Todd was disappointed that he had seen little action at Minisink even as he realized that being out of the thick of the fight probably saved his life. The battle remained a hot topic of discussion at Baird's Tavern on King Street in Warwick. Francis Baird was adamant in his opposition to the British after the Stamp Act had taxed taverns. One night, Joseph opined to his fellow minutemen, "It's a vicious circle with the Indians committing atrocities in response to their loss of land and traditional hunting grounds, followed by the settlers committing atrocities upon the Indians, and on, and on."

He was met with scowls of disapproval from the others, and Ephraim responded heatedly, "How can you say that when the barbarians use their tomahawks and knives to take scalps even of women and children?" Joseph could imagine that the warriors sometimes could not control their emotions in the heat of attacks. But, he let the topic drop.

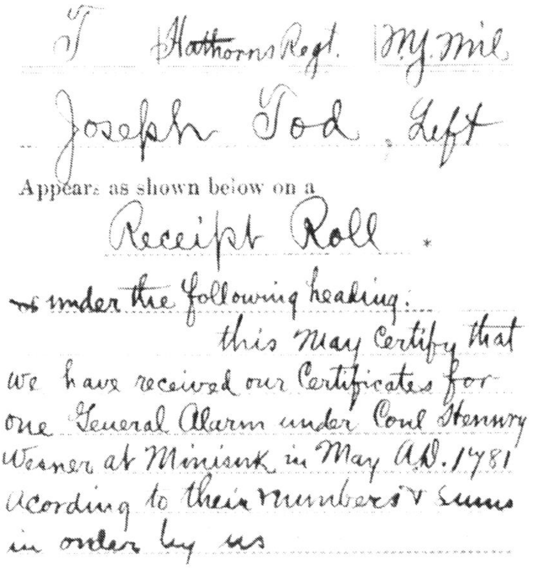

> *of Hathorns Regt. NY Mil.*
> *Joseph Tod, Left*
> Appears as shown below on a
> *Receipt Roll.*
> *under the following heading:*
> *this May Certify that we have received our Certificates for one General Alarm under Conl Henrry Wisner at Minisink in May A.D. 1781 according to their numbers & Sums in order by us*

Troubles from the Loyalists continued even as the Continental Army scored some victories. In 1781, Butolf issued a general alarm and called up the minutemen for patrols. Neighbors John Clark and Henry Brop had been murdered near De Boues Pond. Both men were members of the volunteer militia. Joseph was determined to take his sixteen-year-old Josh, with him this time. Catharine had accommodated to Joseph's being gone but she was reluctant to see her sixteen year-old son go with him.

"Josh is but a boy."

"He's a man, and it's time he did manly things."

"I'm not impressed with manhood." But, at the same time, Catharine was well aware of how close to home these attacks had been, and she acquiesced.

Josh was tall with a big chest like his father, but had not yet been successful in reproducing his father's big, broad, brown mustache, and he still had the look of a boy about his face. They had no uniforms, just the homespun blouses and breeches Catherine had sewn and patched as best she could to make them last. Joseph also carried a small tent that they would share. Catherine stuffed some johnnycakes into the men's packs when they were not looking.

When Butolf addressed the men gathered before him in Warwick, there was emotion in his voice. "Two of our fellow minutemen have been murdered. This has gotten completely out of hand. Everyone in the valley is frightened. If the Tories are now targeting us, we are all in grave danger. I see that our ranks are less than before. I suspect that some are staying home to protect their families, and some are simply derelict in their duty. I thank you all for coming."

"What's our strategy?" asked Joseph.

"We will break up into small groups and patrol randomly to make our armed presence known. If someone is attacked, we can respond quickly. Lieutenant Todd, you come with me." Butolf marched south toward the New Jersey line and arrived in the vicinity of Clove's Tavern. To bolster morale, they usually managed to bivouac near taverns. Joseph opened his knapsack and found Catherine's johnnycakes. He felt Cat's love in this small token.

Joseph was known as a storyteller, though as often greeted by groans as laughs. "What is George Washington's favorite tree? Give Up? Infantry." The men snorted, but it helped pass the time.

For weeks, the patrols did not discover anything out of order, but Colonel Hathorn thought that their mere presence kept the peace. But then, Joseph's small group came upon a makeshift shelter in the woods near the pond. Joseph and his friend Ephraim circled around to the back while the rest approached the front. Butolf called out for anyone inside to come out and state their business. Just then, Joseph, Josh, and Ephraim noticed a movement in the brush. Perhaps some men had returned to the shelter to find the militia around it and slunk back into the woods. For a moment, a man was visible and Ephraim raised his musket to fire. Joseph grabbed his arm and said, "Wait! We do not know who it is, and we don't want innocent blood on our hands."

When Butolf came up and was told what happened, he stridently rebuked the two men. "We found stolen property in the shelter. You are of no use if you will not shoot these thieving murderers when you have the chance. If they were honest men, they would've identified themselves and not stolen away."

But Joseph stood his ground, replying, "It is no use fighting for our security and independence if merely suspicious behavior is cause for death. Just because these men were in the vicinity where a murder took place does not prove their guilt." Joseph knew he was right, but he burned with the captain's harsh words spoken in front of his son.

To calm his emotions, Joseph went hunting. He bagged a deer and planned to take the skin home to be tanned at the tannery in Warwick. At least he would have something to show for his summer's work. He knew he would not be paid for his service, just more certificates that would probably be worthless as New York lacked the funds to make good on them. Joseph was dismayed that many of his countrymen were in favor of independence but did not want to serve in the military or tax themselves to pay for it. Joseph also thought it curious that the certificates were denominated in British pounds and schillings.

Upon his return home in the late fall, Joseph abed with his wife, snuggled up and caressed the back of her neck. He loved it when she let her hair down for the night. Then his hand rubbed her back and went steadily, but unhurriedly down to her thighs. Catharine, at age forty, was still an attractive and desirable woman, even if days in the field had roughened and wrinkled her skin. Her inner thigh, however, was smooth as silk. Catharine stiffened and did not respond to his touch.

"Is that any way to treat a man on his first night at home from soldiering?" he cajoled.

"You can't come marching in here after leaving me and the girls to do your work in the fields and expect me to be enthusiastic. I'm exhausted."

"I know it's been hard for you, and I will try to make it up to you." He continued his caresses, and finally Catharine rolled over to face him and then pulled him on top of her. He entered her, and the long days of sleeping on hard, wet ground were forgotten.

When Joseph got around to reading the old papers at the tavern in Warwick village, he learned that while he was gone in September of 1781, Washington had defeated Cornwallis at Yorktown, Virginia, with the help of the French. It was rumored that the Brits at the Battle of Yorktown sang a song entitled, "World Turned Upside Down."

If buttercups buzzed after the bee;
If boats were on land, churches on sea;
If ponies rode men and grass ate the cows;
And cats should be chased to holes by the mouse;
If the mammas sold their babies to the gypsies for half a crown;
Summer were spring and the t'other way round;
Then all the world would be upside down.

Catharine was not sure whose world the song referred to even after the hostilities appeared to have ended. "The hardships of war are not over for us. It is all fine for Washington to say he would give his 'fortune and sacred honor' for the cause, but we are modest dirt farmers with little to spare. Surely, that is the end of the war and we can get back to our normal lives."

"I'm relieved as well," said Joseph. He had been moved by his wife's honest expression about the hardships she'd known. He did not share with her his awareness that despite many Loyalists having left for Canada, the bitterness between the Tories and the Rebels in their community would not dissipate immediately. And even after the surrender at Yorktown, the main British army still occupied New York City. It might be some time before a peace treaty was signed. Joseph was all too right. Local attacks continued and the militia was called out again in April, 1782, just before Samuel, was born, meaning another season of planting interrupted for the Todd family. The Brits did not evacuate New York City until the Treaty of Versailles in 1783, they would control Detroit and create trouble in the West with help from Joseph Brant's Indians for many more years.

Still, life in Warwick Valley went on, slowly resuming the ordinary patterns of the days before the conflict. Catharine valued reading even if she could not write her name. She jumped at the chance to meet Noah Webster at his school in nearby Goshen and purchase a copy of his 1786 *The American Spelling Book* from which she taught her children with the help of a neighbor. The purchase required considerable sacrifice by Catherine, but she was determined to improve her family's opportunities and education. The years ticked on, and more children came, eight in total. One day, Elizabeth, the oldest, came running into the house breathless. "There is a man outside who says he is here to take the census. What's a census?"

Catharine welcomed in the enumerator, whom she knew to be one of the more respected residents of the county, and she and the children listened as he read the relevant authorization:

"Representation and direct Taxes shall be apportioned among the several States which may be included within this Union, according to their respective Numbers. The actual Enumeration shall be made within three Years after the first Meeting of the Congress of the United States, and within every subsequent Term of ten Years, in such Manner as they shall by Law direct."—Article I, Section 2 of the Constitution of the United States

"Our family will be in the very first one, now in 1790," Catherine pointed out. The other girls were rather proud. The boys ignored the whole thing. Thus, it was recorded for the household of Joseph Todd in the year 1790: two free white males under sixteen, one free white male of sixteen years and upwards, including heads of families, and six free white females including heads of families. Catharine registered a mild protest because the females were all lumped together regardless of age. Son Josh, now twenty-five, was head of his own household of three located next door.

In the new nation, Joseph took his citizenship responsibilities seriously. He'd been on the Warwick, Orange County, tax rolls since 1774 and at the town meeting he allowed his name to be put forward for the offices of road master and fence viewer. The district road master organized work crews to maintain the roads and served as keeper of the pound for stray dogs and other animals. Fence masters settled any arguments over split-rail fence building and maintenance. It was the custom that property owners on each side of their common boundary were responsible for half of the fence. Joseph was disappointed when he was not selected for either post. Later, he kept his complaints to the minimum when the town assessed each taxable male to contribute to the fund, totaling one hundred pounds, to benefit the poor. He was grateful that he and his family need not be among the recipients. Another tax levied on dog owners funded an indemnity paid to anyone whose sheep were killed by dogs. At least now, the citizens could vote on their own taxes.

Joseph had been pleased when his former commander-in-chief, Washington, was inaugurated as the new country's first president in 1789. He was proud of his role in his country's birth, giving rise to a belief in a future that was boundless and full of opportunity. He did not want to miss out. Settlers were streaming into the former lands of the Iroquois, and Joseph wanted to be among them. The most common topic at the tavern in Warwick was the prospect of better land further west. Joseph's best friend and neighbor, Benjamin Whitney, spoke of nothing else. Joseph asked Catharine if she thought they could better their lives by moving further west. "We have been scratching in this dirt and stones since 1774, and our family has grown to a size that our present land cannot support. Our children will never have farms of their own here. I've had this vision of going to Michigan."

"Where is Michigan? I never heard of it."

"It's virgin territory to the west across Lake Erie. I hear tell that the land is rich and there's enough for all our children to have farms. But, first we will settle in western New York."

Catharine was silent for a few minutes, then replied, "I really don't want to go. We have a good enough life and our house is big enough now that some of the children are married. I really do not relish the idea of starting over and living in lean-tos and rough log cabins. Couldn't we all be comfortable here? What is this land hunger you have?"

"I am mindful of what you say," Joseph said as though he had not really heard her, "but we really do need more land for the children."

"As much as I like having them close by," Catharine countered, "they could go by themselves if they've the mind."

"I'm sorry, Cat, but this is something I have to do." Joseph had made his commitment to a future his wife did not wish for herself, but she recognized the futility of fighting the powerful urge men seemed to have to always be seeking more and better land.

Joseph also consulted Reverend Montague at the Baptist Church in Warwick village, whose good judgment he and many others in the community trusted. A person did not make these moves alone. A small group of families befriended through their militia ties—the Hortons, Ketchums and Whitneys—joined the Todds to discuss going out together. Joseph's premonition that his children would marry into the families of his militia comrades was being borne out. Daughter Elizabeth married William Lobdell, Hannah married Joseph Lee Horton, and son Sam married Hannah Whitney.

Joseph and Catharine traveled to Hannah's house where they discussed possible routes west with their daughter and son-in-law, Joe Horton. "Overland on the frontier is out of the question," said Joe. "There are no roads, and besides there are the impenetrable mountains." He suggested following the Mohawk River in northern New York, which was the route favored by the Indians through the barrier of the Appalachians.

Hannah added, "I've read that major improvements have recently been made to navigation on the Mohawk." Joseph took these improvements as a sign that he should now get serious about going west. Together the men carefully mapped out their route. First they'd take horse-drawn wagons east to the Newburgh landing on Haverstraw Bay of the Hudson bordering Orange County, then take boats north up the Hudson to the mouth of the Mohawk above Albany. There they would portage around the twenty-foot Cohoes Falls to Schenectady and then boat up the improved Mohawk to Wood Creek and down to Oneida Lake. This would put them just sixty miles from their interim destination in Palmyra, New York, a manageable distance by wagon. It looked simple on a map, but Joseph knew it would be arduous in fact.

"I'm not leaving without all of the household goods we have managed to acquire." Catharine continued to insist. "I'm not sleeping on the floor again."

"But that will overload the wagon, making the boats hard to maneuver over obstacles."

Not to be put off, Catharine said emphatically, "Then get another wagon, and I'll drive it."

The Todds sold their one hundred eighteen-acre farm to Benjamin Horton for $3,125. Thus began the historical process of farm consolidation. He was Hannah's brother-in-law, who had chosen to stay behind. Part of the money was used to buy another wagon and team. The party that embarked for the western frontier in the spring of 1804 included Joseph and Catharine, each driving a wagon, the families of sons Josh, thirty-nine, Jonathan (twenty-six), Samuel, twenty-two, and daughter Hannah (thirty-three) plus unmarried Catharine (17); daughters Elizabeth, Margaret, Anna and Sarah with families and various other Whitneys and Hortons would come later. They headed east to a landing at Newburgh where they unloaded the wagons before they were lifted by crane on board the Durham boats they'd hired.

Of the same design that had carried George Washington across the Delaware in 1776, the boats were pointed on each end, sixty feet long and eight wide and only drew twenty-four inches of water when loaded. A twenty-foot sweep provided steerage and forward motion. The boat had a square sail that could be used when the wind was right, but most locomotion was provided by four men who pushed the boat forward, using twenty-foot iron-tipped poles with knobs at the end. They walked along cleated boards the length of the boat. It was risky work, and the boatmen sometimes fell overboard. At the mouth of the Mohawk above Albany, the boat was unloaded and the wagons moved overland to the terminal at Schenectady.

Upstream in 1795, a mile-long canal had been built around Little Falls with five wooden locks rebuilt with stone in 1803. A mile-long canal at Herkimer avoided two troublesome rapids. Above Rome, the Mohawk turns north and on tiny Wood Creek, the only connection to Lake Oneida, four timber locks were built, turning the shallow stream into a series of navigable pools. There were still dangerous rifts caused by gravel washed into the Mohawk from connecting streams. One was at the mouth of Canajoharie Creek. When Joseph's Durham boat passed the mouth of the Canajoharie, he could not help but think of his former adversary, Joseph Brant, who had once farmed there. At Canajoharie, a glacial river had once cut through shale, dolomite and limestone to create a three-mile gorge just west of The Noses. The glacier cut a large, circular pothole into the solid rock near the lower end of the gorge, inspiring the name Canajoharie, which was the English version of the Mohawk's word meaning, "the pot that cleans itself."

"The Noses," a rocky passage through the Appalachian chain dropped ten feet in a short distance. This gap in the mountains made the Mohawk the favored path for the canoes of Indians and traders from the Great Lakes, but it was hell for boatmen. Boats and their cargoes were often destroyed when they got crosswise in the current and were battered against the rocks. But the worst was Keator's Rift at Sprakers, just past The Noses.

The Noses on the Mohawk River

Sammy, the youngest grandchild, asked his grandfather why there were scraps of lumber amongst the rocks. "Those are what's left of some of the boats that went before," Joseph explained.

"Grampa, could we crash?"

"No, don't worry," Joesph tried to reassure him, "but, I can't answer any more questions. I must grab a pole and help the boatmen keep the boat in the upcoming narrow passage between the rocks. Go to the center of the boat and hang on with your sister."

Joseph had just joined the boatmen on the cleated walkway when the boat was caught in a violent eddy and turned helplessly broadside. The boatmen tried to absorb the shock of pushing off from one rock after another, but one man in the front was knocked off his feet and fell into the raging, boiling water.

"Man overboard!"

"Throw him a line."

The boatman disappeared beneath the foam. His pole bobbed up and continued past the boat. Sammy screamed and clung to a rope that anchored some of their supplies to the deck. When the boat straightened out, Sammy asked, "Grampa, where did the man go?"

"He must've hit his head on a submerged rock." As the boat cleared the last of the rapids, Joseph tried to shield his son's eyes so he could not see a body still bobbing behind them, going under, popping up, then disappearing again.

"Won't we stop to recover the body?" Joseph asked the captain.

"No, too dangerous. We must go on."

Later, they passed a large stone storehouse. The captain said it belonged to the Kane Brothers who had the best stock of goods west of Schenectady as well as providing an assembly point for western products of wheat and potash moving east. Joseph knew that this transportation system made possible by river improvements would make the western lands where he was headed more valuable by providing markets for their products.

Spraker's Tavern

After passing The Noses and Keator's Rift, Spraker's Tavern was a welcome relief for Joseph and his party. They had encountered a strong headwind and even with the men of the party helping the crew, it seemed to take forever to reach it. The tavern was a two-story white clapboard house with nine windows in each story facing the King's Highway alongside the river. The Todd extended family overloaded the rooms of the tavern and many had to sleep on the floor. Catharine was especially pleased to get off the boat and into a bed, even if it was a bunk crib shared with her three youngest grandchildren. Joseph found himself bedded down crosswise with three other men in a bed, but at least they were relatives. The prices of bread, butter and milk at the tavern were outrageous, a consequence of monopoly. "Eight pence for a quart of milk?" Joseph asked incredulously. He and the other men mined the captain and others at the locks and tavern for information on the lands to the west.

Everyone assembled after breakfast the next morning to again board the boats. In good matriarch fashion, Catharine counted noses, and to her dismay, grandson Sammy was missing. "Hold the boat," she screamed. She and Hannah frantically ran back to the sleeping rooms, searched the common room, but no Sammy. They knew the boat captains would not wait long. Crying, "Sammy, Sammy!" at the top of their lungs, they ran around to the back of the tavern and found the boy innocently playing with a new puppy. They each grabbed him by the collar and half-dragged him back to the boat. They were too out of breath to reprimand him, but his father cut loose with heaps of condemnation in words Catherine had not heard him speak before.

The grandchildren never tired of watching the boat enter a lock, seeing it fill, lifting them up to the next level. It seemed almost magic. Finally on land, driving to lay claim to promising acreage in Palmyra, Joseph had misgivings for the first time. The enormity of beginning again suddenly hit him. They would be living in a lean-to as they cleared the land and built a log house. The task was made a bit easier by the fact that his married children and their families were close by. Their bodies were strong, while his was weakening. Several other families from Warwick who shared the patriot bond had also settled at Palmyra.

Joseph continued to talk to his sons about moving on to Michigan, but Catherine shushed him, "How can you even think of going to Michigan when the Brits still command the lakes and Detroit?"

"I know I'm ahead of my time, but when the territory opens up, we are in position to take advantage of new opportunities for land.

Palmyra was to be as far west as Joseph would go. He died there in 1808 at the age of sixty-three. On his deathbed, Joseph blessed his children and haltingly patted the heads of his grandchildren one by one. He whispered to sons, Sam and Josh, "It's up to you now to plant the Todd flag in far Michigan." Then to Catharine he said with emotion, "I don't regret moving here, though it has been but a few short years since our arrival, but I do regret leaving you alone again."

Catherine brushed back her tears. "Remember back in Warwick, when we discussed your joining the local militia and leaving me alone to do the farm work? And then, I objected to moving west. I want you to know that I respected your decision. I admire you even more now. We did the right thing for our family and future generations."

"Thank you," Joseph whispered. "Hold me tight one more time." He pulled up the bed covers and breathed out his spirit without a sound. Despite what Catharine had told Joseph, she had enough of pioneering. When some of her children moved west, she remained in Palmyra living next to her son, Jonathan, and his family until she died at age eighty-seven.

Joseph's old enemy at the Battle of Minisink, Joseph Brant, had died in Canada the year before. The Indian leader had died, broken and discouraged by the collapse of his beloved, once mighty Six Nations of the Iroquois. One people hopeful of new opportunities, while another mourned its losses. Would this pattern be repeated, or would the Indians finally keep a homeland further west?

~4~

On To Michigan

Joseph's son, Josh, was the first Todd to leave New York for Michigan Territory, becoming one of Oakland County's first settlers in 1818. When Commander Perry eliminated British control of Lake Erie and General Harrison defeated the British Army and their Indian allies abandoning Detroit in the Battle of the Thames, Josh took it as his signal to fulfill his father's dream of moving to Michigan.

Josh's younger brother, Sam, and wife, Hannah, tried farming in several New York locations over the next decade, but none completely satisfied the younger man. After the opening of the Erie Canal in 1825, half of the people in New York State seemed to be headed for Michigan. So in 1830, Sam also decided to take up his father's dream of relocating to the rich land in the west.

Sam and Hannah's last home in New York was on the Erie Canal, and Michigan territory seemed within reach across Lake Erie. Sam loaded his family, oxen and wagon full of necessities on a canal barge and made the short trip to Buffalo. The Todds purchased their tickets for the Detroit-bound steamer Niagara at the Canal Coffeehouse in Buffalo. The steamer was powered by waterwheels at its sides and had two masts from which sails could be rigged when the wind was right, which was hardly the case on the Todds' journey. The Niagara had fifteen berths, weighed three hundred tons, had fourteen crew members and carried one hundred cords of wood to fire the boiler. Hannah had argued for berth passage, which included meals, but the cost was eight dollars compared to only three for deck passage. Sam reasoned, "We need to conserve our cash. We got six hundred dollars for the farm in Palmyra, but we need it all to buy land in Michigan."

As it turned out, the deck passage was perfectly adequate, as no one left the deck anyway during their first day out and no one felt like eating. Not long after the steamer left Buffalo, it sailed into a storm with fearsome, fierce winds. The ship rolled and pitched, and waves broke over the top deck. Soon everyone was heaving over the sides except Sam himself. The smelly vomit was washed off the decks by the breaking waves. Sam struggled up to the pilot house and shouted over the howling wind to Captain Pease. "How much longer do you think the storm will last?" He knew it was an unanswerable question. The captain, bracing himself, replied, "In all my days on Lake Erie I have not seen anything like it." Recalling the loss of the steamer "Walk-in-the-Water" in a storm a few years earlier, the captain announced, "We're going to anchor at Erie town and remain there 'till this storm is over."

At Erie, the passengers were allowed to go ashore. Hannah moaned, "Let's go back home. I have never been so wretched in my life. Maybe your brother Jonathan made the right decision to stay in Palmyra." Sam tried to comfort her, "I know you don't really mean it. We will soon be in Michigan, and besides we have no option. We have sold the New York farm, and there is no going back."

It did not help that Hannah had not been enthusiastic about moving to Michigan from the start. More than once she recounted the travails of bearing her family during relocation after relocation, hoping to impress upon her husband the seriousness of her objections to yet another move. "After your father died, we farmed at Palmyra where Sally and Ransom were born, and then we moved east to Ovid, Seneca County, between the Finger Lakes where Edwin, Alfred and Morris were born. Then we came west again to Shelby Township only forty-five miles from Buffalo where our last child, Alanson, was born in 1820. Now he is just ten years old. Every time we build a livable house, we move again. This is too much. I agreed to move to Shelby because my brother, James, was there. I didn't know then that he, too, was soon going to Michigan. Just because your own brother followed your father's wish doesn't mean you have to, too." Sam had to admit that he was partly influenced by the desire not to let his brother outdo him, but he expected his wife to recognize the wisdom of finding more prosperous land for the next generation.

The next morning, the lake was calmer and so was Hannah. Once aboard, the passengers began to sing to buck up their spirits, and though Hannah did not join them, she couldn't help but feel more hopeful when hearing the words they sang:

> My eastern friends who wish to find
> A country that will suit your mind,
> Where comforts all are near at hand,
> Had better come to Michigan.
>
> Here is the place to live at ease,
> To work or play, just as you please;
> With little prudence any man
> Can soon get rich in Michigan

The steamer landed at Detroit on a Sunday at noon. A mile before they arrived, a small cannon on board the steamer was fired to announce their imminent arrival to the villagers. On board, Hannah scanned the few rough buildings in the town. A short distance below the wharf was one pretty house, which they learned belonged to Territorial Governor Cass. "Sam, I see a hotel near the wharf," Hannah said. "Could we stay the night and let me recover from the rough lake?"

"We'd better not," he replied. "We need to conserve our money, and I couldn't sleep anyway as I would have to guard all of our baggage." Sam also wanted to continue onward toward their claim during the remaining daylight hours.

They boarded a schooner and headed just south to Monroe at the mouth of the River Raisin. There they waited for the unloading of their oxen, wagon, milk cow, one crate containing a cock and four hens and another with six young pigs and many barrels containing flour, salt pork and household goods. Heeding the schooner captain's warning about ruffians and thieves at the dock, Sam kept his rifle and powder horn prominently displayed. And both parents said sternly, almost in unison, "Children, keep close and don't wander around."

The party was headed forty miles west to the area where Hannah's brother, James Whitney, had scouted out good land in the fall of 1827. On the way back to New York, James had stopped at the land office in Monroe and purchased four hundred acres west of the River Raisin for himself. The following May, he'd sold his farm at Shelby where he had lived since 1813 and moved with Mary and their children to Adrian in Michigan Territory. Once settled, James found additional land that he recommended to Samuel and Samuel's oldest son, Ransom, who was now married. Other members of the Whitney clan would follow—siblings John, Nathan, Sarah and Elizabeth with their spouses.

When Sam, Hannah and the children pulled onto the road to Adrian, Hannah protested again. "You call this sloppy, muddy path a road?" Sam did not tell her that such as it was, it ended at Adrian and beyond that there was only raw wilderness and Indians.

The good news was that a hotel named The Exchange had been built two years before and another, The Franklin House, had just been constructed in Adrian. They could stay at The Exchange until a cabin could be built on their land. Hannah was pleased to learn that a school already had been established by Miss Dorcas Dean in a frame schoolhouse on the west side of Main Street at the junction with Winter Street. The street was named after E.C. Winter, a dry-goods merchant who had previously been a successful Indian trader.

The Todds had no sooner arrived than they were visited by the census taker. Population numbers were critical to the apportionment of taxes and representation on the territorial legislative council. The legislature had provided that as soon as a town had twenty families, three commissioners of common schools should be selected to lease the school lands and apply the proceeds to the support of the schools.

After filing his land claim, Sam and his brother-in-law worked together to build the Todds' cabin and farm buildings. Trees were felled, and logs twenty-two and eighteen feet long were selected and notched at the ends. Red oak logs were split into thin flat shakes for the roof. Pegs were also split and carved. Sons, Edwin, twenty-two, Alfred, eighteen, and Morris, sixteen, could do a man's work. Even little ten-year-old Alanson had a job gathering moss and clay from the nearby creek to use to fill the chinks between the logs.

Sam and the older boys worked every day from sunup to sundown, but not on Sunday. Sam's only break from endless labor was walking to neighboring farms on Sunday afternoons to play ninepins with homemade pins and a ball carved from a burl of a tree. Hannah complained that such frivolity was inappropriate for the Sabbath and she was triumphant when she learned that the legislative council had declared playing ninepins illegal. Sam defended himself and said he would continue playing. "This is my one break from the monotony of plowing and a chance for a bit of socializing. I need it to keep sane. The sheriff is not going to scour the countryside looking for bowlers. Sometimes I think we are over regulated, though I do appreciate setting the price for grinding grain into flour. Besides, now we're playing with ten pins, not nine."

"Samuel Todd! Are you mocking me?" fired back his angry wife. "You miss my point."

"I get your point, Madam. Just give me some space."

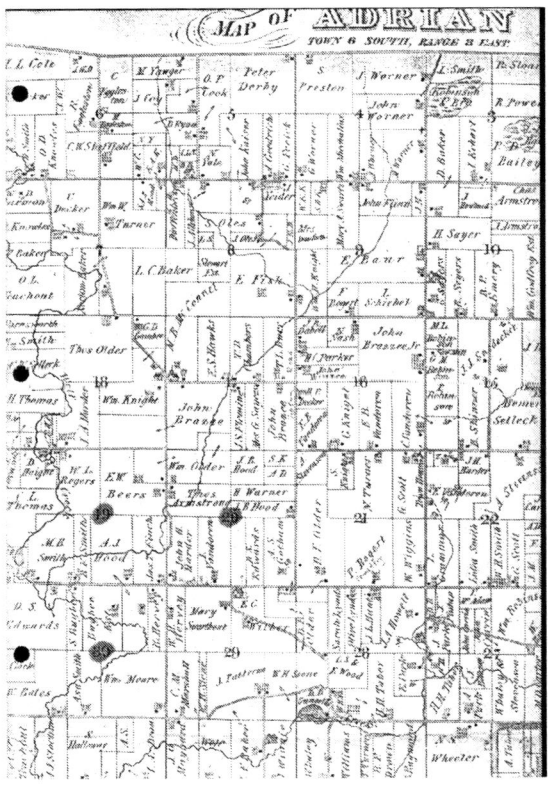

On New Year's Day, 1831, Sam was issued a patent from the Monroe land office for eighty acres in Adrian Township for which he paid one dollar and twenty-five cents per acre with banknotes obtained from the sale of his farm in New York. The property was identified on the patent as East Half of the North East quarter, Section 30, Township 6-S, Range 3-E, on the Michigan-Toledo

Strip, Lenawee County, Michigan Territory. When Sam showed the certificate signed by President Andrew Jackson to Hannah, he admitted "Well, the president probably did not sign it himself, but someone signed his name."

Son Ransom and wife Sally Ann sailed close behind Sam and Hannah but they'd paused briefly to work in Ypsilanti where their first child, Sarah Jane, was born in April, 1830. First son Luther Lindsley was born in Adrian in January, 1832, and the next year Ransom purchased one hundred sixty-acres across the road from his father. Wolf Creek, which ran through both properties was a highly valued asset, as it provided water for their livestock.

Close proximity to family made all the difference on the frontier. Sam teamed up with his brother-in-law and rented a bull plow for clearing some of the land. The plow had a beam six feet long with a forged iron coulter shaped like half of a lance head attached vertically for slicing the earth ahead of a curved moldboard that turned the furrows. With two teams of oxen hitched to it, the bull plow would cut through roots up to four inches thick and overturn small stumps without stopping the oxen. The plowman had to be very careful, for the roots would sometimes snap and recoil backwards. Sam and James worked together, with one man walking just to the side of the oxen to guide them while the other controlled the plow.

Once the ox yokes were hooked to a chain attached to the plow, Sam gave the command, "Get up," and the massive animals leaned into their yokes. Oxen have a large muscle in front of the shoulder, and it is this muscle that provides the pulling power. Sam had raised and trained his team back in New York. After letting two bull calves develop some muscle, he castrated them so that they would remain tractable even as they grew larger. Horns were left on so the yoke does not slip off when backing up. Training was a slow and somewhat tedious process of repeating the commands "gee" for a right turn and "haw" for left while pulling on a rope attached to their halters or pushing against their shoulder to turn them in the desired direction. The animals liked to be petted and developed a trust in their owner. They relied on their driver to direct their movements, and if Sam got too far behind, the near ox would turn his head to check on him.

After the ground was plowed and the broken and protruding roots chopped off with an ax, the plot was harrowed with a triangular wooden frame from which iron spikes protruded. Once they'd worked the rough ground sufficiently with the harrow, the men made shallow furrows about three feet apart and planted corn. Little Alanson's responsibility was to spend each day walking through the field to keep the crows from eating the seed before it could germinate and come up. After the corn was about a foot tall, it had to be cultivated with a shovel plow pulled by the one horse Sam owned for his lighter driving and riding needs. Corn was a staple of the Todds' diet. When the dried kernels were ground into meal, it was cooked as johnnycakes, corn mush and corn fritters or, when the whole kernels were processed with lye, it became hominy.

Each fall the Todds butchered four hogs, cut them up and salted the large cuts in wooden barrels. Scrap meat was ground, made into sausages and smoked. The fat sliced from the carcasses went into a large kettle and was rendered to liquid form over an outdoor fire, then poured into five-gallon ceramic crocks. When it cooled and solidified, the hog fat turned white and served as shortening for baked goods and fat for frying. Everyone loved Hannah's pie crusts made with lard.

Sam and his family were no sooner settled in than the threat of Indian warfare raised its ugly head. The Potawatamies in the southern part of the territory were relatively peaceful, but the settlers were always nervous about them. A treaty had been signed in Wisconsin in 1830 ceding over twenty-six million acres east of the Mississippi to the United States government. But Blackhawk, inspired by Tecumseh, did not sanction the sale of land that had included the village where he lived. He led a party of Sauk and Fox Indians in attacks on settlements in southern Wisconsin and northern Illinois where he believed earlier treaties had granted the land to his people.
Exaggerated rumors of Indian atrocities spread like wildfire, and the Illinois governor called out the militia. A regiment from Adrian set off along the Chicago road, but by the time they reached Niles on the St. Joseph River in August of 1832, the war was over. Blackhawk tried to surrender, retreating back to Wisconsin. Many in his band including women and children were massacred as they tried to cross the Mississippi.

     Sam knew enough history of Indian resistance that he found the name of the nearby village of Tecumseh to be bit ironic, as it honored such a bitter enemy of the Kentucky settlers. Blackhawk's rebellion succeeded in wreaking wider havoc than the settlers ever anticipated. An epidemic introduced by federal troops sent from Virginia to Chicago via Buffalo proved much more deadly than the Indians attacks. A cholera epidemic had spread through Europe the year before, then found a foothold among the thousand soldiers before they started on the westward march. By the time the troops reached Chicago, only three hundred able-bodied men remained. Many of the rest had died or deserted. In the process they spread the disease, and a large-scale epidemic leapt across many regions of the country by 1833. Thousands died in New York State. The symptoms of cholera were bilious diarrhea, vomiting, cramps and general dehydration accompanied by a purple discoloration of the skin that physicians called cyanosis. The *Free Press* of Detroit suggested the following treatment and prevention: temperate drinking, avoidance of green vegetables, avoidance of night air and general cleanliness.

     Hannah was very concerned for her family and declared, "No one will go into the village until this plague has passed." Sam respected her judgment and shared it with Ransom and his family. Sally Ann was already worried sick after news from back home that her brother Jeptha was deathly ill with the disease. Finally, a second letter from her mother reported that he'd survived but that he was in such a weakened condition he'd never be able to follow his late father's profession of surveyor. The legislative council authorized villages to restrict travel from infected areas, and towns closer to Detroit, such as Pontiac, Rochester, and Ypsilanti, posted sentries to turn back travelers from the larger settlement where the disease was rampant.

One of Sam and Hannah's neighbors braved a trip to town and brought back a letter.

2 Dec 1833
Dear Brother,
The biggest topic of conversation in Palmyra involves our neighbor Joseph Smith. After publishing his Book of Mormon, he continued to report visions and revelations. I don't know why, but Peter was motivated to sign an affidavit swearing that Smith was a liar and fraud. As you know sister Margaret's husband sold Smith some land a few years ago. I wish we weren't involved with this crazy man.

The big family news is that the twins are now six years old and what mischief one does not think of the other one does.

Fortunately, we have escaped the cholera so far.
Affectionately,
Catherine (Mrs. Peter Ingersol)

Despite periodic, disrupting epidemics, the settlers built the institutions around which the community grew. John Whitney, Hannah's brother, who'd come west about the same time as the Todds, had been one of the eleven founders of Adrian's Baptist church in 1831. The first baptism, which took place the following January, was testimony to the members' deep faith. After the church service held in the Adrian schoolhouse the entire congregation trooped down to the River Raisin for full immersion in the freezing water. In 1837, a brick church was erected and dedicated on Broad Street in Adrian. Ransom Todd became very active in the church and was selected to be a deacon.

John Whitney was also elected to the Constitutional Convention of 1835. The new constitution limited the right to vote to white males over twenty-one who had lived in Michigan for at least six months. Samuel and Ransom voted for adoption of the constitution. Hannah and Sally Ann reluctantly accepted that voting rights were not given to women.

"Do you understand why we have a constitution and still have not been admitted to the Union?" Hannah asked Sam. "I read in the paper that Ohio sent a survey party to draw the boundary between Ohio and Michigan starting from the northernmost cape of Maumee Bay only thirty miles southeast from us. The paper said our boundary, as established in the Northwest Ordinance of 1787, was to start from the bottom of Lake Michigan and run in a straight line, due east, to Lake Erie. That would put the mouth of the Maumee and the town of Toledo in Michigan, not Ohio."

"I don't understand all of the fine points and political moves and countermoves, but the essence is that Ohio has representatives in Congress and we don't," Sam explained. "Ohio is holding our statehood hostage to a brazen land grab. Things are heating up now that a Lenawee County judge issued a warrant for the arrest of the Ohio survey party, and our sheriff's office took a posse of thirty men and captured Ohio's surveyors. What a mess!"

Michigan became a state in January 1837 after a compromise gave Michigan land of the Upper Peninsula including Sault Sainte Marie in consolation for losing the Toledo strip. Sam and Hannah were not sure it was a good trade, but they realized that Michigan had little choice. Further armed confrontation between the two states did not seem like a good idea.

With statehood granted and fear of Indian attacks a thing of the past, the settlers turned their full attention to their farms. The Todds primarily grew corn. Wheat did well, but that crop was occasionally lost if wet conditions in the spring caused rust to damage the grain or the Hessian fly rampaged through the crop. From the *Michigan Farmer,* the farmers learned that if they planted their winter wheat after the first frost in the fall, the fly larvae would be destroyed. Wheat was broadcast by hand from a bag suspended by a rope tied to one corner and carried on the shoulder. Sam would put a stick at the ends of the field to guide him, moving it over the width of his throw when he completed each pass. Some of the local corn crop was made into whisky by the county's four distillers. However, the Baptist Todds would not sell to the distillers because they knew that much of the whiskey was intended for sale to the Indians, who, as the popular phrase put it, could not hold their liquor very well. Instead, they had their corn ground at the Red Mill, a large two-story building in Adrian built by A.J. Comstock and Isaac Dean in 1829. By 1837, there were fourteen such mills in the county along with thirteen sawmills.

Samuel and Ransom began to understand that rich land and productive livestock were not enough for an improved life. They struggled to earn enough cash to pay their taxes. Sam's original crate of six little pigs had multiplied into a nice herd of thirty hogs. He and brother-in-law, James, had bought a boar together and bred their sows. The family had all the pork they could eat and more. Using salt that came in from Syracuse over the Erie Canal, they had no problem producing salt pork to sell. Marketing the salt pork was the problem. The Erie Canal offered the promise of access to eastern markets, but first someone had to buy their produce and get it to a port on Lake Erie. Things began to look up when the Erie and Kalamazoo Railroad installed thirty-three miles of oak rails from Adrian to Toledo late in 1836 for horse-drawn coaches. Just a year later, iron straps were laid over the rails, and a steam engine pulled the cars. Merchants in Adrian now had shipment options for the grain and pork they might buy from the local producers, but commerce between the western frontier and eastern consumers still faced an intractable obstacle. Sam learned firsthand about the problem the day he rode into Adrian with a proposal for Isaac Dean, a local merchant from whom he had bought supplies on credit.

"Will you buy salt pork from me so I can pay back the credit you gave me?" Sam asked the merchant.

"No," Isaac replied bluntly, "but if a deal that I have been working on comes through, it will amount to the same thing. My problem has been that my suppliers in Boston and New York will not accept the notes of our Adrian bank. But, I think I have found a way around it. I expect a pork broker from Boston in a month. He will have a draft from a New York bank that is evidence of a deposit he has made in that bank. I will exchange my Adrian banknotes for that draft and use the draft to pay my Boston suppliers. The broker will buy salt pork from you and pay you in local currency, in effect paying you with what was once my money. He will ship the salt pork to Boston over the Erie Canal and when it is sold to a merchant in Boston for New York banknotes, the broker will be able to deposit them in the bank, and the process can start over again with a new draft. So, my advice to you and a number of other local farmers is to slaughter your hogs and pack the bacon and hams in salt in barrels made by a cooper here in Adrian so you are ready when the broker comes. There is some risk, but I think it is worth taking."

Sam agreed, though he was not entirely sure how the system worked. The flow of real goods was clear enough: Michigan farmers sent pork east, and eastern manufacturers sent hard goods to Michigan. Somehow, a less understandable flow of paper made this exchange possible. He vaguely understood that social inventions were as important to his welfare as mechanical inventions and the development of new seed varieties. It seemed that money was just debt that depended on the reputation of the players. The New York bankers had a reputation for reliability in the eyes of eastern manufacturers and wholesalers, and Adrian bankers did not. Although suspect to the easterners, the reputation of Adrian bankers was good enough for Sam to accept their notes for his pork and good enough for Isaac to accept when Sam wanted to buy a new ax head and some iron chain.

Several banks sprang up in Lenawee County, but the Todds did not trust them. They did not fully understand how banks worked, but they were aware that in 1837 a financial panic gripped the whole country. Some speculators bought land with borrowed money, never intending to farm and hoping only to profit after the land appreciated in value. When, instead, land values fell and many of the speculators went broke along with the banks who'd made them the loans, the hardworking Todd men had no sympathy. Ransom was especially bitter toward anyone who tried to get rich without actually working and sweating as he did. Wildcat banks had made more loans than they were authorized to make and had less metallic currency than required. They had gotten away with their shoddy practices because of little supervision by bank examiners. "Excess and greed always breed disaster," Ransom observed. The Todds were not directly affected by the panic, as they had no savings deposited at this point, but the financial turmoil did slow trade in grain and salt pork.

"Hannah, I'm mighty glad we bought our land when we did," mused Sam as he discussed the banking situation with his wife. "Then we were able to use banknotes, but in '36, President Jackson ordered that payment had to be made only in specie—gold and silver—or in banknotes that were redeemable in specie. I don't know where we would get that amount of hard money today."

The next year, Sam went to Adrian and talked to the teller at Erie & Kalamazoo Bank to understand what was going on. The teller proudly said that his bank was one of sixteen chartered by the state. He explained that while the Bank of the United States was operating, it would redeem its notes in specie and that competition caused most other banks to do likewise. But Jackson vetoed a bill to extend the charter of the bank because he thought it elitist and played political favorites. Jackson had withdrawn federal funds and redistributed them to banks in the states. It was ironic that the policies of Jackson, who believed himself to be a hard-money, anti-debt man, ultimately caused one of the most speculative periods in American history as banks across the country used the new money to expand their unsecured loans.

"I voted enthusiastically for Jackson because he was a man of the common people," Sam admitted, "but I never thought much about his specific policies."

The teller explained what happened when the Bank of the United States closed. "The Michigan Territorial legislature passed a law that allowed anyone to start a bank without a state charter. They only needed fifty thousand dollars in capital, but part of that could be in real estate, the value of which was largely a matter of assertion. By law, they could begin to issue notes only when thirty percent of its capital had been paid in." The teller added, "They are supposed to have a certain amount of specie in their vault as well, but I understand that many of the banks that have sprung up at every crossroad in the county pass around a box of gold coins just ahead of the bank examiner; and even then, the supposed box of gold could be filled with ten penny nails under the top layer of coins. Banks are supposed to print banknotes in amounts only two and a half times greater than the amount of capital paid in to them."

"So what's the problem?" asked Sam who was having trouble following all this.

"I suspect many of them exceed that limit. The notes of one of these wildcat banks are used as capital by another. A bank examiner once told me, 'Gold and silver flew about the country with the celerity of magic; its sound was heard in the depths of the forest. Yet, like the wind, one knew not whence it came or whither it was going.'" The teller swelled with his own eloquence. "The Bank of Palmyra just down the road claimed they had enough specie when the examiners came, but the examiners played a trick on them and came back in a few days to learn that the bank only had thirty-four dollars in hard cash while they had issued more than twenty thousand dollars in banknotes."

"I think I am beginning to see that all of this works only as long as land prices are escalating and no one actually asks for specie in exchange for their banknotes."

"But, now the house of cards has come tumbling down." The teller added, "In spite of all this, if these wildcat banks had not created credit to allow farmers and merchants to expand, we would have no railroad, and we would all be living only on what we could scratch from the earth with our hands. It is greed and excess that have ruined the country. Still, I wouldn't put my money in any of these banks, Sam."

Sam laughed and said, "If I had any money I would not put it in any bank, but maybe the reason I have none is because our banking system is crazy."

When Sam got home eager to tell Hannah what he had learned about banking, he found she had taken to her bed. She had been ailing for days. Now she was running a fever, evident in her flushed face. After another day without the fever abating, Sam became alarmed and rode his horse into Adrian to fetch the doctor, who returned with him, expecting to be paid not in money by these penniless farmers, but with a cured ham or stewing chicken. When he examined Hannah and diagnosed typhoid fever, he admitted there was little to be done. The next day Hannah was barely hanging on and weakly spoke to Sam, "Ask Ransom and his wife to come over. I think I might die, and I want to see them."

"Of course; right away. But don't talk like that. You'll beat this yet." Sam ran down the road to Ransom's place and luckily they were at home. They all hurried back and arrived at Hannah's bedside out of breath. She was still breathing and opened her eyes and smiled faintly, but she could not speak. The next morning with family gathered round her, she died. The year was 1837 and she would have been fifty-two.

Sam had never given any thought to what life might be like without her. His mind was in turmoil as he spoke to Ransom. "Maybe Hannah was right," he admitted. "We moved too many times, and life as a pioneer wore her out. Maybe I became too obsessed with my father's vision of the frontier." Ransom tried to assure him that it was a good move for all of them, but the question haunted Sam for the rest of his life.

Samuel Todd died in 1850 at the age of sixty-eight. He and his brother Josh had fulfilled their father's vision of moving to Michigan. But, old Joseph and even his boys could hardly imagine that the frontier would continue to move west and that his descendants would catch up with the Indians once more.

With Samuel's death, Ransom became the patriarch of the family. The Baptist Church was a big part of Ransom's life, and Sally Ann was very supportive. "I'm proud of you, Ransom, for the work you do as deacon for the church. I can see that it is your passion."

Ransom smiled and said, "I'm pleased to do the Lord's work, but my passion is you and the children—Sarah Jane, Luther Lindsley, Henry James, Alvira, Cynthia Lee, Susan Maria, Martha Alphena, Newel Delno, Elmore Llewellyn and little Rosa Seraphine. I guess our ten children are proof enough of my passion."

"Ransom, you old dog," cried Sally Ann. "That's not what I meant!"

Sam stopped with the teasing to tell her truthfully, "We have raised a fine family, and now our oldest daughter is about to be married."

The joy of Sarah Jane's wedding to Gideon Hendrick was followed the next year by her death in childbirth. Ransom was inconsolable. "Why has God taken my beautiful daughter? My firstborn. I have never questioned my faith, my God, before, but I just don't understand it. In my work as deacon, I have consoled many a fellow parishioner upon a death in the family, but this has struck close to the bone.

He remembered neighbor Austin Robinson who fell off the back of his hayrack when his oxen bolted from the sudden appearance of a wolverine. He was only twenty-three. "I made many visits to his family reassuring them of God's love and wisdom. I'm not sure I can do it anymore. Untimely death seems to be everywhere."

Sally Ann struggled to keep her own composure. "God does work in mysterious ways. He has left us with nine wonderful children. We must keep our eyes on our blessings. I can't dwell on it long; I have hungry mouths to feed." It was some time before Ransom escaped the dark cloud that dominated his days and robbed him of sleep. He thought again and again of the beautiful hope chest that he had made for his daughter before her wedding. He had saved the walnut lumber just for this purpose when he first cleared his land twenty-four years before and Sarah Jane was no more than three. Now there was no daughter and no grandchild.

Knowing that the young widower had no money to bury Sarah Jane, Ransom purchased a large cemetery lot just down Hunt Road from his farm. Neighbor John Bogert had fenced off a corner of his farm along the road and donated it for a cemetery. "That is where we shall be buried as well when the Lord comes for us," Ransom told Sally Ann.

Lenawee County Farmland at edge of Bogert Cemetery

Ransom had learned carpentry and joinery before he left New York, and he worked at his old trade in the winter months to supplement his farm income. He decided to put his skills to work building a better frame house for his family to replace the cabin they'd built when they first claimed their land, and he taught his oldest son, Luther, the trade as they raised a new home.

Luther was married to Margaret Snyder of Grand Rapids in 1853. Margaret Ann died in childbirth just one year later. The scourge of young women had struck the Todd family again. Ransom had not recovered from the death of his daughter just three months earlier. He felt like the family was cursed. Yet within three years, Luther married again to Adelphi Hodge, and soon after the couple moved west to Leavenworth, Kansas. There, Luther put his accountancy training to work in Citizens Bank, and Adelphi gave birth to two healthy children, Frank and Belle Lutherine. When news of their first grandchildren reached Ransom and Sally Ann in Michigan they were filled with joy.

Ransom and Sally Ann would never go further west, but they were a part of their sons who did.

~ 5 ~

Missionary to the Indians--Michigan

While the Todds and the Whitneys were coming into southeastern Michigan, the Indians were already under pressure to leave the southwestern part of the territory. With the Treaty of Chicago signed at Fort Dearborn in 1821, the Ottawa, Chippewa and Pottawatomie had ceded most of the territory south of the Grand River. In addition to an annuity, the Indians were to receive the services of a blacksmith, teacher and farmer. Territorial Governor Cass appropriated one thousand dollars for these positions. The Board of Management of the Baptist Convention sent the Reverend Isaac McCoy to establish an Indian mission in southwest Michigan. It was called the Carey Mission in honor of a Baptist missionary to India. McCoy was to be the government's teacher. A party of thirty-two including Isaac and wife Christiana and children had walked eleven days from McCoy's previous mission at Fort Wayne, Indiana, over icy ground in December of 1822. They had driven before them fifty hogs and five cows, animals the Indians had not seen before. On the way, a wagon broke and capsized when one ox got mired in a stream. The crippled animal was left for the Indians to eat. All in the party were afflicted with violent ague, fever, delirium and pleurisy. A site on the St. Joseph River was selected in the land of the Pottawatomi. The Indians called the river O'sang-e-wong-se-be. On New Year's day 1823, Chiefs Chebass and Topenebee conducted a ceremony of welcome that they'd learned from French traders. It involved much handshaking and kissing. At the risk of offending the Indians, McCoy declined the kissing.

Three years after establishment of the mission, a young twenty-one-year-old by the name of Jotham Meeker, who for the previous seven years had been a printer's apprentice in Cincinnati, decided to become a missionary after hearing Michigan missionary, Robert Simerwell, speak. Meeker was sent to help teach school at Carey. He arrived in November 1825 and soon had thirty-seven boys and sixteen girls as his students. At the same time, a blacksmith named Crosley arrived. In addition to a schoolhouse and blacksmith's shop, five hewn-log cabins were constructed plus a milk house and a stable. Meeker found McCoy to be a likable man with exceedingly good manners. "When he looks at you, you feel there is no selfish scheme in his mind," Meeker told Crosley during a discussion of the mission leader. "He is always thinking what he could do for others."

An old Ottawa chief named Mak-a-tapw-shah, the Indian term for Blackskin, was introduced to the youthful new teacher and said that he found

Meeker a difficult name to pronounce. "We therefore desire to give him an Indian name," the chief explained to McCoy. "and we have decided that his name shall be Mano-keke-toh, He that Speaks Good Words. We hope he will remain with us to teach us and our children good things."

Upon hearing the esteem with which he was being welcomed, Jotham replied, "I'm deeply honored." He resolved to learn the Indian language so he could converse with the people he had come to serve.

Within the year, four young, unmarried women—Miss Thompson, Miss Day, Miss Bond and Miss Richardson—joined the mission as teachers. The seventeen-year old Eleanor Richardson was, like Jotham, from Cincinnati, a connection that seemed to draw the two together.. Jotham thought it curious that in a time when women were sheltered and denied many occupations because of their presumed frailty, it was acceptable for them to become teachers in a strange and hostile land. But, he was mighty glad for female company.

Eleanor wrote to her mother in verse:

Dear Mother, I'm set down to write
Although it's very late at night.
My cousin going home
You may be sure I've some distress
Here in a savage wilderness
And left almost alone.

Some trials now I do expect
But I cannot this work neglect.
In faith I feel so strong
I can do all things, I can bear
All sufferings while my Lord is near
for him I left my home.

Chief Blackskin's initial welcoming attitude toward the missionaries soon turned to antagonism. At the same time, a chief of another band named Nawequageezhik or Noonday urged McCoy to establish a new mission farther north at the rapids of the Grand River. Nawequageeshik believed bringing a mission to his people would enhance his prestige if he could be seen as dispensing cattle, metal tools, oxen and plows to his band. Rivalry among chiefs and with French Catholics confused the Indians. Were not all of the new religions representing the same great spirit? The Catholic traders and their allies opposed the Baptists because they profited from selling whiskey to the Indians, which the Baptists opposed.

McCoy contracted with a provision source in Detroit to deliver flour and other goods by boat up Lake Huron and down Lake Michigan to the mouth of the St. Joseph. But, the captain found a better price for his cargo en route and never arrived at the wilderness outpost. A second contract was made, but when the boat arrived, a severe storm swept the vessel out into the lake, and in the end only a few barrels could be set ashore. McCoy never lost heart. He kept singing lyrics from a Baptist hymn by John Newton:

> The birds without barn or storehouse are fed—
> From them let us learn to trust for our bread;
> The saints what is fitting shall ne'er be denied,
> So long as 'tis written, 'The Lord will provide.

The young Meeker, who often went hungry, could not help blurting out, "Too bad we are not birds!"

McCoy saw his work at his missions undercut by the availability of alcohol. He thought that the Indians would be better off if they moved to a country of their own, far away from the traders who provided the alcohol. He lobbied Washington for removal of the Indians to west of the Mississippi and Missouri Rivers. When the Pottawatomi chief, Leopold Pokagon, fully understood McCoy's intentions, he severed all ties with the Baptists, and Carey Station was closed. In keeping with the Pottawatomi culture's use of mutual gift giving to forge bonds of solidarity, Pokagon purchased a Sioux captive from the Sauk and gave the boy to the Baptists for services the mission had rendered to his tribe. Satisfied that his obligations to the previous benefactors had been met, Pokagon turned to the Catholic French who were content to trade with the natives without any additional ambition to reform or remove them.

In August, 1827, Jotham and Eleanor left Carey for Thomas Station that had been established two years before by missionary Leonard Slater below the rapids of the Washtanong or Grand River at the village of Chief Noonday. Among other things, the one hundred fifty Ottawa Indians there were to be taught to raise hogs now that their hunting land had been lost. The Ottawa land extended south to the Kik-ken-a-ma-zoo River that the whites called the Kalamazoo. Noonday, whose shortened Indian name, Qua-gee-zhik, literally meant "noon," was a striking figure six feet tall and of fine physique, a friendly and industrious man who had built his own log house. He was solemn, dignified and quite willing to admit that he had fought with the British in the War of 1812.

Slater's mission on the west side of the river boasted a one hundred sixty-acre compound with several hewn-log buildings: a twenty-by-twenty-four-foot dwelling, a schoolhouse of the same size, a separate kitchen and another two-story general purpose building with a stone chimney, a small stable and a sawmill.

Chief Qua-gee-zhik (Noonday)

Slater's Mission on the Grand River

McCoy's attention to building up the mission was diverted when the government appointed him commissioner to accompany representatives of several tribes to explore the suitability of land in Kansas for a reservation. Among the tribal representatives was Chief Noonday. When the party reached St. Louis in July 1828 several Indians got drunk. Chief Noonday apologized profusely, and the incident confirmed McCoy's belief that the Indians must be removed far from the white man if they were to survive.

Upon returning to Michigan, McCoy increasingly came into conflict with Slater. The mission founder had learned the Ottawa language and had become devoted to helping the Ottawa stay in Michigan, a stance directly opposed to McCoy's grand plan to move all Indians west.

Meeker was intrigued with Ottawa culture and recorded what Noonday told him about their religion, dances, death ceremonies and the like. Eleanor asked Jotham, "Why are you spending so much time recording the ceremonies of these heathens?"

"I can't hope to change them to our religion if I don't understand where they are coming from," Jotham explained. "There are some similarities between Indian and Christian beliefs. Their creation story describes the Great Spirit making man and woman from clay. They believe there was a time when a great flood covered the earth, and one of their leaders saved all the animals in his big canoe, just like Noah. Their ceremonies have a lot of songs that you might call hymns. We can build on that."

"I've heard drums and rattles during their dances. What are they for?" Eleanor continued to press.

"I don't think I will add drums to my services, but they are used to make sure that the Indians' prayers are heard by the Spirits." Jotham told her. "Their Great Spirit seems more modest that our God. He admits to mistakes in the process of creation and asks for advice from the lesser spirits."

"I notice that food sacrifice plays a major role in their dances," Eleanor pointed out in her practical way "They often have so little that I hate to see them waste it."

"Perhaps the sacrifice of something precious shows the strength of their commitment. In our Lord's Supper, we supply the symbolic food to the people, while the Indians supply the gods. There is another difference that intrigues me," Jotham continued. "They believe that if they follow the rules set down by the Great Spirit, they will live a long life and die peacefully without pain. In contrast, we promise everlasting life only in heaven."

"The Indians' expectation of a painless death holds a certain attraction to me as I am often sick," Eleanor admitted, "and if it keeps up, I'll die in a lot of pain."

"If you will allow me to tease you a bit," Jotham said, "the Indians have a story similar to our creation story where the woman tempts her husband with an apple picked from a forbidden tree. There are many lesser spirits, but only one is female."

"I guess their religion is male dominated like ours." Eleanor teased him back. "I promise not to tempt you with sin."

"The one female spirit is Mother Earth, and all life springs from her."

"They have that right."

Eleanor may have been only eighteen years old, but she could hold her ground. Jotham admired that kind of spirit, but he did not tell her so. He didn't know what had come over him. He had never teased a woman before, and he did not know how to react to a woman's flirtations.

Noonday allowed Jotham to witness a medicine dance called Me 'ta 'wuk. Each person assembled in the temporary dancing house (twenty by sixty feet) carried a complete otter skin, including the head. When stitched closed it made a sack with an opening in the throat for holding sacred medicine used only for festive occasions. Metal artificial eyes glistened, the teeth were exposed, and the sides of the mouth were decorated with soft feathers dyed red. Porcupine quills were added to the tail, and small brass thimbles and bells were attached to the feet. After many speeches, the skins were held up with two hands and rattled while the Indians danced ending with everyone standing around the wall facing in. Two principal men then danced around the house, each carrying a gourd rattle and accompanied by drums. Crying Ho-o-o in quick, frightful bursts, they punched one of the men in the circle with their otter skin, whereupon the person dropped to the ground lifeless. After the victims kissed their own skins, they were restored. Every male took a turn circling the assemblage. The females participated in the exercises, but never led. At the conclusion each person had a small bowl into which meat was placed from a large pot.

Meeker could see for himself where the Ottawa buried their dead. At the head of the grave was a post of the same height as the deceased. On one side was carved an animal, such as a panther, that represented the dead person's clan, while on the other side was a drawing of a man. If the deceased had died in war, the drawing would be headless, Noonday explained.

That fall the Indians became very sickly. An Indian came to Meeker and asked for something to give his ailing daughter and son to make them throw up as their stomachs were tied in knots. Meeker followed the worried father to the nearby Indian village where he gave the children some tartar emetic. The little girl vomited in response to the potion, relieving her distress, but the boy did not respond. So Meeker went back home and returned with Glauber's salts with which he dosed the child. When Meeker checked on the boy four hours later, he found the patient still vomiting, violently and the Indian father accused Meeker of giving him bad medicine. He demanded that Meeker reverse the action. By the time Meeker had run home to get some paregoric, the boy was dead. The father shouted, "It was your medicine that killed him! You gave him too much."

Sweat broke out on Meeker's brow. "The medicine would not kill the boy," he told the distraught father. "It must have been part of the disease that sickened him in the first place." The father was obviously unconvinced, and Meeker was shaking with the thought of what the Indian would do next. Would he kill Meeker in retribution?

"Bring him back to life," the man demanded. "His breast is still warm."

Meeker called for some warm water and bathed the boy's feet arms and chest, but it was clear that he could not be revived.

"You must give me burying clothes for the boy," the father demanded when he was convinced of his child's death. "A blanket, leggings, shirt, breechcloth, moccasins, a handkerchief and a small tin kettle."

Hoping to mollify the grieving man, Meeker agreed. He was afraid that the Indians would now withdraw their children from his school, fearful that they would be harmed by their teacher's incompetence. As he walked slowly back to his house, he prayed, "Oh my God, have mercy on me and forgive me. May this affliction be sanctified to me, and may I be enabled to live nearer to thee than I have done hither to."

The next day the Indian father sent his older son to ask Meeker to make a coffin for the dead boy. Meeker, a goods craftsman, was glad to comply. The messenger also said the chief was asking for wood for his village because all their women, the usual gatherers, were so busy taking care of the sick that they had no time to fetch it.

Meeker was learning that being a missionary was much more than preaching or even ministering to the sick. It required diplomacy. To replace hunting, he persuaded the Indians to pool their annuities and use the money to hire men skilled in agriculture and fence building to teach them, rather than to squander their money on whiskey. The Indians agreed to ask Territorial Governor Cass to hold their money until a missionary could come for it. Meeker set out for the Grand Saline 120 miles southeast where annuities were paid. Indians had used the salt springs there as long as anyone could remember, and it was a convenient gathering place where six trails converged. Meeker planned to continue on from there to Detroit to hire two laborers and a cook for the thirty-some mouths at the mission. Meeker traveled with two Indians who planned to continue on to Fort Malden, Ontario, to receive their annual presents from the British. After riding four days, they arrived at the Grand Saline. The agents had not been apprised of the Grand River Indians' wishes to have the tribe's money held for a missionary and would not hand over the annuities to Meeker. Instead, they insisted that he accompany them to the Rapids. Meeker was frustrated and torn. He really needed to go to Detroit and hire some help for the mission, but the government agents were unmovable. Meeker reluctantly gave up his plan and returned with the agents to the Rapids.

It turned out that the annuity was negligible anyway: two dollars to each Indian in the villages of Noonday and Blackskin. The Indians gathered for a council in the mission schoolhouse, and afterwards Noonday reported that, because the payment was so small, they had decided to abandon hiring any outside help.

"Governor Cass and McCoy will be greatly disappointed and will not have any enthusiasm for helping you further if you do not pool your money for farm improvements," pleaded Jotham, but, to no avail. Later, after more thought, Meeker could understand their response to such meager payment.

Young people far from home tend to gravitate toward each other. Eleanor wrote to her sister, Maria in Cincinnati:

Thomas Station, August 2, 1828
    I am going to mension something that you will expect I think, and that is this. I expect to change my name from Richardson for such a name as Meeker. I have given my consent to be married the first opportunity with Mothers consent. I expect it will not be before Brother McCoy returns from the west whitch will be if he is blessed in his undertaking sometime in December next.
    I trust if we never meet again in this world we shall meet in the next where parting will be no (more). O that that we may be prepared for the hour of

Death and at last be received into heaven to cut bread in the kingdom of God, there we shall be happy forever more.
Farewell Sweet Sister Maria,
I remain your loving Sister,
(s) Eleanor Richardson

Another letter was sent after Eleanor fell in the river and became quite ill:

Thomas Mission Station, April 20, 1829
Dear beloved Mother,
Once more I am permitted the unspeakable privilege of communicating to you, the inexpressible goodness of our great and merciful Preserver to sinful me, He is pleased in his own good time to enable me to inform you that my health is tolerable, and humbly hope it is mending daily, for which I have great reason to be truly thankful, and send for the praises to him in the highest.

Bro Meekers foot which he informed you he cut, is just got so he can walk without his crutches, except his feet, his health has been very good. And he is improving very fast in learning the language, he is able to converse with the Indians without the need of an interpreter. There are a number of Indians whom we trust are anxiously inquiring after wisdom.

I received a letter from the Dr. with directions and advice. He advises me to start for Cincinnati, in the first vessel which we expect will be at the mouth of Grand river by 15th of May. He says it will be indispensably necessary, for me to take a journey this summer, for the sound recovery of my health. I have made up my mind to start in the first vessel, accompanied by Mr Meeker if the Lord will permit.

Monday morning, goodby—Mother and Sisters, try to find out what I want to say if you can.

Return address:
Pogwatigue, Michigan

Many of the Potawatomi were forced to move west of the Mississippi by the Indian Removal Act of 1830. The Thomas Station was closed for a period, but later was reopened by Brother Slater just to the south at Prairieville. Some Indians escaped the order by moving to Michigan's upper peninsula or to Canada.

The two missionaries were married in 1830 in Cincinnati. Eleanor's mother, also named Eleanor, wrote a poem to celebrate the marriage:

Rejoice my friends, with me rejoice
'Tis a delightful day
My Daughter hears the Bridegroom's voice
And with delight Obeys.

Meeker retired from missionary work to support his new wife and mother, Lydia, and returned to the printing trade. But, McCoy sent him an urgent message in 1831 asking him to come to Arkansas Territory to work with the Cherokees on the Arkansas River. McCoy had made two exploratory trips in 1828 at the request of the Department of War that allowed him to explore mission opportunities at the same time. He favored establishing a mission in Arkansas Territory because he thought it offered the best possibility for a permanent home for all Indians. It could be a place where the Indians could establish their own independent local government without pressures from settlers. Meeker was reluctant to go, but hated to disappoint his mentor. Leaving his wife and mother in Cincinnati, Meeker made an arduous journey of more than a thousand miles by water to join McCoy on the Arkansas River. The last twenty-five miles was across open prairie in December. Jotham tried to protect his face against the bitter oncoming wind. By chance, he met a stranger going the other way who called, "Hello friend. What you doin' out here?"

Meeker said, "I'm going to a mission among the Cherokees on the Arkansas."

"Well, if you ask me, it's a waste of time. Those heathens are beyond help. By the way, I see your face is patchy white with blisters. You're in danger of frostbite, my friend."

"Thanks," replied Meeker. "I wasn't aware of it. It came on slowly and the numbness fooled me."

"I just passed another man who was suffering from the cold and had built a fire in a grove about a half mile back," the fellow reported. I will retrace my steps with you and see that you get warmed up before I return to my own path."

Meeker was amazed by the Christian charity this stranger afforded to another in need while at the same time being so dismissive of the value of a "heathen's" life or soul. I guess some people don't see Indians as humans, he thought.

When he finally completed his journey, Meeker found that McCoy was very pleased to see him. "I want you to stay two or three months, then return to Ohio and bring your family to settle here. This location is the best opportunity to establish a permanent settlement for all Indians."

Meeker's face told of his struggle to accept McCoy's plan. "I have learned the Ottawa language well enough that I can teach and preach without a translator," he said. "I feel that missionaries must speak the Indian's language to gain their trust and be successful. If I'm going to continue as a missionary, I want to return to Michigan and follow the Ottawas and their close relatives, the Chippewas, north."

"I deeply regret your decision and think it injudicious," said the elder missionary. "But, if our mission board approves, I will not interfere. I will leave for Kansas shortly to establish a mission there for the Shawnee. Perhaps you will join me there in the future. We are much needed where, I'm told, over four thousand Indians have died as a result of smallpox." Despite McCoy's hopes, Kansas was not to be a permanent land for the Indians.

Upon his return to Cincinnati, Meeker requested permission from the mission board to return to Michigan with his wife. In the late summer of 1832, Jotham, Eleanor and the Reverend Moses Merrill arrived at a new post with the Ojibwa and Chippewa at Sault Sainte Marie in the upper peninsula where a mission had been established three years before. The Meekers had traveled from Cincinnati by steamboat upriver to Portsmouth then north on the newly completed Ohio and Erie Canal to Cleveland on a horse-drawn barge. Finally, they boarded a schooner to cross Lake Erie first to Detroit, and from there sailed northward to the Sault.

Sault St. Marie, Nov 8, 1832

My Dear Sister Emeline,
      Through much mercy and goodness of our Heavenly Father I am again permitted to address you from heathen ground. Many have been the scenes which I have witnessed since I saw you walk from me on the wharf, never shall I forget my feelings at that trying moment when I could see you no more perhaps forever, but I endeavored to cheer up under the blessed anticipation of meeting you with those who are gone a little before us, in that happy world where the heart-rending stroke of parting with those who are dear unto us by the strongest ties; is never known. But, I must not dwell on this any longer, but must give you a little of what I have seen and heard since I saw you. Mr. Meeker wrote you while at Detroit informing you how we got along that far. We stayed two weeks waiting the arriving of the vessel, during which time we purchased provision to bring with us, together with what things we should need for housekeeping.
      We started from Detroit on the 12th, on the 15th we had a very rough sea, the vessel tossing very much, all sick except Sister Brown and myself. We lost our way on the lake and were obliged to wander about on the Lake all the next day. Just before we found our way out, we struck a reef of rocks which caused great alarm not knowing what the results would be. We were in sight of land, but it is more than probable that some lives would have been lost had the vessel sunk as we all expected it would for 15 or 20 minutes, but we have great reason to thank our great Preserver for his helping hand in that time of need. I felt at that time the great importance of being prepared for death when God in his providence should see proper to call us hence.
      I am much better pleased with the place than I had anticipated. There is quite a village besides the Garrison. We have English and Indian meetings on Sunday, prayer meeting on Monday and Wednesday evenings, female prayer meeting on Thursday with the Indians and on Friday with the Presbyterian sisters, and on Thursday even, Indians prayer meeting. The people here, all appear very friendly. I have been asked to a number of places, but I have been so busy sewing that I have not been to see them. There are six women of us, Miss Mccomber, Miss Rice, Mrs. Bingham, Miss Brown, and Mrs. Merrel from the East came in company with us from Detroit.

We have nothing of the cholera here, but I fear we shall hear that it has reached Cincinnati. There were a number of cases in Detroit whilst we were there.

I know not how to stop writing but I must as the last vessel this season is now about ready to leave for Detroit.

I remain your sincere friend and sister,

(s) Eleanor D. Meeker

Jotham added a note:

We will send letters to, and receive letters from Detroit every 6 or 7 weeks, so that you can write any time, and we will get your letters in two months or less after you write them.

After watching his wife struggle with her emotions as she finished the letter to her family, Jotham said, "Eleanor, I know you are deeply attached to your Mother and sisters and desperately miss them."

"Yes, and I'm so concerned about my own health that I'm often convinced I will never see them again," she admitted. "At the same time, I'm deeply committed to saving the souls of the Indians. God have mercy on us."

~ 6 ~

The Missionary and the Indians--Kansas

After the 1794 defeat of an Indian confederacy at the Battle of Fallen Timbers in northern Indiana, the Shawnee war chief, Tecumseh, thought the only way to regain their lands was a larger alliance that included southern and western tribes. He resurrected an idea first promulgated by Mohawk Joseph Brant during the Revolutionary War that the Indians were of one nation and no land could be ceded without the consent of all. He was aided in his crusade by his brother, Lowawluwaysica, The Noise Maker, who had renamed himself, Tenskwatawa, The Prophet in 1805 upon the death of the previous prophet. While unskilled as a hunter and warrior, he could hold an audience spellbound for hours. He talked of the importance of the Indians being united and rejected the white men's dress and their alcohol. He and Tecumseh organized a new village southwest of Fort Wayne, Indiana, at the confluence of the Wabash and Tippecanoe Rivers that became known as Prophetstown. Some whites thought the name of the river had to do with canoes, but it was actually a corruption of the Indian name, Ke-tap-e-kon.

The Prophet had spoken vaguely of a darkness that would envelope the earth. When a total eclipse of the sun accommodated him in June 1806, he proclaimed his great powers. His following increased, and more than a thousand Indians made a pilgrimage to Prophetstown. The Prophet made a series of fiery speeches in the Detroit area. He spoke of his visions of great victory. He convinced the Indians that they were invulnerable. In Tecumseh's absence, the Prophet allowed his followers to commit a number of aggressive acts against settlers in the area.

Tecumseh, whom many regarded as a savage, was a complex man. While he rejected white culture, he learned English and could read. His favorite book was Hamlet which he read upon frequent visits at the home of white settler, James Galloway. Tecumseh listened attentively as Galloway read from the Bible. At age forty, he fell in love with the Galloways' sixteen-year old daughter, Rebecca, who took it upon herself to improve his English. He asked her to marry him in the summer of 1807. Her parents, after much anguished debate, consented if Rebecca wished it. Tecumseh asked Rebecca, "Will this I tell you be for you and you only?" When Rebecca agreed to keep his secret, Tecumseh told her of his great plan to unite all Indians and reclaim Ohio. While the young girl had deep emotion toward him, she had demands of her own before agreeing to marriage. "I fear the hard life of a Shawnee wife," she told her suitor, "and I can't accept the multiple marriages that the tribe practices."

"I assure you that you will not be expected to work as the others, and you will be my only wife." Tecumseh promised.

"I will marry you if, on your part, you will adopt my people's mode of life and dress," Rebecca insisted. In this small way she hoped to divert Tecumseh's energy and power to peace, rather than war, and she left him to ponder her final demand.

The next moon, Tecumseh returned with his answer: "I will not come back again, Rebecca. I cannot take you as my wife under your conditions. To do as you require would lose for me the respect and leadership of my people." The call of his mission overcame his passion for this young woman.

Tecumseh's mission would not be unopposed. General William Henry Harrison, getting wind of an Indian uprising, assembled an army in Vincennes, Indiana, and marched north toward Prophetstown in November 1811. While Tecumseh was seeking alliances in the south, the Prophet had whipped his followers into a frenzy. When Harrison's army met the Prophet's warriors on the Tippecanoe River, the Indians attacked with abandon, believing that bullets could not hurt them. Even as many were dying, the Prophet shouted, "Fight on! It will take a little while for the prophecy to be fulfilled. I will raise my voice to encourage it." As Indian casualties mounted, they deserted, and many tribes went home. Harrison's troops prevailed, and the general would later ride his victory to the Presidency, using the campaign slogan, "Tippecanoe and Tyler Too."

The Prophet was still full of himself, declaring that he was "second only to the Great Spirit." Upon his return to his tribe, Tecumseh repudiated the Prophet who had destroyed in one day all his brother had worked for years to build. But Tecumseh was not finished and decided to abandon his dream of an all-Indian force to expel the whites and in desperation to align himself with the British. The United States had declared war on the British in 1812 because of naval blockades of east coast shipping. Some eastern states withheld their militias and Congressional funding was inadequate.

In his campaign to rally all the tribes, Tecumseh had prophesied that a great sign would occur signaling the will of the Great Spirit to begin the battle that would free the Indian lands. On November 16, 1811, a meteor flashed across the cloudless midnight sky. This was followed a month later by an earthquake that caused great damage. This was powerful medicine. This was the same quake that frightened Lucy Byram in Kentucky.

Tecumseh moved north to join British forces at Fort Malden, Canada, across the river from Detroit. Several tribes responded to Tecumseh's prophecy. A combined force of British and Indians approached Detroit, and the American commander capitulated without a fight in August, 1812, just after President Madison declared war in June.

British strength depended on its naval dominance of Lake Erie. When this was broken by Commander Oliver Hazard Perry with a decisive victory, the British realized they could no longer hold Michigan, and the British commander abandoned Detroit and Fort Malden across the river in Canada, retreating to the River Thames in Ontario, east of Detroit, with his 1,300 Redcoats and Indians.

The Indian force included Chiefs Noonday and Saginaw from the rapids of the Grand. Tecumseh was inclined to give up his grand plan, but the Sioux and Chippewa chiefs objected, and Tecumseh remained to fight even though he expected to die. "I have no fear of death," he asserted. In October, 1813, General Harrison attacked the British forces with three times their numbers. Tecumseh stripped himself of anything that might identify him. A mounted battalion led by Colonel Richard Johnson rode toward the Indian lines. With a whoop, Tecumseh charged, armed only with a club, and tried to knock Johnson off his horse. But Johnson managed to discharge his pistol into the Indian's chest. Within five minutes of their leader's death, the rest of the Indians evaporated into the woods.

None of the Americans knew what Tecumseh looked like, so long-time Indian fighter Simon Kenton of Kentucky was summoned to identify the body. Kenton did nothing to disabuse those who'd found a dead Indian dressed like a chief of their conclusion that it was the body of Tecumseh. Unaware of the misidentification, the soldiers stripped the body with a vengeance and cut it to pieces. In the night, a small band of Indians, including Noonday, returned and found Tecumseh's intact body and buried it, intoning over the grave, "Tecumseh will come again." Was it wishful thinking, or would a new leader emerge now that the alliance with the British had failed?

Years later, a white settler living near the Baptist Mission at Gull Prairie, Michigan, asked Noonday, "Were you near Tecumseh when he fell?"

Answering in his native language Noonday replied, "Yes, directly on his right."

"Who killed him?"

"Richard Johnson."

"Give me the circumstances."

Noonday then proceeded to tell his version of the story. "Johnson was on a horse and the horse fell over a log, and Tecumseh with uplifted tomahawk, was about to dispatch him, when Johnson drew a pistol from his holster and shot Tecumseh in the breast. Tecumseh fell dead on his face. I seized him at once and with the assistance of Saginaw, bore him from the field. When he fell, the Indians stopped fighting, and the battle ended. We laid him down on a blanket in a wigwam, and we all wept; we loved him so much. I took his hat and tomahawk.

"Where are they now?"

"I have his tomahawk and Saginaw his hat."

"Could I get them?"

"No, Indian keep 'em!"

Noonday also recalled his meeting with President Buchanan and Vice President Richard Johnson at Washington . "I went with Lewis Cass to the President's great wigwam, and when I saw the same man I see in battle, the same man I see kill Tecumseh. I had never seen him since, but I knew it was him. I look him in the face and said, 'Kene kin-a-poo Tecumseh,' that is, 'You kill Tecumseh.' Johnson replied that he never knew who it was. Another Indian in the party spoke up, declaring, 'That was Tecumseh. I see you do it.' "

The dreams of Tecumseh and Tenskwatawa to unite the Indian nations had seemed ill-fated from the beginning. Central authority was inimical to Indian culture, which was tribally and clan based. The Indians were not the only people in history that might have remained self-determining if they were united.

With the death of Tecumseh was lost any possibility of a force large enough to stop the onslaught of white settlement. Tecumseh had made one prophesy that proved to be particularly prescient:

Where today are the Pequot? Where are the Naragansett, the Mochican, the Pocanet, and other powerful tribes of our people? They have vanished before the avarice and oppression of the white man, as snow before the summer sun ... Sleep not longer, O Choctows and Chickasaws ... Will not
the bones of our dead be plowed up, and their graves turned into plowed fields?

While some white settlers would have been pleased if the Indians disappeared from the face of the earth, others were committed to their well-being. Two of these were Jotham and Eleanor Meeker. They had ministered to the Indians' spiritual needs first in southwest Michigan, then, in 1832, they'd moved northward as the tribes were pushed to the unpopulated Upper Peninsula in the area of Sault Sainte Marie. Meeker knew the appointment there would be temporary, as the Indian Removal Act of 1830 was already in place, requiring the Indians to relocate farther west. The Baptists would not desert them, but would the Meekers' devotion be enough to save them and ease their burdens?

Eleven thousand Indians, including Shawnee, Pottawatomie, Ottawa, Chippewa, Delaware, Kickapoo, Wyandotte and the Iowa, Sac and Fox, were uprooted and sent west. In the spring of 1833, the mission on Lake Superior was abandoned. The mission board had agreed with McCoy that it was a waste of resources ministering to unsettled Indians that would probably have to move again. That summer, Meeker was to go to Boston to meet with his superiors who wanted him to take a printing press along with him to Indian territory to print religious materials for the Indians.

After leaving Michigan, Jotham and Eleanor traveled to Cincinnati where he left her to give birth to their first child at the home of her mother, and he set out on the arduous trip to Boston for his instructions from headquarters. On his return via Cleveland, he learned there that his son, John Ells Meeker, had died in Cincinnati, at just twenty-six days of age. When he finally reached Eleanor, he burst into tears. "Eleanor, my sweet Eleanor. I'm so sorry," he confessed. I left you alone to bring our child into this cruel world. God is testing us again."

"Don't chastise yourself too much," Eleanor consoled him. "My mother gave me a poem she wrote after losing five of her own infant children.
Five infants from my bosom torn
By Death's resistless hand;
But why should I reflect and mourn,
'Twas done by God's Command.
My mother's poem has helped me cope. I hope it helps you."

In Cincinnati, Meeker purchased his printing press, a used 1817 model that had twenty stars on its frame, the number of states at that time. By September 11, 1833, the press was packed and ready to go, and Jotham and Eleanor were on their way by river steamer down the Ohio and up the Missouri to join the Indians in the wilderness of northeastern Kansas. The dock at Independence Landing, Missouri, was built up against the muddy bluff, and the landing and unloading of the heavy press was problematic. Yet God's special blessing seemed to be guiding it to its destination, sparing it the steamboat disasters that were common on the Missouri.

The printing press and their other supplies were loaded on a wagon, and Jotham and Eleanor struck out westward across the Blue River to a place referred to as Shawanoe. When they arrived on October 2, 1833, they joined other newcomers, Alexander Evans and the Reverend and Mrs. Moses Merrill. Robert Simerwell, with whom they had worked in Michigan, arrived shortly thereafter. The Merrills were soon sent two hundred miles north to work with the Otoes where the Platte joins the Missouri River, and Simmerwell went off to the Potawatomi. The Meekers were welcomed by Isaac McCoy, superintendent of what came to be called Shawnee Baptist Mission, and Dr. Johnston Lykins and wife Delilah, who had erected the mission building the year before. Delilah was McCoy's daughter. The first winter was nearly the death of them all, with government provisions sparse and the temporary shelters cold and damp.

Once settled in, Jotham marveled at the nearby council house of the Shawnee. It was of hewn logs, about thirty feet wide and eighty long, one room, no windows, with a door in each end. Two rows of pillars held up the roof and sides. The pillars near one door were carved with a rattlesnake about five feet long on one side and a snake without rattles on the other. At the other door, one pillar had a human face, partially painted, and the other a turtle with metal eyes that were kept polished.

On December 28, 1833, Meeker unpacked the printing press, and he printed the first pages in January. Jotham was determined to put his skills learned as a printer's apprentice to use in printing parts of the *Bible* for the Shawnee and his Ottawa (Odawa) in their language. The printing press was central to the Baptist strategy for converting heathens around the world. They believed that the Indians, Africans and Asians would be easily converted if they could read the word of God. Because of the missionaries' devotion to the printed word, the Indians called them "paper men."

Meeker began working on an orthography for the spoken Shawnee language, but, for now, a new system of letters and spelling had to be delayed until Jotham could build a permanent log house for his family. And even when the first tasks of settlement were completed, work on the alphabet had to be squeezed into the candlelit hours after the garden was tended and his regular sermons and visitations were finished. He was often sick and weak. Only the dogged help of Eleanor, the generosity of the Indians and God's grace made it possible for him to eventually publish parts of the *Bible* and some hymns in a form that the Shawnee would learn to read and interpret for themselves. Holding a monopoly on Biblical interpretation did not suit Jotham's temperament nor the principles of his church.

In April, Eleanor wrote to her sister Emeline

Shawnee Mission, April 11, 1834
My dear dear Emeline,

If this new mode of teaching the Indians to read in their own language shall continue until the scriptures shall be given to them in their own language, who can tell what good may be done within a few years. We must believe that a blessing will follow whenever a full circulation of the word of God is given to the heathen.

The Indians attend meeting better that they did and pear to take much pleasure in singing hymns which have been printed in their language. We have preaching in Indian every Sunday. There have none joined the Church since last Fall. We hope for better times. On account of the house being small, we are obliged to meet under a stately Oak which stands in the door-yard, it has stood the stormes for centuries but has probably never had the praises of God ascend from its shade until now.

I want you to write and tell me all your situation, let it be what it may. I did intend to write more but must stop for want of time.

I remain you Sister and friend,
(s) Eleanor D. Meeker

Printing for Shawnee readers was not a straightforward matter. Jotham had to first invent a Shawnee alphabet. One could not just imagine the English spelling of the Indian words and then utilize the available standard typefaces as th

e English did for Chinese. Several Indian orthographies had been created, but they used special symbols for some syllables. Special symbols made it impossible to use standard typefaces. Jotham used eight ordinary print characters to represent certain positions of the mouth and tongue and twelve others to represent every uncompounded, distinguishable sound used in the Indian language. Some letters were assigned arbitrarily to sounds used in the Shawnee language. For example, Jotham's system included the following phonemes:

    The letter "b" represented a consonant sound equivalent to "th" in the English word *their*.
    The letter "a" was sounded as the "a" in *mane*.
    The letter "i" represented sound of "a" in *far*.
    The letter "e" was sounded as "e" in *me*.
    The letter "o" represented the "o" pronunciation in *no*.
    The letter "w" stood for another version of "o" as in *move*.
    Pronunciation of the letter "t" required that the end of the tongue be pressed hard against the roof of the mouth.

    In Jotham's orthography, each alphabetic symbol represented only one sound so that the usage was unfailingly consistent. He'd seen the difficulties posed to students of written English by the multiple sounds represented by each letter of the English alphabet. McCoy was very enthusiastic about his colleague's system and told him, "Jotham, you have created something wonderful that no one else has been able to do. I think it could be used to advantage with any language and would be of great use to our missionaries in Asia."

    "Thank you, Isaac," Jotham responded. "Your praise makes my labors worthwhile."

    The few young Indians who chose to study under the new system learned to read in a couple of weeks with minimal instruction. An additional advantage of this orthography was that an English speaker could read a Shawnee text out loud in the Indian language without actually understanding the message conveyed in the unknown tongue. Meeker's teaching method failed to catch on throughout the Kansas missions, however, because of jealousies among the different denominations working in the territory, The Presbyterians and Methodists opposed using the orthography even though the Indians were pleased to be able to read in their own language. The different denominations competed for the Indian souls in many ways.

    The Baptists and Methodists differed in their approach to Indian improvement, and the Shawnees themselves were split as to which they preferred. The Missouri Shawnees had voluntarily given up their hunting lands in Kentucky and accepted the offer from the Spanish to settle at Cape Girardeau, Missouri, in 1793 before the Louisiana Purchase. They had become good farmers after the Missouri resettlement, but they could not prevent white settlers from using their land and appropriating their improvements. Finally, almost fourteen hundred Indians were forced to move on to Kansas in 1831. Chief Fish had had good experiences with Methodist missionaries, and after his tribe's move to Kansas, he asked for the Methodists, who set up a mission about five miles from the Baptists in 1830. Isaac McCoy had also served that group when he moved from Michigan to Westport, Missouri, just across the territory line.

A second group, the Ohio Shawnees, had within it two opposing factions. One had fought with the British in the War of 1812 and participated in the British defeat at the Battle of the Thames. After Tecumseh's death there, The Prophet, remained in Canada for nearly ten years. The other group had stayed loyal to the United States and remained in Ohio on the Maumee River during the hostilities. That faction followed old chief Black Hoof, called Cutewecusa in the native tongue, who hated Tecumseh and distrusted Tenskwatawa. After leading his tribe in many battles against white settlers, including the Byrams in Kentucky, Black Hoof had decided that the Shawnee could survive only through peaceful adoption of white culture.

After the old chief's death, the leadership passed to the younger Black Hoof and Cornstalk, or Wynepuechsika. As a result of the 1817 Treaty of Fort Meigs, Ohio, negotiated by Michigan's Territorial Governor Lewis Cass, they received patents on reservations at Wapakoneta and Lewistown, Ohio. Cass later regretted his decision and persuaded the Shawnees to trade for greater acreage in Kansas. Cass allowed The Prophet to return from exile in Canada to the United States if he would help persuade the Shawnees to leave Ohio.

The Ohio Shawnees had experience with the Baptists. Part of them started for Kansas accompanied by The Prophet in September 1826, traveling via Vincennes, Indiana, Kaskaskia, Illinois, and St. Louis, Missouri. They received some help from William Clark who had been appointed Indian commissioner after his successful exploration of the Northwest with Meriwether Lewis. From St. Louis, the Indians followed the south bank of the Missouri River, finally arriving in Kansas in May 1828. Many died on the trip, and those who survived suffered from lack of supplies, exhausted horses and white depredations. Isaac McCoy visited the new Shawnee village and told them of his plans to build a mission to serve them. Tenskwatawa supported the idea. But McCoy distrusted his motives, recognizing that The Prophet was no longer revered as a religious leader by his people and that he was looking for means to regain his reputation. The old Indian failed to recover his status and would die in obscurity in Kansas not long after wandering artist and author George Catlin painted his portrait.

Because of the Indians' different experiences and demands, Methodist, Baptist and Quaker missionaries arrived to serve the tribes displaced to Kansas. The Methodists focused their primary efforts on agriculture and the industrial arts, including fence building, operating mills and running shops. They took Indian children from their parents and placed them in the mission's boarding school, using the children's labor for agricultural improvements. Lacking other funding, the Methodists tried to use the children's labor to make the school self-sufficient, and they sold trees from Indian lands for lumber. The Methodists used the boarding-school approach to break tribal bonds and family ties, and they limited their aid to those willing to give up their tribal affiliation.

The Methodists, like many military victors, partially adapted their ceremonies to those of the vanquished. The Shawnees' green corn festival and their feast for "our grandmothers" resembled the Methodists' own camp meetings. The Indians gathered for several days around a central preaching site. Joint historical dramas incorporated the creation stories of both Indian and Christian. Methodist leader Thomas Johnson judged that "the grand object was to bring the Shawnees to a correct understanding of our language, and enable them to speak it fluently." The green corn dance originally occurred when the chief declared the corn ready to eat in the early summer. No one harvested any roasting ears until after the dance, which was organized by the women who prepared a variety of corn dishes from the fields they tended. In the fall, the bread dance that gave thanks for the harvest and the first hunt of wild game was organized by the men, balancing the responsibilities of the genders. Reflecting European culture, the missionaries wanted the Indian men and women to adopt new roles. Men were to become farmers and women to be submissive household managers. The Indians resisted this radical change, and the concept made them reluctant to adopt Christianity.

In contrast, the Baptist missions let the children remain with their parents and tried to educate both generations together, hoping that some parents would, in time, become teachers themselves. Farming played a lesser role. Learning English was given equal emphasis with learning to read in their own language with the aid of Meeker's orthography and printing press. Making books and a newspaper available in the native language let the Indians adopt concepts and practices of their own free will. The Baptist approach also helped them retain a sense of cultural identity.

Neither manner of dealing with the relocated tribes came to grips with their immediate problems: lack of food, clothing and agricultural implements. No matter how appreciative the Indians might be of their education and Dr. Johnston Lykins' vaccinations, they were, above all, hungry. Removal of the woodlands Indians to the prairies made them dependent on government annuities. The failure of the government to deliver was not the missionaries' fault, but the missionaries took some of the blame. The Shawnees gathered in council in October 1834 and requested that all missionaries be withdrawn from their lands. Wanting to stay and hoping to placate the Indians, the Methodists reversed their emphasis on the exclusive use of English in their mission, and Thomas Johnson asked Meeker to print some Methodist hymns using his orthography. When Meeker got the request, he was torn. "I'm reluctant to accommodate the Methodists after they condemned my system," he told Eleanor, "but I guess it would be un-Christian, and it would look bad if I openly fail to cooperate."

"God will sort it out," his wife replied.

Unexpectedly the Indians demanded that the missionaries leave. McCoy and Meeker were deeply troubled. McCoy focused on the source of the demand, rather than trying to understand its cause. In a discussion with Jotham, he said, "I think the demands come from only a few Indians dominated by the ever-contentious Prophet and also from white men who want to eliminate missionary support for Indian lands so they can move in themselves."

"You are probably right," Jotham responded "The differences among the Indians have simmered and remained unresolved since the days when Tecumseh and Tenskwatawa wanted to drive the white settlers from Indian lands in Ohio. Remember how others, such as Black Hoof, came to advocate accommodation to the white culture. History bites deep into the trajectory of the future."

"Still, I wonder if we should ask ourselves if the Indians have a legitimate complaint," McCoy pondered. "Have we missionaries been a force for Indian unity that many desperately desire? Or has the competition among denominations in seeking Indian allies only contributed to the division and resentment among the different Shawnee subgroups?"

McCoy was in no mood to discuss it further.

"But I am thoroughly committed to saving the souls of these Indians," Meeker persisted. "I can understand their reluctance to abandon their old religion. They have their own creation story and a kind of salvation if they follow the rules of the Great Spirit. They have been moved from their homes several times. I understand that they feel like they have no control over their lives. They're not allowed to make any important choices. We'll have to give them a lot of love along with religion."

"You have more patience than I," said McCoy whose own supply was running out.

"But men without choices are no men at all," Jotham had to add. "They will resort either to desperate violence or sink into resignation, withdrawal and drink."

"Jotham," counseled his mentor, "too much philosophy may get you into trouble."

Amidst the moving and settling in at the Kansas mission, Eleanor Meeker realized she was pregnant again. Both she and Jotham were apprehensive, remembering the death of their first baby in Cincinnati the previous summer. Still, Eleanor kept her counsel and continued her heavy workload until she felt the first pangs of labor. On September 4, 1834, attended by an Indian midwife, Eleanor gave birth to the first white child born in Kansas at the Baptist mission. The baby girl screamed her way into the world with something like an Indian war hoop. They named her Maria.

"Isn't she beautiful, Jotham?" asked the exhausted mother. "Look at these perfect little fingers and toes."

"Yes, she is the most precious thing in the world," he agreed. "I just hope that we can provide for her."

"God will provide," assured Eleanor, displaying her unflagging faith once more. Jotham, daunted by the prospects of providing for his wife and new babe, wrote in his journal only that "Mrs. M. was delivered of healthy looking daughter today."

The next spring, Jotham built split-rail fences to keep out marauding animals and set about cultivation of his land. He put out cabbages early in the season and spent most of July tending to the small grain crops that would feed his livestock and his own family. In November, he killed and dressed a hog and purchased fifty bushels of corn to be ground at a mill built by the Delaware. He went to look for a cow who'd recently freshened to provide the family with milk, but he found none. He walked forty miles to the river the French had named Marais des Cygnes, meaning Marsh of the Swans, to examine a possible location for his future home and mission for the Ottawas. On his return, he took the wrong trail and wandered an extra two days before finding his way home.

Upon his arrival, there was both pity and peeve in Eleanor's voice. "I was worried sick when you did not return as expected," she told him. "The prospect of being left alone on the prairie with Maria and no husband alarmed me."

"I knew you'd be fretting, but what could I do?" he asked. "As I walked along, I was thinking of what I wanted to make for Maria."

The next day, he was very busy with his carpentry tools with which he fashioned a rocking cradle and a miniature chair for his daughter.

"The chair is premature for such a small babe," Eleanor chided him, "but I suppose she will grow into it."

Besides seeing to the Indians' spiritual needs, Jotham spent much time providing for his family. In January, he killed and salted three hogs. In February, he managed to print the first book and the first newspaper in Kansas called the *Shawnee Sun* in English and *Siwinowe Kesibwi* in the native language. The Baptists hoped the *Sun* would, indeed, help the Indians see the light and convert.

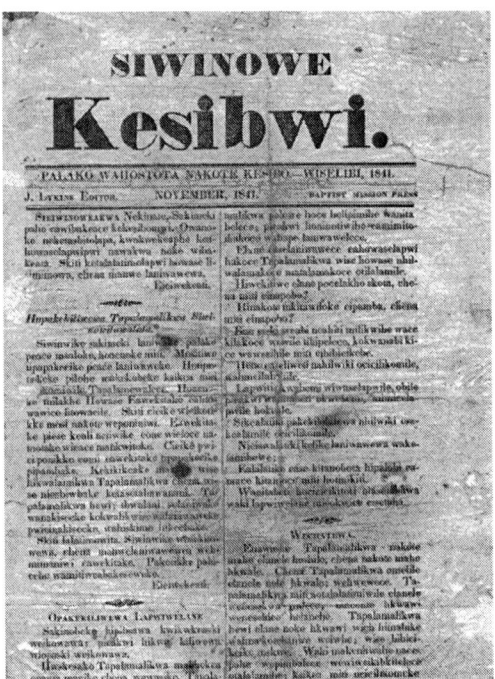

The Shawnee Sun, 1841

Meeker's Press, c. 1935

    During his second season on the Kansas land, Jotham planted potatoes and corn in April and in June purchased a horse at Isaac McCoy's store in Westport. He made beehives from which to collect honey, their only source of sweetener. There were no maples for sugar as in Michigan. September found him spending two weeks haying, digging potatoes, harvesting a load of pumpkins and always helping neighboring Indians. He went to the Methodist mission to buy winter shoes for himself and Eleanor. In November, he hauled firewood, and again in December, he killed and cut up his winter pork, thus completing the agricultural cycle.

    A highlight of the next year was teaching Blackfeather and Henry Bluejacket to write in their own language. Later, the two Indians delighted in writing a message for the Sun. Blackfeather and Joseph DeShane spent many hours at the Meekers' home going over Jotham's translation of the Bible, helping him name and translate the major concepts, such as God and Hell. Blackfeather contributed Tapalamalikwe, the Shawnee word for the Great Spirit, for God and miceminato for the Devil's domain. In doing so, Blackfeather subtly injected Shawnee meaning into the Bible they would be using. The Indians thereby were not wholly converting from the pagan spirit to a new god, but rather were merging the two deities.

    For the Shawnee, miceminato meant "bad snake," the embodiment of evil in the form of a giant horned snake that inhabited the depths of rivers and lakes. The Great Spirit was creator of almost all things on earth except the evil snake that had been made by a lesser spirit gone bad. This errant spirit was also the creator of mosquitoes and weeds. The Great Spirit regretted giving the lesser spirit the power of creation, but the error became obvious only after it was too late to do anything about it.

The same round of backbreaking farm chores followed year after year. One year after stacking hay in August, Jotham became ill and could not work at all in September, causing him much concern about provisioning his family during the long winter ahead and about his own ability to continue in the frontier service. In his diary he wrote, "I have become an invalid." Dr. Chute prescribed blistering and cupping to remedy the pain in his spine. Boils on his shoulders caused him considerable discomfort.

During his incapacity, Jotham received a letter from his mother that caused him greater pain than his boils. Jotham's father Randolf had died in 1809, and his mother Lydia remarried Daniel Bradstreet. With her second husband, she had Jotham's half-brother, John Milton Bradstreet. Lydia and Daniel proved to be incompatible, and Daniel paid her three hundred dollars to initiate a separation.

But, without a sustained income, Lydia had been forced afterwards to live with a series of relatives. His mother's letter revealed how intolerable her dependent state had become:

College Corner, Butler County, Ohio, October 1835
Dear Son,
　　　　I sit down to write a few lines to you to let you know my health is tolerable good. I could not live with your uncle any longer with any comfort. It seems like altered times since your aunt's death. I think your uncle is a little hard with me. He says he will not keep me for less than a dollar a week and his health is but poor. He was going to Hamilton and I packed up and came with him as far as Martin Millers that married your cousin Casander Yaman. I do not know how long I shall stay there. Milton wrote to me that he could not keep me well. He still lives in Cincinnati. He thinks he is not able to keep me he thinks. I had better live with you but you live so far. I do not know what to do, the distance is so great. I cannot go by land and I am afraid to go by water. It costs me a great deal to move so much. I had to pay 20 dollars to move me out and more to move me back besides my expenses my money seems go.

　　　　I shall not have very much money left when I settle with your uncle. He says he cannot pay me all that he owes me until next fall. I have not received a letter from you since June 5. When you write to me direct your letter to College Corner, Butler Co Ohio. If you could send me some money it would help me. Just now when you write to me I will write to you again. It has been a very sickly season all over. I live about 18 miles from Hamilton.
I remain your affectionate Mother,
(s) Lydia Bradstreet

More letters followed, heaping guilt upon Jotham with claims that he loved his Indians more than his poor mother. Finally, Jotham traveled to Cincinnati in 1836 to fetch his mother who overcame her fear of boats and water and returned with him to Kansas. The Baptist Mission Board gave him a supplement to support his mother so that he'd be able to remain in the field.

Lydia helped out by teaching the Indian children and assisting with the care of baby Maria. In a letter to her sister Emeline, Eleanor bragged, "Maria talks quite plain, she knows some letters, she is a complete mimic. I know you would be glad to see her jumping about."

In 1837, the Ottawa of Blanchard's Fork on the Auglaize and of Roche de Boeuf on the Maumee were removed from Ohio to a tract measuring ten by twelve miles, including thirty-four thousand acres, and watered by the Marais des Cygnes River in Franklin County, Kansas. There they joined other Ottawa who'd moved four years earlier from west of Lake Michigan following the Second Treaty of Chicago. These Indians had moved west just as the Todds arrived in Lenawee County, Michigan, from New York. Joseph Badger King, one of the transplanted Ohio Indians, described Kansas in glowing terms: "The swelling upland prairies and wooded valleys were not only beautiful to the eye, but they were teeming with wild game, which of course, made it rich to the Indians' way of thinking."

Jotham was eager to establish a mission of his own for the Ohio brothers of his beloved Ottawa to whom he had ministered on the Grand River in Michigan. But McCoy would not allow him to leave Shawnee Mission until a replacement could arrive to take over his printing operation. Mary Walton Blanchard, wife of Ira at the Delaware Baptist mission, wrote to a friend, Olivia Evans, taking Meeker's side. "It does seem altogether wrong that brother Meeker, after having spent six years of hard labor in acquiring a knowledge of the Ottawa language, should be kept from them by work that another could just as well perform while there is probably no man upon earth that can, without spending much time in conquering an unwritten language, fill his place among a people with whom he can converse and over whom he has gained an influence." This was Meeker's thought as well, though he never voiced it.

When Brother John G. Pratt arrived at the Shawnee Mission, he took over the printing and freed Jotham to work with the Ottawa. Jotham scouted land and selected a building site on the north bank of the Marais des Cygnes River. In March 1837, he had laid out a five-acre field, sowed grass seed and dug a shallow well in anticipation of his move. He returned in May and planted corn. He tried to buy a wagon, but found them scarce. When he returned later, he found that birds had dug his corn seed out of the ground, so he had to replant. He settled his accounts with A. J. McCoy's trading post in Westport and prepared to move his wife and daughter to the new Ottawa mission in the spring. Jotham felt obliged to trade with McCoy's son rather than Albert Boone who often had better prices.

As the longtime colleagues discussed Jotham's new mission, Isaac McCoy reminisced about his life's work. "I began as a missionary in Indiana at age nineteen," he told the younger man. "I married sixteen-year-old Christiana and we served a frontier church near Vincennes, Indiana, for a while. But, I always knew I wanted to serve the Indians, not the whites. I worked with the Delaware with only a one-year-contract from our mission board. I borrowed money and made frequent trips to appeal to congregations in Ohio for funds. Can you believe that my wife's mother and sister were once briefly taken captive by the Ottawa when the family first settled in Indiana? Still, she is as committed as I to the Indian's welfare.

"You have been here long enough to learn that the life of a missionary is not easy," the older man continued. "It is hard on a man and his family. My wife and I had fourteen children, eleven of whom died during the time I was a missionary. My firstborn daughter, Mahala, the apple of my eye, died when she was only fourteen. I know you do not expect a comfortable life, but I can understand that you might be concerned about providing for your family in old age."

"What do you mean exactly?" Jotham asked.

"I remember saying to myself when I was a young missionary in Indiana, I shall never be able to lay up by personal service, a shilling for my widow and orphans, which I shall probably in a few years, leave in the middle of Wabash or Arkansas country. Worse, I feared dying without seeing the fruit of my labors, knowing only that I had prepared the way for others to follow." Jotham hardly knew what to say in response to his mentor's frank confession that continued, "In my dark moments, I justified having no nest egg by thinking I shall not live to old age anyway." This hit Jotham hard. Finally he said, "We must focus on the here and now, doing the Lord's work and bowing to his will."

"I have long been troubled by the Indians' use of ardent spirits. It ruins their lives," McCoy went on to his most enduring concern. "I keep hoping the Indian agent will find a solution. It is illegal to sell whiskey to the Indians, but the law is not enforced. Can you believe that after the first Treaty of Chicago in 1821, the government gave the Indians seven barrels of whiskey which shortly after produced ten murders? A drunken Indian once nearly killed one of my daughters. According to Indian custom, I could have taken his life in revenge, but, we decided to leave vengeance to Him to whom alone it belongs. I had a vision that if the Indians could be brought to the West, far from white influences, these temptations could be avoided and the Indians could live in peace. I was one of the main lobbyists in Washington for the Indian Removal Act of 1830 proposed and signed by President Jackson."

Meeker pressed McCoy, "Many think Indian removal was cruel. Among them missionary Jeremiah Evarts who thought that removal and abrogation of their treaty rights was immoral and unfair."

"To the contrary," McCoy replied stridently. "I believed getting them apart from white culture was their salvation."

"I guess the white settlers and traders moved west faster than you anticipated."

"When I came out here with a party of Indians in 1828 to explore sites where the Indians might settle, there was nothing but prairie. Chief Noonday and the other Indians liked this land. Their only lamentation was the lack of trees in general and the lack of sugar trees in particular, since they were used to the woodlands of Michigan, Indiana and Ohio."

"I rather miss the maples myself," Jotham concurred.

"My vision hasn't been realized," McCoy admitted "and that preys on my mind even more than any hardships that I and my family have endured."

"We can only ask for God's guidance and do our best with the situation we now have."

"I sometimes get discouraged by the lack of support from the mission board," McCoy confessed. "They are far more interested in saving souls in Asia than among the Indians here."

"It's easy to understand," opined Jotham, "Americans can be generous when they do not covet the land of the souls to be saved."

"For the last ten years, we would have had to abandon our work if it hadn't been for government support," continued McCoy. "Treaties provide money for teachers, blacksmiths and agriculturalists. I got my first appointment as a teacher to the Potawatomi. You took my place when you came to Carey Station. The government does not object to our adding religious teaching because we organize it all, and it would be hard for them to get regular teachers to make the necessary sacrifices to live in Indian country. Excuse my rambling on, but this new mission of yours has set me to reflect on my own career."

Jotham took his mentor's reflections as an acceptance that his course was now approved. He would be moving to a mission of his own.

Eleanor, Maria, and Jotham Meeker

~7~

A Mission of his Own

Jotham's excitement mounted as the day of their move neared. He really was going to have his own mission for his beloved Ottawas. He would no longer be laboring in the shadow of other missionaries. In June, Jotham and his little family began its move to the site he had chosen earlier on the Marais des Cygnes River. They made eighteen miles the first day, and camped the night on the prairie. Made twenty miles the next day, and after seven more the following day, they finally arrived. They lived out of their wagon while Jotham set to work making a cabin.

The next year, 1838, Jotham's labors for the church resulted in his being ordained at Shawanoe. His pleasure was dulled by continuous struggles against illness. Still, he managed to clear the land and extend his plantings. In November, Jotham turned thirty-four. Meeker's Indians also suffered from sickness. Mr. Roby, the Indian agent, reported to his superiors: "Out of about six hundred emigrants, more than three hundred died within the first two years, because of exposure, lack of proper food, and the great difference between the cool, damp woods of Ohio and the dry, hot plains of Kansas." The natural increase in population never equaled the mortality numbers. Meeker added coffin making to his repertory of skills.

The first months of 1839 found Jotham discouraged by excessive drinking among the Indians and their reversions to pagan ceremonies. In the midst of the Indian debaucheries, Eleanor gave birth to their second daughter Emeline in September at Ottawa Mission. She was the one joy in Eleanor's taxing work life. Eleanor's domestic chores included raising the children, cooking, cleaning, sewing, baking, gardening and making soap and candles. She was also responsible for teaching the Indian women new methods of cooking, sewing and knitting. She made medicines and helped nurse the ill. Eleanor could speak the Ottawa language fluently. In October, Jotham and Eleanor harvested potatoes, turnips and pumpkins to store in their root cellar for winter food for their growing family. December again found them dipping two hundred fifty candles, collecting firewood, killing hogs and dressing and salting pork.

The Indians' pagan reversions created a conflict between a conjurer and a convert named Waseem, who was dying. Jotham made a woman seeking church membership throw away her medicine bag. In the midst of their drinking and fighting, the Indians would not attend school. There was more talk of driving all the missionaries out of the country. "The devil seems to be let loose upon us," reflected Jotham to Eleanor. Otto-wu-kee, a principal Ottawa chief and three others took an open stance in opposition to Meeker and threatened to destroy his property. The threat did not deter those who had been born again and joined the church, including David Green who was a zealous convert. Some weeks later, Otto-wu-kee sent for Meeker. The chief was in obvious discomfort with cholera, having severe pains in his bowels followed by vomiting and cramps. His family thought there was nothing that could be done for him. The chief reached out his hand and asked Jotham to be merciful. Meeker ran home and returned with some medicine. A week later, the chief seemed to improve and most in his tribe thought that this was a sign of the power of the Baptists' God. Jotham remarked to Eleanor, "I think the chief will fear to oppose us further. The Lord works in mysterious ways."

With this good experience fading, Meeker felt that God was testing him again when, in the space of just one day, baby Emeline was sick, two of his best horses died, and he experienced a severe attack of ague, with much aching alternating with malarial chills and fever. Still, he and the baby recovered, and he soon managed more translations of English texts, including St. Matthew, into Shawanoe and started building a new house, laying in fuel, and buying cows, chickens and pigs. In January, the temperature fell to eighteen degrees below zero.

Meeker wrote to the Baptist Board making a case for paying convert Brother Green to assist him in his missionary work. He cited Green's accomplishments and ability to argue with the chiefs and medicine men who opposed his mission. "I hope the board will not compel him to leave any part of his missionary work by sending him home to work for his family." But, the board only provided money for a third of Green's time.

Meeker's troubles with Otto-wu-kee were not over. The partially revived chief and his sub-chief Kompchaw again began to agitate for removal of the mission, claiming that it was never the wish of the Indians that a mission be established there. But Brother Green came to the defense of the mission by saying he had witnessed the Indians' request to the Commissioner of Indian Affairs at Washington. Otto-wu-kee was not dissuaded by this testimony and called a council meeting to plan on the mission's removal. The next Sunday while Jotham was preaching and the congregation was singing hymns in their language, the chief held an otter skin medicine dance within earshot and with much drumming. The exertion of the ceremony seemed to cause the chief to relapse, and he soon died. Meeker continued his ministry and admitted several more Indians to the church and led them to the river for baptism.

As Maria became of school age, Eleanor insisted that she get a good education, a task that was impossible in Indian country. "Jotham, we must send her away to school. It will tear my heart out to see her go, but it must be," she told him. "Will the mission board give us an allowance for her education?"

"I think so," Jotham replied, "but first we can send Maria to Brother Pratt's school at Shawanoe. I was denied the opportunity for formal education, and I also want more for Maria."

Jotham hardly noticed the passing of his thirty-seventh birthday in November of 1841. He spent the day translating the St. Matthew Gospel. He made a trip to Shawanoe and when he returned he found Eleanor and the two girls sick.

Mother Lydia Meeker was not happy in the far west. "This place is uncivilized and no place for an old women. Milton has sent me some money, and I would like to move to Westport," she told Jotham. She had already stayed longer on the prairie than he had expected, but he kept the thought to himself. She remained in Westport, the closest town, for a year, and then Milton offered to keep her at Cincinnati. The next May, Jotham took his mother back to Cincinnati, accompanied by Eleanor and the children. Maria would be left there to go to school.

Eleanor described the perils of the trip in a letter to her sister Emeline in Darke County, Ohio, whom she'd not been able to see during the Cincinnati trip:

Ottawa, Aug. 9th 1842

My dear dear sister Emeline,

I feel more anxious to see you than ever and feel that it is more probable that I <u>never</u> shall. Before we got ready to leave home, baby Emeline was taken very sick; we did not expect her to recover, but when the disease broke she began to mend very fast, and we again made preparations to start. On the 10th of May we left home. Arrived at the Shawanoe Mission on the next day. On the 12th we went to the river, encamped two days waiting for a Steamboat—at length one came, we embarked, and on the 22nd found ourselves safely landed at Cincinnati. Emeline's health had been improving until that day, at which time she again caught a severe cold and gradually grew worse until June 2nd at which time she was taken down with a disease on her lungs, and was three weeks not expected to live.

I was heartily gratified to find that Brother Miller of our church was willing to take our little Maria into their family. Three Female School teachers very kindly offered to teach her free from charge, and they board and clothe her free from our expense, which we are very grateful for.

We left on the 24th of June with heavy hearts. Yes I need not tell you that I found it truly heartrending to give up seeing you and give my parting embrace with one arm to my Maria whilst I held in my other as I then thought my almost dying child. After we started she grew worse. When we got to St. Louis, we thought we should have to stop and bury her there. Mr. M. was also very sick, but we found a good boat was to start up the Missouri, and that there would not be another for some days; we thought that it would be much harder to bury our little one on the way. Our passage was very quick up the Missouri, but when we got to the Westport landing they put us ashore at the wrong place in the night, the only alternative was to sit and wait for morning. Mr. M wrapped us up in an armed chair which a friend gave me in Cin. When daylight came he left us sitting in our chair whilst he went on search of a wagon—he found an ox wagon—we had left our box of cooking utensils on the boat, and therefore left without anything to eat or drink. We put what things we could in the wagon and got in and later arrived at the Mission.

I hope you will remember us, and the benighted people among whom we live, and if we never see each other again, in this wide world of sin let us try to live so that we may meet in that world of happiness where parting will be no more.

As ever Yours
(s) E. D. Meeker

Lydia would live with her son, John Milton Bradstreet who by then had a successful mercantile business in Cincinnati. He would later create a credit-rating business and move to New York City after his mother died. Eventually this firm became Dun & Bradstreet. Maria was left in Cincinnati to continue her education. She returned home in the following November.

From travelers, Meeker heard of the trouble with the Mormons at nearby Independence, Missouri. On the road to Independence, he met twenty-five armed and mounted men returning from pursuing some Mormons. Meeker learned that Joseph Smith founded Mormonism in Palmyra, New York (where the Todds once lived before moving to Michigan in 1830). There the Book of Mormon was published in 1830. Smith had a vision of a temple for his followers in Jackson County, Missouri. Many Mormons left New York for Kirtland in southern Ohio, but as Smith pushed the idea of the temple, a new Zion awaiting the second coming of Jesus, many moved into the area around Independence in Jackson County. Mormon beliefs provoked an unusually strong reaction among followers of the older religions. They feared influence of one man on his followers, though a foreign Pope never engendered the same level of suspicion of Catholics. The opposition was also political. The Mormons would soon have a majority of votes in the county, and they voted as a block. Additionally, they welcomed free blacks and were friends with the Indians, neither position being popular among many Missouri residents.

Armed mobs had attacked the Mormons in 1833-34, burned their houses and demanded that they leave the county. Some Mormons thought that the locals just wanted to appropriate their land without paying for it. The Indians sympathized. Meeker heard that the Mormons filed a suit in the county court against those who attacked them. Sixty militiamen guarded the petitioners, but it was clear that their plea could not go forward and they retired. In July, mobs tarred and feathered Mormon leaders and destroyed homes, shops and a printing press. Meeker called it a "Reign of Terror." In November, the Missouri militia was called out, but it gave no protection to the Mormons as the militia commander had been previously active in the mobs. The Mormons appealed to the Governor and the president for protection, but their pleas were ignored. Many left the county and moved north across the Missouri River to Clay in the newly created Caldwell County, establishing a community they called Far West.

Some Mormons had had enough and fought back; armed bands on both sides roamed the countryside. When a Mormon paramilitary unit attacked an official militia, thinking it an anti-Mormon mob, the Missouri governor, Lilburn Boggs, ordered the removal of the Latter Day Saints in 1838 declaring, "*The Mormons must be treated as enemies, and must be exterminated or driven from the State if necessary, for the public peace—their outrages are beyond all description.*" Protection of minority rights had no popular support.

Three days later, a mob attacked the Mormon village of Haun's Mill and massacred dozens of men, women and children. Meeker was deeply disturbed and asked in his sermons, "Why can't people be tolerant and live in peace? God commands us to love one another as he loved us."

In the dead of winter, many Mormons were driven away to Nauvoo, Illinois, near the Iowa-Illinois border. The same prejudices followed them there, and Joseph Smith was murdered at the age of thirty-eight (Meeker was forty that year). After years of persecution, Brigham Young then led twenty-five hundred believers to Winter Quarters on the Missouri river at Omaha, Nebraska, in 1846-'47, where they waited to make the trip to Utah, which was then Mexican territory. During the trek across Iowa, Young agreed to provide five hundred men to fight in the Mexican War. They marched to Santa Fe.

The Mormons, like the Indians, sought a land far enough away from other settlers to allow them to pursue their own culture. Church leaders learned from the Indians' experience that Mormons must have the majority of voters in the new territory. Young gave voting rights to women to offset the arrival of non-Mormons when silver was found on the western side of the Rockies. The Mormons had ten years of peace in Utah before the rest of the world caught up with them. Young was appointed territorial governor in 1851 but was replaced in 1857 when federal troops arrived to enforce the prohibition of polygamy.

The Mormons were more successful than the Indians in establishing a self-governing state, but still they could not escape the dominance of the federal government, as evidenced by the Mormon War and the Army of General Johnston enforcing the prohibition of polygamy. Supplying this army enriched the Byram Brothers' freight business operating out of Nebraska City in the 1860s. The Mormons and Indians suffered similar prejudice, but, in establishing a self-governing state, the Mormons had two advantages going for them that the Indians did not have. First, they put a mountain range between themselves and the advancing settlers, giving them time to get established and become the local majority. Second, they had a centralized, hierarchical leadership, making collective decisions easier and more coordinated. The Indians never were able to join together to resist the whites.

Meeker helped Chief No-tin-no write a letter to the Superintendent of Indian Affairs in St. Louis. No-tin-no pointed out that the government had promised plows and harness years ago when the Indians were living on the Maumee River in Ohio. The plows still had not arrived, and he thought his next step was to write the great White Father in Washington. The chief ended his letter with a plaintive cry, "If he shall refuse to pay any attention to my request, I shall drop the subject and be convinced that my Father not only wishes to throw me away, but that he also intends to defraud me of that which is my own." No-tin-no gave Jotham a ceremonial pipe decorated with an eagle feather and used in the sacred medicine dance for generations. The chief also gave him a beaded purse. Jotham felt deeply honored by this expression of good will.

One June day in 1844 it started to rain. And it rained and it rained! The clouds hung around for three weeks and could not contain themselves. The nearby Marais des Cygnes River that drained a large basin began to rise, and rise and rise. The floodwater surrounded all of the Meeker farm outbuildings and then the house. When they went to bed, Jotham told Eleanor to be mindful of possible water inside their cabin. "Surely, it will stop rising soon," she said. In the middle of the night, Eleanor, awakened Jotham and exclaimed, "Jotham, I can hear water running." She swung out of bed and her feet recoiled when they touched several inches of water on the floor. "I'll dress and then gather the chickens while you drive the cattle and hogs to the hill."

When Jotham returned, they gathered up an old tent, blankets and bedding and other salvageable items, prepared to leave their house. In the afternoon, with the water continuing to rise, Jotham realized they could wait no longer. "Eleanor, there is only one canoe within five miles of us," he told her. "I will blow the emergency horn and hope someone will bring the canoe to us."

When the small canoe arrived, paddled by one of their Indian neighbors, the water was knee deep. There was room for just two adults and the small children and Jotham had to make a difficult decision. "Eleanor, put the girls in the canoe. The current has become so strong, I will have to help paddle. I will return for you."

Eleanor sat on the table that had been pushed to the wall, fearing for her life. "Lord, have you forsaken us?" she cried. When Jotham and the canoe returned, the current was so swift and strong, it was hard to maneuver the canoe close to the cabin door. Jotham strained with all his might to hold it steady. "Hold on to the side of the canoe and I will help you in." But, he could not get her in without capsizing the canoe. "Hang on to the side, Eleanor. I can't get you out of the water." Paddling like a madman with terror in his eyes, Jotham aimed toward the bluff with Eleanor clinging to the side of the canoe in the raging water. As they approached, Eleanor lost her grip. She was so tired that she could do nothing but let her body drop. Then she felt her feet touch bottom and she managed to wade ashore using the last bit of her energy against the current. On shore, they both collapsed on the grass gasping for breath. When they had recovered a bit, they erected their tent as night was falling. Both of them were completely drenched, and Jotham, exhausted, fell asleep on a wet blanket. Eleanor, shivering in spite of a blanket she drew around herself and the girls, sat up, comforting the children and keeping them as warm as she could.

In the morning, they watched the flood sweep away all of their outbuildings: the smokehouse with a year's supply of pork and hard soap, the bee house with seven hives, the chicken house with one hundred birds, the stable, the corncrib with one hundred twenty-five bushels of corn, the kitchen with cooking and table equipment, the garden fence and four hundred rails stockpiled for fencing. All of their crops were destroyed, and even the orchard was uprooted, with the exception of one forlorn-looking peach tree. The Meekers, soaked by river water and the relentless rain, spent several nights in their tent on the high prairie near a cleft in the rocks. Finally, they returned to the Shawanoe Mission on a wagon brought by Brother Pratt. They traveled nearly a mile in the floodwater with driftwood cruising by. They realized now that building in the flood plain was a mistake. The convenient access to water had blinded them of its danger.

They had not slept soundly for a week, and Eleanor had lost hope. "Jotham, I am so discouraged," she told her husband. "I had just done my spring cleaning and washed all our clothes and bedding. Now, much of it is lost, and the rest is smelly. I'm so sick, so weak, I don't know if I can begin anew. Just when I thought we were making some progress, this had to happen. A few years ago we fought prairie fires, and now we are flooded." Jotham was also of heavy heart. God was testing him again. He could find only one thing to be thankful for. They had been spared the tornado that had devastated Westport.

Kansas City was completely inundated, and the Missouri River was reported to be fifteen feet higher than it was ever known to be. When the water receded, Meeker could see that the plowed ground was washed away as deeply as the plow had penetrated. The cellar wall and chimney of their house had collapsed. The Meekers and the Indians surrounding the mission faced starvation. Meeker went in search of corn for the Indians, but could find little. Many Indians left for the west to hunt. Many more died of cholera and malaria.

Jotham replanted his potatoes. He planted turnips at night, since the flies were unbearable in the day. In the fall, the turnip patch yielded only twelve bushels and the potatoes yielded nine, the extent of his crops that year. In the fall, they rebuilt on higher ground with donations from the Baptist Mission Board and churches. These gifts saved the Meekers' lives and those of many Indians. When they moved their salvaged furniture, their furnishings seemed to Eleanor to be more meager than ever—three double beds, a clothes press bureau, three cupboards, a table and four chairs. The Meekers' annual salary was three hundred fifty dollars.

The next year, Jotham was stricken with severe headaches. He medicated himself with a homemade syrup of one grain quinine, one grain rhubarb and a half grain blue mass. Blue mass was widely used for tuberculosis, constipation, toothache, parasitic infestations and the pains of childbirth. It was made of thirty-three parts mercury, five parts licorice, twenty-five parts Althaea (from the marshmallow plant or hollyhock), three parts glycerol and thirty-four parts rose honey. The drug was known to cause loss of teeth and hair. Jotham did no printing that year. In fact, he and the rest of the family were frequently incapacitated with intermittent fevers. Jotham read medical books, searching for remedies for his family and the Indians. He subscribed to several newspapers to keep abreast of the political and medical news. He continually ordered medicines from Boston.

"Jotham, I didn't know that you were a pharmacist," Eleanor observed one day. "You make for yourself and the Indians hundreds of Cook's pills each week. But sometimes I wonder if we are overdoing it. There's calomel, Brandreth's pills, Lee's pills, Eberle's pills, Moffat's pills, Turner's Cerate and quinine. Sometimes after taking a dose, we feel better, but maybe our bodies would have recovered anyway. And, a few days later, we are sick again."

"Sometimes I feel so helpless," he admitted. "I, too, wonder about the effectiveness of our medicines, but I keep hoping that there will be a new one that will work. Above all, we must trust in God's grace." Meeker mostly suffered his prolonged illnesses in silence, but his frailties caused him to reflect on God when he discussed his ailments with his wife "Remember, Eleanor, the Indians believe that if they follow the righteous road and sacrifice food to the spirits, they will secure good health and die a peaceful death in old age."

"That goes further than our God," she said. "I sometimes pray that I might die in my sleep."

"Still, one can observe that Indians suffer from malaria, smallpox and cholera and often die horrible deaths. They seem to expect too much of their Great Spirit."

"I can see why their faith now wavers," Eleanor concluded, "but, I'm not sure it makes their conversion any easier. It seems rather to make them despondent."

Eighteen forty-six was another eventful year. Jotham made a lengthy trip to Baptist Mission Board headquarters in Boston, with Eleanor and the two children accompanying him partway. When Jotham traveled, he wore his only suit, black with wide lapels. His white shirt emerged well above the collar of his coat. A loosely tied, wide black ribbon was at this throat. Eleanor's dark hair, parted in the middle, was always neatly tucked into a white bonnet with rucking that tied under her chin. Her dress was black with a small collar of white lace at the neck. They traveled by all means of transport available at the time. They took a steamer to Cincinnati where Eleanor and the children remained to visit with Eleanor's sister. Jotham continued on the steamer, The Talisman, to Pittsburgh, then took the steamboat Consul on the Monongahela to Brownville. From there he boarded a stage to Cumberland, Maryland, then a train to Baltimore, where he took another steamboat to Philadelphia. Finally, he boarded a train again to reach New York City, then rode on to Providence and, at last, to Boston. The mission board ordered him to revisit his former post in Michigan to help persuade the remaining Indians there to move to Kansas. McCoy asked him to deliver an accounting of his use of government funds to Secretary of War Lewis Cass in Detroit on his way. Jotham wrote to his wife in Cincinnati:

Cleveland, Ohio, Friday June 5, 1846

Dear Wife,
I wrote to you last Monday from New York City, in which letter I informed you that the board had directed us to go to Mr. Slaters Ottawa Colony, to use our influence to get his Indians to consent to remove on to the Osage, and vicinity in Kansas.

I have made no disposition whatever of Maria. The Board gives me 50 dollars a year for educating our children. The boat is about starting, and I must close. May the blessing of Heaven still attend us all.

Your affectionate husband,
(s) Jotham Meeker

Jotham's return from Boston was by a different route and means: by train to Buffalo, via New York City and Albany, then from Buffalo to Detroit on the Lake Erie steamer Constitution and finally overland by wagon to Kalamazoo, with the last fifteen miles on foot to Slater's station.

Meeker was greeted with open arms by his former associate. "It has been fourteen years since we were together on the Grand," Slater said. "What brings you here? I'm sure this is not a social call."

"I come with a heavy heart and a duty to perform that is repugnant to me," Meeker admitted. "I am charged by the mission board and Brother McCoy to persuade you to take your Indians to the West."

"Yes, Cass has continually pressured me to move," Slater replied. "Cass is convinced that the Indians are inherently savages and cannot be assimilated."

"We know that's not true," Meeker assured his colleague. "But since Cass uses Schoolcraft as one of his authorities on Indian character, what else could we expect? Schoolcraft was biased when he was the Indian agent at the Sault, Cass himself had no firsthand knowledge of the Indians such as we have."

"He claims the Indian language is not capable of expressing complex ideas and that is evidence of their being less than human," Slater said.

"Such a falsehood!" Meeker cried. "I have translated the scriptures into the Ottawa language, and it is quite capable of rendering complexity."

"I'm afraid that these arguments have less to do with fact than with political rhetoric. Cass has already been rewarded for his pro-removal arguments by being named Secretary of War by President Jackson. People believe what they want to believe." Slater remarked. "I will put the question of removal to the Indians in council, but I can predict their answer."

"So be it," said Meeker with regret. "I have done my duty."

The Grand River Ottawa continued to resist removal. A party of Michigan Indians had traveled to Kansas and reported that there were no sugar maples and the climate was bitter cold in winter and boiling in summer.

However, Ottawas from La Arbcroche were willing to sell their ancestral lands and went to Washington to negotiate. The Grand River clans sent along some representatives to try to stop the sale. The representatives were specifically chosen from non-chiefs who had no authority to sign any treaties. Some Ottawas gave Slater cash from their annual government payments to buy land in Barry County so they could stay in Michigan. The irony of it all was not wasted on Slater nor the Indians: The Indians were having to buy back land that had always been theirs.

After a few days of visits with Slater and the Indians, Meeker began his trip home, returning first to Detroit. From Toledo, he traveled the Miami Canal to Cincinnati via Piqua and Dayton. At Cincinnati, Jotham arranged for Maria, just eight and a half years old, to attend the Female School on the Walnut Hills, two miles from the city. Friends in Cincinnati helped to pay for her schooling and boarding. Leaving Maria behind in Cincinnati to continue her education, Jotham, Eleanor and Emeline. boarded the steamer Swiftsure bound for St. Louis and, for the final leg, they rode the Saluda to Westport. The entire trip took eighty-nine days, fifty-eight of which were in transit. Both of these steamboats later sunk. The boiler of the Saluda exploded in 1852 with the loss of one hundred lives, mostly Mormon immigrants from England and Wales.

On his way back, Jotham learned that his old mentor and role model, Isaac McCoy, had died at Louisville, where he served as director of the American Indian Mission Association. Isaac's death brought a flood of memories of their work together. Jotham told Eleanor, "Isaac was a loving man. When he looked at you, you felt there was no selfish thought or scheme working in his mind but that he was thinking what he could do for you, for your benefit. I wish I had told him how much I admired him while he was still alive."

"I think he knew, Jotham." Eleanor assured him. "Sometimes you don't need words. I am pleased that you have forgotten your differences with McCoy after he aligned himself with the pro-slavery Southern Baptists."

Whenever this trip to Boston was related to future generations, the family would recall that their Byram and Phillips forbears had traveled part of the route in reverse sixty years before from Cumberland to Brownville, but they had walked from Cumberland to Brownville, then used a wooden boat to float down the Ohio to Kentucky while under occasional Indian attack.

Jotham wrote to daughter Maria away at school with news of home:

Dear Daughter Maria,
All are well at Mr. Barkers, Mr. Blanchards, Mr. Pratts and Mr. Simmerwells. Mr. Fuller died last week. Kup-pash-kum-mo-qua is dead. Sally is very sick. Keotowahba is married to Seseel. Kesiswathba is married to Wau-wau-sum-mo-qua, and As-si-bos is married to Mio. We this year have plenty of corn, potatoes, pumpkins, beans, melons, onions, beets, cucumbers, and such things. We have had a great many wild blackberries and plums. While in St. Louis we bought every thing necessary to finish off our meeting house.

You know, my dear daughter, that it is hard for you and hard for us, to be separated. Emeline says, Tell Maria I feel very lonesome for her every day—

sometimes I dream about her in the night—sometimes I get out my little box of dishes, and my dolls, and Maria's doll that had its head broke off. Tell her that our dog got to be a big dog, but he killed chickens and we had to kill him.

Your mother and sister wish to send you all the love this little letter will hold.

From your affectionate father,
(s) Jotham Meeker

.

At home again, Jotham adapted to Indian culture by organizing extended church meetings at which the Indians brought their own food and camped. On Sunday, July 4, 1847, Meeker ignored the national holiday, but preached two sermons to one hundred persons at the edge of the river. He baptized three Indians, including Sophia Big Knife, and administered the holy sacraments to fifty native members. Four other members of Sophia's family joined later. The Meekers adopted an Indian boy called Pontiac, who was the great grandson of the noted chief of the same name who had led an uprising against the British in 1763. They renamed the boy Robert Merrill.

Mr. Roby, a local trader, was accused of fraud and Meeker was called to testify before a grand jury of the U.S Circuit Court in Cincinnati. Jotham and Eleanor seized the opportunity to leave Emeline at a school there. They got their teeth filled with gold foil and had a set of false teeth finished off for Eleanor, all paid for by Cincinnati Baptists. Jotham visited Dr. Peck who gave him homeopathic medicine for his painful sciatica. For a bit of diversion, they went to see the famous dwarf, General Tom Thumb, who, at age sixteen, was twenty-eight inches tall and weighed fifteen pounds.

While Eleanor visited her sister Emeline Clough, Jotham borrowed a horse and tack and rode to the country to see Meeker relatives. He visited the graves of his father, sister, uncle, cousin and both grandfathers at Hopewell, Ohio. He knelt on the grave of his father and prayed, then visited the farm where he was born. Afterwards, he and Eleanor boarded the steamer Declaration bound for St. Louis. There they took passage on the Cora. They were on the river for eight days traveling from Cincinnati to Kansas.

A third daughter, Eliza, was born in 1849, ten years after Emeline. Eleanor reflected on the many children the McCoys had lost. "I thank God that he has given us three children." She never mentioned the death of her own son after one month in this unwelcoming world.

"This new babe will fill a hole left when Maria and Emeline are at school," Jotham said, "I know that your pillow is sometimes wet with tears thinking of them."

Eleanor's great, great, great grandfather, Samuel Richardson, was a Quaker and friend of William Penn who appointed him first alderman of Philadelphia when the city was first chartered in 1691. He was elected by a vote of the people as alderman in 1705, and served until his death. He owned considerable land including a thirty-acre parcel in the heart of the city, commencing at Market Street and running some distance up the Delaware River. The English brought with them their system of land tenure wherein land was not sold outright, but was leased for ninety-nine years, renewable forever with the payment of annual ground rents. Samuel's will bequeathed the ground rents to his wife and others, along with his "Negro Woman Dinnah." Somewhere along the line of inheritance, the ground rents ceased to be paid. A sharp lawyer looking for business discovered this and contacted Samuel's heirs. He sent a contract to Eleanor and Jotham in 1846 proposing that he bring a court action to recover the rents and the property. He offered to do this for one-half of the recovery.

"Eleanor, this is mighty tempting, given our poverty," Jotham offered. "We could give much of it to the Church."

"I don't trust lawyers in general, and this one seems especially greedy. Half of what he recovers seems excessive," said Eleanor with some indignation. "More to the point, I do not want to profit by someone else's loss. There are unsuspecting people living or making a business on this property, and I would not want to dispossess them."

"I agree, we could use the money, but it is not right. I could not do it in good conscience," Jotham conceded. "I pray to God to deliver me from this temptation. God would not want this money."

That put an end to the proceedings. But, Eleanor's brother, David, many years later in 1857 after Eleanor's death, was still pursuing the gold. The legislature of Pennsylvania passed a law that all old claims must be adjudicated before 1858 or be extinguished. David traveled to Philadelphia to better pursue his interest. He was excited to learn that the Ridgeway Hotel located on the property was sold for one hundred sixty thousand dollars, and since clear title could not be delivered, the sale price was dropped by forty thousand. That meant that ninety thousand in ground rents had accrued. David offered to pay Eleanor's children's share of the lawyer's costs so that they could share in the recovery. Maria's husband, Nathan Simpson, paid one hundred twenty-five dollars to the lawyer, N. H. Sharpless, as one of the five sets of heirs pursuing the case. Nothing came of it.

Cholera was ever present in the lives of both whites and Indians. A chief of the Sacs and Foxes told Jotham how cholera had found the Indians on a buffalo hunt just fifty miles west of the mission. The party counted about two thousand, including women and children who always accompanied the hunters to cut up the meat and process the hides. "In the course of a day or two, twenty or thirty died. We feared that the rest of us would take the disease and die. We left the dead and dying," the Indian related. "The hunting party left behind food and a tied horse. The chief said to the sick, 'If you get well, you can untie your horse and ride home; if you die, by and by your horse will starve to death, on whose soul you can ride to the world of the spirits.' Thus, men left their mothers, their wives and their children to die."

"That's awful, but I understand you had no choice," Jotham responded. He knew then that the missionaries had done little to change the religious beliefs of many Indians, but at the same time he realized that their religion, just as his, helped them deal with life's vagaries. He heard that great numbers were dying of the contagion among the Pawnees, Otoes, Osages and, further west, the Rocky Mountain tribes.

Some Ottawas had stayed in Ohio, but the United States Commissioners continued to pressure them to leave. A treaty was drawn up to that effect in 1833 on the Maumee river as it empties into Lake Erie. Ah-sho-wis-sa seeing his chiefs and headmen about to sign the treaty announced, "I will kill the first Ottawa who puts his name to the treaty." Everyone was afraid of him, and the treaty was postponed. However, the next day the chiefs got him drunk, and while he was indisposed, they sold the last foot of land they owned east of the Mississippi. When he became sober and saw the treaty was concluded, he withdrew his death threat. He went with the rest to Kansas in 1838, remaining a violent enemy of the white man throughout his life.

Those of Ah-sho-wis-sa's compatriots who had been influenced by the Baptist missionaries kept urging him to adopt Christianity. Meeker visited him many times, and the Indian slowly was convinced and sought religious knowledge. Ah-sho-wis-sa was nearsighted and Meeker bought him a pair of glasses so he could read the Bible in his own language. Meeker also taught him to write and cipher, keep accounts and correspond with others. Meeker visited the old man on his deathbed and found his scripture translations on his pillow. "I am fearful that my fervent desire for heaven is a sin. Do you think so?"

Jotham assured him it was not.

"I do not want to appear before God with any earthly debts hanging over my name." He gave Meeker enough money to pay all he owed.

When Jotham returned home, he told Eleanor the story. "These experiences are enough to compensate us for all our toils and ills."

Meeker held a successful all-day quarterly meeting of the mission church in October. About one hundred attended. The Ottawa chief, Pahtee, spoke, as well as Shawboneda. It was the time of the government's annuity payments as specified in the treaties associated with the Indians' removal from Ohio. Jotham, like the whiskey sellers, took advantage of the fact that the Indians had cash in their pockets. He collected any debts owned him by the Indians and solicited donations for the church. Thirteen Ottawa brethren subscribed six dollars each, Brother Tuay Jones gave ten, and Jotham also put in ten, bringing the total to ninety-eight dollars. The previous week, Brother Kendrick brought back Jotham's press and types from the Delaware mission, and soon Jotham printed the *Ottawa First Book* and the *Ottawa Hymn Book*.

Eleanor wrote to her sister in February 1850 to give her news of her one daughter at home. "Our little Eliza eight months old on the 12th inst. is very healthy, active and playful child, gives very little trouble, is a good deal of company for us while we are so far separated from our other loved ones. My greatest desire for my girls is that they may be useful in society and prepared to meet their creator with joy."

On March 18, 1850, Meeker left for Cincinnati to get his two children who were attending school there. He reached St. Louis on the 25th and there he renewed his subscription to the *Missouri Weekly Republican*. He arrived in Cincinnati five days later, and he and the girls left for home on April 4. The steamship Pike was crowded with California gold seekers with their mules, wagons and complete outfits. He left St. Louis five days later on the Bay State among three hundred bound for California and on April 13, they arrived back in Kansas. During May, many gold seekers passed the mission every day on their way west.

When Jotham told Eleanor of the gold seekers, she said, "Jotham, I can't understand how thousands are trying to land their *bones*, at least, on the barren plains of the far west or in the precious sands of gold dust. How strange is human nature that intelligent men are so carried away with a hope of obtaining momentary riches.

"It's strange indeed, Eleanor, but remember my brother Samuel is one of those in the Coloma Valley of California."

"Sorry, I didn't mean to criticize your family."

"That's all right. I see you feel strongly."

"I think this inexhaustible wealth will ere long prove to be the greatest curse ever to befall our happy, boasting America."

"We could surely use a bit of that wealth."

"Who can think without emotion of the thousands of immortal souls who, leaving their bodies to moulder in the regions where gold lies deep, will appear in the presence of Him who has said, 'Lay not up treasures on earth'?"

"I don't want to lay up treasures, but we could use a new wagon."

"Jotham, are you taking me seriously?"

"Of course, but I'm just mindful of our own perilous situation."

In July, Meeker printed more copies of the one hundred twenty-seven page Ottawa Hymn Book while the mercury hit one hundred two degrees. Then as the temperature rose to one hundred five, eleven-year-old Emeline helped her father plant an acre and a half of turnips. The fall was very dry, and the creeks stopped running. There was danger of prairie fires.

After Emeline returned to school, Eliza thought she should take her place, offering in her sweet way, "Mama, me set table." Eliza loved to sing, and as she finished with one song, she'd ask, "Mama, would you like me to sing more?" Eleanor missed Emeline's help, but her sagging heart was lifted by her lively youngest daughter's songs.

With a branch of the Santa Fe Trail running by the Meeker house, visitors frequently stopped at the Ottawa mission. They ranged from congressmen to teamsters. Eleanor wrote her sister, Emeline Clough now living in Indiana and complained,

On Thursday evening just as I was getting ready to write a few lines to you, in came a family of nine. I got supper fixed and all in bed and then began to think about getting breakfast for 12 persons including some hired men who are digging a well. I had to turn away four more that came that morning."

The swelling in my throat continues much the same. My eyes are not so painful as they were last year. My teeth are all gone except five and no two of them meet, so you know that I am poor for grinders. I am continually reminded that my fabric is decaying and must soon fail, but I still feel anxious to do what I can for my family and others until I am called to stop.

Maria was sent to school at Westport in March. She wrote back that she was much pleased with her teacher. Eleanor was encouraged and told Jotham, "I also want to send Emeline as soon as possible."

"Expenses will be high, but let's try it for a while. If we can't manage it, we can send her back to Cincinnati next spring where friends help pay her tuition. Why did Maria not want to go back to Cincinnati?"

"Because she hated to go so far away when my health is so poor. Also, I'm in favor of parents keeping an eye on their children if possible."

Oversight is never complete. In May, Eleanor received a letter from Maria and relayed the news to her husband. "Maria, has fallen in love with a young man named Nathan Simpson and plans to marry. I am taken aback, but it looks like a good match. She says he is of good character and much loved by those who know him. Maria's friends say she could not do better if she should hunt the world over."

"What is the occupation and situation of his father?"

"He has been a merchant in Westport for sixteen years and is quite rich. There is only one thing that gives me hesitation. His family owns slaves. Maria was very troubled by it at first, but Nathan has promised her that he would not have many slaves, and that those he did have would be treated well."

"I guess the world is not perfect, and we all have to make some compromises."

"I am equally concerned about the wealth of the young couple-to-be. I fear she will be too enthralled with the glittering things of the earth and forget that she is but mortal."

"I'll pray that she can overcome temptation."

Daughter Maria was married at the age of seventeen to Nathan L. Simpson of Westport, Missouri, on December 10, 1851. The marriage had to be performed in groom's hometown, as legal marriages could not be conducted in Indian territory. Emeline attended the wedding and reported to her parents and little sister that the bride and groom each had two attendants and that a grand party was given by Nathan's father.

In a letter to Maria, Eleanor proposed that she and Nathan come out so the young man could get acquainted with his new in-laws:
"Nathan could do some hunting on the river while at Ottawa and if he could do nothing more than to scare some wolves, chase a wild goose, or kill some chickens and bring them for supper, it would be about as cheap a way to sow your wild oats as any other. And if he should wander off some distance and a storm should be threatening, he would only have to rally and set out to reach the harbor where his own blue-eyed Bird might per chance be sweetly at rest."

After the newlyweds had left, Jotham found Eleanor bent over her stitchery. "I see you very tired from your daily work, yet you are finishing some quilts you had started before."

"Yes, I feel I must make some things for Maria in her new home," Eleanor replied.. "I am determined to finish these quilts and make some sheets and pillowcases for her."

"I worry that you endanger your health with even more overwork," her concerned husband told her.

"I worry about you also. You preach every Sunday, hold a prayer meeting at an Indian's house each week, visit the sick, make caskets and conduct funerals and have religious meetings all over God's creation. And, then you do translation and printing. That's not to mention the farming and gardening, digging a well, butchering our meat and making and mending fences to keep our stock out of our crops."

"I know; I know. I spend hours looking for our stock that wanders off over the prairie. The saving grace is that I get to see the beautiful prairie flowers like the bunch I brought you the last time I was out."

"That reminds me, I don't think I even thanked you for the flowers, I was so busy at the time baking. You're romantic, even if you are a preacher."

Jotham and Eleanor's first grandson, Duke, was born in September 1852. "Grandchildren are the best," Eleanor told her husband. "I just wish we could see him. Exchange of letters is not enough." Maria and family finally came to visit a year later. When they left, little Eliza was hurt that Nathan had gone without kissing her goodbye. "I s'pose Nasen don't love me much," she told her amused parents. She moped around for days, and Eleanor asked her what was the matter. "Why I want to see Sissy and Nasan's little boy so bad it makes my stomach ache, and I don't know what to do."

Some years the rains failed and the Meekers and the Indians barely survived. But 1852 was a bumper year. in which Jotham harvested two hundred fifty bushels of corn from ten acres and forty bushels of oats. He brought in twelve wagon loads of pumpkins, one of which weighed ninety pounds, plus forty-seven bushels of potatoes. "God has blessed us," he said. "We will have much food to give the Indians when they attend our quarterly meetings." The next year was even better, producing seven hundred fifty bushels of corn. "Let's celebrate and thank God with a Thanksgiving feast on the newly created holiday," he suggested to Eleanor.

At forty-nine, Jotham was already beginning to feel his age. He confided in Eleanor, "I am entering the list of old men. I am more and more hiring help as my sciatica is killing me." For the next two years, Jotham devoted himself mostly to farming and did little printing. He reproached himself for loss of missionary zeal. He did translate the old Ottawa treaties at the request of Shawboneda so that the Indians could determine the provisions contained in the documents without having to rely on translators who might not have the Indian's welfare at heart. Meeker was concerned about a swarm of new settlers now occupying Indian lands, many of whom seemed of undesirable character. However, the desire for land even captured Jotham, and he made an entry for title to one hundred sixty acres. He had to admit that as he approached the end of his life he had become more worldly. Emeline had been attending the Female

Academy on the river eight miles north of Weston. She was now to attend the Christian College in Columbia, Missouri. Jotham wrote to the Principal, Professor J.A. Williams in September 1853:

> We have decided, in accordance with your offer, to send to your care, during the next Collegiate year, our daughter Emeline. By examining her, you will decide what class to place her in. We wish special attention given to improvement in Orthography, reading, writing, geography and Eng. Grammar, together with lessons in vocal music and instruction in composition. In case you shall decide that she ought to take lessons in drawing & painting, and that she can do it without interfering materially with the more important branches, as above, you may give her them—but nothing more this year.
>
> We prefer that she be kept from all pleasure parties, all company with young men, and whatever else shall have a tendency to draw her attention from her studies. We are Baptists, and of course, would prefer that our daughter should attend Baptist Meetings, but do not require it. Our daily prayers shall ascend for her and for you. My friend and brother, D.W. Simpson, into whose family our oldest daughter is married, will make you, the customary payments, etc. for us. May heaven bless you and our child.
>
> Your brother,
> (s) Jotham Meeker

Eleanor oversaw Emeline's preparation for her move to the college. A partial list of articles the young scholar would take included the following:

1 chest	1 shawl	Bible
1 trunk	1 white bonnet	Christian Psalmist
3 pr. shoes	1 gingham bonnet	Comstock's Philosophy
1 overshoes	4 linen handkerchiefs	Whipley's Comprend
5 pr. Cotton stockings	1 fine pair mits	Kirkham's Grammar
2 quilted skirts	4 neck ribbons	Comstock's Botany
3 white cotton skirts	1 green veil	Davies Arithmetic
1 white flannel skirt	2 gingham aprons	Blake's Astronomy
4 pr. drawers	1 worsted dress	Morse's Geography
5 chemises	2 calico dresses	Slate
4 nightgowns	1 calico gown	

"Eleanor, the number of clothes seems more than a modest girl needs," Jotham remarked when he saw the trunk and its contents. "She has more clothes that we have all together."

"She'll no longer be living on the prairie," Eleanor explained, "and she needs these things to live in polite society. And, besides, Maria and her husband are paying for everything."

"Nevertheless it seems extravagant to me. It is so far beyond our means that it's embarrassing."

There were three missions to the Shawnees only a few miles apart—Baptist, Methodist and Quaker. Thomas Johnson of the Methodists was very aggressive in pursuing the dominance of his church. He had been a slave-owning Virginian and continued to have slaves at his Shawnee mission. Quaker missionary Richard Mendenhall thought it peculiar that the Methodists used slaves to civilize the Indians. "Is not this the climax of inconsistencies?" he asked. Those Indians, who thought themselves modern, copied the Methodists, and some of the wealthier ones became slave owners themselves. The Methodist Church itself was divided into North and South branches, and the affiliations of border churches were contested. The North church sent its own missionary, Thomas Markam, to the Shawnees in 1850 at the request of eighty-five Indians. Johnson tried to undermine Markam and called him an "abolitionist," a word calculated to elicit emotional opposition in northwest Missouri. But, Markam continued his work for a time.

The demand of white settlers for Indian lands continued to grow. Illinois Senator Stephen Douglas, who later would contend with Lincoln for the U.S. Presidency, insisted that "hostile savages" blocked the country's development and that the "Indian barrier must be removed." This stance belied the fact that the Indians along Missouri's western border were peaceful. Lies that stirred the emotions persisted. Missionary Johnson, also an entrepreneur with a freighting business and real-estate trade in the newly formed Kansas City, added his support to the cries for Indian removal. Many thought that Johnson viewed the breakup of the Indian reservations as a chance to get rich in land speculation, the most tried and true road to riches throughout American history.

In 1853, Congress, authorized negotiations with the Kansas tribes to extinguish Indian title and open the land for settlement. This alarmed many Indians who pointed out that the previous treaties gave them this land forever. They were to learn that "forever" meant only until the majority whites wanted to change it, a lesson already learned from their experience in Ohio.

On the portion of the Santa Fe Trail passing near the Meeker's house, someone counted eight hundred wagons and ten thousand head of cattle driven past as companies of emigrants headed to California. Sometimes the herders were not too careful and incorporated some of Jotham's cattle into their herds, and Jotham had to ride after them and bring back his stock.

Johnson became active in politics and was elected to the territorial legislature and served as a congressional delegate. In Washington, he lobbied Indian Commissioner and fellow Methodist George Manypenny to negotiate the sale of Indian lands. The fate of the Indians was sealed by passage of the Kansas-Nebraska Act, signed by President Franklin Pierce in 1854, opening Kansas for settlement. There was an eclipse of the sun May 26, 1854; maybe it was a sign to commemorate the signing of the Kansas-Nebraska Bill. Senator Douglas was instrumental in destroying the Missouri Compromise and instead allowing the voters of the two states to decide whether they wanted slavery or not. Since it was never clear who was eligible to vote, this provision set off election fraud and violent intimidation that led to the term "Bleeding Kansas." It is ironical that Johnson was murdered in 1865 at his home in Missouri by

Southern sympathizers who were angry that the canny businessman had pledged allegiance to the Union at the start of the Civil War. Johnson's motives for swearing loyalty probably had more to do with protecting his business interests than anything else.

The Shawnees were also divided and conflicted. The Ohio Shawnee and the Missouri Shawnee each struggled for power and influence in Indian affairs and used the missionaries for their own political ends, and vice versa. Ohio Shawnee Chiefs Joseph DeShane and Blackfeather allied with the Baptists. The cagey Blackfeather, who originally demanded the removal of all missionaries, later sponsored church meetings at his village to gain the missionaries' favor, though he never converted.

Jotham asked the chief, "You have been very sympathetic to my ministry among the Indians, but you have not yourself converted. Why not?"

"You have your God, and I have my Great Spirit," Blackfeather explained. "Our creation stories have some similarities. The Great Spirit made us and all of the living and non-living things on earth. I pray to him and ask for his blessings. My messages are heard by the spirits in the four winds and carried to the Great Spirit. He asks for sacrifices of food, something like your lord's supper."

"Yes, I have been aware of these similarities ever since I heard of your ceremonies and traditions from Chief Noonday back in Michigan."

"I admit that following your god is tempting because I see that the white man is defeating the Indians. But, I am confused when I hear different interpretations of your god from you and the Methodists and the Quakers. We Indians have followed the ceremony of the otter dance for generations."

"I see you have given it a lot of thought," Jotham conceded.

"There is another thing that bothers me. I can't make any sense of being dunked in the river."

"I guess that we both have ceremonies that don't make sense to the other."

There was something else that Blackfeather did not share with Meeker. He really would prefer that all missionaries would go away, but, if they had to remain he thought it was better for his Indians to associate with the congregational approach of the Baptists.

To compound and confuse matters, there was a schism within the Baptists missions. Reverend Francis Barker, ministering to the Shawnee, Meeker to the Ottawa and John G. Pratt to the Delaware represented the Baptists' traditional congregational approach. Each local church and, by association each local tribe, should be independent. Barker wanted local church members, not missionaries, to determine standards for church membership.

It was this congregational approach that had appealed to the Byrams and Phillips in Virginia and Kentucky at the end of the Revolutionary War as they rejected the centralized, hierarchical power of church and state. Some Indians saw the local congregational approach as supporting the retention of their cultural and tribal sovereignty. McCoy, on the other hand, with his vision of a pan-Indian state, preferred a strong central, denominational authority. Thus, the Shawnee chiefs such as Perry and Black Hoof with national leadership ambitions allied themselves with McCoy and Methodist Johnson. With the help of these missionaries, these chiefs enhanced their tribal power by being the ones who distributed the government's annuity payments to their followers. McCoy had shifted his allegiance from the Boston-based Baptist Missionary Board to the Southern Baptist Conference, which greatly troubled Meeker because of its pro-slavery orientation.

Some Shawnees thought their lands had already been lost and their timber stolen and that they had to make the best deal possible and move. Chief Joseph Parks, though not a hereditary chief, used the government and the missionaries to ascend to a leadership role. Claiming to speak for all Shawnees, he said the tribe was willing to sell but unwilling to move. He again reminded the government of their sovereign promise to protect Indian property. The whites, he said, are "like the prairie wolves, prowling and stealing." The 1854 Treaty ceded more than one and a half million acres, keeping only one hundred sixty thousand acres for the Indians.

The treaty and subsequent agreements enabled Johnson and the pro-slavery Methodists to rule the missionary field. Two thousand acres of land were given to the Methodists which Johnson eventually took for himself. The Quakers received three hundred twenty acres to support their work and the Baptists got only one hundred sixty. Baptist missionary Francis Barker objected to the inequitable distribution of the Shawnee school fund. In a letter to Meeker, Barker hinted that Johnson had bribed three Shawnee treaty delegates to gain their support. Johnson and Parks attacked Barker and used their influence with the government's Indian agent to have Barker removed from the reservation. In a letter to Solomon Peck, Meeker wrote, "The Shawnee agent and the Shawnee principle chief have joined Johnson in his deadly hatred to our brother Barker." In the competition for Indian souls, Barker baptized some Methodist Indians who had become dissatisfied. The Methodists claimed these Indians were undesirable criminals and drunkards. Barker was evicted from the mission in early 1855 by the Indian agent, as was the missionary of the anti-slavery Northern Methodists.

Barker's fate was on Jotham's mind when he preached at Shawanoe, "How common to the practice for Christians who call themselves Baptists and Christians who call themselves Methodists or who are called by some other name to stand as completely disconnected as regards loving one another. We are plainly told that 'He that saith he is in the light, and hateth his brother, is in darkness.' How much better would it be for us to agree to allow our brethren to differ from us in some matters of faith and practice and to love them still."

Meeker also questioned the allocation of school funds and told his mission board that they might as well close the Baptist Shawnee Mission. The inequality in the distribution of government money showed in their respective buildings. The Methodists had two-story brick buildings, while the Baptist Mission was of crude construction. Meeker struggled to follow the Biblical injunction to not hate or envy his enemies.

Eleanor went to be with Maria for the birth of her second grandson, James Meeker Simpson in March 1854. She stayed seven weeks and afterwards, wrote to her sister Emeline about other matters of concern, including the return of her daughter Emeline to college:

"It is truly hard to part with her so much, but I value an education too highly to allow my feelings to overcome my judgment, and am willing to exert myself to the end of my strength in order to give her a chance at school. As to our prospects about the future, every thing continues uncertain. The Ottawas refuse to sell their land—so we may not have to make any change for some time yet. Most of the tribes have sold their land, or at least the most of it—and White people are pouring in from every direction with the expectation of finding our barren Prairies to be the very garden of Eden."

Jotham, having struggled with ill-health since his days in Michigan, died at the age of fifty on January 12, 1855. It was some days before Eleanor was composed enough to write her daughter away at school of her father's passing.

Ottawa Mission, Jan. 29th 1855

My dear Daughter,
On Friday morning about five o'clock, his hour of rising, after we had worked over him all night he awoke from a state of stupor in which he had been lying for some hours owing to the medicine which he had taken and said I am dying. He then called for his pocket book and spectacles but he found that he was blind. He said that he was intending to write to you and to Mr. Williams in regard to you. I told him that he was not able to write but to tell me what he wanted to say to you. It was difficult for him to speak, but he raised his voice as loud as he could and said, My dear, dear daughter Emeline, I can not tell how much I love you. Your mother has always loved you exceedingly but I do not think that her love has been stronger for you than mine has been.

He then called Eliza and said my dear little daughter Eliza you will soon have no father. I am going to die now and leave you. I have always told you that there were three for you to obey but I tell you now that there will be only two for you to mind, God and your mother, obey what God says and what your mother tells you. He then said come to me my dear, dear Eliza. You know that father never kissed you while he was well but I want to give you a dying kiss. Now my dear, dear daughter farewell. After he had bid me farewell he then called for Thomas Wolf, his assistant.

O my dear child, I hope you and I will try to feel as Eliza often says, "Father can never come back to us again but I will try to be good and when I die I will go where father is in that happy land far, far, away." She can sing all that hymn very sweetly. "There is a happy land."
As ever yours,
(s) E. D. M.

Jane Jones, wife of Meeker's assistant Brother Tuay Jones, wrote to Maria immediately after Jotham's death.

Ottawa Mission House, Jan. 14, 1855

Dear Maria Simpson

The painful duty devolves to me to inform you of the death of your beloved Father he expired on Friday at twelve o'clock Your afflicted Mother has been in suspense ever since hoping you or husband would have come last night She Therefore sends an express this morning come in hopes he may meet you on the road but if not go to your house, and if the child is so that you cannot come or if you can come let Moses take that fresh Poney give him an early start so that he can get home here by noon tomorrow we have decided to keep the precious remains until Monday three o'clock in the eve. It was your Father wish to be interred at his Post of labor directly in the rear of the Pulpit, where he has so long and so faithfully preached the ever lasting Gospel.

(s) Jane H Jones

Maria did not come to the funeral because her two boys were sick. When she did come home, her boys contracted whooping cough upon arrival. Duke, the oldest, was the sickest and was still ill when they returned to Westport four weeks later. Later, Eleanor wrote to Maria and advised her to stop giving Blue Mass to her son. "I think that Duke would not have taken cold so easy if he had not taken Blue Mass so much." Maria and Nathan eventually had eleven children, some born in Nebraska City where Nathan worked as a clerk for Russell, Majors, and Waddell, freighters.

Eleanor later also wrote to her sister:

Dear Sister,

I suppose you will want to know how I expect to get along, or dispose of myself and girls. It is more than I am able to do, till at present. The way seems dark and gloomy to me now. I have concluded however, to remain here until the Board should make some inspection of the Station. I do not expect the Board will be willing to give me anything after the expiration of this year. Maria wants me to live with her, but I am not willing to take Eliza among slaves if I can get along any other way. It would be hard for me to live among slaves.

I fear that I shall not live long any place on earth. I have reason to fear that I shall never see you again on earth. I am almost down. I have a severe cough, have but little strength left. I am afflicted with Bronchitis. I have not been able to speak above a whisper, more than two weeks. I make out to keep up through the day but of the tedious, gloomy nights, here I sit alone, no friend to say a word, my little pet Eliza fast asleep. My eyes turn to the vacant spot where my dear husband sat for the last time to read the word of life, and where we knelt together. How lonely the rude hearthstone looks to me now, where for many years everything looked happy, and cheerful. When Mr. M. was at home, there seemed to be nothing of consequence wanting.

As to the poor forsaken Indians I know not what to say. They feel that they have lost a true friend, and will never find another. In addition to this, they

are in a suffering condition. On account of the great failure of the crops last season, they are left without anything to eat. Some of them are now living on roots. I fear that many of them will die with hunger. Provision is very high here. The white people who are settling around us, are some of the worst in the world, and are standing ready to injure the Indians in every possible way in their power.
(s) E. D. Meeker

Later, Emeline, away at school, wrote to Eliza:

Columbia, Mo. March 24th 1855

My Dear little Sister,
So do you ever think of me or talk about me. Oh! Let me not be forgotten, by any one. I have been taking music lessons all the session, Mr. Williams is making me a present of them. I can now play a great many little pieces. I am a regular Sophomore and will be examined as one of that class. Where do you suppose we will live next year? I have no idea without it is at Nathans

Tell Ma that if she thinks she has time, I would like very much to some very nice underclothes some of all, and if it is not too much, tell her to please get the latest fashion. The girls in my room are keeping so much fuss I can not write. Tell the Indians that I want to see them so bad. The picture you see is our school, it is not near so pretty as it is.
Excuse these blots,
(s) Emma Eugenia Meeker

Jotham was prescient when years before he told McCoy that he probably need not worry about a source of income in old age. His prediction also applied to Eleanor. She died the next year at the age of forty-six, literally worn out by her work. Eleanor was buried next to Jotham in the Ottawa Indian cemetery along with many they had taught and loved, including Chief No-tin-no and Chief Compchau. That the Indians buried them there is a testimony to the regard they felt for the missionary couple.

The Indians gave Eliza and Emeline each eighty acres as an expression of their esteem for their parents, formalizing the gift by treaty in 1862. Emeline and Eliza went to live with Maria and Nathan in Westport. Before Eliza moved, she wrote to her sister describing how her bereavement affected her, "I know not one half of any time, what I am doing. I have endeavored to look to that fountain from which all blessings flow, and I hope to be fully resigned to my bereavement, knowing God is love, and that he does not afflict us willingly. I want to say at all times, Not my will Oh Lord, but thine be done, but my frail nature must weep. It relieves the aching breast. Jesus wept. My greatest desire now is to live, and act in such a manner, as will prepare me to meet a peaceful death, as my companion's was. He had nothing to do but to die and go to rest."

After Jotham's death, the mission farm was managed by John Early, a full-blooded Ottawa. Meeker's assistant, John Tecumseh "Tuay" Jones, a partial blood Chippewa, became the religious leader of the one hundred-strong Ottawa Baptists. The total tribe numbered three hundred twenty-five. McCoy had brought Jones to the school at Carey Station, Michigan, and sent him to be educated in Hamilton, New York. Jones then found his way to Kansas at the same time as Jotham. He acted as an interpreter and accumulated some wealth operating a trading post just south of the Marais des Cygnes. Tuay was married to Jane Kelly of Maine who had come to Kansas as a missionary to the nearby Delawares.

Prior to the Civil War, the Jones's home and lives were threatened by bushwhackers favoring slavery, but Tuay escaped to a cornfield as the border ruffians broke in. He'd helped the ill-fated abolitionist John Brown, then he and Jane founded Ottawa University for the Indians in 1860. The Indians originally gave twenty thousand acres of land to support scholarships for fifty Ottawa children each year. Tuay died in 1879 of dysentery and was buried in the same Ottawa cemetery as the Meekers. The Jones gave their estate to the university. This was a legacy of McCoy and Meeker's work.

Indian Commissioner Manypenny summed up the land seeking that drove most of the Indians out of their homes once more. "From highest to lowest amongst the people in Kansas, there has been one continued, persistent, determined effort to plunder the Indians, and by force or fraud to deprive them of their lands. Amongst all their differences, the squatters have uniformly agree in this." He was in a position to know. Even the Fort Leavenworth soldiers got in on the act before the removal treaty was signed. They organized a town company and laid out lots, encouraging illegal settlement. The military gave no aid to the Indians in protecting their land.

The Indians were never afforded the protection of the law. They had no standing in court and their testimony against people who murdered their fellows and stole their lands and cattle did not count. This was also the problem of the Shawnees who went to Missouri voluntarily and without treaties or government annuities in 1793. In spite of their efforts to play by the white-man's rules, they were pushed off their lands in Missouri and Arkansas. Some would go to Oklahoma and Texas, and others to reservations established for them in Kansas.

There were influential whites who tried to help the Indians keep their lands and realize a pan-Indian separate state. William Clark was a champion of Jeffersonian ideals. He believed that Indians who adopted the yeoman farmer ideal should be full citizens of the United States. As the appointed Missouri Territorial governor, Clark ordered the territorial militia to remove squatters from Indian lands, but the commanding officer refused. When Clark ran for governor of the state in 1821, his opponent labeled him as "pro-Indian" and "anti-squatter." Clark lost in a landslide.

The guerilla battles between Indians and squatters were a kind of civil war, only in this case the Indians did not want to secede from the Union. They wanted to accede. The bulk of the Kansas Shawnees relocated to the Cherokee Nation in northeastern Oklahoma after 1854. Only a few stayed on the Kansas reservation. The Ottawas held on a bit longer, then moved in 1867.

The Meekers had endured droughts, floods and disease, but for all of their personal sacrifices and devotion to the Indians, they and other missionaries were overwhelmed by a greater force--an avalanche of settlers. For all of their efforts to adopt an agricultural and settled culture, the Indians were not accepted into a racist white society. The vision of a separate, pan-Indian state held by many Indian tribes, Isaac McCoy, William Clark and others was not to be realized. The scales of justice never balanced for the land's original inhabitants.

The fate of the Indians was now clear. Settlers could not be stopped from occupying Indian lands, neither in the Mohawk Valley of New York, Pennsylvania, Ohio, Kentucky, Michigan, Missouri nor Kansas. In the absence of massive, concentrated and carefully orchestrated violence by united Indians or the U.S. military, the settlers kept coming. Neither King George, Brant, Pontiac, Tecumseh, Blackhawk nor Meriwether Lewis could do it. The inexorable land seekers won. The Indians could not even stay in Kansas but were again promised "permanent" land in Indian Territory, Oklahoma. But this promise was no better than the previous ones. Much of their Oklahoma land was later opened to white settlement. Thousands of the land hungry lined up on the border and ran or rode hell for leather to claim the best parcels in 1899. Oklahoma became a state in 1907, but the Indians did not become U.S. citizens until 1924.

~8~

Civil War Soldiers: The Cavalryman

The Fugitive Slave Act of 1850 was one of the things that particularly irritated people in the North, including Michigan residents. The idea that it was a crime to help slaves escape was repugnant to Ransom Todd. He knew that people in Lenawee County were helping the slaves. He had many conversations with his pastor about slavery. "Pastor, I think it is simply morally wrong for one man to own another. I have talked to people in the Raisin Valley Friends Church, and while they are cautious in their conversations, it is clear that they are part of the underground railroad helping slaves get to the Second Baptist Church in Detroit and on to Canada. I gave them a small donation for food to help them out."

Pastor Allen whispered, "I hear that Laura Haviland of the Lenawee County Female Benevolent and Antislavery Society and of the Raisin Church has been so effective that southern slave owners have offered a three thousand dollar reward for her capture. It is dangerous work. I know that she has opened a school for Negro children here in Lenawee County. We will do what we can to help her."

The slavery question had been a major topic of conversation among Ransom, Sally Ann, and their children at the supper table. The whole family vehemently condemned it. It was no surprise, then, that sons Henry and Newell Delno wanted to enlist when the call for volunteers went up after the Confederate shelling of Fort Sumter in April 1861. Sally Ann struggled with herself and confided in Ransom, "I am an abolitionist in principle, but now possibly sacrificing two sons for the cause creates a dilemma for me."

Henry pleaded with his mother, "I have heard family stories about Todd men fighting for their country. Great-grandfather Joseph was in the Revolutionary War and grandfather Samuel was ready to fight the Indians."

This argument did not carry much weight with Sally Ann, but Ransom understood what his son was saying. "Perhaps this is the price of manhood," he explained to his wife.

"Oh, pshaw! You and your manhood," Sally said with scorn.

To his son, Ransom said, "You are twenty-nine years old and have no family responsibility. So do as your heart commands." With his father's blessing, Henry enlisted in the 5th Regiment of the Michigan Cavalry.

But before Henry could serve, he died of pneumonia. Deeply saddened, Ransom added Henry's stone alongside that of daughter Sarah Jane. He never thought he would put two children in the ground before his own stone was erected. Ransom called upon every fiber of his faith in God, but it was shredded and torn. His flag was limp, and he could only mutter, "May God protect him."

That left Luther Linsley, thirty-one, and Newell Delno, eighteen, as the adult children in Ransom and Sally's family. Luther was not interested in being a soldier. He had married ten years before and lost his wife to disease, then married again. Newell had always been in the shadow of his much older brother. He saw military service as his chance to emerge and do something grand on his own.

The next fall, Newell made his case to enlist. Sally was completely torn up now that Henry was dead. Ransom felt weak and fatalistic at this point. Newell enlisted in Company H, 11th Regiment, Michigan Volunteer Cavalry in October 1863. The only comment that Sally could muster was "At least he knows how to ride and take care of a horse." Several in the extended family also answered the call. Ransom's brother, Morris, and two of his brother Alanson's sons, Ira and Samuel Warren enlisted. (Ira later died, and Samuel Warren and Morris were discharged for disability.) Ransom's son-in-law, George Harvey Todd, age twenty-four and husband of daughter Susan, enlisted at Adrian in the same company as Newell. Ransom found it remarkable that he'd ended up with a son-in-law also named Todd but from an unrelated line.

Ransom's cousin, Abel, donated fourteen thousand dollars so that no man would be forced from his home by a draft as long as there were men willing to serve in their place for the bounty.

It was a cold, blustery, December day when the whole Todd clan gathered at the Adrian depot to see Newell and George board the train for Kalamazoo. The local band was playing as families said goodbye to their sons with a mixture of pride and trepidation. "Make your ancestors proud," said Ransom as he embraced his son. Sally choked back her tears, kissed him on the forehead, and said, "Take good care of yourself and keep close to George." A shiver ran up her spine. The company was ordered to Lexington, Kentucky, just days before Christmas.

"Some Christmas this will be," said Sally Ann, "with three empty places at the table."

In January, the company was busy organizing its equipment and becoming familiar with their mounts. Newell thought he looked grand in his dark blue waistcoat with its row of brass buttons and gold piping. His trousers were of a lighter blue. The uniform set off his full, dark mustache and seemed to add to his average stature. He was issued a pistol and a breech-loading Sharps carbine rifle with its barrel shortened to make it easier to use on horseback. The Sharps was a single shot and held moisture-proof cartridges with built in primer that were much better than the long-range Enfields and Springfields used by the infantry. His light steel saber hung in its scabbard at his waist attached to a leather belt hanging diagonally from his shoulder.

When Newell enlisted, he had given no thought to carrying a sword into battle as opposed to showing it off in parades. Now that he held it in his hand, he realized he would be using it in close hand-to-hand fighting. It would be kill or be killed.

Once assigned his mount, Newell pondered the horse. "George, I have it: His name shall be Mosnar," he burst out one day in the stable area.

"Where did you come up with that strange name?" his brother-in-law asked.

"It's Dad's name spelled backwards."

"The deacon will be honored," George said with a smile."

Each cavalryman rode with half-tent shelter, blanket, poncho, ration-filled saddlebags, canteen, four horseshoes and prepared nails strapped to his saddle. Under good conditions, the daily ration consisted of twelve ounces of salt pork, plus hardtack, possibly potatoes, beans or peas, and coffee. Newell had not drunk coffee before enlisting, but it was a communal ritual among the troops, and it seemed to pick him up after a hard day in the saddle. Often the cook put the salt pork in a kind of soup mixed with hardtack and vegetables, which, in winter, were dried in blocks. This dehydrated fare was officially called desiccated vegetables, but to the soldiers they were "desecrated vegetables." Pack mules carried the rest of their essential equipment: nosebags, currycombs, brushes, replacement saddles and bridles, revolvers and swords.

In the field, cavalrymen often pooled their rations, and Newell learned to make baked beans when they camped for a day. A hole was dug in the ground and a stone placed in the bottom and a fire built in it to last for several hours. Water and a teaspoon of soda were added to a quart of beans in a mess pot and cooked over the flame for twenty minutes. The water was poured off, then replenished and boiled again until the beans were soft. A chunk of salt pork and pepper were added. The hot coals were removed, the covered pot placed in the hole, and the coals arranged around it. A preheated stone was placed on top and covered with green saplings, some sacking and finally a layer of dirt. When prepared in the evening, the hearty bean dish would be ready for breakfast.

The company practiced firing their rifles while their horses were running full tilt on loose reins. Newell was a bit slower than George in the rate of his fire. They were taught to fight either mounted or on foot in a staggered skirmish line. When dismounted, one man held the horses, while three other troopers were on the firing line. Each company consisted of one hundred men commanded by a captain, and ten companies made a regiment under the command of a colonel. Each regiment had its own blacksmith and surgeon. Four or five regiments constituted a brigade. Three or four brigades made up a division, totaling twelve to fifteen thousand soldiers. Usually, three divisions made a corps or army. The 11th Michigan Cavalry Regiment was a part of the First Brigade, First Division, Army of the Ohio.

The usual practice was that a prominent man in a community would organize a company and become its captain. Twenty-nine year old Henry Bowen of Adrian commanded Newell's Company H. In April, their first assignment was to escort a large drove of cattle to Nashville, Tennessee. Newell thought this service was a bit mundane. Had he come all this way to herd cows? Though he would not admit it, he was glad to have some time to become familiar with his horse and practice shooting and swordsmanship. And, while they were driving cattle, they ate well. "Not so bad," he remarked to George. As they passed an infantry company resting by the side of the road, the soldiers raised their feet and shouted, "Boys, here's your mule."

"Never mind them," said Newell. "The web feet are just sorry they ain't riding." Newell had to laugh and patted the neck of his horse. "Good boy."

On their infrequent days off, the troopers relaxed, wrote letters and played card games such as euchre and faro. In a letter home, Newell wrote:

April 10, 1864
Somewhere in Kentucky

Dearest Mom and Dad,

Army life is not so bad. We are eating well. Had roast beef and Boston baked beans last night. My horse and I have become good friends and my shooting has improved. I have half of a dog tent that is put together with one of my buddies and we sleep under it on top of our ponchos. The canvas is about five feet long and four and a half wide. The only problem is that I am five feet, ten. Three edges have buttons and button holes so that we can put our tent halves together. There are loops at the bottom for tent pegs to keep the thing from blowing away. We cut some saplings for ridge poles that we connect by a length of rope.

Don't worry about me, George and I look out for each other.
Your affectionate son,
(s)Newell

Newell wrote "Soldiers Letter" on the envelope, and it would go for free. What Newell did not tell his parents was that he had diarrhea for a couple of weeks. "Damn," he complained to George, "it's hard to mount and dismount every ten minutes to take a runny crap. The regimental surgeon offered to bleed me, but I asked for a few days of sick leave instead."

"Yeah, the flux. Half the company has it! But, I'll be damned if I'll take the Blue Mass that our doctor prescribes. It's worse that the shits."

Nor did Newell tell his parents that sometimes when the hardtack got wet it would be covered with maggots. He knew that they would not believe that he'd crumble it into his coffee so he could skim off the maggots. You do what you have to do.

"I remember Grandpa and Dad telling me that they built their houses and dug wells away from the privy and the animal pens," Newell remarked to George,. "Sometimes the horses and we are using the same water when we are camped. I wonder about that. Oh well, what does a private know?"

"Well, I know a good riddle," said George with a grin.
"Let me have it."
"Why is a beautiful girl like a hinge?"
"Because she needs oil or she will squeak"
"No, because she's adored."
"George, you've been in the saddle too long."

The Army of the Ohio was charged with protecting the eastern portion of Kentucky. During the spring and summer, they engaged in a number of small battles along with carrying out their scouting duty. In October, the regiment, led by General Burbridge, participated in a raid on Saltville tucked in between the Alleghany Mountains and the Blue Ridge in southwest Virginia. The five thousand-man regiment all came from Kentucky except for the two regiments from Ohio and Michigan. Saltville was one of only two large sources of salt in the Confederacy. Salt was a strategic resource needed to preserve meat for the army. Bad weather delayed the Union regiment at Clinch Mountain and Laurel Gap, allowing Brigadier General Alfred E. (Mudwall) Jackson to concentrate his Confederate forces north of the town where the rebels dug in on the high river bluffs.

As the cold, foggy day of the battle dawned, Newell roused from his tent to feed and water his horse. This would be his first big battle, and he spoke softly to his horse as he saddled up. Was he reassuring his horse or himself? As they approached the enemy barricades, at 10 that morning, the bugle sounded "Boots and Saddles," and Company H and the others formed into lines of attack.

They began with a series of charges upon Chestnut Ridge. Just beyond lay Cedar Ridge and the town of Saltville. A brigade under the command of Colonel Robert Ratliff was composed of the 12th Ohio, the 11th Michigan and the six hundred-man 5th Colored Cavalry (USCC) composed of volunteer ex-slaves from Kentucky. The colored cavalry had been issued untrained horses and Enfield infantry rifles that were useless to mounted cavalry. On the march to Saltville, the colored unit was subjected to taunts from the white soldiers. Insulting remarks were made, caps were pulled off and even some of their horses were stolen. The Colored Cavalry did not respond in kind. When Newell voiced his objections to the taunting, he got into a fight with a Kentucky trooper. The white cavalryman kneed Newell in the stomach, and he crumpled to the ground with the air gone out of him. Newell had no experience with this kind of fighting and was mighty glad when George and others came to his rescue. George admonished Newell, "Maybe you had better keep your opinions to yourself."

"Not on your life!" Newell cried in frustration. "What are we fighting for if it is not for equality and freedom?"

"OK," George conceded, "but don't forget that a soldier from our regiment was shot in the head by a soldier from the 6th Kentucky Cavalry over just this sort of thing." An officer of the black regiment reported that there were acts of intimidation to his men almost daily.

Kentucky was a slave state but did not secede from the Union. Kentuckians continued to own slaves because Lincoln's Emancipation Proclamation applied only to slaves in the rebel states. The Union did offer freedom to slaves and their families in Union states if they would enlist in the Union Army. This offer accounted for the Colored Cavalry unit. Kentuckians were split over Negro soldiers. The state had trouble meeting its quota of enlistments, and the slave volunteers reduced the pressure on whites to enlist.

Saltville Battle-field, Oct. 2nd, 1864.

At Saltville, the Union cavalry were to attack dismounted because of the strength of the enemy. Newell hated to be on foot. They charged uphill toward the rebel position and were repulsed by the Butternuts' long-range rifle fire. They charged again and fell back. Ratliff ordered a final all-out assault to get close enough for their Sharp's carbine fire to reach the enemy. Finally, by force of numbers and rapid fire, the cavalry breached the rebel line and drove them back to the top of the ridge. Newell could see that the colored units next to his were fighting fiercely. But so were the rebels, who seemed incensed by the appearance of the colored troops. After six hours of intense fighting, Ratliff's brigade was dangerously low on ammunition. At five o'clock, a bugle called retreat, which was hastened by the arrival of Confederate reinforcements.

"George, we've got to get the hell out of here!" Newell called to his brother-in-law. "Run for the horses."

Just as they approached their mounts, an artillery shell exploded nearby, killing Newell's horse. "Quick jump up behind me," yelled George. As they rode out of range, George shouted over his shoulder, "Hey, you're holding me so tight, I can hardly breathe."

In their hasty retreat, many dead and wounded were left behind by the Union army. That night in camp, a grizzly story made the rounds. A group of

Rebels methodically toured the battlefield and killed the black wounded. Five blacks were taken from the medical tent of a Union surgeon who had stayed behind to care for them. They were murdered. The distant firing could be heard in the Union camp all through the night. Newell then understood the intensity of hatred, or was it fear, that southerners held for the blacks. The most disturbing product of their imagination was of their homeland threatened by armed Negroes. Deep emotions caused the rules of war to break down.

As Newell tossed in his tent in a fitful sleep after the battle, he realized that war was a crapshoot. If a bullet had your name on it, you were dead or severely wounded through no particular action of your own. What had once been glorious adventure turned into what seemed like endless slogging and wondering when the bullet with your name would arrive. The regiment received a commendation from General Burbridge in general orders. Newell and George each received a promotion to corporal. George offered his congratulations. Newell made light of it. "If you survive, they give you a promotion," he said. "The less fortunate of our friends die as privates."

Newell was given a reserve horse that he named Mosnar II, and the cavalry returned to Kentucky. General Burbridge interpreted his charge to be to discourage guerillas in the Kentucky countryside by any means necessary. Newell and George were aware that Burbridge arrested suspected Confederate sympathizers and had them shot.

"This makes my stomach hurt," Newell confessed to his brother-in-law. "Hundreds are being shot without formal charges."

"I hope the butcher is replaced," George replied. "He even kills people he imagines might not vote for Lincoln."

"Being killed for what someone imagines you are thinking is not what we're fighting for," Newell protested.

"I'm afraid excess breeds excess. Kentuckians will try to avenge these insults rained down by the butcher for years to come."

Lincoln would replace the Kentucky general early the following year for his misguided efforts on the president's behalf. But, for the time being, district commander, General George Stoneman, wanted Burbridge to lead the second attack on Saltville because he already knew the area.

Just before Christmas, Newell and George were part of the Union forces attacking Saltville again, under the command of Major General Stoneman, who devised a grand plan he did not share with his officers and men. He knew that the salt works would be well defended with thousands of well-entrenched rebels, so as his cavalry drew alongside Saltville, he kept them moving.

"What's going on here? Why aren't we preparing to attack?" asked Newell of his protector and buddy.

"I don't know, but you can bet the old man has a plan," George assured him. "If it's a mystery to us, it must be doubly so to the Rebs."

"I don't relish charging uphill into the teeth of a fortified hill, but do you suppose Stoneman and Burbridge have gone soft?"

Scouts reported that the Confederate General Breckenridge had three thousand infantry and several hundred cavalry on the top of the ridge outside of town. Soon, the master plan began to unfold. When Stoneman kept on going toward Wytheville and its lead mines, the rebel commander felt obliged to send his cavalry to try to head them off. Separated from their infantry, they were no match for Stoneman's thousands and suffered crushing losses. Stoneman had his troops destroy the lead mines at their leisure, then turned his men toward nearby Marion to attack the foundry there for good measure. He sent some of his force in a feint back in the direction of Saltville.

Breckenridge felt he must come to the aid of Marion and abandoned his fortifications and heavy guns and moved east to engage the Union troops before they could reach their new target. The battle raged for thirty-six hours.

"Damn, George, we're on foot again, Newell complained. "These Butternuts are tough, and I'm sure glad we're not fighting them uphill."

"Keep your head down, Corporal, and reload as fast as you can; our lives depend on it."

"Our arms give me confidence that we will prevail."

"The fact that Stoneman is here on the ground fighting with us gives me heart."

Stoneman sent one of his brigades around the Confederate left, which cut Breckenridge off from the town. Sensing he might be surrounded, he broke off engagement and escaped. George and Newell breathed a sigh of relief as they saw the enemy withdraw. The next day they had a lot of fun destroying two thousand kettles used to boil down the briny water from the salt spring. They also captured and burned two arsenals filled with ammunition, thirteen cannon, five locomotives and eighty train cars, dealing a severe blow to their enemy.

"Lee is going to be eating a lot of spoiled meat from now on," George remarked, bringing smiles to the exhausted troopers around him.

"The word is that we are going home, back to Knoxville," another fellow reported to even wider grins.

"Surely, we deserve it," Newell muttered to his comrades.

The elation of victory proved short-lived as they approached the snow-covered Cumberland Mountains, marched across the Clinch River and struggled through Pound Gap into Kentucky. "I don't think our horses are going to make it," one of the cavalrymen said with alarm on the third day of their march through the frigid wasteland. "There's no forage."

When the order came, "Dismount and lead your horses," Newell's wet boots were frozen in his stirrups. He took his sword and beat on his boots to free them, and he felt nothing below his ankles. Newell's horse stumbled, fell, and no amount of urging could get him back on his feet. Tears welled up and cascaded down Newell's face as he took his rifle out of its holder and aimed it at his horse's twitching head. Whangg. The shot echoed down the ridge, soon followed by many more gunshots all around. In camp that night, George managed to remove Newell's boots and first soaked his feet in lukewarm water, then slowly, slowly increased the temperature of the baths. Finally, feeling returned to Newell's feet.

Sherman had reached Savannah in his march from Atlanta to the sea. He had promised Lincoln the City of Savannah as a Christmas present. The Union forces now under the unified command of General Grant were closing in on Lee in Virginia. Still the South fought on.

Newell's unit was to be part of General Stoneman's expedition in the early months of 1865 through east Tennessee, western North Carolina and southwestern Virginia. Their assignment was again to destroy Lee's supply sources and to cut off his retreat west. Their start on the mission was delayed for months at the great displeasure of General Grant. Replacement horses were scarce, and incessant, record-breaking rains slowed preparations. Newell's unit was issued new repeating Spencer carbines, the most advanced in all the Army. The .56 caliber weapon could fire eight shots before reloading. There were not enough of the new rifles and horses to supply all the men, and Newell felt sorry for some of the companies that got left behind. "These Spencers have enough range that they ought to help us avoid being pinned down like we were at the first battle of Saltville," George told Newell.

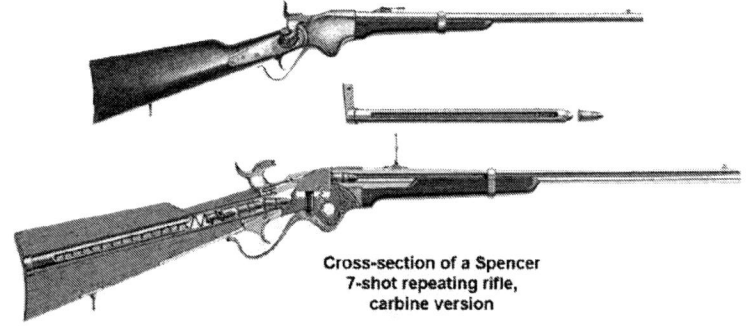

**Cross-section of a Spencer
7-shot repeating rifle,
carbine version**

"I hope so, I don't want a repeat of that hell," the younger man replied.

Once out of Knoxville, the Union Army followed the East Tennessee & Virginia Railroad, tearing up track to deny supplies to Lee at Petersburg. The days and battle sites began to blur in Newell's mind: Hazel Green, McCormick's Farm, Morristown, State Creek, Mt. Sterling in Kentucky; Clinch River, Cobb's Ford, Bristol, Paperville in Tennessee. In Virginia, they raided Abingdon, Wytheville, Mt. Airy, Marion, Seven Mile Ford, and Jonesboro. Crossing into North Carolina and heading south, they raided sites that were manufacturing goods vital to Lee's troops: Danbury's Moratock Iron Works, Statesville, Morgantown, Swannanoa Gap, Asheville and Hendersonville.

Newell's mind was numb, and he just rode on, following orders, forgetting any great cause and focusing on the care of his horse and loyalty to his fellow troopers. He did ride with more determination when he learned that their next objective was Salisbury, North Carolina. "The prison there is reputed to be more deadly than Andersonville." he said with bitterness.

"Yes, I hear stories that one in three prisoners have died there from malnutrition and putrid water."

The boys were disappointed upon arrival to find that most prisoners had been moved further south. In their fury, the cavalry destroyed the prison and large stores of industrial supplies, military equipment and arms, unaware that Lee had already surrendered and the war was over. Not only did their destructive raids play no role in Lee's surrender, but they made the coming reconstruction harder.

When news did come of Lee's surrender to Grant at Appomattox, Virginia, in April, Newell felt only relief, but none of the elation of victory. His mood blackened further with the assassination of Lincoln. Up until now Newell had resisted joining in the looting of private homes, but with the murder of Lincoln, his mind lost its usual controls. In Statesville, the 11th behaved badly and broke store windows. Like many others Newell found a bag and filled it with merchandise. When he returned to camp that evening, his conscience kicked in, and he gave it all away, explaining ,"I can't bring this stuff home; my mother would kill me."

Retracing their steps, they pushed through Saluda Gap in the Blue Ridge and entered South Carolina. A magnificent view opened up. Their lieutenant ordered, "Hey, rein up a minute, Let's enjoy this."

In awe, Newell remarked, "The mountain peaks are beautifully blue in the haze. Each receding ridge is a different hue."

A bald eagle riding the thermals wheeled overhead, and Newell said to no one in particular, "I wish we could travel as effortlessly as that bird."

"I have a new sense of the size and majesty of this country that we are defending," George said.

"I never dreamed of such a thing growing up in Michigan."

Newell couldn't resist carving his initials into Caesar's head, a stone formation that seemed to resemble a person's head. "We're not the Romans, but I guess that destroying the seceesh supply sources is what cavalry is good for."

After skirmishes with bushwhackers and marauding ex-Confederate soldiers at Pickensville and Anderson's Courthouse, it was time to go home, his Michigan home.

But first, the cavalry had new orders from Division Headquarters:

One hundred thousand dollars reward will be paid to any person or persons, who will apprehend and deliver Jefferson Davis to any military authority of the United States. Several million dollars of specie reported to be with him will become the property of the captors.

"I don't care about any reward, but I hope we find him so I can personally kick him off one of these cliffs," Newell declared. But another unit captured Davis, and the 11th was finally headed home.

Newell's regiment had lost twenty-four men killed and mortally wounded plus one hundred fourteen to disease. No mention was made in the official reports about the man shot by a Kentucky trooper in an argument over Negro soldiers. And no one in Michigan gave much thought to the fact that Kentucky's tobacco crops were reduced by one half in 1865 because of severe labor shortages. The state had over two hundred twenty-five thousand slaves in 1860. Now, Kentucky had forty regiments—forty thousand men—of black soldiers. Many more freed themselves and moved to the cities in spite of violence against them and the hesitation of whites to hire them. Newell had a lot of sympathy for both white and black families caught in the mess of postwar Kentucky. Perhaps because of Burbridge's cruelty, Kentucky failed to support the 13th amendment freeing the slaves, but it was nevertheless adopted nationally in December. Newell was proud that Michigan was the third state to ratify it.

Newell and George mustered out in October and returned to Adrian. When the young man embraced his mother, tears came, and she said, "I have been singing 'When Johnny Comes Marching Home' every day since you left, but I substituted Newell for Johnny."

Newell lived with his sister, Cynthia, in Morenci, Michigan, until he married Hulda Aldrich in 1871 at the Baptist church. Newell was a handsome chap in his black wedding suit with his carefully trimmed full, dark mustache. His high-collared white shirt had a fat black knot at the neck. Newell liked the way Hulda wore her hair in a bundle of curls above her forehead and the rest combed back into a bun at the back. Newell thought her aquiline nose reflected her strong character. Hulda's ancestors were part of the Massachusetts Bay Colony that had settled in Mendon in 1631. Later they became Quakers, rejecting the Puritan combination of church and state, predestination and the dominance of scriptures for instruction. As succeeding generations moved west, they became Baptist and returned to the Bible for guidance, but rejected infant baptism. Only an adult could testify to being born again.

One of the first things the newly married couple did was to invite George and Susan for supper. Newell bought one of the hams hanging in his father's store, and Hulda prepared it with some potatoes and peas. At supper, the men reflected on their admiration for General Stoneman. "We owe our lives to that man," Newell remarked. "His strategic deployment helped us to avoid a lot of firefights against a concentrated enemy."

"How'd he do that?" Hulda asked.

"By keeping the enemy in the dark as to the places we would attack next. He advanced over the countryside in a huge zigzag pattern, often causing us to retrace our steps."

"For example, in Salisbury, the enemy withdrew several thousand troops just before we changed direction and attacked," George added.

"Those are fine points of military maneuvering I know nothing about," the new bride confessed. "I'm just thankful it worked and you two are home with all of your limbs."

"I just read about race wars in Memphis and civil rights disputes," Newell remarked as the conversation turned to politics and reconstruction. 'Did we bring equal rights to the Negro or not?"

"Well, it's complicated," George explained. "The Fourteenth Amendment tried to wrest power from the old local elite slave holders by prohibiting rebels from holding public office."

"Sounds good, but there's a problem," Newell countered. "I read what our old top commander, General Schofield said, 'It is folly to bring back a revolted people by disenfranchising all the leaders in whom they trust and confide.' "

"I understand that white vigilantes and guerillas take the law into their own hands and scare the Negro into not voting," Susan chimed in.

"Yes, it was a lot easier just to shoot the crap out of the Rebs!" Newell said to the disapproving looks of the ladies. Then he added, "I'm not proud to have been a Stoneman Raider. We ruined the mountain economy and made many people destitute. And, for nothing; the war was ending anyway."

"We can't take on that guilt load," George counseled. "Stoneman couldn't have known when he started that campaign, and he carried out his orders very well, as did we."

"Yes, I suppose if the war had still been on, destruction of war-material production would have helped end it."

"Thinking in terms of 'ifs' and 'might-have-beens' can drive you crazy," added Susan.

Hulda   **Newell**

"Enough! No more politics, except I want to say one thing," interjected Hulda. "If the war was about equality, it is still going on, and it can be lost."

No one could speak for several minutes. Newell, his head hanging and voice barely audible, said, "Up till now I hadn't thought much about it. Our brigade stole a lot of things from the relatively wealthy and left everyone without food. Though once, we left a lot of food in a town square for the Negroes, but then we rode off and abandoned them."

"It's time to think again on why we volunteered," George reminded them.

"For me, I fought to free the slaves following the moral reasoning of my father, the deacon," Newell said.

"There's a lot of talk now that the North's purpose of the war was primarily to preserve the Union, while the South says they fought for state's rights and freedom to secede to achieve self-governance."

"In their enthusiasm for freedom, many in the South forget about freedom for the Negro," said Newell, still pondering the irony in the Confederate rationale.

Hulda rose, served her husband another slice of ham, and kissed him on the back of the neck. "You will be my hero forever."

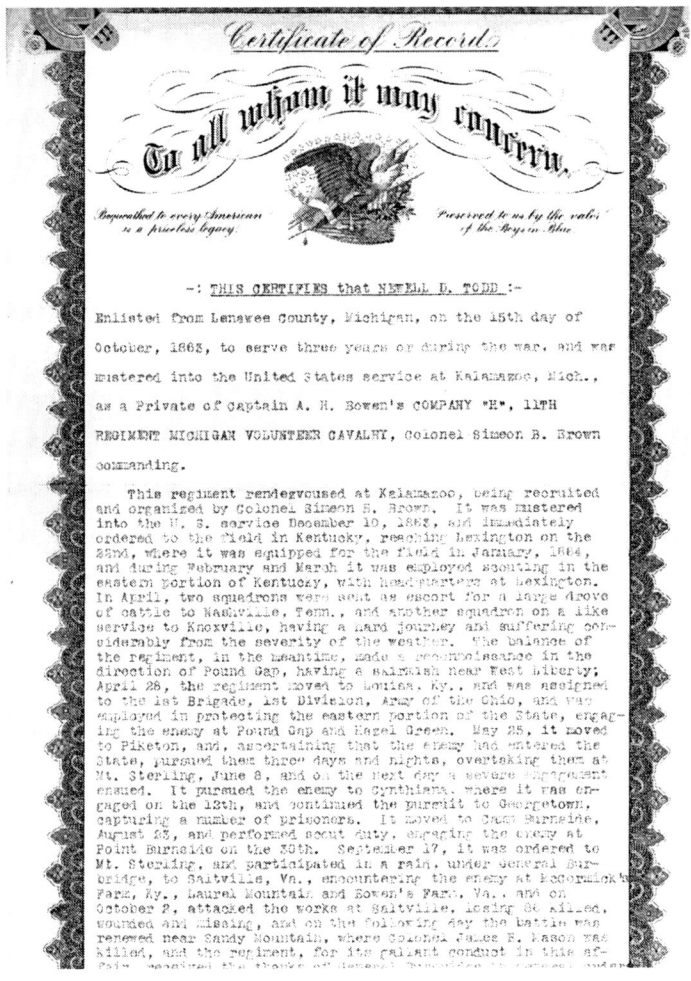

They lived at Morenci, a village of nine hundred inhabitants, where Newell was a druggist and grocer with his father and brother Luther who had moved back to Michigan from Kansas for a while. The *Michigan State Gazetteer & Business Directory* for 1867-8 listed:

Morenci List of professions, trades, etc.
Todd, R. & Co. (Ransom, L. L. and N.), drugs and groceries.

Newell was not pleased that Luther had come back and he remarked to Hulda, "Maybe we should think about moving. Maybe west." But then Luther moved back to Kansas in July 1870, and Allen Beach, sister Cynthia's husband, joined the firm, and the name changed to Todd and Beach, Druggists.

Out in Atchison, Luther stayed in the drug business until June 1874, when family connections paid off again. Uncle Wade was generous with his in-laws and offered Luther a job in May 1875 as cashier of the American Bridge Company, a position he held until the opening of the Chicago & Atchison Bridge in September. Erection of the bridge across the Missouri River at Atchison had begun in August of the previous year. The stone used for the piers and abutments, upon which the bridge rested, came from the quarries at Cottonwood Falls, Kansas. The one thousand one hundred eighty-two foot-long bridge was built by the American Bridge Company of Chicago, which was owned by Luther's mother's brother, Jeptha Wade of Cleveland.

The bridge itself was built of wrought iron, nineteen feet, six inches wide, with five-foot sidewalks on either side. It was composed of three fixed spans and a middle section that pivoted on a circular pier sunk to the bedrock. The fixed spans were each two hundred sixty feet long, and the three hundred eighty-two foot long pivoting section allowed one hundred sixty feet of clear water on either side for passage of taller vessels. As the bridge was nearing completion in July, a celebration and dedication were held that included a grand parade, fireworks, displays, speeches, balls and concerts in the evening.

After completion of the bridge, Luther was appointed superintendent. That fall, Newell and Hulda moved to Atchison where he would work as toll collector of the bridge. After they settled into a small rental house, Newell remarked to Hulda, "I'm again in the shadow of my older brother who is the superintendent. I can't seem to stand in my own right.

"I know this has always bothered you," she said, "but at least it's a good job."

"And it has let us move further west. I think there is more opportunity in fast-growing Atchison than in Morenci."

"I can hardly believe that when our ancestors came to Michigan, it was the wild frontier," Hulda remarked. "Now to get any space and opportunity, we have had to move west to Kansas."

"Yes, and before all I knew about Kansas was that it was Indian Territory."

Newell chafed at having his older brother for a boss, but upon Luther's death in 1887, Newell was named superintendent, finally emerging from the domination of his brother. Newell now felt guilty for his enmity toward his brother, and he and Hulda named their first son Luther Anson after Newell's overbearing brother and Hulda's father. As superintendent, Newell moved his family to a bigger house and entered into community affairs, becoming a Knight Templar in the Masonic Fraternity. His income afforded him the luxury of hunting and fishing vacations with friends at Spirit Lake, Minnesota. He even saved enough to invest in farmland.

Newell's brother-in-law and comrade in arms, George, and sister Susan Maria moved to Burlingame, Kansas, after the war, then later to Pleasant Hill and Butler, Missouri. They, like so many others, responded to the pull of the West and the opportunity to start anew.

~9~

Civil War Soldiers—The Surgeon

When Newell was in the Civil War, he remembered the story of his great-grandfather, Joseph Todd, who had acted on the bond he felt with his neighbors by faithfully serving in the New York militia during the Revolutionary War. Todd's comment, "You never know who your children will marry, and I would not want their in-laws to think I was a coward," had been passed down through the generations. Newell could not help reflecting on a future descendant who might have had ancestors who also served in the Union army or even in the Confederate army. He could not have known that his son would one day marry the granddaughter of John G. Miller. At age forty-one, Miller had been appointed assistant surgeon for the 11th Iowa Infantry by Governor Kirkwood in 1862. At the end of 1864, when Newell was taking part in the capture of Saltville, Virginia, Miller was with General Sherman in Savannah. If you believe in numerology, you could make something of the fact that both the Michigan and Iowa regiments were number eleven. And, you might make something out of the fact that Miller was born in Gettysburg, Pennsylvania, though he was not present at that famous Civil War battle.

In 1861, President Lincoln had directed state governors to appoint a surgeon and an assistant surgeon for each new volunteer regiment supposedly "after having passed an examination by a competent Medical board." This order was honored more in principle than in practice, and political appointees were often incompetent doctors who had little or no formal training. This was not the case with Miller, a graduate of Oberlin College, who first studied medicine in a physician's office in Ohio and then graduated from Castleton Medical College in Vermont in 1853. He was a handsome devil with fire in his belly and good enough prospects to marry a riverboat captain's daughter in 1854.

His thirst for knowledge was nearly insatiable, causing him to seek further training at New York Medical College, later renamed Belleview Hospital, and also attend lectures at Philadelphia's venerable College of Physicians. He was aware that two hundred fifty pro-slavery students at the latter college had left in December 1859 and headed for Richmond. They had been promised funds to defray their travel expenses by the Virginia governor. Philadelphia was the home of the American Anti-Slavery Society. The southern students were particularly incensed when John Brown's body was paraded through the city's streets as an abolitionist martyr. The students threw stones and rioted before leaving for Richmond, where they were welcomed by a band playing "Carry Me Back to Old Virginny." Miller thought it was good riddance.

When the war broke out, Miller and his young wife, Ruthanna Bennett, whom he called Annie, and daughters Lillie and Mary were living in Iowa where he was practicing medicine. Miller was a peripatetic soul and already had practiced in Ohio and Kansas and had spent some time in San Francisco as part of the gold rush excitement of 1849. He believed in the Union cause, but fundamentally, he was restless to move on to something new, something to define who he was, something through which he could make a real difference.

Before seeking the assistant surgeon appointment from the governor, he learned all he could about what to expect. The rationale for political appointment of surgeons on a regimental basis was the idea that soldiers would prefer to be treated by locally known doctors. The result was a decentralized medical corps with surgeons treating only men in their own regiment. The transport of each regiment's equipment required one wagon for medical supplies and another to carry hospital tents, cooking utensils and the surgeon's baggage. The hospital tent had straight side walls that could be rolled up for ventilation and was tall enough to stand up in. It could shelter twenty patients, but was often overcrowded. The two surgeons had a smaller wall tent of their own.

The ambulance drivers were organized under the quartermaster who often used the wagons for nonmedical purposes. This lack of central command may have been somewhat satisfactory at the war's outset, but the result was chaos and inefficiency when large battles produced thousands of wounded soldiers. The chaos was evident at the Battle of Bull Run and the Peninsula Campaign of General George McClellan. Gathering the wounded and delivering them to their respective regimental surgeons was impossible. Later the ambulance service and hospitals were reformed on a division and brigade basis.

Ambulances

Miller stood five feet, eleven and a half inches tall, had brown, almost black eyes and was of dark complexion. He thought he was quite handsome in his surgeon's dress uniform with his sword at his side. He caught up with his regiment in July after it had participated in the Union victory at Shiloh, Tennessee, led by Ulysses Grant, and the siege of the vital rail center of Corinth, Mississippi, by the troops of Major General Henry Halleck. Miller immediately was pressed into service caring for the wounded of that battle. In July, Miller was ordered into detached service at Corinth:

Headquarters 6th Division
July 28th 1862
Special Order No. 19

    Assistant Surgeon J.G. Miller of the 11th Iowa Vols. is hereby detailed as assistant surgeon to the 6th Division General Hospital and will report immediately for duty to Dr. G.F. Huntington, Surgeon in charge.

    Dr. Miller will be responsible for the safe return of the Hospital tents left in his charge by the 11th Regt. Iowa Vols.
        By order of
        Gen. McArthur
        S. B. Davis
            Staff Surgeon, 6th Division

    Medical practice in the Civil War was the same as it had been for one hundred years. Its tenets were to bleed, blister and purge. The dominant theory was that disease was caused by an imbalance in bodily fluids that could be corrected only by getting rid of much of this fluid by bleeding. Blistering also caused loss of body fluids, and the intestines were emptied by strong cathartics, primarily calomel and tartar emetic, which produced explosive diarrhea and volcanic vomiting. Physicians thought that if these "heroic" measures were not taken, the patient would surely die. The fact that many died anyway with exhaustion, extreme salivation, inflamed gums and tongue and open sores did not reduce devotion to these measures in this prescientific period.

    Bleeding was so common that it was often prescribed for seasonal allergies and postnasal drip by civilian doctors. The attractiveness of these invasive measures was partly due to the fact that physicians could be seen doing something. This supplied psychic balm during a period when physicians had little beneficial treatment to offer. In medieval days, doctors were not expected to intervene and were paid to simply name the disease. So these more active measures were seen as a modern advance. Such was the training that Miller had received in medical school.

The second Battle of Corinth, Tennessee, was fought in early October as Confederate General Braxton tried to prevent Major General Don Carlos Buell's Army of the Ohio from joining Grant's Army of the Tennessee. Under the overall command of Grant, Rosecrans' army defeated the Confederates, but lost twenty-five hundred killed and more than eighteen hundred wounded. There was plenty of work for Miller and his colleagues. Miller had conducted only one amputation some years before when a man caught his arm in some machinery. Now he was doing dozens a day, each one taking ten to twelve minutes. The saw he used looked like any common hacksaw. His nurse laughingly remarked, "After the war, doctors will be known as "old Sawbones."

"That's not funny," responded Miller with irritation in his voice. Anesthesia was used but was rarely available. The amputated arms and legs piled up outside the operating tent. Miller followed the methods employed by the lead surgeon of his regiment. A slosh of water was often used to rinse off a bloody operating table, and sponges were used over and over. If a bullet had penetrated the body deeper than could be reached by the surgeon's finger, it would be sought with a metal probe. Bullet forceps or a scoop was used to remove it if found. A bullet deep in the chest or abdomen was fatal; surgeons soon knew that opening body cavities was quickly followed by coma and death.

Miller was a free spirit and a bit of a rebel. One day for sport and to relieve the monotony of continuous surgery, he asked Asa, his nurse, if he would like to practice using his revolver. Asa reluctantly agreed. "Wait here and I'll grab my haversack from where I keep it."

They walked to the far edge of the camp and beyond a grove of trees. Miller passed the revolver to Asa for his inspection. "It's quite heavy," remarked Asa. "Where did you get this thing?"

"I appropriated it from a Rebel captain who was brought in for surgery. I figured he didn't need it anymore."

"What are these six notches on the handle?"

"The son-of-bitch must have been keeping track of the number of our men that he shot."

"Do ya know how to load it?" Asa asked. "It seems quite complicated?"

"Well, I think so. I watched an infantry captain load his one day." Miller sat on the ground with the butt of the gun on the ground between his knees. "First you pour black powder from this flask into a chamber. Then you add the ball and tamp it in with the integral loading lever that is hinged beneath the barrel."

"That's rather painstaking. Now what?"

After filling all the chambers and pointing the revolver down, Miller put a tiny percussion cap into the back of each chamber in the cylinder. He fumbled one and lost it in the dirt. "Damnation!"

"Now I see why it's called a cap-and-ball revolver'" said Asa "It takes a lotta time to load. If you fire six shots in the field, you're done for the day."

"OK, we're ready. You fire first after I put this empty bandage box out there about twenty yards for a target."

Asa raised the revolver and tried to hold it steady, but it wavered in his hand. The loud retort made them both jump. "Damn," said Asa when he saw that the target was undisturbed. "If that was a Reb, he would still be coming for us."

Miller took a turn and had the same result. His surgeon's hand was steadier, but only on his last try did an edge of the box splinter. "I hope no one saw us," he said. "They sure as hell could hear us."

Head Quarters McArthur's Div.
Left Wing, 13 Army Corps
Yockune Station, MS.
Dec. 19, 1862
Special Field Order No. 42
Placed under arrest for shooting in violation of orders.
By order of McArthur, Brig. Gen'l Commanding Div.

Dec. 20.
released from arrest until such time as he can be brought before a Court Martial.
By order of McArthur, Brig. Gen'l

Miller's Cap & Ball Revolver

Miller had another dilemma. The head surgeon of his regiment resigned when he could no longer tolerate the long hours and gore, and Miller knew that it could be months before the news filtered back to Governor Kirkwood that a replacement appointment was needed. Even then, there was no assurance that some doctor in the Iowa state capital might not capture the appointment instead of himself. "I need to put my case before the governor in person," Miller thought, "but, how can I travel north without being AWOL? I am in enough trouble already." In a copy of army regulations, he found an obscure clause that he thought might work: He could muster out, then muster back in once he got the appointment as head surgeon.

However, when he returned with his promotion, the regimental adjutant general gave him a hard time. After much maneuvering, Miller finally prevailed and not only got his payroll started again but had the shooting infraction dismissed as well. He told his assistant surgeon, "I guess the army is smart enough to not want a good surgeon wasting away in the stockade." He managed to say it with a bit of bravado, but inside he was greatly relieved. His promotion provided an opportunity to employ more of his own thinking and called the division officers' attention to his qualifications.

Grant conducted his central Mississippi campaign from November to January 1863, then he moved on that spring to Memphis. Miller wrote of his brigade's experiences in a letter to his hometown newspaper, *The Union Sentinel,* in Osceola, Iowa:

Camp at Lafayette, Tenn.
Jan. 9th, 1863

Mr. Editor:- thinking that anything connected with Iowa troops would be interesting to the people of Iowa, and having a little leisure, I will give you a few items in relation to the whereabouts and doings of the Iowa Brigade. We are in McArthur's division: our commanders are all fighting men and will as well, as the men, give a good account of themselves whenever and wherever tried.

I take them to be such men as Scott represents Edward Bruce to be when he says – "Whose desperate valor oft' made good Where prudence might have failed."

Let me give you an instance or two of McArthur's desire to be 'up and at them.' We were in front in our advance on the enemy's fortifications on the Talahatchie. McArthur, as I have been informed, asked permission of the general commanding, to storm their works, proposing to do the business up in half an hour. The general thinking "prudence – the better part of valor" denied the request. That night the enemy evacuated and destroyed the Bridge. McArthur was ordered to repair it so that the army could cross, but so eager was he to be after the rebels that he had it fixed merely so that his division could get across before it gave way, for which we had to remain behind and build the railroad bridge, which took us nearly two weeks. We then moved on through Oxford to Tycona, where we arrived on the 19th of Dec. and expected to soon take our place in the advance, but on the evening of the 20th we were ordered to be in readiness by 7 o'clock the next morning to retrace our steps. Various rumors were afloat as to the cause of our retrograde movement, but none were satisfactory. In the morning three days rations were issued with orders that it must last six; and at the appointed time, suddenly and in silence we commence our march northward; cursing the supposed or real incompetency of the planner of the expedition. We had hoped to spend the holidays in Jackson, Miss. And when more than half way there, to be compelled to march back again, was to say the least, very annoying.

We remained in Holly Springs until the 30th, and though only half rations were issued, no one suffered for eatables, as there was plenty in the adjoining country, of cattle, hogs and sheep, corn sugar and molasses, and the boys helped themselves.

Lafayette is a very small village on the Memphis and Charleston Rail Road, just 31 miles from the former place, the country around is very good, though rather flat. There is an abundance of forage of every kind, and nearly every day the boys come in loaded with chickens, turkeys, geese, sugar, molasses, honey, pork and beef; though when we first arrived here it was dangerous to go any distance from camp, as guerrillas abounded; several of our boys were taken prisoners by them, and two were reported killed. As we were in Tennessee, and it being considered a loyal State, we were ordered not to forage off of the country when we first came here, but since they have taken our boys prisoners, the General tells them to take anything they can make use of.

The health of the 11th is excellent, not having a patient in the regimental hospital. Wishing well to all friends, I remain,
(s) J.G. Miller

The only important military stronghold remaining was Vicksburg that controlled passage on the Mississippi River. Grant crossed the river south of Vicksburg and won battles at Port Gibson and Raymond and captured Jackson, the Mississippi state capital. Attempts to halt the Union advance at Champion's Hill and Big Black River bridge were unsuccessful. Confederate commander Pemberton withdrew to avoid being outflanked by Major General William T. Sherman coming from the north. Pemberton burned the bridge at Big Black River and took everything vegetable and animal to sustain his troops while they were holed up in Vicksburg waiting for reinforcement.

After making a number of frontal attacks with huge losses, Grant's forces could not penetrate Vicksburg's extensive fortifications. To avoid more casualties, Grant reluctantly settled into a siege in May. Union cannon bombarded the city as did Union gunboats on the river. The odor of dead men and horses rotting in the fierce southern sun fouled the air, and the wounded cried for medical aid. Pemberton proposed a truce to recover the wounded and dead. Grant at first refused, thinking it a show of weakness, but then consented. The medical corps from both sides mingled peacefully for a few hours as they dealt with the casualties.

In early June, a Confederate force under the command of Major General John Walker attacked at Milliken's Bend up the Mississippi. They were trying to cut Grant's supply lines but failed. The lack of food in the city had a devastating effect, and by June, half of the Confederate soldiers were sick or hospitalized with scurvy, dysentery and diarrhea. Horses, mules and dogs disappeared from the streets. On July 3, Pemberton surrendered. Grant did not want to feed thirty thousand hungry Confederates in Union prison camps and offered to parole all prisoners, thinking that in their starving and diseased state, they would not fight again. Union casualties exceeded forty-eight thousand.

      Physicians were not immune to the same diseases plaguing the soldiers. In October, Miller was sick with bilious dysentery followed by chronic diarrhea, rectal prolapse, enlarged prostate and irritable bladder.

Headquarters Seventeenth Army Corps
Department of the Tennessee
Vicksburg Miss. Oct. 30th 1863.
Special Orders, No. 246
"On Surgeons certificate that it is necessary to save life or prevent permanent disability, leave of absence for twenty (20) days."

      The Regimental Staff and Muster roll of December 19, showed Miller "Present, returned from sick." The march from Vicksburg to Meridian and back in March with inclement weather was hard on Miller. He contracted synovitis of the right knee, resulting in floating cartilages in the joint that would plague him the rest of his life.

      While Miller's training was of the bleed-blister-and-purge school, he was a keen observer. When he was overwhelmed with surgery, the sick could not be treated in the customary ways. Miller began to notice that men with similar symptoms that received only good food recovered as well as those who received the standard treatment. In fact, their overall vigor seemed better. Accosted by doubts, Miller eased up on the invasive interventions. To eliminate them entirely would make him a renegade, and he perceived that renegades did not advance in the military. He did not make a big deal of it, but he used the standard treatments less and less and taught others by example rather than words. In May 1863, William Hammond, Surgeon General of the Army in Washington, issued Circular No. 6, referred to as the Calomel and Tartar Emetic Order. It prohibited the use of these minerals, and the agents were removed from the medical-supply list. The directive was like a bombshell and was received with mixed reactions. Miller was quietly pleased, but many of his colleagues ignored the order. The few homeopaths in the army were greatly pleased as they did not believe in large doses of anything, in particular these minerals. Raging debates over these treatments split the medical corps.

      The army admired order, and Miller showed he was a good organizer. His regimental hospital tent was orderly and clean. He did not let severed limbs pile up and rot in the sun but saw to it that they were quickly buried if at all possible. Common sense told him that piles of limbs were bad for morale, regardless of the medical implications. And, soldiers just felt better in clean clothing and bedding than not. He sent a request to the captain of the bummers to scour the countryside and keep him continuously supplied with clean straw for the floor of his tent.

Miller was not shy and retiring. When he needed help in cleaning up after a day of surgery, he was not afraid to order men in camp to help clean up even if he did not have the authority to do so. Age and demeanor went a long way if you were willing to exploit them. He was not above cajoling the able-bodied men. "You are lucky to be alive," he'd remind them. "Now give me a hand to help out those less fortunate."

Major General William Tecumseh Sherman was named after the Shawnee chief Tecumseh, whom his father had admired. He led the Atlanta Campaign in the summer of 1864, forcing Confederate General Joseph E. Johnston to retreat to Chattanooga, Tennessee, and then to Marietta, Georgia. Johnston's performance lost him his command, and he was replaced by John Hood. Sherman's 17th Corps was commanded by Major General Frank P. Blair. The Battle for Atlanta began July 22 after the Battle of Kennesaw Mountain allowed the shelling of Marietta in June. The Union suffered almost three thousand six hundred fifty casualties, while the Confederates lost eighty-five hundred, but they still held the city. Sherman settled into a siege.

Miller knew that cleanliness and order could be more easily seen by his superiors than any long-term survival rate of those he treated. It worked. Also, reforms were under way to move more care to the division and corps level so that doctors could specialize. The order for detached service and greater responsibility came in August during the siege of Atlanta. The wounded were sent back from the front lines to Marietta.

Headquarters Seventeenth Army Corps,
Department of the Tennessee,
Before Atlanta Ga, August 9, 1864
Special Orders No. 197
Surgeon J.G. Miller, 11th Regt Iowa Infantry Vols is hereby relieved from present duty and is assigned to duty as Surgeon in charge of the 17th Army Corps Hospital at Marietta Ga.
By command of Maj. General F. P. Blair

Miller read the order again. Did it really say "in charge of" and not simply "attached to?" Recognition had come faster than he dared hope. Marietta was well suited as a hospital center because of its proximity to railroads upon which the wounded would eventually be sent north.

The siege ended September 2 when Hood retreated eastward. Hood could see that he was outnumbered and unable to prevent Sherman's further advance into Georgia. He felt his only hope was to circle around behind Sherman and cut his supply lines. With the approval of Jefferson Davis, Hood attacked Federal supply depots and forced Sherman to the defensive. The 11th Iowa was part of the force that left Atlanta to pursue Hood into Alabama in October. Hood presented Sherman with a dilemma. All along, Sherman had wanted to march across Georgia to the sea. But, he could not disengage from Hood while Hood was close to Atlanta without being perceived as cowardly. Hood originally planned to follow Sherman and nip at his heels if he headed toward Savannah. Hood changed his mind and headed northwest with the intention of recapturing Nashville. Sherman's specific plans were always evolving. Grant's grand plan was to destroy the Rebel armies rather than to capture territory. Still, Sherman persuaded Grant to permit him to advance through Georgia while living off the land which would free him of concerns about securing supply lines at his rear.

In November, the Union hospital was evacuated. The 17th Corps was spread out in encampment around Marietta when the order came to march east. Miller watched Sherman's command group march through Marietta on its way back to Atlanta. Union forces were split into two wings, with the 17th Corps as part of the right wing. Sherman ordered the destruction of everything of military value, but explicitly prohibited the use of fire. However, the order was not enforced. Boys do like to play with matches, and Marietta, like Atlanta, was burned as Sherman planned his march to the sea. Miller could not suppress a shudder as he watched the columns of black smoke reach for the sky. The soldiers were in a good mood, and Miller could hear them singing, "John Brown's soul goes marching on."

As Miller watched the last of the Union wounded loaded on a train headed north and oversaw the loading of his hospital tents and supplies, he remarked to one of his nurses, "The war is over."

"What do you mean?"

"Atlanta was the South's major industrial city, and its loss will greatly reduce military supplies to Lee," Miller explained. "There is every reason to believe that Sherman will be successful in reaching Savannah, and the South will be cut in two. Lee can't hope to win after that. I keep hearing that he is a man of honor. Well, if he had any honor he would surrender and stop this bloodshed. Why waste any more lives, both north and south, on a hopeless cause? This is all vainglory."

"I doubt if he's that big of a man," the nurse replied. "Southerners would think he was a traitor, and his name would live in infamy. His reputation will be better if he suffers a conclusive defeat. The same goes for Jeff Davis."

"And take tens of thousands of soldiers to their graves?" the doctor countered.

"You're thinking too rationally for this sad world."

Sherman's victory in Atlanta was a great help to President Lincoln who was fighting for his second term against Democrat and former Commander of the Army of the Potomac, George McClellan. After a lackluster performance at Antietam, Lincoln had fired McClellan for being too timid and slow. Miller's sympathies were with Lincoln. McClellan favored reunification of the Union, but his Democratic party was in favor of negotiating a peace with the Confederates, and this caused great confusion in the party and resulted in Republican Lincoln's overwhelming victory.

Sherman believed that southern civilians were not aware of how poor their military prospects were, and he wanted to send them a clear message of their vulnerability. Sixty thousand Union troops began a scorched-earth campaign that would cut a sixty mile-wide swath of near-total destruction. Only localities that offered no resistance would be spared. Sherman ordered his men to stay out of homes and to leave enough food so that farmers would not starve. One item in Sherman's Special Field Order No. 120, issued on November 9, 1864 just before leaving Atlanta, read: *VI. As for horses, mules, wagons, &c., belonging to the inhabitants, the cavalry and artillery may appropriate freely and without limit, discriminating, however, between the rich, who are usually hostile, and the poor or industrious, usually neutral or friendly.*

Foragers known as "bummers" gathered food from local farms and destroyed the railroads and manufacturing. Rails were heated and twisted around trees, earning them the term, "Sherman's neckties."

Later in November, before abandoning the capital at Milledgeville to Sherman's army, the Georgia legislature called for Georgians to "Die freemen rather than live [as] slaves." When Miller heard about it, he could not understand that mentality. "We are freeing slaves, not making more," he remarked to his steward. "I can understand why slave owners would fight to protect what they call their property, but what I can't understand is why non-slave owners, the predominant small farmers and villagers, are willing to die to sustain the economic interests of a few rich slave holders."

"It's like when we were in school and a leader chose sides for a game," his steward responded. "You had no control over whose side you were on, but as the game unfolded, the 'you' and 'them' emerged as animosity toward the other side grew. And, remember that Southerners call this the War of Northern Intervention." In fact, not all of the able-bodied Southerners had enlisted in the Confederate army, much to the disgust of President Davis, who insisted that they could still win if all would devote themselves to the cause.

As Sherman's troops swept across Georgia, ten thousand slaves left their plantations and followed the Union troops. Unfortunately, many died of hunger and lack of water. Upon his arrival on the outskirts of Savannah, Sherman sent an ultimatum to the city and on December 21, he telegraphed President Lincoln, "I beg to present you as a Christmas gift the City of Savannah, with one hundred and fifty guns and plenty of ammunition, also about twenty-five thousand bales of cotton." If Hood had not abandoned his original plan in favor of attacking Nashville that turned out to be unsuccessful, Sherman might have been considerably delayed. If the southern cavalry had attacked in force Sherman's supply wagons that often extended for thirty miles, delays would have ensued. The military outcomes are often a matter of if, if and if.

Early in the war, the ambulance service was a disaster. But now with well-trained drivers and ambulances under the control of the Medical Corps rather than the Quartermaster, the wounded were recovered with efficiency. An ambulance train brought the Union sick and wounded to Savannah. Four hospital steamboats were waiting with supplies in the Savannah harbor.

The boats also brought mail for the troops, tons of it. Miller read several letters from his wife, Ruthanna. He had trouble connecting. Annie was having the same problem. "You have been gone so long," she wrote. "I can hardly remember what you look like." Miller was especially puzzled by one line that asked, "Are you coming home?" Not *when* are you coming home, but *are* you coming home. Of course, he was coming home; why would she ask that? After finishing his duties for the day, he felt at loose ends and wandered about the town. His walk took him down by the waterfront past a row of two-story brick houses. There was something unusual about them. Every window had a beautiful young woman sitting there, smiling. Most of them were black. To himself he said, "Get thee behind me, Satan." But, he was a long way from home.

Sherman did not fancy taking thousands of Negro camp followers with him. It did not make for a fast-moving, flexible fighting force, and the logistic problems were staggering. He hit upon a solution: Give them land, and they would stay in Savannah. The general issued Special Field Orders No. 15 that read as follows: *The islands from Charleston, south, the abandoned rice fields along the rivers for thirty miles back from the sea, and the country bordering the St. Johns river, Florida, are reserved and set apart for the settlement of the negroes now made free by the acts of war and the proclamation of the President of the United States.*

Sherman now headed north through the Carolinas to apply pressure from the south to Lee who was resisting Grant's attacks at Petersburg, Virginia, just north Richmond. During the march through the South Carolina swamps in January, it rained four straight days. All the wagons bogged down, and Miller had never been so miserable, and he could only think, "Right now I wish I was back in Iowa."

An orderly from headquarters delivered new orders to Miller when he was in the middle of an amputation. Pointing to a small table covered in instruments Miller said, "Put it over there if you can find a spot without blood covering it."

"I think you'll want to read this right away," the orderly urged.

"Put it over there," Miller insisted. "Can't you see I'm busy?"

"Yes, sir," and the orderly turned on his heels and departed.

Later that night when Miller read the order, a faint smile came to his face.

Head Quarters 17th A. C.
Medical Directors Office
Rivers Bridge S. C. Feb'y 4, 1865
Special Field Order No. 10
Surgeon J.G. Miller, 11th Iowa Inft. Vols. is relieved from duty with his regiment, and is assigned to duty as Surgeon in charge of the Division Hospital of the 4th Div. 17 Army Corps.
By order of Major Genl F. P. Blair
    J. W. Boucher
    Surgeon USV, Medical Director, 17th Army Corps

Miller folded the order and put it in his pack and spoke to his tent mate, "I've been given more responsibility. If I wasn't so tired, I'd celebrate, but given the number of soldiers who I couldn't save today, it wouldn't be appropriate anyway."

"Congratulations, sir. We're all doing the best we can," his colleague reminded him.

Sherman had a particular enmity toward South Carolinians, as they were the first to secede. He ordered that Columbia be burned to the ground. The soldiers were given license to plunder. One slightly wounded soldier came into Miller's surgery carrying a pillowcase filled with gold watches, silver of all kinds and jewelry.

"What is all this?" the doctor asked.

"It's my share of what we took from the chivalry of the city. The company gets two-fifths and the officers get the rest. I understand Sherman has enough gold to start a bank. You'd better hurry and get yours."

"That's disgusting," Miller replied. "We're no better than the barbarians who sacked Rome."

Grant's strategy for ending the war was falling into place. He was coming down on Lee from the north and east. Philip Sheridan cleared out the Shenandoah Valley and was approaching Petersburg from the west, as was General Stoneman from eastern Tennessee, whose troops included a cavalry corporal named Newell. The siege had lasted nine months before Grant's army of one hundred twelve thousand finally broke through the Confederate line. Grant had fought a dogged war of attrition, losing forty-two thousand men to Lee's loss of twenty-eight thousand.

Sherman had repelled rebel General Joe Johnston's army at the Battle of Bentonville, North Carolina, in March and advanced on Raleigh. The two generals negotiated terms of surrender of Johnston's almost ninety thousand troops. President Davis did not like the terms covering only a military surrender and ordered Johnston to disband the infantry and escape with mounted troops to continue the fight as guerillas. Realizing the cost of prolonged war, Johnston disobeyed his orders on principle. "War can no longer be continued by us, except as robbers," he said "I would avoid the crime of waging a hopeless war." Finally, there was some rationality in place of vainglory, thought Miller, when he heard the general's comment.

After the loss of thousands of lives on both sides in Grant's siege of Richmond and Petersburg, Lee abandoned the cities. The Rebels experienced another ten thousand casualties at Sailor's Creek before Lee headed west, hoping for time enough to be joined by General Johnston. Miller spoke with his nurse, "Lee's strategy was hopeless as Sherman had cut Johnston off at Bentonville." Sheridan had come from the northwest and squeezed Lee between his troops and Grant's.

"Maybe he thought he could get supplies at Lynchburg," the nurse suggested.

Miller shrugged and said, "Maybe so, but we know that General Stoneman's raiders had destroyed much of the rail lines and supply sources to the west. Do you remember when I told you at Atlanta that the war was over?"

"Yes. I asked you why you thought so, and you said that Lee was cut off from the rest of the South and would be even more so after Sherman took Savannah and destroyed the Carolinas. You said if he had any reason, he would surrender and stop the slaughter that was going to ensue in the final months of the war. And I said Lee was not a big enough man and that reason was in short supply."

"You were right," Miller agreed. "In the battle between honor and reason, saving honor wins." Lee even made one last offensive move at Appomattox the day before his surrender. He did it even when it was clear he was surrounded by superior Union numbers and his troops were tired, hungry and dressed in rags, and there was no place to go even if he momentarily broke out.

"What a vain gesture!"

"Vanity! All is vanity, and human life be damned."

Both men were aware that Grant probably manipulated those last engagements to allow Lee to choose the place of surrender, all for the sake of the vanquished general's "honor." With bitterness and resignation, the nurse remarked, "Generals never consult the poor bastards whose life is going to be sacrificed."

"Agreed, but the soldiers seemed to go along," Miller replied. "It never ceases to amaze me. Lee's soldiers seemed to regard him as if he had godlike qualities."

"How men can be deceived."

"I consider Lee's delay of surrender as nothing short of murder," Miller declared.

"Those are strong words."

"I can't help it. That's the way I see it."

Lee surrendered at Appomattox Courthouse, Virginia, on April 9, 1865, but the elation of victory was short-lived. On April 16, Lincoln was assassinated. In short order, Miller felt as if the ground had been cut from beneath him. What was his purpose now that the war was over? Who would guide the future without Lincoln? As he sat outside his field hospital, he could smell lilacs in the air, but he did not experience the joy he usually felt with spring in Iowa. He began to realize that he was going from being someone important performing important work to someone ordinary, again treating run-of-the-mill ailments of farmers and townspeople.

Sherman's army and Miller marched to Washington via Richmond in time for the May 24th Grand Review Parade. Sherman's troops bivouacked around the Capital building, hung in black crepe with its flag at half-mast. Concerned that his ragged, sunburned army would be outshone by General Meade's Army of the Potomac, Sherman ordered some practice drills before the parade. Miller could not have cared less about appearances. There was still work to do in the hospitals. It was a bright, sunny day in Washington, not yet beset by summer heat and humidity.

"It's a good thing, given the amount of horse manure that will soon be dropped on the streets today," Miller remarked to his assistant surgeon.

"Still, the smell of slaughterhouse offal dumped into the Tidal Basin everyday makes me gag," the younger man replied. "I'll be glad to get home to my little village."

Ambulances in Grand Review Parade

Sherman's sixty-two thousand-man Army passed in review before President Johnson for six hours and made up for its lack of precision with bravado. Bringing up the rear was an entourage of medical workers, laborers, freed slaves and a collection of farm animals appropriated during the march through Georgia.

Miller returned to duties at the Army's General Hospital, where the work differed from battlefield operations. Now he was cleaning up medical failures, cutting away gangrenous tissue and amputating limbs where resection had failed. He learned that half of the amputees in the field had developed infections and died. Instead of dealing with a tent full of injured soldiers, he now faced a huge ward of the injured every day. They continually cried out in pain. Miller heard them in his sleep.

Taking a break from his duties, Miller asked an orderly, "Who is that long-bearded man who is here every day ministering to the soldiers?"

When the response was "Walt Whitman, the poet," Miller approached the volunteer nurse and introduced himself.

"Yes, I know who you are," Whitman replied. "I have seen you do surgery. You're one of the best in this sad place."

"Thank you. I'm doing mostly repair work now. We lose too many fine men to infection," Miller admitted. "I think your attention to the patients does more for them than we surgeons. How long have you been here?"

"I came three years ago," Whitman explained. "My brother was wounded at the Battle of Fredericksburg, and I came south to find him. Seeing the wounded soldiers and heaps of amputated limbs motivated me to try to help them, so I came to Washington to do whatever I could for these sad specimens. They are desperate for some expression of affection. Sometimes all I can do is hold the hand of a dying man."

"Both of us feel inadequate to the immensity of the task," Miller replied. "How do you support yourself? I see you here often."

"I was a clerk in the Department of Interior, but I was fired because the Secretary thought my *Leaves of Grass* was indecent. Don't worry, I'll find something else."

"Damn moralists," Miller responded, then asked, "Would you recite one of your poems for me?"

Whitman's face took on an inward expression, as he recited to the doctor and surrounding patients a poem they understood all too well.

Surgeons operating, attendants holding lights, the smell of ether,
    the odor of blood.
The crowd, O the crowd of the bloody forms—
    the yard outside also fill'd;
Some on the bare ground, some on planks or stretchers,
    some in the death-spasm sweating;
An occasional scream or cry; the doctors shouted order
    or calls;
The glisten of the little steel instruments catching the glint
    of the torches;
These I resume as I chant—I see again the forms,
    I smell the odor;
Then hear outside the orders given, Fall in, my men,
    Fall in ….

Headquarters Seventeenth Army Corps, Department of the Tennessee,
Washington D.C. June 3, 1865
Special Orders No. 141
Surgeon J.G. Miller 11th Iowa Inft. Vols. in charge of 4th Division Field Hospital will remain in Washington until he can turn over the medical and Hospital property in his possession, when he will rejoin the Corps at Louisville Ky reporting to the Medical Director.
By command of Maj. Gen; F. P. Blair

But, even after leaving Washington for Kentucky, Miller's work was not yet done.

Head-Quarters, Seventeenth Army Corps,
Medical Director's Office,
Louisville Ky June 25th 1865
Special Orders No. 34
Surgeon J.G. Miller 11th Iowa Inf. Vols. in addition to his duties with his regiment is assigned to duty as one of the Medical Pound for the examination of disabled soldiers for discharge.
By order of Maj. Gen. F. P. Blair
(s) J. W. Boucher, Surgeon U.S. Vols, Lieut. Col. and Med Director, 17th Army Corps.

Finally, Miller was individually mustered out at Louisville, Kentucky, on July 10, 1865. He returned to Iowa and Ruthanna and his daughters, and in a night of passion, sired a son, William. But, he was a changed man. To survive months of bloody amputations, he had distanced himself from the humanity involved. The wounded and dying men became mere commodities to be processed. Now at home, he seemed disconnected, even with his wife and children. He spent a year and a half in the Pennsylvania oil region practicing medicine and dealing in oil.

While he had been successful as an Army doctor, he was not satisfied with his skills. Within the year, he moved his family to Pleasant Hill, Missouri, and enrolled in the College of Physicians and Surgeons in Kansas City, graduating in 1873. He moved again to Atchison, Kansas, and opened a practice. There, daughter Lillie married W.W. Hetherington, the banker's son. But, Miller's wanderlust and fortune seeking were still not satisfied, and in three years the family went to the Black Hills of Dakota Territory where, for four years, he was a surgeon for the Homestake Mining Company and in charge of the Hospital of the Holy Cross controlled by the Sisters of Mercy. The work paid well, and he came back to Atchison and built a new house at 500 Riley at the corner of North Fourth across the street from the home of W.W. Hetherington.

"I'm glad to be close to our daughter and, I appreciate our spacious new house," said Ruthanna, but for all the words of gratitude there was a hint of testiness in her voice.

"If I hadn't gone to the Black Hills," her husband replied "we couldn't have built this house."

"I understand, but I'm telling you now, I'm sick and tired of moving around."

The ultimatum was not completely heeded, and Miller spent the summer of 1881 in the mining region of Gunnison, Colorado, where investors from Atchison and Leavenworth, including L.L. Todd, had organized the Prospect Mining Company. Gold and silver had always acted like a magnet to Miller, and miners paid high fees for his medical services. In the fall he returned to his office above Breman's Drug Store at 421 Commercial Street, Atchison.

500 North Riley, Atchison Kansas

In later years, Miller stopped his adventuring and was devoted to his wife's welfare. When she became ill in 1892, he decided the mild climate of San Diego would be beneficial, and they set out on the journey from Kansas. But, his own health collapsed first. While aboard the California-bound train, John Miller died near Yuma Arizona.

~10~

Civil War Soldiers—The Confederates

Neither Newell D. Todd nor John G. Miller could have imagined that their descendants would intermarry with relatives of descendants of the rebels. Later, they would hear stories parallel to their own from the other side of the conflict. Milton Jeffries Byram, Jr., was the grandson of William Byram of Stafford County, Virginia, who married Susan Phillips and migrated to Kentucky in 1785. Susan used her mother's maiden name, Jeffries, as her son's middle name. Milton, Sr., had moved west along with his cousin Augustus and nephew Peter, and he purchased two hundred forty acres of Missouri land from the government in 1846. The elder Milton Byram was a slave owner, and because of the family's stake in the maintenance of slavery, Milton, Jr., enlisted in the 3rd Regiment, Missouri Infantry, CSA (Confederate States of America). In 1861, he fought at Wilson's Creek, southwest of Springfield, Missouri, in the first major battle west of the Mississippi in what he and his compatriots called the War of Northern Aggression. It could be described as Blue against Grey, except that most of the rebels at Wilson's Creek had no uniforms.

The Missouri Compromise in 1820 essentially had allowed Missouri to be admitted to the Union as a slave state, while banning slavery in the rest of the former Louisiana Purchase. Then in 1854, the compromise was effectively repealed by the Kansas-Nebraska Act that allowed the citizens of these areas to decide the slavery question for themselves. The act had been written by Illinois Senator Stephen Douglas whose planned bid for the presidency made him sensitive to maintaining Southern support. Lincoln was opposed to the compromise, believing as he did that slavery was immoral and should not spread to more states. Further, in the *Dred Scott v. Sandford* decision of 1857, the Supreme Court ruled that Congress did not have the authority to prohibit slavery in territories and that the act admitting Missouri to the Union did not qualify Blacks as citizens.

Missouri's citizens were divided on the question of slave ownership. The governor was sympathetic to the South and organized the Missouri Militia under the command of General Joe Shelby to attack the U.S. arsenal at St. Louis. But the arsenal's commander, Nathanial Lyon, forced the militia to surrender and went on to capture the state capital at Jefferson City where he installed a pro-Union state government. At the end of July 1861, the Missouri State Guard planned to capture Lyon and regain control of the capital. When the opposing forces met in a bloody battle at Wilson's Creek, the rebels prevailed, and the Federals retreated to Springfield. Still, Missouri remained under Union control.

Soon after the Battle of Wilson's Creek, Milton Byram, Jr., took fever and died.

Milton was not the only Southern-sympathizing Byram to die as a result of the conflict. Alvin M. Byram, son of William, a resident of Lexington, Missouri, was killed by Union troops in 1862. As the troops marched through the town shooting off their firearms, a stray bullet hit Alvin. The troops claimed it was an accident. The war touched soldiers, families and civilians, or more accurately "hammered" them.

The guerilla warfare that had started in Missouri and Kansas prior to 1861 continued after Confederate secession, with small bands of mounted raiders wreaking destruction on each other and innocent citizens. Residents of Lexington showed their allegiances by flying either the Union stars and stripes or the Confederate bars and stars. The city council banned all flags in an attempt to keep the peace, but the U.S. Postmaster kept his flag flying. A crowd of armed Rebel sympathizers assembled at the flagpole and chanted, "Postmaster. Postmaster." A bespectacled man in green visor and white shirt, sleeves held by elastic bands, appeared. "Take down the flag, or we will," the crowd yelled. The postmaster tried to answer above the din, "No, the flag must fly above all federal offices." The crowd surged forward, and while one man tried to climb the pole, the mob chanted, "Kill the postmaster."

Alonzo Slayback, a native of Lexington who had recently established a law office in his hometown, was married to Alice Amelia Waddell in 1859. Alice was the daughter of Susan Clark Byram Waddell, formerly of Stafford County, Virginia. Slayback was a known rebel sympathizer. When he heard the shouting that day, he left his office and walked to the post office. At first he stayed on the edges of the demonstrators, but as things grew ominous, he waded into the crowd and shouted, "I will kill anyone who harms the postmaster." Being a known secessionist, his act confounded the anti-Unionists, and they began to disperse without harming the federal employee.

No one was surprised when Alonzo offered his services to Confederate Major General Sterling Price in 1861. After victory at the first Battle of Lexington, Alonzo was commissioned by the Missouri governor as a colonel of a State Guard Cavalry Regiment. While campaigning in Arkansas, he contracted typhoid fever. Although they had been married only a few years before Alonzo left to fight with the rebels, Alice Amelia attempted to obtain a pass through Union lines to care for him. When her request was denied, she thought of a scheme. She knew that Union officials banished women who were known to support guerillas. She made sure everyone was aware of her sympathies. Her subsequent "banishment papers" got her through the lines. Upon arrival in Arkansas, she discovered Alonzo had been moved to Shreveport and was so weak he could not raise his head off the pillow. Alice spent three months in Louisiana nursing him back to health.

In 1864, Alonzo organized a regiment called the Slayback Lancers attached to Joe Shelby's Iron Brigade. Slayback was a red-haired, handsome and dashing officer who inspired his men to boldness and bravery. While serving with General Marmaduke in Arkansas, he deliberately rode into the Union line and shouted, "I challenge anyone to single combat." Immediately, a Union captain rode forward and when within twenty paces fired on Slayback who returned the fire. Slayback's bullet wounded the captain in the leg. Two others came forward to replace him, and one of Slayback's men joined him in exchanging two rounds of fire. The result was another Union cavalryman fallen, while no Confederates were touched. Slayback liked the pomp and flash of war and thrilled to danger. He confided the effect combat had on him to one of his lieutenants: "I have never felt more alive. Would that this war could be settled by personal combat in a large amphitheater with thousands looking on."

Alonzo was part of Price's ten thousand-man Rebel army that fought the Battle of Westport just west of Slayback's hometown. On October 22, 1864, Price's men, along with General Joseph Shelby's troops, fought their way across the Blue River at Byram's Ford and other crossings, driving the Federal's Jennison back to Westport. Slayback had crossed the Blue at Hickman Mills below Byram's Ford. Later his Missouri cavalry was at the center of Shelby and Fagan's Confederate line facing General Curtis's Union line south of Westport and Brush Creek. Curtis set up his headquarters in the Harris House in Westport. Price brought his supply train of five hundred wagons and thousands of cattle with him. The western end of his line was at Shawnee Mission, where Jotham Meeker once ministered to the Indians, and the eastern end was at Byram's Ford.

The next day, Union General Pleasanton, who had been dogging Price, crossed at Byram's Ford, and his men fought their way up from the floodplain to a fifteen foot high limestone ridge that the Byrams' called Potato Hill. There, they flanked Marmaduke's Rebel forces whose sharpshooters were firing from a

Potato Hill

fencerow and two log houses near the crest of the hill, homes once occupied by Augustus and Peter Byram. Pleasonton pressed the attack relentlessly, yelling, ""Rebels, Rebels! Fire, fire, you damned asses!" at Marmaduke's force fleeing northeast across the prairie. In the three-hour battle, four hundred men died at the hill, causing Union Commander Blount to name it Bloody Hill. Now with his main force flanked and unable to penetrate the main Union line along Brush Creek, Price retreated all the way back to Arkansas, burning his wagons, denying them to the enemy. Missouri was now firmly in the Union even though guerilla outbursts continued until the end of the war.

Slayback and his immediate commanding general, Joseph Shelby, did not surrender after the war ended. "I can't live in this new America with its loss of freedoms and states' rights," Alonzo confided to Shelby. Thus he left Alice Amelia alone back in Lexington and, with other Rebel officers, escaped to

Mexico in search of land and a new life. The Iron Brigade veterans crossed the Rio Grande at Piedras Negras on July 4, 1865. They ceremoniously furled their battle flag and submerged it in the river. Alonzo composed these lines: *"Its cause is lost. And the men it led on many a glorious field, in disputing tread of invader dread, Have been forced at last to yield, But this banner and plume have not been to blame, No exulting eye shall behold their shame."*

Things did not start well in Mexico. Slayback became ill and was robbed of everything but his horse and pistols by members of his own party. The prefect of the City of Mexico heard of his plight and brought him to the city to convalesce. During his stay, Slayback met Maximilian, the Austrian newly installed as Emperor of Mexico, and they became good friends. Slayback taught him English in exchange for Spanish lessons. He was named Duke of Oaxaco. The French had used force to put Maximilian on the throne after Benito Juárez had declared a moratorium on foreign debt payments, but when the French departed and Juárez returned to power, Slayback's benefactor was doomed. Maximilian was executed in 1867.

Slayback's mother was anxious for her son to return to America. On his way to Havana where she awaited him, Alonzo stopped to visit with Generals Price and Shelby at the Confederate Colony of Cordova that had been granted them in 1866. The land grant was revoked upon the execution of Maximilian, and the generals later returned to America. Alonzo and his mother went on to Washington to seek a pardon. Upon his return to Alice Amelia in Missouri in 1867, he fathered a daughter, Minette, and set up a law practice in St. Louis. He became a delegate to the Democratic Presidential Convention of 1876 and was elected vice president of the Bar Association of St. Louis.

Alonzo and his brother were St. Louis boosters and wanted some event rivaling Mardi Gras as celebrated in New Orleans. Together they created the Veiled Prophet Ball with much pageantry that attracted fifty thousand participants. One debutante was to be crowned the Queen of Love and Beauty by the Veiled Prophet, whose attire was similar to the Ku Klux Klan regalia. Of course, the first Queen of Love and Beauty was Alonzo's daughter, Minnette.

Alonzo, a charismatic and much sought-after speaker, was asked to deliver the address at the decoration of soldiers' graves at Jefferson Barracks National Cemetery near St. Louis in 1873. The audience seemed to share his view when he said, *"The Union soldiers and officers of St. Louis having in charge the preparations for this celebration, passed a resolution, prompted by their own lofty and humane generosity, to the effect that surviving Confederate soldiers are invited to participate with them in the ceremonies of the day, and that the graves of the soldiers who died in the one cause should be decorated the same as of those who fell for the other."*

He continued, giving the reason he and his comrades in arms had made peace with their side's loss: "*It is apparent that outside of a few heartless agitators each party was sincere in the belief that the other party was inimical to the principles of the Constitution. It was this devotion to Constitutional liberty, as the respective sections had been educated to regard it, that impelled each party to the dreadful onset, and it was this same principle that made peace possible ... Life is too short. They have no time to waste. The present urges. The future beckons. They have something better to do than to cherish revenge. They cannot recall the past. They cannot bring back the dead. They cannot be enemies, and since they have determined to be countrymen, they have resolved to be friends. This day decides that resentment shall not mar the future of our beloved country.*"

The speech emphasized that the war's outcome was the maintenance of the Union and states' rights. No mention was made of slavery or of the *de facto* denial of civil rights to former slaves. Slayback's sentiments could not eliminate instances of desecration of the graves of Union soldiers in the south and Confederate graves in the north.

Slayback had a fateful confrontation with the editor of the St. Louis *Post-Dispatch* in 1882. Believing that the newspaper had impugned the honor of his law partner, Slayback stormed into the editor's office demanding an apology. The editor, a former Union soldier, feared for his life and pulled a gun from his desk. He shot Alonzo in the chest, killing him instantly. The jury at the subsequent trial did not convict the editor, perhaps believing the story going round that a gun had been found in Alonzo's overcoat pocket. Later, an eyewitness came forward with the fact that the gun had been planted. No matter, Alonzo had died as he had fought, seeking honor and devoted to principle as he saw it, asking and giving no quarter. He was survived by his wife and six children.

Despite his violent end, Slayback's conciliatory speech at the national cemetery in the previous decade probably helped heal the wounds of war in that divided territory, as did intermarriage between descendants of Union and Rebel sympathizers in the generations to follow. The participants in the war, North and South, were forever marked by their experiences: Newell, George, Henry, Ira, Morris and Samuel Todd; John Miller; Milton and Alvin Byram; Alonzo Slayback. They were all kin whether knowing or not.

~10~

The Wagon Master

Maysville Kentucky was the port of arrival of the Phillips and Byram families and their slaves in 1785. Maysville and nearby Washington were centers of the slave trade between 1825 and 1840. Unneeded slaves from Virginia and, later, Kentucky were assembled there, some to be auctioned. It was the sight of a slave auction at Washington that inspired Harriet Beecher (not yet married to Stowe) to write *Uncle Tom's Cabin*. Some of the slaves were marched overland to Natchez, and many others were shipped downriver to New Orleans, inspiring the expression "sold down the river." The sight of a coffle of forty enslaved Negro men, women and children in chains was sickening. On his way to Washington one day, Valentine Byram, the hatter son of Lucy and Peter, witnessed a coffle passing by, and, led by a fiddler, they were singing:

O come and let us go where pleasure never dies,
Jesus my all to Heaven is gone,
He who I fix my hopes upon.
His track I see and I'll pursue
The narrow road till him I view.
O come and let us go,
Oh come and let us go where pleasure never dies.

Shadrach, one of Valentine's four slaves, was moved to tears and spoke out, saying, "Massa, dat's not right." Few slaves would dare speak like that to their owners, but the two men had an unusual relationship. When they passed the slave pen run by John W. Anderson just outside of town, they could hear the cries from inside. The little log cabin had formerly been Anderson's slave quarters, but he now used it as a kind of miserable jail where slaves were held until enough were gathered to make the trip south to the cotton and cane fields of Mississippi and Louisiana worthwhile. The slave pen was twenty-one by thirty feet on the ground and twenty-six feet high. Anderson wrote to a colleague in 1831, "I want you to find and purchase all the Negroes you can of a certain description—men and boys from twelve to twenty-five years old and girls from twelve to twenty and no children. Don't give more than four hundred to four hundred fifty dollars for men seventeen to twenty-five years." When Anderson died in 1834 there were thirty-two slaves in his inventory.

Anderson's Slave Pen, restored

In downtown Maysville there was a large two-story brick building with arched windows. One day as Shadrach was passing by with Valentine he asked, "What goes there? I sees a lot of well-dressed men enter from time to time?"

"That's a slave pen of sorts, too." Valentine responded, then, not knowing exactly why, he added, "I have been told that there is a section of the building that is like a nice hotel. Young, attractive women, mostly mulatto, are kept there for buyers to inspect in pleasant surroundings. I understand they're called "fancy girls."

Shadrach looked incredulous and blurted out, "I bet they are taken as mistresses and prostitutes. Massa, dat's not right!" Valentine could not look Shadrach in the eyes and felt ashamed.

The Byrams and Phillips had been slave owners for generations, and it seemed natural to them. But time brought changes for descendent William Phillips, who built a magnificent new house with a two-story pillared porch in downtown Maysville. The townspeople called it Phillip's Folly and were unaware that Phillips had a secret tunnel built that led to the Ohio River. His neighbors did not know that he sheltered runaway slaves and helped them make the two hundred-yard journey across the river to freedom. He was not the only one in Maysville with such secrets. John Paxton was an attorney and innkeeper who catered to the slave traders that came to town. A narrow hidden staircase in the inn facilitated his work on what came to be called the Underground Railroad. This double-dealing did not bother his conscience.

Philips Folly

The town of Ripley, just down river on the Ohio side, was the home of John Rankin, a Presbyterian minister, his wife and thirteen children. His home was high on a hill above the town. Ripley was a center for abolitionists, and Rankin was one of abolition's early advocates. Rumor was that he had helped more than two thousand slaves escape to the North. The slaves walked from Ripley to Lake Erie and, with the help of sympathetic ship captains, entered Canada. The Federal Fugitive Slave Law made Ripley's work dangerous and illegal. Kentucky slave owners offered a cash reward of twenty-five hundred dollars for his murder. Rankin believed his success in eluding capture and death was a miraculous gift of the Lord. Fellow abolitionists, Harriet Beecher Stowe and her father Henry Ward Beecher, frequently visited Rankin.

As long as there was a frontier in the United States, there was always hope that something better lay further west. The Byrams had left Virginia seeking more and better land in Kentucky. Most of their Phillips relatives, including William, were satisfied with their Kentucky lives, but now the Byrams were on the move again, this time heading for Missouri. Would it finally satisfy them?

Lucy and Peter Byram's sons, Augustine and Valentine, were born in Mason County, Kentucky, and there they married Fletcher sisters. Augustine and Catherine Fletcher had six children before she died, then Augustine remarried to Sally Toulson in 1816 and had six more children with her in Nicholas County, Kentucky, including sons Peter and Augustus, Jr. The elder Augustine followed the lead of Daniel Boone and his son Daniel Morgan Boone and, in 1835, headed out to look for land in Missouri. When the census taker arrived in 1840, Augustine was living alone in Jackson County, Missouri, clearing land with his young slave couple and their son. Sarah had remained temporarily in Kentucky with five of their children. Augustine's next door neighbor was Daniel Boone, grandson of the frontiersman, and his wife and children. Nearby was his mother Sarah, widow of Daniel Morgan Boone. Other Kentucky Byrams, all descended from William Byram and Moses Phillips of

Virginia, also moved to Missouri. Among them was Milton Jeffries Byram whose namesake son served and died for the Confederacy in the Civil War.

Brothers Augustus, Jr., and Peter were twenty-three and twenty-one when they moved on their own in 1839 to Kaw Township, in northwestern Jackson County just south of the Missouri River. They brought a slave family with them to help them farm. They had just settled in when gold fever erupted. "Peter, I know you've heard of gold being found in California," Augustus remarked. "There's sure to be money to be made out there."

"There's money to be made right here," the more practical Peter countered. "We're doing OK."

"Yes, but this work is tiresome," the older brother said. "I'm going for the big money. So much that I won't have to work for the rest of my life."

"You've always been a dreamer and risk taker," Peter replied. "It's too much for me."

"You're a stick in the mud of the Blue River down there," mocked Augustus pointing down the hill.

"So be it. When will you go?" Peter replied.

"Next month. Time's awastin'. I'm goin' with a group of others from Independence. You know Linville and Upton Hays and their dad Boone over at Westport?"

"Are you actually going to dig? You know the best sites will probably be claimed by the time you get there."

"I'll size up the situation when I get there," Augustus said with convincing confidence. "We're taking a herd of cattle to sell, and I'll probably set up a mining-supply store and let other poor bastards do the work. I'm taking my share of our savings so I can stock the store. Do you want to invest some of yours in a partnership?

So Peter threw in his lot with his adventurous brother, and as more than a year went by, he did not hear a word from Augustus. He invited his sister Elvira and husband Hiram Widener and their children to help him farm. "Vi, you know Gus could be dead, and we wouldn't know it," he told them. "And there goes my money with him."

After two years, a wagon stopped on the trail below their house. Peter saw a well-dressed man get out and start up the hill, and his face lit up when he recognized his brother.

"Vi, come quickly! Our brother's home."

The three siblings hugged each other, laughed and cried, and the homebodies demanded to hear all about Augustus's experiences. "We were a party of nineteen wagons and sixty men, so we had no problems with the Indians," he recounted. "We followed the Santa Fe Trail, and then followed the Rio Grande River south to the beginning of the Old Spanish Trail, and on to California," the adventurer told them. Like I said before I left, I started a store and did very well. I even staked several miners who I thought had promising claims. That's the way to go with the law of averages. For every five men I outfitted, one is likely to find gold. If you are an individual, and you fail, it's all over and you go home with less than you started with."

"OK, smart guy," Peter said with a bit of irritation in his voice, "Did you come home with gold in your pocket? I see a gold watch and chain dangling from your vest."

"I sure did, I more than tripled our original money," Augustus shot back. "Did you triple yours digging potatoes?"

"Well, no, but I didn't worry about being scalped by Indians on the way out or killed by a drunken miner celebrating his luck or drowning his sorrows."

"Peter, you're no fun! Now that I'm back, I'll be looking for new opportunities to use our capital."

"I'm sorry to tell you that Poppa died just after you left, and I bought his land here in Jackson County from our other sibs."

"Great," Augustus told him. "We still have some capital left."

"We could buy still more land," Peter suggested from his farmer perspective.

"No way. I'm looking for big money and less hard physical labor."

"I bought Poppa's slaves as well, so you won't have to work very hard," Peter offered by way of convincing his brother.

Elvira just shook her head knowing that her brothers couldn't be more different. She wondered how long they could remain partners.

After Augustus returned from California, the brothers continued to farm for a few years. When two of their hired men, Dennis and David, became seriously ill, Peter sought help from Doctor James Parker in Westport. Doctor Parker visited them a dozen times during the month of August 1853, charging Peter forty dollars for his services. Peter thought the treatments were worse than the disease, as the doctor was of the bleeding, purging and puking school of medicine, but the men did recover.

Among Doctor Parker's other patients were J.C. McCoy, Jim Bridger, Daniel Boone's grandson A.G. Boone and the family of Alexander Majors. Peter often purchased supplies from Boone's General Store on Westport Road as well as from McCoy's store. Boone sold everything from groceries to slaves, and McCoy was the son of Reverend Isaac McCoy from Shawnee Indian Mission on the other side of the river. Bridger later left his farm ten miles south of Westport to become a well-known mountain man and guide.

One fine summer day, Augustus and Peter sat on their front porch on a rise overlooking a ford across the Blue River that was used by freighters hauling goods from nearby Independence through Westport to Santa Fe. "You know, Gus, we could be freighters instead of scratching out a living in this damnable dirt," Peter admitted. "Yes, I know that our ancestors have moved steadily west in the search of better land, and now we have succeeded beyond any of them. But times are changing, and perhaps it's time to switch from farming to business. With our combined capital, we have enough to start something else."

Byram's Ford today

Alexander Majors, who was active in the Santa Fe trade, encouraged the brothers to become freighters. Majors' fine house in Westport, built from freighting profits, stood as visible proof to the brothers of the prospects in such a change. The brothers sold some of their land to buy mules and wagons, hired some teamsters and began a freight route from the U.S. Army post at Leavenworth, Kansas, to El Paso, Texas, which they made their headquarters. They expanded with a route hauling military supplies from Leavenworth to Fort Kearney in Nebraska Territory.

Majors joined with W.H. Russell of Lexington and, in 1855 and '56, carried government freight from Fort Leavenworth to western forts. On one trip, cholera felled their drivers who abandoned their wagons at a great loss. Nevertheless, their profits reached three hundred thousand dollars. Russell and Majors got a new contract in 1857, but the goods they were to transport reached Fort Leavenworth late in the summer. Having started off without sufficient time to cross the Rockies before the first snows, the wagon trains were forced to winter over at Fort Bridger where many animals perished from starvation. Majors and Russell lost all the profits they had earned in the previous years.

Freighters were experimenting with different northern routes west beginning in Omaha, Nebraska City, Brownville, St. Joseph, Atchison and Leavenworth, all of which were on the Missouri River and were served by steamboats. The route out of Nebraska City was attractive because it avoided crossing the dangerous mudflats of the Platte River and had excellent access to timber and grass along the way. The city's boosters promised to improve the levee and roads to make better access for the haulers.

An epidemic of Texas fever killed eighty-five of the Byrams' cows in 1858. Gus recognized the tenuous financial situation they were in and told his brother, "We're too small to bear these risks. We need to be part of a larger outfit."

Peter agreed. "Let's use our acquaintance with Majors and ask for a job at his new depot at Nebraska City. We now have experience that would make us valuable to him," he suggested to his brother.

"And, we have something else going for us," Gus expanded on the idea. "One of Russell and Majors's partners now is Bill Waddell, Cousin Susan's husband. This is what families are for." Susan Clark Byram's middle name had been chosen in honor of George Rogers Clark, a famous Kentucky soldier whom her father admired.

The brothers saddled up and headed for Nebraska City where Susan was surprised but happy to see them. "Welcome cousins; good to see you," she said in greeting. "Of course, you'll stay for supper. Bill will be home soon."

"Well, thank you." Peter replied. "Actually we'd like to stay in town much longer. We are looking for jobs in the freighting business."

"You've come to the right place; we are always looking for good men that we can trust. You men wash up and rest a bit while I prepare supper."

Susan Clark (Byram) Waddell

Before Bill got home, Susan told the story of her courtship and life to date. "Bill came to work for your uncle William in Kentucky. He was smitten with me, and I with him. After a two-week courtship, we were married. No use waiting. Father was pleased with the marriage and gave us several Negroes, sheep and fifteen hundred dollars."

"Hey, that's more than we got from our father whose estate was split ten ways," said Peter.

Just then Bill arrived, and Susan told him of her cousins' interest in jobs.

"You couldn't have come at a better time," he responded enthusiastically. "Can you start tomorrow?"

"Sure, we're not going back to Westport and raising potatoes."

As the evening continued, Bill completed the account of their journey to Nebraska. "We operated a dry-goods business in Mayslick until 1835, when we decided to go west to Lexington, Missouri, which was thriving with trade on the Santa Fe Trail and later those heading to the California goldfields."

"I was part of that movement to California, too," said Augustus. "I opened a store for miners."

"That was smart. That's using your head instead of your back," Bill replied with admiration in his voice.

Susan took over the story of her husband's success. "At the age of twenty-nine, Bill built a store near Jack's Ferry where he did well as both a wholesaler and retailer," she told them. "He traded in produce, hemp and grain. He had a lot of self-confidence, and I admired his judgment and cool reasoning ability. We met William Hepburn Russell at Reverend Warder's Baptist Church and became lifelong friends. Russell lived just across the street."

Bill jumped back into the narrative. "Before long, I joined Russell and Majors in freighting out of Leavenworth. We supplied some of the goods from our store and kept their accounts. They built offices, warehouses, a blacksmith shop and a sawmill. It was pretty big business with seventeen hundred men on the payroll. Ten-year-old William F. Cody was hired by Majors as a messenger to accompany him on freighting trips to Utah. The boy would take messages from Majors to other drivers in a long train."

"You don't say!" Gus chimed in. "He done growed up since."

Russell, Majors, and Waddell

Bill went on to explain how much of their business came from the Mormons. Thousands of the believers in the new religion had streamed along the Oregon Trail to Utah from Omaha, following the north bank of the Platte River in Nebraska Territory. The Mormons would not agree to be bound by U.S. law, including the prohibition of polygamy. There was a clash between federal judges and the Mormon Church's own court system. President Buchanan sent twenty-five hundred troops from Leavenworth to Utah under the command of Colonel Albert Sidney Johnston, who later gained fame as a Confederate officer. In February 1858, the Majors and Russell firm received a contract to supply the federal troops involved in this action, and before it was all over, they had carried more than sixteen million pounds of freight to Salt Lake, Utah, using thirty-five hundred wagons, forty thousand oxen and four thousand men. The contracted price was from a dollar and a quarter to three fifty-five per one hundred pounds per one hundred miles to Fort Kearney, then slightly higher for the remainder of the route to the Great Salt Lake.

"Your firm must have made a wagonload of money," said Peter with a smile for his cleverness.

"Yes, but we then ran into a heap o' trouble, too. The Panic of '57 meant that a lot of unemployed men were available, but few were experienced teamsters. Advertisements for teamsters pointed out that the job was a good way to get to the goldfields of California."

"Poor Bill, he was tearing his hair out," Susan told her cousins. "The first wagon train that we sent out was a disaster. Indians made off with a herd of eight hundred beef cattle. Then three trains of wagons and supplies were burned by raiding Mormon militia, with nine hundred oxen lost and costing the firm almost a half million dollars." Obviously, Susan was from a long line of Byram women who kept track of what was going on.

Early in 1858, three-thousand more troops were sent out from Leavenworth. Only Russell, Majors and Waddell (RM&W) were capable of moving the huge amount of necessary supplies—sixteen million pounds. "With higher prices in the new contract, the firm recouped its losses and made loads of money," Susan pointed out. "My Bill sold the farm and built us a mansion in town on the same street where Russell lived. Bill made four trips to the west all together."

Yes, and I loved it," Bill recalled rather wistfully. "There was something exciting about sitting in the lead wagon."

"We left our Lexington business to our boys Milton and George," Susan continued. There was quite a contrast between my ever-calculating, careful husband and Russell with his flamboyance. He is quite a schemer and plunger."

"I just hope it's not the ruin of us all," said Bill, his face momentarily clouded with worry.

"Russell established a new depot at Nebraska City, and Majors brought out his new wife and family, and so here we all are," Susan told them. She went on to say that Majors was frank, honest and affable. He was also a religious man who gave each employee a Bible and hymnal and required him to sign an oath foreswearing profanity and drinking. Once he brought a Cumberland Presbyterian minister to Nebraska City to speak to his men. Yet his religious beliefs did not keep him from owning six slaves, who all managed to run away in 1860, just a year before the Nebraska legislature outlawed slavery. Of course, she didn't know that behind Majors' back, the teamsters made fun of him in song:

> Oh! I'll tell you how it is when you first get on the road:
> You've got an awkward team and a very heavy load;
> You've got to whip and holler (if you swear, it's on the sly)—
> Punch your teams along boys—root hog, or die.

"Let's get back to why you came," said Bill. "Gus, with your business experience, I can offer you a yardmaster position. At fifty dollars per month. And Peter, we need more wagon masters who can manage the teamsters and the animals."

Bill went on to explain that the yardmaster was in charge of organizing the freight and the loading of the wagons at the RM&W depot while the wagon master headed out with the train, keeping the men, animals and equipment moving and making the critical decisions on the trail.

"You'll have a lot of financial responsibility weighing on you," Bill told Peter. "Each wagon costs us about two hundred dollars, and a yoke of oxen goes for around seventy dollars, depending on the supply. I'll send an experienced assistant with you on your first trip."

In a few days Peter was on the trail headed for Denver. He rode ahead of the train on a mule while his assistant rode at the rear. The roundtrip was uneventful, and Peter learned fast. Each evening he practiced with a whip, and by the time they arrived back in Nebraska City, he was an expert.

The wagon master supervised the loading of the wagons and decided where to camp for the night. He roused the men in the morning before dawn and started the train with a loud shout of, "Roll out," usually followed with a string of swear words to make sure he was heard and sufficiently feared. Wagon masters were paid three times as much as the drivers, who were called bullwhackers. And whack the bulls they did, with whips that could reach to the first of a four- or five-yoke hitch.

By his second trip, Peter felt like a veteran as he worked with many new drivers. He enjoyed teaching them to use the fourteen foot-long whip with its rawhide popper at the end. "Now look here, you greenhorns," he instructed as he held the coiled lash in place with his left index finger. "You hold it with both hands and move it quickly above your head. If it is fast enough, the coil will cut loose straight out. That's when you jerk it quickly, and it will pop like a pistol shot." The greenhorns could never get their whips to make that cracking sound, and Peter would goad them further with a challenge. "I'll bet a dollar to anyone that I can cut a small piece from your pants with the whip at twelve feet

without drawing blood." Few took him up, but once in a while a brave soul would accept Peter's challenge, only to find a new tear in his pants and a dollar less in his pocket.

In 1857, RM&W had an inventory of six hundred forty-five wagons worth approximately one hundred twenty-two thousand dollars. Just a year and a half later, they owned thirty-five hundred wagons. Typically, an RM&W supply train contained twenty-five freight wagons plus a cook wagon. Fuel for cooking on the tree-scarce plains was largely from dried Buffalo and ox dung, what the French called *bois de vache*. Each wagon carried two and a half to three tons of freight. The power came from six spans of oxen per wagon. Extras oxen were driven along with the train for replacing animals that went lame or got sick. The bullwhackers walked on the left side of the team next to the nigh ox who was yoked with the off ox. The train averaged about fifteen miles per day. The bullwhackers generally dressed in red or blue checked shirts or plaid flannel, and they carried one or two pistols and a Bowie knife strapped at their sides. The men became covered with dust and filth and had no opportunities to wash any of it off during their long treks. Their diet consisted of fresh buffalo meat when they encountered a herd, plus bacon, beans, dried apples, rice and baked or fried bread, which had been leavened by saleratus or soda. A teamster with a good aim might have the luxury of meadowlark broiled on toast. The wagons often bore painted-on names, such as Old Kaintuck or Lorili, as mementos of some past life. A pair of oxen were fitted with a wooden yoke resting just in front of the hump of their shoulders that were held in place with two bent bows encircling their necks. The removable bows were held in place with a key. Chains connected the yokes to the wagon tongue. Yoking the ox pairs prior to hitching was hard labor for new teamsters, and Peter would patiently show the greenhorns how to move the gear to their oxen by carrying the yoke on their own backs, holding the heavy chains and ox bows in their hands and clasping the iron keys in their teeth.

When the trains had to pass through hostile Indian Territory, twenty to fifty armed guards might go along as well as. Luckily, Peter never had a serious fight during his passages, as the size of his trains tended to scare off the typically small raiding parties. He heard of one train whose men would scalp any Indian they killed and trade the scalps in Denver to Jews for suits of clothes. The Jews then took them east and sold them as relics.

Peter was more than busy organizing and overseeing RM&W trains to Utah. He and Gus had also started a small freighting company of their own. Long days on the trail gave Peter time to reflect that he was thirty-two years old and not yet married. Then in May, he was putting together a train of wagons four abreast in front of RM&W headquarters on main street of Nebraska City when he looked up to the second story and saw a pretty young woman sitting at the window watching him. He swaggered a bit on his mule knowing that she was taking him in. And indeed, she was. After the train left town, Mollie Dorsey inquired as to the wagon master's name. The young woman had come to Nebraska with her family when her father obtained land under the Preemption Act of 1841 The Dorsey family had traveled by train from Indianapolis to St. Louis, then took a steamboat to Nebraska City. The farm was on the Little Nemeha just thirty miles south of Nebraska City, but Mollie had moved to town to keep house for Mrs. Burnham, a family acquaintance.

Wagon Trains forming up, Nebraska City

When Peter returned from Utah, he sent his compliments to Miss Dorsey and asked to call before leaving on the supply train heading out in July 1858. On the day before her suitor was to call, Mollie broke a tooth. She had no time to visit the dentist for a replacement, but Mr. Burnham assured her that she could fashion such a realistic-looking tooth of white wax that Mr. Byram would not know the difference.

With her wax tooth in place, Mollie welcomed Peter as Mrs. Burnham withdrew from the parlor to leave them alone. Their conversation covered many topics, but Mollie did not tell Peter that she was already engaged. A bit of flirtation never hurt anything, she thought. Unfortunately, after Peter told her a raucous story, she laughed so hard that the wax tooth fell out. Covering her mouth, she bolted from the room. After a short time, Mrs. Burnham returned to the parlor and explained, "Miss Dorsey has been taken ill. Please call again another day."

Peter was not discouraged by the girl's strange behavior, and a year later when he was in town, he visited Miss Dorsey at the school building where she was now a teacher. He had thought about her many a cold night on the trail and was anxious to make her his bride. By then, he knew about her fiancé, but since she was teaching school, she wasn't likely to be married anytime soon. Standing in front of the teacher's desk, Peter wasted no time in getting to his mission.

"I have a good job with Russell, Majors and Waddell," he reminded her. "I could make a good home for you, and you could be done with teaching."

"But, I enjoy teaching," Mollie replied. "I'm quite independent."

"You can't be a schoolmarm forever, living in a bedroom in someone else's house," Peter insisted. "Will you marry me?

Mollie was taken aback. "I won't accept your proposal. You insult me. Goodbye, and I don't want to see you again!" The following year soon after her twenty-first birthday, Mollie married Byron Sanford and moved with him to Colorado. Byron never had a good job and finally joined the Army to obtain a secure income.

Undaunted, Peter kept up his hunt for a wife. It happened that a RM&W clerk named Nathan L. Simpson had been married to Maria Meeker since 1851 and for about half of the marriage he'd also had Maria's little sister Emeline in his household after their missionary parents' deaths in 1855. One day when Peter was in the freighting office, he asked Nathan to introduce him to Emeline. This time Peter went slower and applied more charm. He would be sure his intentions would be evident to the young lady before he put forth a proposal. Using a purchasing trip to Independence, Missouri, as an opportunity to express himself clearly, he wrote Emma the letter he had promised her before leaving.

Independence Mo, May 8th, 1859

Miss Emma Meeker,

Dear miss, it may possibly surprise you a little when you cast your eyes to the bottom of this letter and see from whom it comes, but be you surprised, offended, or pleased; as I always had a desire to make known to you the high estimation and esteem I had for you but being exceedingly bashful myself in such matters and knowing your aversion to flattery, and thinking that you might not appreciate the compliment (if such you take it to be) in the true sense in which I would have offered it; I never intentionally made known my feeling in the matter; but being here at a safe distance, and knowing that I am prompted by none other, than the purest motives, and knowing that I am prompted by none other, than the truest motives, I feel that if I should possibly incur your displeasure, the enathemas that you might heap upon my innocent head would be of no affect. But why should I feare thus? I who have always looked upon you (though unknown to you probably) with feelings of admiration and spoke of you always in the highest terms of praise, when occasion presented itself, I fear that I am doing you an injustice to think that you would get offended at me, yet I know and feel my unworthiness, when compared to yourself, so strongly, that I could not help my fears arising. You know that I told you that I would write to you when I got down here, but from the language of your countenance at the time (if I did interpret it right—which I hope I did not) I inferred that you did not beleave I would, nor did you much care weather I did or not although you sayd "well" had you even said no, I nevertheless would have written a letter to you, and felt confident that you would condesend to read it from curiosity, if not from a kind and just appreciation of the motives which promted me to write, which are the same that promts every one to make known these feelings, which, under certain circumstances, and at least once in the life of every individual, are aroused in his bosom by some unseen power, and often continue to dwell there long after the object which, excited it, has faded away, and even when his better judgment tells him, that it is all folly, and useless to waste those feelings in placing them upon an object which they could not expect to gain, for it is all "loves labour lost."

What ever influences may have been brought to beare upon your mind against me, by the agency of other persons, or by my conduct at particular times, from which you may have formed an opinion, of me, either good or bad, I shall always look upon you, as nearest to my ideal of perfection, a being who I always have had pictured in my mind, the perfect embodiment of purity,

loveliness, and virtue and all that is noble and generous in the female caracter. I regard you as one who at all times and under all circumstances, should command the respect, admiration which I have formed in my emagination, or not, I don't think that I could find one that comes nearer to it than yourself, and as my opinion is, to a certain extent governed by their opinion of me did I now that the feelings which I entertain for you was reciprocated, or was echoed back, even half as fervently my ideal of perfection would be complete in you, and I would look no more on this earth for it.
(turn to the next sheet)

The last page was missing. It had been torn off in the mail. But Emeline knew who it was from and she read it with more than idle curiosity. She showed the letter to Maria. "Sister, Sister, what shall I do? He's not much of a speller, but I do like him a lot."

"Follow your heart and instincts," came the reply. When Peter returned to Nebraska City and called on Emma, they had a good laugh about the missing sheet and even though Emma asked him what the rest of the letter said, she didn't wait for his reply. "If it is a proposal of marriage," she told him with candor, "I accept."

Peter and Emeline were married at the Simpson residence in Nebraska City in December 1859 by Reverend Giltner. All of the Majors, Simpsons and Waddells attended the wedding, including Nathan's brother, Richard, who was married to Missouri Amanda Majors, daughter of Alexander Majors. Intermarriage among the families connected with the firm of RM&W was common. Business brought families together, and family ties provided trustworthy employees.

Emeline had been well educated, beginning at age ten at Wesleyan Female College in Cincinnati, then the Female Institute in Camden Point, Missouri, and finally Stephens College in Columbia, Missouri. She followed a course of study including natural philosophy, mental and moral philosophy, astronomy, botany, chemistry, physiology, geology, history and ancient and modern languages. Emeline's superior education proved to be a point of contention between her and her unlettered husband. "Pete, I'm bored in this uncultured town," she complained. "There's nothing but forty-something swearing and drunken bullwhackers in our boarding house."

"Hey, those teamsters help buy our groceries," replied Peter. "If you want some culture, you're going to have to organize it yourself."

"OK, that's just what I'll do," Emeline asserted. "I'll start with women's groups at church and organize some literary discussions and maybe put together some evenings of piano and song, plus some plays."

Emeline's days soon became quite full with the births of their first child, Claude, in 1861 and, two years later, of Eleanor named, of course, for Emeline's beloved mother.

Augustus also married in 1859 to Eleanor Wetzel of Missouri, the sister of his boss's second wife, Susan. Their first three children were born in Nebraska Territory: Fanny in 1860, Henry the following year and Sarah in 1863. Fanny would marry Calvin C. Burnes in Atchison, Kansas. There, Burnes would develop eleven business blocks, including the Byram Hotel named after his wife's family.

Gold was discovered on Cherry Creek near Pikes Peak, Colorado, in 1858. Activity was greatest the following year when one hundred thousand Fifty-Niners, as they came to be called, flooded into the territory. The rush continued until 1861. Individual wagons filled with would-be miners headed west bearing signs that declared, "Pikes Peak or Bust." Some of the prospectors later returned with the signs rewritten to say, "Pikes Peak Busted." These miners, like the Utah army before them, needed supplies. Among the Pikes Peak provisioners were the Byram brothers who hauled ten thousand sacks of flour to Denver trailed by 2,000 head of cows. There was a difference of opinion whether oxen or mules were the best draft animals. Some liked oxen because they were docile and the Indians did not try to capture them. But, for trade to Denver, Peter and Augustus preferred mules because they were faster, and timely arrival in Denver could be the difference between profit and loss. Once, the Byrams' one hundred wagonloads of flour arrived in Denver during a shortage of that essential foodstuff, and the brothers made a magnificent profit.

At that same time, RM&W were expanding their company to include retail stores, express lines and mail services as well as freight hauling. Their stagecoach line was officially the Central Overland California & Pikes Peak Express, but the employees reinterpreted the acronym COCPPC as "Clean Out of Cash and Poor Pay Company." The stage service required a huge investment in stations and fifteen elegant Concord coaches that ran between St. Joseph and Salt Lake, and they borrowed money to make it possible. Ironically, the Byrams' independent company freighted the material to build and supply these stations.

Majors had his own small freight line and also supervised RM&W military freighting from Westport, Kansas City. With Majors spending most of his time in Kansas City, Peter acted as his agent in Nebraska City while running his own line as well. The Byrams would accept freight delivered to St. Joseph by the Hannibal & St. Joseph Railroad and haul it to Nebraska City. Peter boasted that he could deliver St. Joseph freight to Denver one week sooner than shippers using other routes. The railroad being built out from Chicago to Omaha had reached the middle of Iowa in 1861.

Russell, the plunger, had the romantic idea of carrying mail by horseback from St. Joseph, Missouri to Sacramento. The ever-practical Susan Byram Waddell thought the idea was risky and insisted that if her husband was going ahead with the idea that he first deposit one hundred thousand dollars of their money in an account in her name only. Thus the Pony Express was born in April 1860, following some of the route and stations belonging to the COCPPC. Among the large crowd attending the inaugural departure in St. Joe was Alice Amelia (Waddell) and husband Alonzo Slayback who had drawn up the partnership papers for the company. The rider tucked the letters into pockets, or mochila, on a specially made saddle, and he was off to a cheering crowd. The first letters took ten days to reach Sacramento via Salt Lake, compared to twenty-five days on the southern route used by the Butterfield Overland Mail stages. The speed came at quite a cost. The riders, including Bill Cody who rode one section, suffered terribly from the weather and rugged conditions, and soon reliable replacements became hard to find. Russell had paid one hundred thousand dollars to set up and equip the service, and monthly expenses were thirty thousand plus miscellaneous costs. Indian attacks resulted in losses of another seventy-five thousand. The Paiute chief, Winnemucca, hated the whites for taking his land. His raiding bands attacked all mail carriers and destroyed every rest station between California and Salt Lake. The government should have reimbursed RM&W for the Indian damages but it didn't. Federal receipts and subsidies came to only about five hundred thousand, not even enough to cover the total monthly operating expenses during the company's brief run.

Even as the Pony Express captured everyone's imagination, Susan's fear proved well-founded. The firm went bankrupt and ceased operation in the fall of 1861 after being in operation for only sixteen months. Russell's idea was a good one, but it had come too late. Thanks to the likes of Jeptha Wade and Western Union, the transcontinental telegraph made the Pony Express obsolete, and transcontinental train service was pushing its way toward completion.

By 1861 RM&W was dying. Unable to recoup the cost of establishing the Pony Express and the Overland Stage, Russell was desperate and persuaded a government clerk to loan him some bonds. The trouble was that the clerk had no authority to do so, resulting in a scandal and Russell's arrest for using stolen goods. He was acquitted, but the firm's creditors foreclosed, and he and his once-rich partners were suddenly impoverished. Majors, only 46, struggled on. Russell found new partners with whom he freighted and ran a stage out of Leavenworth until after the Civil War.

The Byrams were becoming more and more independent and Peter felt a flush of pride when he saw his name in the paper. The *Nebraska City News* of May 25, 1861 noted that "Messrs. Byram will send out two or three heavy trains a week to Pikes Peak guarded by thirty armed men. ... Drawn by six to twelve yoke of oxen and loaded with three to five tons of freight, the heavy wagons carried an amazing variety of goods: food, grain, clothing, whiskey, mining machines, lumber, arms and ammunition."

The Civil War touched the lives even of those far removed from the battles. Peter and Augustus joined the Union League and swore an oath of allegiance to the Union. At a meeting to raise money to pay bonuses to Otoe County draftees, Peter pledged two hundred dollars. The brothers realized their loyalty was suspect since they and their former employers were all slave owners, and they made clear their Union sympathies.

The Byrams recognized their opportunities as RM&W's fortunes plummeted. Augustus told his brother that he wanted to buy all of the failing firm's wagons and livestock. Peter's more conservative nature made him leery. "Wait a darned minute," he responded. "We have expanded little by little. It was Russell's rapid growth with borrowed money that got them into trouble. What makes you think that we could succeed where RM&W failed? We have a good business; why take on a huge risk? Why be greedy?"

"You're going soft on me again," Gus taunted. "Their freighting was fine. They just made a huge mistake with the Pony Express."

"You can say that again," Peter agreed. "A blind man could hear the telegraph coming that would spell the end of horse-carried mail."

"Now you're making my point. The problem was the ill-advised Pony Express, not the freighting business."

With Peter's reluctant agreement, the brothers bought RM&W's wagons and stock and became completely independent freighters in 1861.

By this point, Majors' business holdings had dwindled to a single small freighting company owned by his wife as protection from creditors. He was frequently a subcontractor for the Byrams, his former employees. Whereas RM&W had freighted mostly military goods, the Byrams carried private freight. They also entered the stage-express business, incorporated as the Nebraska City, Fort Kearney and Denver City Freight and Express Company.

Peter's conservative approach seemed to find support with Augustus as the brothers discussed the plight of their old employer and wondered what lessons were to be learned. "They expanded too fast on borrowed money. Then when cash flow fell, their creditors descended upon them," Peter reiterated. "I know the temptation for RM&W was to respond immediately to the government's needs to supply a large number of troops for the Mormon War. I'm not sure if I could have refused the contract and told the government that such a large amount of freight was impossible to move to Utah in a short time. Russell and Majors should have demanded a substantial amount up front before a pound was moved. Instead, the firm 'bet on the come' to finance the Pony Express, but the government never came."

"Let's resolve to finance all of our big outlays for equipment and warehouses out of our accumulated earnings," Gus proposed, setting their business on a course of slow, sensible expansion. In 1862, the brothers built an immense warehouse on the levee in Nebraska City. They expanded their business to include salt manufacture at Salt Springs near Lincoln on the Nebraska City-Fort Kearney Road. Their wagons transported as much as all other Nebraska City freighters combined, and they hauled three million pounds of goods to Denver. In the winter of 1861-'62, they wintered two thousand head of oxen and cattle in Colorado, and when they brought them back to Nebraska City, the herd numbered five thousand. They built a two-story fireproof warehouse in Denver and went into wholesaling. But all was not roses and honey. A heavy snow in late April 1862, killed a thousand head of their beef cattle The risk of ruin was always present. Peter was always aware that if it happened to RM&W, it could happen to them.

During one of Peter's business trips to Denver in 1862, who should he run into on the street but his first love, Mollie Dorsey Sanford. In cordial small talk they revealed that they were both happily married. Peter asked if Mollie would like to go home to Nebraska to visit her folks. She admitted she was very homesick, having not seen her parents since moving to Colorado. Yet Peter's offer to give her a pass on any of his stagecoaches was met with a sharp rebuff. Mollie was not going to be in his debt even after years of deprivation with her poor husband. Both still had unsettling memories of that summer afternoon when Peter had awkwardly proposed.

The later years of all three partners of RM&W were marked by hardship, penury, and obscurity. After the bankruptcy of the Pony Express, Bill Waddell and Susan went back to Lexington, Missouri, to their spacious house at the corner of 13th and South Street. Bill never engaged in business again and their savings shrunk. They were caught up in the shifting tides of the Civil War. One of their sons was killed on the steps of their house defending a young slave. Their home was raided several times by each side, and Bill was accused of being disloyal to the Union. He signed an oath of allegiance to the United States to quiet the charge. Bill was doubly suspect because his sister, Alice Amelia, was married to Alonzo Slayback, a Confederate officer. The firm's angry creditors challenged him and he had to sell some of his land for taxes. He died a broken man in 1872 at age sixty-five at the home of their daughter. His widow did not have enough money left to meet all of their debts. Alexander Majors moved to Salt Lake and furnished railroad ties for the Union Pacific. He witnessed the driving of the Golden Spike upon completion of the transatlantic railroad. He was penniless when Buffalo Bill Cody found him in Denver, and took pity on his old boss and brought him into his Wild West Show. Majors died at age eighty-six in 1900. Russell lost his twenty-room mansion with its formal garden, stable and coach house before his death in 1872.

The Byrams, on the other hand, did very well from 1859 thru 1863. But they could see that the glory days of freighting from Nebraska City were numbered by the coming of the railroad. Nebraska City's role as a transportation hub was going to lose out to Omaha, where continuous rail service between East and West was realized when the Chicago and Northwestern Railroad reached the Union Pacific line in 1867. But the brothers had already moved on to Atchison in 1864, choosing the town for its rail connections to the East and the westbound Smoky Hill Trail that took a more direct route across central Kansas to Denver than the Platte trail out of Nebraska City. The Byrams also foresaw the business implications of the western freighting boom that came as the war ended and western migration picked up and new mines were being developed in Utah and Montana. An economist would later call their adaptability "creative destruction" in which a businessman had to be nimble to remain on the creative rather than the destructive side of economic movement. Atchison's newspaper, *The Freedom's Champion*, welcomed the Byrams as "men of capital, energy, and experience who were said to have realized profits to the amount of $50,000 annually for the past five years."

Peter had discussed the relocation with Emeline. "We could keep moving west to Denver or even Montana and Utah," he told her, "but I'm getting tired of being away from you and the children, of hard living, poor food and miserable shelter."

"You don't have to convince me. Further pioneering on the frontier does not appeal to me either," Emeline replied. "It is time to settle in a more civilized place, to put my education to better use and to raise our family."

"Atchison will put us closer to the traditional haunts of the Byrams and Meekers," Peter concluded.

Peter and Emeline's life was full as seven more children were born in Kansas: Edward, Theodore, Ruth, Paul, Virgil Parker, Albert and Warren Peter, whom everyone called Jim for reasons unknown. The nickname would stay in the family for generations, again for reasons unknown. Atchison at that time was the terminus of rail lines from the east while trade over the southern wagon route to Santa Fe remained viable for a few years. The Atchison Commercial Directory of 1865 at the close of the Civil War included a listing for the brothers' business: *A.&P. Byram, Government Contractors and Freighters, Trains Run to Montana, Utah, Colorado and All Points West. Private freight will be forwarded by our trains to all points by which our trains run. Office in Price's Block.*

Returning from Fort Laramie, a wagon train of twenty-six wagons owned by Peter and his partner, Howes, along with two other immigrant parties, were attacked along the Platte at Plum Creek between August 7 and 9, 1864. A hundred Indians killed several of the men in the party and abducted one of the women in what became known as the Plum Creek Massacre. When Peter learned of the attack, he was mighty glad he was no longer a wagon master.

The company continued to freight from Atchison and Leavenworth to New Mexico until 1868. That year, Peter returned to his first love, farming, and bought one thousand acres five miles west of Atchison near a crossroads community called Shannon. He built a two-story, white clapboard house in the Italianate style, complete with cupola. It was comfortable but not pretentious. He finally had a house of his own as fine as Majors' mansion in Westport, fulfilling the ambition that had attracted him to the freighting business fifteen years before.

Four hundred acres of Peter's farm were under cultivation, with an additional four hundred acres in tame grass and the rest in one thousand forest trees. He now called himself a stockman and farmer. "I quit farming to become a freighter, and now I am a farmer again," Peter recalled to Emeline. "I guess I am still seeking land." At the same time, Peter hadn't entirely cut himself off from commerce, in 1866 joining Gus in a partnership with William Hetherington in the Exchange Bank of William Hetherington of Atchison. They also became partners with G.W. Gillespie dealing in native lumber, lathe and shingles, materials in great demand by builders in fast-growing Atchison.

Papa's home. Shannon - Byram Farm

    In 1870, Eliza Meeker was twenty-one and living with her sister Emeline and brother-in-law Peter on their Kansas farm. Orphaned at a young age, she had finished her schooling at Brownell Hall in Omaha in 1864. The girls' school, established by the Episcopal Bishop of Nebraska City, was a place of fashion and frivolity as well as education. The older girls wore braids either coiled at the back or around the head. Hoop skirts, full dresses, undersleeves and lace collars, turbans and nubias were in style. The girls made up riddles and wordplay for their amusement. One riddle asked, "Why is one of the young ladies of Brownell Hall more to be admired for her virtues than Moses? Because she is Meeker." After Eliza's graduation, she visited her oldest sister Maria in Nebraska City on her way via steamboat to Atchison where she would live with the Byrams until she married and moved to Byars, Indian Territory, Oklahoma. Eliza was aware of the irony that she, the daughter of Indian Missionary Jotham Meeker, was part of the white invasion of the last Indian Territory promised as permanent lands to the Kansas tribes.

Augustus Byram had no inclination to become a country gentleman like his brother. He was a full-fledged capitalist, always hungering for more wealth and power. Now he was planning to run for statewide office.

"Gus, why do you want to get into politics?" Peter asked him. "Don't you have enough to do with all of your business interests?"

"Politics and business go together. The rules of the game can make or break a business," Gus explained. "Remember how much time Russell spent lobbying in Washington."

"Yeah, and it got him into a heap of trouble," Peter recalled with sarcasm. "But I might as well save my breath. You never listen to me."

"If I listened to you we'd still be digging potatoes at Westport," said Gus, getting in the last dig, as usual.

Augustus was elected to the Kansas Legislature in 1868, the year his fifth child, Alice, was born. Their household included three domestic servants, one of whom was born in Ireland. The immigrant Irish now filled the role formerly occupied by slaves.

The brothers had anticipated with the completion of the Santa Fe Railroad to the Colorado border in 1872 that the days of the Santa Fe Trail as a main southern transportation route to the West would be over. The iron horse had replaced mules and oxen. Augustus was one of the incorporators of the Atchison and Nebraska Railroad. "If you can't beat 'em, join 'em," he remarked as he considered the demise of their freighting business.

Augustus withdrew from his partnership in the Bank in 1871 to invest in other ventures. On one of Augustus's several trips west, his interest in the potential of mining resumed. In 1875 two miners, James Ryan and Samuel Hawk, sank a shaft in Beaver County, Utah, near the town of Milford and found chlorargyrite silver only ten feet from the surface. The silver-rich rock was the color of horn, and shavings produced with a pocketknife curled like a ram's horn, inspiring the property's name--the Horn Silver Mine. Although the mine would become one of the richest mines in the West, even the world, the prospectors were fearful that the deposit was not very extensive, and sold out the year after they discovered it. The mine went for twenty-five thousand dollars to a partnership of Allen Green Campbell, Matthew Cullen, Dennis Ryan and Augustus Byram. Campbell, the most experienced of the partners, had made a lot of money as a placer miner in Montana. The partners erected charcoal kilns and smelting works and developed the ore body, extracting twenty-five thousand tons of high-grade ore that yielded from seventy to two hundred ounces of silver per ton.

Augustus borrowed twenty-five hundred dollars from William Hetherington & Co. to buy his way into the partnership. The contract provided

Horn Silver Mine, Utah

that Hetherington was to receive a one-eighth interest in the mine. From 1876 to 1879, total value of mine production was more than two and a half million dollars, of which almost fifty percent was paid out in dividends.

The Byram brothers' relationship had grown strained and they rarely conversed, but when Peter ran into Gus on a trip to Atchison he couldn't help but ask Gus about his business practices. "There are rumors around town that you borrowed money from Hetherington to help buy the mine and now refuse to honor your contract," he said pointedly. "This reflects on our good name."

"Contracts, contracts," Gus replied dismissively. "Don't believe all you hear."

After that encounter, the brothers stopped speaking entirely.

Augustus had, in fact, paid back the twenty-five hundred-dollar loan, but he refused to acknowledge Hetherington's claim to one-eighth interest in the mine.

If the Horn Silver were going to reach full potential a railroad stub line had to be built to the mine. There was no water at the mine and no fuel for the smelter, all of which had to be shipped in by wagon. Lycurgus Edgerton, an associate of Jay Cooke, a railroad tycoon who'd suggested that the Union finance the Civil War by issuing bonds, called Cooke's attention to the mine, and together they traveled to Utah to inspect the property. Even though Edgerton died of a heart attack en route, Cooke continued with the inspection and liked what he saw. Unfortunately, the financial genius, happened to be broke after the Franco-Prussian War and the Panic of 1873 ruined his promotion of bonds to construct the Northern Pacific Railroad. A panic had followed a period of overextension, speculative excesses and fraud, notably the infamous Crédit Mobilier scandal. As a result of the financial collapse, even Cooke's mansion near Philadelphia had been taken by creditors. Nevertheless, he was a great organizer as well as visionary financier, and he persuaded the mine owners and the Mormon Church to each provide a quarter of the capital needed for building of the railroad spur to the Horn Silver Mine.

Then Cooke went to the Salt Lake City office of Sidney Dillon of the Union Pacific to get the rest. There he was greeted as an old friend. Cooke had forgotten that he had met Dillon once before, but Dillon had not. "I remember well the twenty thousand you loaned me when I was in financial trouble" he said. "What can I do for you now?"

Cooke explained the need for a rail extension to the mine. Dillon excused himself from the room and returned with a short, black-bearded man. "Let me introduce Jay Gould," he announced to Cooke. Cooke outlined the plan for the mine and explained that a rail line to service it could be built for ten thousand dollars per mile. Gould liked the plan and, together with Dillon, guaranteed the remaining half of the necessary capital. The Utah Southern Railroad, with Gould and Dillon as major stockholders, was completed to Frisco, Utah, in 1880.

The partners gave an option to Jay Cooke in exchange for his promise to build a railroad to the mine. In negotiating the sale, the four mine partners chose Allen Green Campbell to go to New York to meet with Cooke and deliver the mine title. When Campbell was asked to sign the report describing the mine at the meeting, he refused, saying, "I can't sign that report." Cooke was stunned and after a strained silence asked, "What could you sign?" Campbell said "I could sign a truthful report," and he proceeded to describe the mine in great detail that only someone deeply familiar with mining could do. He described the size of the laterals, the assay of the ore, the costs of mining, hauling and smelting, all as the basis for calculating the mine's value. Cooke's accountant made the calculations and concluded the mine was worth at least three hundred thousand more than the agreed-on price. "I am not asking for more," Campbell told them. "I just wanted to have the facts straight in the report. We agreed previously to five million dollars." The financial wizards who had never lifted a shovel gained new respect for the uncultured western miner.

The Horn Silver deal was a godsend for the bankrupt Cooke. He sold his share to Charles Francklyn plus receiving a commission of one million dollars. Cooke set about reacquiring his lost homes and was back in business again. He was thoughtful enough to give some shares to Edgerton's widow. It was Edgerton, after all, who brought his attention to the mine.

The small-town financier who'd stood to gain a fortune from his early involvement was not so lucky. Yet Webster Hetherington, the bank founder's son, showed amazing acceptance whenever his wife pressed him about pursuing his rightful return from Augustus Byram.

"I know, Lillie, it's hard for you to accept," he told her. "Lawyer Balie doesn't understand it either, but money isn't everything. We have enough. What would I do with much, much more? Big money just corrupts. And besides, I don't want to sue a former business partner and create a big scandal. It might not be good for my bank."

Lillie could not be satisfied with such an offhand attitude toward the loss of a fortune. "Would you please bring me the contract from the office," she insisted to her husband. "I would like to read it."

At supper the next evening, she took the contract in hand and read it out loud.

Atchison, Kansas, Feb. 7, 1876

Received from Wm. Hetherington & Co. twenty–five hundred dollars as purchase money for one-eighth interest in a silver mine situated in Beaver County, Utah, in the district of San Francisco, owned at this time by the firm of Hawk and Byram, and I hereby agree to return to Wm. Hetherington & Co. deed to one-eighth interest in said mine, and hereby acknowledge receipt of said twenty-five hundred dollars.

(s) A. Byram

"That seems pretty clear to me, an open and shut case.," Lillie went on. "I've spoken with your cashier at the bank, and he said that Horn Silver stock is now worth three dollars and twenty-five cents per share and paying big dividends. If the contract were enforced, you would be entitled to two million dollars and retain a million dollars of the stock besides."

"Let it be, Lillie," Web said with a firmness in his voice that announced the case was closed.

Once comfortably established in their new farm home, Emeline had a yen for assembling family and friends. "Peter, let's have a reunion of all our family and the folks from our days in the freighting business in Nebraska City," she suggested.

"That's a great idea," Peter agreed, "But, are you sure you are strong enough? "

"Yes, this is something I really want to do."

"Well then I will hire neighbor women to help you."

"We could invite Maria and her husband who now live close by in Westport. They can bring Nathan's brother and family," Emeline stated enthusiastically. "It's been a long time since sister Maria was here. Then there is your cousin Susan and Bill Waddell over at Lexington, and your sister Elvira and husband Hiram here in Atchison County. And, of course, your brother Gus."

"I don't see much of Gus. He's always traveling looking for properties to buy."

"He must be home occasionally since he and Eleanor just had their fifth child. It would be good to see as many of our family's children as possible. I want to show off our own children."

"Do you think Russell and Majors would come?"

"I hope there are no hard feelings after we bought their wagons and stock when they went broke," Emeline said. "We can invite J.P. Brown. You knew him when you were both freighting out of Atchison before he helped the railroads take over moving goods to the West."

"We can have a grand picnic here in our yard and everyone can stay a few days here at the farm or in Atchison," Peter added. "We can slaughter a couple of hogs and have a barbecue."

The reunion was a grand success. When all the guests were assembled, Gus was conspicuous in his absence. After the great feast, J.P. Brown rose and offered a toast that he remembered from his hungry days in Ireland: "May your hand be the hand that sticks the pig, and may the pig be yours."

Peter asked J.P. to explain. "When neighbors got together to butcher a hog, it was an honor to be asked to bleed it," he told his host. "And, since few had meat, it was even better if the pig was yours." After that, it was a contest to see who could tell the tallest tale of their days driving wagons west. As the reminiscences continued, the trail got dustier, the bullwhackers more belligerent, the Indians fiercer, the breakdowns more frequent and the profits larger.

"We are the successful survivors, and it would be easy to conclude that we were smarter than those who failed," J.P. opined, "but I know there's a lot of luck to it—a certain randomness to the world."

"No, I give myself more credit than that. Some of those who failed took on debt too fast, and I never did," said Peter.

"Don't forget my partner who got shot by thieves coming back from Virginia City," J.P. countered. "It could have happened to any of us."

"You have a point. I tend to forget my own narrow misses—the blizzards, Indians, breakdowns, price changes," Peter conceded. "They slip from my mind because I never told my wife about them."

All present chuckled.

This was to be Emeline's last grand affair. She died in 1880 at age 40. Perhaps giving birth to nine babies, one dying in infancy, was too much for her. Peter was disconsolate and drew his children around him.

Peter and Emeline Byram

The late nineteenth century was marked by the beginning of the organized labor movement and the strikes called to put some clout into workers' demands for improved working conditions. One hundred men struck the Horn

Silver Mine in March 1882, taking possession of the works and holding the management under guard. Mine Superintendent Hill petitioned Utah Governor Murray to halt the strike through either a court order or by military action. The right to collective bargaining was not yet established, and any kind of group action by labor was regarded as a conspiracy against the business corporation which was accorded rights as if it were an individual to be protected by court injunctions and finally the police or army.

Mining is dangerous work, and profit-driven owners often skimped on safety features. A major cave-in at the Horn Silver Mine occurred in 1885. Rain and snow had soaked the ground, and the extra weight caused the mine tunnels to collapse. The night shift had come to the surface and the day shift was preparing to go down when mine officials stopped them after becoming aware of trembling in the mine. The cave-in was so violent that shock waves broke window glass fifteen miles away in Milford. Fortunately, no lives were lost, but a new shaft had to be constructed. In this era before workplace safety regulations, workers were presented with take-it or leave-it employment at the owners' whim. Each year, approximately a third of all miners were killed on the job, and only half of their families received any compensation .

The boom town of Frisco, named after the nearby San Francisco Mountains, had risen near the mine, and much to the chagrin of the Utah's Mormons, it was a den of inequity, containing at least twenty saloons, plus houses of prostitution. There were so many murders that city officials contracted to have the slain hauled to Boot Hill. One writer of the day referred to Frisco as "Dodge City, Tombstone, Sodom and Gomorrah all rolled into one." When newly hired Marshall Pearson arrived from Pioche, Nevada, he announced that he would not be making any arrests. Rather, he would shoot anyone found breaking the law. It took seven such deaths to bring order to the town.

When the Horn Silver Mining Company incorporated in 1879, Augustus remained a director, as did Dennis Ryan, Matthew Cullen and Allen Campbell, the original partners who bought out the mine's founders. Sir Bache Cunard, a major stockholder better known for his steamship line, installed Charles G. Francklyn, a relative, as company president. After a time, it came out that Francklyn had lent himself over six hundred thousand dollars of the company's money. He was held in the Ludlow-Street Jail, a Federal prison in New York City, but managed to secure his release. The other stockholders sued the Directors including Augustus in 1887 claiming that they were liable as the people who had hired Francklyn in 1880.

Not only did Augustus stiff Hetherington, he refused to acknowledge his brother Peter as a partner, even though it was well known that they always did business together. Atchison was too small a stage for Augustus, and he moved to Chicago, where, in 1882, he built a mansion at 2909 South Michigan Avenue designed by Burnham and Root in the Chateauesque style combining the Italian Renaissance and French Gothic traditions. The mansion's asymmetrical façade, steep hipped roof, elaborate chimneys and pinnacled gables stood in elaborate contrast to Peter's modest farm house west of Atchison where he raised cattle and horses.

Augustus Byram   Byram's Chicago Mansion

    Augustus did not treat old friends any better than his brother. Years before on his first fortune-seeking trip to California with his former Westport neighbors, Gus had gotten a loan from Linville Hays, who'd spent most his life as a freighter and farmer. In 1887, Linville visited Augustus in Chicago to collect the long-overdue loan. When Linville broached the topic of the money due him, Gus evaded the subject by inviting his visitor to dinner at the Calumet club downtown. Conversation at dinner was rather strained, and when they returned to Gus's home, Linville finally asked point-blank, "Are you going to pay what you owe me or not?"

    "Now, my old friend, I don't really remember any loan," Gus responded with the tones of an experienced politician. "But, for old time's sake, I'll give you this gold watch and chain."

    "No, I don't want it," Linville insisted.

    "Well, at least take this silver one." Linville accepted the less valuable timepiece but took his leave without shaking hands with the man who still owned him from almost forty years before.

    When Linville returned to Missouri, he told his wife, Laurinda, "Gus wanted to give me a gold watch, but I said a silver watch is enough for me. I didn't want him to think the debt had been repaid."

    In his old age, Augustus suffered great heartache. One of his sons was worthless and committed a number of forgeries until Augustus and Eleanor finally took him abroad to Bohemia, stole off and left him there. Later Augustus defended their action by saying, "If the boy was worth saving he would work his way out." A daughter, Murial, died at the age of twenty-four from a bullet wound in the neck, supposedly from the accidental explosion of a handgun prior to leaving for a hunting trip to California. Gus's second daughter, Sally, married a wealthy man who became president of the Bank of North America in Chicago but who was also indicted for arson. When widowed, the oldest daughter, Frances, engaged in a legal battle over division of her husband's millions, and she died in Paris in 1913, a long way from the family's roots in Atchison. Frances' daughter, Marjorie, who inherited the Burnes' estate from her mother plus eventually a share of Augustus and Eleanor's fortune married Sidney Love, a wealthy stockbroker and dashing polo player. English artist Philip Burne-Jones called her the most beautiful woman in America. She inherited $632,000 from her mother in 1913. But neither the love nor the money lasted, and reports of their bitter divorce and custody battles were splashed all over the pages of the *Chicago Tribune* and the *Washington Post*.

Marjorie Byram Love

All men are mortal, the rich and the poor alike. Peter's time was running out. His daughter, Ruth, wrote to her Aunt Elvira:

Shannon, Kansas, June 9, 1891
My Dearest Aunt,
  I have not much time to write but know you are anxious to hear how Papa is. He gradually grows worse and dropsy has set in. He is very much swollen all over, has a red-sore on one hip and a running sore on the other, they are terrible, he does not suffer as he did for he is getting so numb, but has weak spells and the Dr. said last night that he would be apt to go in one of those weak spells. He is as helpless as a baby. The boys sit up with him at night. As Ed said

last night it will always be comfort to us to know we have done every thing in the world we could for him.

Sister is in the family way, nearly 3 months and Mr. Weeks is in such poor health and she left one of the children, so she felt that she must go home because Papa may linger for several weeks yet.

Love to all,
(s) Ruth

Peter lasted only a few weeks more as Ruth predicted. Augustus came back to Atchison, arriving just before Peter died. Despite their long estrangement, he greeted his bed-ridden brother with forced geniality. "Hello, Pete, you old stick in the mud. What's this I hear that you're dying? You're the youngest, I'm supposed to go first."

Peter struggled to speak. "You always had the best luck."

"I'm sorry I didn't keep in touch," Gus finally admitted.

"No account. The dead hold no grudges," Peter whispered, glad to have a final rapprochement with the brother who'd shared so much of his life.

The family assembled for Peter's funeral and afterwards the reading of his will.

Last Will & Testament of Peter Byram, Deceased
Presented for probate and filed this 29th day of July, 1891, P. W. Bean, Probate Judge
I, Peter Byram, being of sound and disposing mind and memory and fully realizing the changes in my family and estate since the making of a former will, do make, publish, acknowledge and declare the following as my last will and testament, and do hereby revoke all former wills by me made.

It is my will that all of the property of which I may die seized, whether real, personal or mixed and wheresoever the same may be situated shall be disposed of in the manner following:

I. It is my will that all of my just debts and the cost and expense of collecting and settling my estate be fully paid—

II. I give and bequeath to my daughter Eleanor Weeks wife of James Weeks, one dollar, which with advancements here to for made to her, amounts to her full equitable share of my estate.

- I give and bequeath to my daughter Ruth Downs wife of Roy Downs one dollar with advancements here to for made, and certain rents, profits and income set apart to and for her by deed herewith to Edward Byram Trustee will make up her full equitable share of my estate.

- It is my will that the proceeds collected or received from life insurance policy be equally divided among heirs of my deceased wife and that the same shall not be by others as it is not by myself, considered as any fact of my individual estate—and this clause is here inserted to make definite and certain by devise and will whatever may be uncertain if anything in such policy.

- It is my will that the several deeds, this day made and executed and the terms and conditions thereof be fully carried out and executed and that all the rest, residue and remainder of my estate be divided equally among my five sons, viz: Edward Byram, Theodore Byram, Virgil Byram, Paul Byram and Warren Byram, share and share alike.
- I hereby nominate and appoint my sons Edward Byram and Theodore Byram Executors of this my last will and testament, to carry out and execute the same without giving bond as such executors.
- I hereby appoint my said sons Edward Byram and Theodore Byram Guardians of the persons and estates of my minor sons, viz. Paul Byram, Virgil Byram and Warren Byram for and during the minority of my said last named three sons, to carry out the terms and provisions of my will, and I do hereby order, request and direct that no bond shall be required of said testamentary guardians.

In writing whereof I do hereto subscribe my name and acknowledge, publish and declare the above and testament, in the presence of the witnesses, whose certificate is hereunder written and signed at my request,--this 31st day of October, A.D. 1890.

(s) Peter Byram

Witnesses: W. H. Bush, A. L. Charles

Peter's livestock and implements were sold at an administrator's sale at the Byram farm, five miles west of Atchison. The sale bill read as follows:

50 head thorough-bred shorthorn heifers (1 and 2 years old)	4 two year old mules
18 two and three year old steers	5 head of mules
12 one year old steers	20 brood sows
1 Standard Bred Stallion Roadster	75 shoats
18 head of broodmares,	1 lister
8 one and two year-old colts	1 hay rake
3 saddle mares	1 wagon and hay rack
	2 14-inch plows and misc.

Horse-loving Lucy Byram would have been proud of her grandson's string of mares.

Augustus lived a decade longer than his younger brother, dying one year into the new century. His later years brought increasing infirmities that confined him to his Chicago mansion filled with memories of his children gone wrong. His family had made the switch from agriculture to metropolitan life, with a little help from mining. America was changing. What would the next generation do? Would they be even richer? Or poorer? Would they move further west or stay put? And who would they marry?

~12~

The Telegraph King and the Deacon

Jeptha Homer Wade and Samuel F.B. Morse had several things in common. Both lost their first wives, they loved music, and they were artists and mechanical tinkerers. The telegraph made Morse wealthy and famous, but Wade became even richer.

Jeptha was the youngest of nine born in Seneca Falls, New York, in 1811. At the age of twelve, he was apprenticed to a tanner. At eighteen, he was a carpenter in Pottsville, Pennsylvania, before moving back home. Jeptha had made Homer his middle name after reading the epic poet as a young man. He liked the stories of struggles amongst the gods, which reminded him of his conflicts with his father and schoolmates. He enjoyed working with his hands, and he played several musical instruments. He combined those two skills and invented some new instruments. He wanted to be a surveyor and work outside like his father, but a case of cholera nearly killed him during a worldwide epidemic, leaving him too frail to follow that ambition. With a partner, he started a small shop making window sashes and blinds, but impetuously sold his share to finance instruction in portrait painting with Randall Palmer in Auburn, not far from his hometown.

Wade Painting in Cleveland Museum of Art

For a decade, Jeptha was a semi-itinerant landscape and portrait painter in New York, Ohio and as far away as Louisiana and Mississippi, where he preferred to work in the winter to preserve his health. He thought he was a good painter, but it was not a good living, as few people had the time and money to sit for a portrait, and he had no easy access to high society.

He married Rebecca Facer at Seneca Falls in 1832 during his recovery from cholera. A daughter died as a baby in 1833. A son arrived in 1835. Jeptha had been so enamored with his painting teacher that he named his son Randall Palmer Wade. His joy was short-lived. Rebecca died only four years after they were married. Jeptha wrote to his sister, Sally, in Michigan: "I am sad to tell you that my dear Becky has died. I feel like Job. But, unlike Job, I can't retain my faith. If God has forsaken me, then I am through with God." When Sally read the letter to her husband Ransom Todd, a deacon in the Baptist Church, he said, "Tell him to concentrate on the Holy Spirit, and it will ease his pain."

Jeptha wasted no time in looking for a new wife. He began to court Susan Fleming who lived in his hometown. As the courtship heated up, Jeptha told her, "I love you more than I have words to express."

"I've grown to care for you as well, but we're moving too fast. I've lots of things to discuss. Where would we live?"

Jeptha Homer Wade

"The obvious place is Michigan where I have my sister Sally Ann, my brother Gilbert, who's a farmer, and my mother Sarah."

"Yes, I knew them all when they lived here."

"Losing my first wife and child taught me how precious time is. I want to give you the world. My mind is full of you. When I paint a woman's portrait, it turns out to look like you. Will you marry me?"

His blazing eyes penetrated to her soul and bypassed logic and calculation. Susan's resistance faded in the light of Jeptha's charm, commitment and passion and she replied, "Yes, I will love you always, no matter what fortune brings."

They were married one year after Rebecca's death. He was twenty-six and she twenty-three. Jeptha, Susan and young Randall moved to Adrian, Michigan, in 1840. He offered to paint Sally Ann and Ransom's portrait, but they could not afford it.

Jeptha was without steady income, but he was not without hope. My fortune is out there somewhere, he thought. Ever alert to opportunities, he heard of the wondrous invention of Louis Daguerre during a trip to Baltimore. The Frenchman had invented the first commercially viable photographic process that was suited to portraiture. Jeptha learned that Samuel B. Morse, while studying art in Paris, had met Daguerre, and, upon his return to New York, had begun experimenting with making daguerreotype portraits, previously thought impractical because of the long exposure time. Jeptha sought out Morse and purchased a camera and learned the process solely by reading the instructions. Jeptha returned to Michigan and made the first daguerreotypes west of New York.

This was a bit of vanity that Sally Ann and Ransom could afford. The portrait taken by her brother showed Sally Ann with her hair parted in the middle and three deep waves on each side.

Sally Ann fretted over the beautification session with her daughter before the sitting. The curling iron that set the waves required a degree of care. "Now be careful, Sarah Jane," she cautioned. "Be sure to test the heated iron on a piece of paper first. If it's too hot it will burn my hair, and if too cold, it won't set."

"I know; I know. I've done it before."

Sally Ann's pendant earrings complimented her long face and sculptured nose, and she wore a dark dress with a high neck and a white lace ruff. Ransom told her she looked beautiful, and she admitted to herself that she was attractive, at least for a mother of ten children. Ransom was a tall, broad-shouldered man with a full beard, but no mustache. His beard, cut in what was called the spade or Shenandoah style, was bushy but neat. He wore a simple wide black ribbon at his collar with no knot. His coat was open and revealed a gold chain and fob on his vest. This was his Sunday look. For his portrait, Ransom sat steel-rod straight and looked rather severe. However, a bit of wave in the thick hair above his forehead softened his face. Those who knew him informally found him of good humor and easy to work with.

Daguerreotypes provided only a little better living for the Wade family than painting. Jeptha realized he must find still another occupation. Recalling his visit with Morse, he went to Baltimore in 1844 to witness the building of the first telegraph line between that city and Washington. He took it all in, talking to the key operators, surveyors and line workmen, to learn all he could.

Back home in Adrian, Sue was startled one evening by a loud thump on the kitchen wall. "Jeptha, what was that noise?" she called to her husband in the next room.

"That was my code book hitting the wall," he replied. "I'm so frustrated; this Morse Code is impossible. There's no pattern to it, just requires pure memorization. Maybe after dinner you could tap out some words using the code book, and I can practice deciphering it."

"Gladly," Susan responded with interest. "How does it work?"

"For example you could spell your name by tapping out dot, dot, dot; then dot, dot, dash; then finally one dot."

Jeptha eventually did learn the code. He also taught himself to make all of the telegraphic instruments and learned how to construct the lines. "I've mastered all the pieces of telegraphy," he remarked to Sue, "and now all I need is an opportunity to put my knowledge to work." His opportunity came when J.J. Speed arrived in Michigan to promote the building of a telegraph line in the state. Speed was impressed with Jeptha's knowledge of all things related to the telegraph and hired the young man as a subcontractor in the summer of 1846.

Jeptha constructed a telegraph line between Detroit and Jackson along the Michigan Central Railroad right of way. Though he had no hands-on experience and he even had to borrow money from Speed for a handcar and horse, he knew more about the technology than anyone else in Michigan. Jeptha's early experiences as a carpenter and proprietor of the sash and blind shop had prepared him for the hard work ahead. During the line construction, he lived with his men in a tent with a cook.

The line he was building was a part of Speed's Erie and Michigan line and the Buffalo and Milwaukee Telegraph Company. When completed, Jeptha operated the Jackson office for a year, and his twelve-year-old son, Randall, delivered messages to customers. Many young boys of the time, including Andrew Carnegie, got their first jobs delivering telegraph messages. Next, Jeptha was given a contract to build part of the Erie and Michigan line from Detroit eastward. Fifty miles out of Detroit, he encountered O'Reilly's crew constructing a competing line coming from the east. Jeptha muttered to himself, this could be trouble, as he met their agent. But neither crew seemed prone to violence, and in November, Jeptha wrote to Speed, "I trust he and I will get along side by side without any difficulty and leave our superiors to settle any conflict between the lines in their own way."

A community of mixed French and Indian blood lay between Monroe and Toledo. They strongly objected to both lines, fearing fires and harm to their livestock. This impasse was going to require all of Jeptha's diplomatic skills and understanding of human nature. He sought out the leader of the group and offered a bit of soft soap and whiskey. "Won't you sit a spell and try a drop of this fine whiskey?" he asked the local chief.

"Indian not sure can trust white man," came the reply.

"This bottle doesn't care white or Indian," Jeptha persisted.

After sharing a few swallows, the half-breed invited Jeptha and his bottle to supper.

Wade found the "Big Chief's" house after wading through the mud that also covered his host's floor due to the free access of roaming pigs. Skinned, whole squirrels were the main course. Jeptha thought to himself, I can't offend my host by refusing to eat what is offered, so he choked it down. When the meal and the bottle were finished, the chief said, "I'll aid project and even make small investment."

"All I want is your cooperation in persuading your neighbors that the telegraph will not harm them," Jeptha said. "And please note that my line is on the west side of the road while my competitor's are on the east."

The next morning, the chief visited all of his neighbors and advised, "On the west side all right; leef 'em be. On the east side, give 'em hell."

At the start of his enterprise, Morse had been desperate for funds, but all he could offer investors and political supporters was a share in his patent. Congressman F.O.J. Smith of Maine had become a partner of Morse in 1838 and accompanied the inventor to Europe to secure patents there. The English dithered, while the French quickly issued a patent, but decided the system should be public, so Morse returned home empty-handed. Smith became Morse's regional director for New England, New York and the Northwest Territories. Another player was Amos Kendall, who had resigned as Postmaster General to head Van Buren's presidential campaign in 1840. In 1845, Kendall became agent for three-quarters of the Morse patent in the U.S., and the remaining one-quarter went to Smith. When Morse went to Washington seeking government money to build the original Washington-Baltimore line, Smith had exchanged his support for an interest in Morse's patent.

Smith had a vision of a national telegraph system, and in 1847, Ezra Cornell and J.J. Speed became Smith's agents in the Northwest. Smith was not satisfied with his one-quarter interest in the earnings of the Morse patent. He decided he could make more money on the construction side by reducing the price of the patent to encourage more companies to enter the field, then profiting from construction and the requirement that subsidiary lines must connect to his main line. In the words of his contemporary, James Reid, "Smith had a facile pen, sharp, pungent, implacable; and, although occasionally misled by a kind of classic facetiousness, always awkward and often amusing, which dulled its point, yet the weapon was keen, cold, able, savage. He had no moral obstacles to contend with."

In August, Smith sent a directive to Cornell and Speed: "Whenever you can get money enough raised to get a line up, start it, and Patentees will not hurry for their part, and your share of benefits shall be made satisfactory. I want no pusillanimous, or doubting movements made—but dash on with all the battery and thunder and lightning you all can command."

Ezra Cornell, who would later found Cornell University, had been a contractor for Morse's original experimental line between Washington and Baltimore over which was sent the to-be famous message, "What hath God wrought?" Independently, Cornell had built many miles of line in New York state. The Erie and Michigan Telegraph Company, with Speed as president, would connect Buffalo, Cleveland, Detroit, Chicago and Milwaukee. Wade became a telegraph operator for the line in Milan, Ohio, in June, 1848, and combined it with his daguerreotype and painting studio. His annual salary, including the services of his son as delivery boy, was four hundred dollars. But his string of bad luck was not over; his studio burned.

Jeptha became aware of Smith's devious strategy, but accepted and took advantage of it, forming a loose partnership with Speed and Cornell in 1849. Jeptha purchased the use of limited patent rights to the Morse telegraph in Ohio from Smith, with the price to be paid as new lines were constructed. Avoiding the need for up-front cash was strategic. Jeptha formed the Cleveland and Cincinnati Telegraph Company and began to solicit capital for its construction.

Smith was not content to transfer messages from his western lines to Morse's New York, Albany and Buffalo line. Instead, in 1849, he and Cornell completed a parallel service to New York called the New York and Erie. Kendall, representing Morse, objected and pointed out that Smith's authority in using the Morse patent was limited to building subsidiary lines. But Smith was willing to bend the meaning of "subsidiary." He claimed his New York and Erie line was only a subsidiary of his Erie and Michigan line. This was no-holds-barred commercial war of assertions and court suits. One observer remarked, "Having sown the wind, Smith was to reap the whirlwind." The Directors of the Erie and Michigan line withheld stock from Smith until he could clarify his right to the Morse patent. Smith's line to New York would go bankrupt and Cornell, Speed and Wade were shortly to fall heirs to Smith's western lines.

Jeptha had no money of his own except what he earned in construction of the Detroit-Jackson section of the Erie and Michigan. But he was an entrepreneur extraordinaire. In addition to major investments from Speed, he set about to raise money from businessmen who wanted the telegraph to serve their communities. The three hundred fifty-mile Cleveland-Cincinnati line would connect at Cleveland with the Erie and Michigan Telegraph Company, built by Speed, Cornell and Smith. The new Wade Line would give all of its east-bound messages to Smith and Speed's Erie and Michigan. Jeptha used his charm and salesmanship skills to sell stock along the route of the proposed line. The money invested was used to buy poles and wire.

Jeptha assured the share buyers that he had the exclusive right to build the line. As part of his sales pitch, he offered to buy back subscribers' shares if they were dissatisfied. This was mostly bluff as he had no money to repurchase them. "In the early days of this business, all's a matter of expectations, assertions, which if believed, come true," Jeptha confided to his lawyer. "I'm proceeding in good faith and confidence that I can put it all together."

"You have to believe, or no one else will," his counselor concurred.

"You know that Smith, Speed and Cornell and the towns along the route, my investors and the eastern lines all want to make money," Jeptha continued, "and that depends on all the pieces coming together. Right now all the balls are in the air, but I think I can bring them all home without crashing."

"It's risky."

"I know. If I can't make connections to the east, I'm in real trouble."

Jeptha had the kind of personality and appealing face with a friendly but determined demeanor that inspired confidence. He was over six feet tall, a wide-shouldered man with receding, thick hair and full beard, but no mustache. His eyes were deep-set and penetrating when he looked at someone dead on.

Jeptha knew that there were Morse patentees who disputed Smith's rights, so he decided to try to head off any trouble. In September after construction had already begun on the line, he wrote to Amos Kendall who represented the other patentees, and asked for permission to build in Ohio south of Columbus. He offered to pay Kendall's interests what he had contracted for with Smith, but had not yet paid. He got mixed signals from Kendall, leaving him still unsure about his right to use the Morse patent in southern Ohio.

Jeptha was having trouble keeping the balls in the air. Subscription sales were not going well, and without new cash from these advance payments, he could not pay his crew or buy wire and poles. One of his competitors encouraged his creditors to attach some wire Jeptha had purchased in Buffalo. As if the financial and legal problems were not enough, there were technical problems in constructing the line. Opinions varied about the best material for insulators, and Jeptha choose a sulfur cap which soon proved defective, and he had to replace them with glass at his own expense. Jeptha was at his wit's end and running out of bravado. He thought to himself, in times like this, the only ones you can confide in are family. He had already solicited help from his brother, Andrew.

He stopped construction and took a few days off to visit his sister in Michigan. He hated to appear weak before Sally Ann and especially his brother-in-law, but he swallowed his pride and told them his plight. He needed a sympathetic ear among the wild animals that were trying to eat him up.

After a cup of tea, Jeptha explained, "All my life I've worked hard but have come up short."

"I know we were worried sick when you contracted cholera," Sally Ann told him.

"Yes. It left me weakened, and I turned to work that was not strenuous."

"I know you had a natural talent for painting."

"I traveled the country to find clients who could afford a portrait, but there just are not enough of them."

"I know that left us out, but we treasure the daguerreotype you made of us," remarked Ransom.

"New technologies have always fascinated me," said Jeptha, "I'm sure telegraphy will make some people very rich. Probably those who are already rich. I'm now building a small line of my own south of Columbus."

"How are you financing its construction?" asked Ransom.

Jeptha's face reddened into a frown. "Not so well. Any town that gets a line will prosper, but it's hard to get the local business people to see that and put their money on the barrelhead, or, in this case, into poles and wire."

"But you've already constructed many miles."

"Yes, but I'm always scrambling for money for the next mile. Now my creditors have attached some wire I bought at Buffalo. I need that wire desperately." His eyes were wet as he finally admitted, "I'm about to lose again."

"We will think on it together, but now come to the table, and we'll have a good meal like Mom used to make."

The next day, no one mentioned telegraphy, and, instead, the siblings just spoke of good times in their New York childhood. They talked over several days during which Sally Ann could not offer a magic solution, but Jeptha felt better just talking about it. When he was ready to leave, Sally Ann gave him a hug and said, "Don't give up, don't let those damned creditors get you down." Sally was a bit surprised at her own language and emotion. "Here's two hundred dollars that we have been saving. Maybe that'll keep you going for a few more days until you can get some more new subscriptions in Ohio." Ransom kept quiet, seeing his wife's commitment to her brother.

With renewed vigor, Jeptha revisited some of the towns on his proposed route and managed to raise enough money to get the desperately needed wire delivered. Construction resumed, and the entire line was in operation by January 1850.

When the telegraph office in Cleveland opened in the old Weddell House on West Sixth Street, eager onlookers gathered around the instrument. They were startled when the instrument began to act, to all eyes, of its own accord. A witness told a neighbor, "The machine all at once began to rattle like the bones of a skeleton under a galvanic battery, and the line was reported in order."

But Jeptha was not out of the woods yet. He explained to the stockholders of the Cleveland and Cincinnati Telegraph Company in December 1850 that the line was only doing local business because of its unfinished condition and imperfect function of the lines with which their line connected. The company was formally organized that year with Jeptha as president and treasurer. The directors included John J. Speed, a major stockholder, Ezra Cornell and Andrew Wade, Jeptha's brother.

The industry's problems were present at its birth. Morse, in his desire to cash-in on his invention, granted overlapping and ambiguous patent rights in 1845 to several players, including O'Reilly, Smith, Kendall and Butterfield and Faxton. Morse and these men would be in conflict involving suits and countersuits for years to come, creating great uncertainty for investors. From the beginning, Kendall wanted Morse to sell his invention to the government which could then build a nationwide telegraph system in an orderly fashion, as the French later did. But this was not to be. Each company had its own investors and board of directors that did not necessarily share the long-term perspective of the company founders. The boards were often more interested in their own immediate rewards.

Smith's dreams of monopoly transferred to the foreign-news business. Ships from Europe docked first in Halifax, Nova Scotia, before Boston or New York. The European news they brought was transmitted to Boston and New York newspapers ahead of the steamer by the best available means, including carrier pigeons, trains and boats. Smith controlled an essential telegraph link between Portland, Maine, and Boston and tried to use it to eliminate competitors. His "non-intercourse" policy maddened James Gordon Bennett of the *New York Herald* who wrote, "Fog Smith is getting into a thicker fog than ever. With the most consummately impudent pretensions, he proceeds to issue laws and regulations wholly subversive of the rights of the commercial public." The monopoly did not last long, as a parallel O'Reilly line using a non-Morse technology was built.

In 1851, there were over fifty separate telegraph companies in the country. A rival line to Wade's was constructed between Cleveland and Cincinnati. In a discussion with his partner Jeptha pointed out how competition among these small lines had them cannibalizing each other so that no one could make a profit. "We must consolidate," he told Speed, "and I've started negotiations with other companies." Speed nodded in assent. One dreary night Jeptha stopped at a railroad eating house in Shelby, Ohio, on an inspection trip of his Cleveland-Cincinnati line. He saw a man eating alone and introduced himself. "My name is Jeptha Wade of the Cleveland-Cincinnati Telegraph. May I join you?

"I'm Anson Stager, working for the O'Reilly lines," the fellow replied. "Please sit down."

Jeptha scraped some of the viscous, brown stuff off his meatloaf that looked more like axel grease than gravy. They began to discuss their mutual troubles. Jeptha acknowledged that he was making little money. "I can't even buy a decent meal." Stager looked up from his corn-beef hash and acknowledged, "We are both on the wrong side of the profit-loss ledger." The remainder of the conversation underscored Jeptha's belief that consolidation was the only answer.

At his company's annual meeting the next year Jeptha presented his case. "In view of the importance of a general consolidation, and thereby reducing our expenses, increasing business and stopping the rivalry that is now eating up nearly all of our profits, and running many of the lines in debt," he stated, "I would recommend that the stockholders invest the directors with the authority to confer with other companies and make such consolidation and business arrangements as they may think for the best interest of our Company. The public would be better served, stockholders better paid, and the telegraph made to answer in every respect more perfectly the purpose for which it was designed." His recommendation was approved.

Kendall, representing the patentees other than Smith, wrote to Wade that he was agreeable to meet with Speed, Cornell and Wade in New York, adding, "I heartily concur with you in the hope that we may accomplish something for the common good." Jeptha had finally gotten Kendall off his back, and he knew that he was on the eve of a revolution in the business.

But there was much work yet to be done. Cornell, Speed and Wade built up their system and contracted with feeder lines pledged to exclusive connection to the Erie and Michigan. In 1853 they bought out other bankrupt lines including some built by O'Reilly. Wade could see that there were advantages to constructing telegraph lines along railroad rights of way. The railroad station managers could operate the telegraph, and railroad management could use the lines for their own business. Addressing the company stockholders in early 1854 he said, "I cannot urge upon you too strongly the importance of rebuilding, in the most permanent manner, the old line, as fast as the resources of the company will permit, and when suitable arrangements can be made, to get it on to the railroads."

To complicate matters, an alternative technology invented by Royal House had been purchased and developed by Hiram Sibley who had ambitious plans to develop a nationwide system. Even though he owned the rival technology, he preferred the Morse instruments, and he sought access to them through purchase of those rights from another party. .Speed and Wade were ready to deal without even letting their partner Cornell know of their intent.

Jeptha tried to explain to his wife his decision to sell the rights to a rival one night after dinner in their small kitchen. Reaching for her hand, he said, "Sue, I need your help with a business decision."

Sue thought it a strange request. "I don't know anything about business. You never asked me before." She took her hand away.

"This is not a straight business decision. There are issues."

"OK, I'm listening."

"A man named Sibley has a vision of a consolidated national telegraph system. He built extensive lines in the East using the House technology, and now he wants to expand in the Midwest. The House technology is workable, but the Morse system is better, and Sibley wants to switch."

"Jeptha, where do you fit in?"

"Cornell, Speed and I have the Morse rights in Ohio that Sibley needs. He asked Speed and me to name our price for the Morse patent and all our stock."

"So, I don't understand."

"We said fifty thousand dollars. I didn't think he would take us up on it, but he did."

"Isn't that a lot of money? Why is he offering so much when you are hardly breaking even?"

"By itself the line is not worth much, but the patent is the lynchpin to Sibley's grand plan for a national integrated system."

"So what's the problem?"

"Cornell doesn't know about it. I told Sibley that it wasn't fair to Cornell. Sibley said that was his problem, and he would settle with Cornell later. He told me to stay out of it."

"Jeptha, you're really caught in the middle."

"Speed has no misgivings about the deal, but I do. I don't like to do things behind the back of others. This hurts my stomach. I think Cornell will be mad that we left him out." Looking into his wife's eyes, he asked, "Would you be disappointed in me if I go through with this deal?"

She frowned, and her eyes said it all. "I'm not convinced that it's the right thing to do."

"I was born poor, and I am still poor. We've been living hand-to-mouth. This is not what I wanted for you and the boy. There is no assurance that the Cleveland-Cincinnati line that I built will ever make money. Consolidation is the wave of the future. The only question is who is going to do it and benefit from it."

"What would you do with the money?"

"If I had this new capital, I could make investments and become a significant player in the industry. On top of it, I impressed Sibley with my managerial skills, and he has offered me a job as his right-hand man. I feel that being Sibley's protégé is my route to future wealth. I admire Sibley. He's a rags-to-riches kind of guy. I want to be like him, somebody you could be proud of."

"What's really driving you? Have I complained about our income?"

"If not for yourself, how about the boy? Wouldn't you like to see him go to college someday? I would've liked the chance to go to college."

"You have a point there."

"I want the respect of you and my son."

"Are you trying to convince me or yourself? Sure, I would like a better life, fine clothes and a nice house, but not at the expense of someone else."

"Where are you coming from?"

"My father was a small-town butcher. He never cheated anyone." She paused to reflect. "I realize that he had few opportunities. He couldn't have done much, maybe put his finger on the scale."

"Your father shaped your values?"

"Yes, and he was very religious. I know you have no use for religion."

"Is that where you learned that things are either black or white, good or bad?"

"I suppose so. I can't help what I am. Who am I, if I'm not true to my principles?"

"Principles? I believe in principles too. But application of principles has a context. In the real world, principles must have grey edges."

"That's hard for me to accept."

"I know it's hard, but, the choices of a small-town butcher are not like those of big business. The scale is entirely different, if you'll pardon the pun."

"Is there no other way? Couldn't you tell Sibley that he must deal with Cornell now?"

"I don't think so. Cornell probably has other plans of his own. It's either go ahead or the deal is off."

"I see now that you are between a rock and a hard place. I can feel your pain."

"I don't like to get ahead by deception, but if I take the money and the job, I'll be in a good position and can afford to play fair in the future. I know it is a slippery slope. The temptation will be to follow one deception with another, and then another. But, I think I can resist it."

"It won't be easy, even Adam couldn't do it."

"Sue, look at me, your husband, not at the Bible."

"This man Sibley, that you want to learn from, is not exactly a paragon of virtue. After all, it was he who propositioned Speed and you, leaving Cornell out of the deal. Is he going to ask you to cut corners on other deals in the future?"

"Big business is not a game for the faint of heart. There are too many duplicate lines being built over the same territory. Someone will consolidate these lines and develop a rational, national system. Some will lose, and others win, whether I am part of it or not. I would like to be on the winning side."

"This telegraph industry seems to be dog eat dog. Maybe you are in the wrong business."

"This is the only business I know. I've already failed at being a portrait painter. I'm thirty-six years-old, I don't have time to start another career from scratch." He brushed an imaginary crumb from their scruffy kitchen table.

"Maybe you gave up on your artistic side too soon. Maybe business is not your calling."

"I painted for three years before we were married and after until I started to build telegraph lines. It was a poor living for us."

"I don't want to scuttle your dreams, but there must be a better way."

"Sometimes there is no better way. This is not easy for me. We are not the only ones involved. When I was building the Cincinnati line, I ran out of money and had to stop construction. I went to visit my sister in Michigan. She gave me her life savings of two hundred dollars that kept me going a few more days. Sally Ann and her husband didn't have any money to spare. They are just small-time farmers."

"So, what's the point?"

"How can I face my sister and tell her that her money was wasted? I'm still poor. Her husband never liked me anyway. I'm so ashamed." He looked past his wife to the fake lace curtains at the window.

"What do you want from me? I don't know anything about business."

"I want this for you and the boy. Can't you see that?"

"I see a man blinded by ambition, by dreams of Midas-like wealth."

"I admit to ambition, but I don't think I'm blinded. I am considering the plusses and minuses. Without a good income, I'm half a man."

"I know you're suffering, but I can't, I won't, change who I am."

"So be it. Anyway, I want you to promise me that if you see me slipping and double-dealing in the future, that you will yell, STOP. Rap my knuckles. Will you promise?"

"Don't try to fool me by switching the question."

"I've tried to convince you with many good reasons for going through with the deal. But you won't acknowledge any shades of gray, any balancing of conflicting, important values."

"I can't give you what you want. Maybe you can explain it better to your son."

"That was an unkind remark."

"It's just a fact, isn't it?"

"I had hoped that you could bend a little, but I see now it's hopeless. I accept your judgment. I'll just have to live with it." His eyes hardened and he could not look her in the face. "But I'm going to trust my own judgment and complete the deal."

"So be it. I'll have to live with it, too."

"Will you be my conscience in the future?" There was a long, awkward silence.

"I don't think you need me."

He needed her, all right, as the nights ahead were icy cold.

Whatever his wife's judgment might be, his mind was made up. Wade and Speed agreed to a consolidation with the New York and Mississippi Valley Printing Telegraph Company, and although their Morse rights were far from secure, Sibley and his partner Judge Samuel Shelden were willing to take the risk. In April 1854, Wade and Speed sold their stock in the Erie and Michigan, New York and Erie, Cleveland and Cincinnati, and Cincinnati and St. Louis lines along with the western Morse patent rights for fifty thousand dollars.

When Cornell learned of the sale, he wrote to his wife Mary Ann, "Speed and Wade's effort at my destruction by their diabolical sale to the enemy has proved to signal failure on their part, and will produce them a harvest of curses from the very men who were to reap the golden apple of their treachery."

Cornell later confronted Speed and demanded an explanation. "This is the foulest piece of treachery toward me that I have ever known," he shouted. "How could you have done such a thing to me?"

"To make money, by God!" Speed replied with brutal honesty.

Wade's luck took a turn. Sibley did hire him to be his manager and later his successor. Things began to move quickly. In 1854, Wade was living in Columbus, Ohio, as principal agent for Sibley's New York and Mississippi Valley Printing Telegraph Company. Cornell, as might be expected, denied that Sibley had a valid right to use the Morse patent. Because the boards of the various companies were independent of the system organizers, Cornell connived to get himself elected as president of the Erie and Michigan instead of Sibley and his associates who had organized the line.

But soon Cornell realized that Sibley and his Rochester backers were too strong to be driven from the field, and he agreed to consolidation. The Morse rights in Ohio, Indiana, Illinois, Michigan, Wisconsin, Iowa and the Territory of Minnesota were now secure. In 1856, Wade and Sibley put together a thirteen-company consolidation that Cornell insisted be named Western Union with headquarters in Cleveland. A historian would later describe Wade as "suave, persuasive, realistic—was chief negotiator, and he exhibited rare talent in arranging satisfactory terms of lease and consolidation by which lines were to be brought into the Western Union fold." A contemporary, James D. Reid, expressed an equally flattering description of the man: "Mr. Wade was in the prime of life, shrewd, ingenious, persevering, able, and familiar with western enterprise. He at once commenced with sagacity and vigor, the work assigned him." Sibley was president and Jeptha became general agent. Colonel Anson Stager, formerly a Rochester newspaperman and the O'Rielly associate Jeptha had met by chance five years before, became general manager to complete the management team.

The Atlantic and Ohio Telegraph Company now was the only serious competitor to Western Union's hegemony. The Atlantic company had a line along the Pennsylvania Railroad from Pittsburgh to Philadelphia with connections to Boston and New York. Wade's diplomacy consolidated a Western Union line along the railroad with the Atlantic company in 1857. Western Union was now the monopolist of the West with a system that connected Baltimore, Philadelphia, New York, Buffalo, Pittsburgh, Cleveland, Cincinnati, Louisville, Detroit, Chicago, Milwaukee and St. Louis.

Sue noticed that her husband was in a better mood these days. "The new Western Union must be working."

Jeptha confided with an example of how things had turned for the better. "I had a block of stock in a little line from Pittsburgh to Louisville that Western Union obtained a permanent lease for. Western Union paid forty-one hundred cash for each one hundred dollar par value stock."

"I sure hope you had a lot of shares, my dear."

"And lest you feel sorry for my former partner, Cornell, he wound up with two million in Western Union stock for his interests." Obviously, Jeptha's earlier deception of Cornell was still on his mind. In the end, Cornell deserted the other Morse patentees just as Speed and Wade had done earlier.

The road to the so-called Six Nations Alliance of 1857 that divided the country into cooperating fiefdoms of telegraph owners was indeed bumpy and contentious. Economist Adam Smith was correct that it was natural when businessmen got together to conspire toward monopoly. He, however, did not fully understand human nature and the desire and maneuvering of each of the parties to be the top dog and get the biggest slice of the pie. It took all of Wade's diplomacy to steer through the warring parties.

Sibley was busy lobbying for a government-subsidized transcontinental telegraph line. One version of a bill explicitly named Sibley-controlled companies, but rival American Telegraph objected. The Pacific Telegraph Act of 1860 provided for an annual subsidy of forty thousand dollars, the contract to be awarded in open bidding. Sibley promptly entered a bid asking for the full forty thousand, and it was accepted by the Secretary of the Treasury. Initially, lower bids were made by rivals who later withdrew for reasons Sibley never explained.

Sibley sent Jeptha to California to negotiate with four rival California companies. Susan was delighted to be allowed to accompany him, and they departed New York on the steamer *North Star* of the Cornelius Vanderbilt Line with twelve hundred fellow passengers. Eight days later they disembarked in Colon, Panama, and boarded the train that had been built across the isthmus after the Gold Rush and boarded a ship bound for California. Each of the four California companies separately wanted to join Western Union and the transcontinental project. Jeptha could see that an agreement with one would have enraged the others, so he told them they must all agree to consolidate before joining Western Union. Thus, the California State Telegraph Company came into being, and, with Wade's approval, created the Overland Telegraph Company to construct a line from the existing terminus of its San Francisco line at Carson City, Nevada, to Salt Lake.

When Jeptha brought back his proposal to establish the Pacific Telegraph Company to build the line between Omaha and Salt Lake, he ran into all sorts of objections. At the Western Union board meeting in Buffalo in 1861, one director was afraid the Indians would cut the wires and the buffalo would rub down the poles. Another thought the money could not be raised. Wade did not falter in his enthusiasm for the project. "This is a line that must be built, and Western Union must be a part of it," he told the directors. Then to meet the worry over obtaining sufficient financial backing, he moved that Western Union would take half the stock and Wade would place the other half.

Once the motion was approved, Jeptha quietly said, "Gentlemen, I will take the other half myself."

"How will you pay for it?" an incredulous director asked.

Without blinking, Jeptha replied, "That's my lookout. I'll pay my part as fast as the Western Union pays hers."

Sibley and Western Union established the Pacific Telegraph Company with Wade as its president. The line would follow the Platte River to Fort Kearney on to Fort Laramie, then up the Sweetwater River to South Pass in the Rockies and on to Salt Lake. Construction out of Omaha was organized by Edward Creighton, who would later endow Creighton University in Omaha.

The contract for the eastern portion specified twenty-five poles per mile, galvanized iron wire, and the use of Wade insulators. Wade still enjoyed working with his hands and invented a glass insulator covered with a wooden cap to make it less attractive to riflemen. The crew out of Omaha employed four hundred men equipped with rifles. The materials and provisions were carried by one hundred wagons with the draft power of five hundred head of oxen and mules. The first pole was set on the fourth of July, the same day that C_' appropriated the subsidy money and authorized Lincoln to recruit an army the Civil War. Lincoln saw that a communication link with California would help keep that distant state in the Union.

When Creighton was building the line in Utah, he realized that cooperation of Brigham Young, the Mormon leader, was vital to success, and he assured his support by making a contract with Young's son to supply poles. Later, the son told Creighton that his bid had been too low and he was losing money, whereupon Creighton promptly wrote a new contract at a higher price. Not long after, Creighton received an invitation from father Young for a meeting.

"Is it true that my son entered into a contract with you to furnish poles for the telegraph?"

"Yes sir."

"Is it also true that the price agreed upon in this contract was subsequently raised?"

"Yes."

Young asked to see the two contracts, read them carefully, then threw the new one into the fire. "The poles will be furnished by my son in accordance with the terms of the original contract," he told Creighton.

Another possible construction roadblock was the western Indian tribes. James Street was sent to confer with Shoshone chief, Shokup. After listening to an explanation of the project, the chief referred to the line as the white man's "wire rope express" and pledged his cooperation. The eastern section of Creighton's line was complete in October, but the builders of the western portion ran into trouble finding poles in the mountains. There was timber in the high mountains, but the men would not cut it, fearing they'd be caught by snow. The company bosses traveled by stage to the site and threatened the men with forfeiture of their back pay if they did not continue. The men agreed to work when crew chief James Gamble and his assistants said they would accompany the men into the mountains. Men usually accept risks if their leaders share them, whether it be civil or military. At the end of October 1861, just a little over four months after construction began, a message was sent to President Lincoln: "May it be a bond of perpetuity between the states of the Atlantic and those of the Pacific." The line was later moved to the right of way of the Union Pacific Railroad that began construction in Omaha in 1865. News of the planting of the Golden Spike connecting eastern and western rail lines was transmitted by telegraph in 1869. Europe and America had been successfully linked by an Atlantic cable in 1865 after several failures. The world was being knit together by wire and dots and dashes.

In 1866, Sibley had resigned and his protégé, Wade, became the president of Western Union that would become the largest corporation in America. Wade made an agreement with William Orton, the president of Western Union's rival, the United States Telegraph Company with extensive holdings in the East and in the Gulf states. At first, Orton thought that Wade's offer of twelve and a half percent of the combined stock was too low. But, Wade had done his homework, and the offer reflected the relative revenues of the two companies. The American Telegraphic Company was an even bigger rival, having consolidated with Morse's Magnetic Telegraph Company. American merged with Western Union, June, 1867. After completing this landmark deal, Wade resigned, and Orton succeeded him as president. Western Union had fifty thousand miles of lines that carried two million news dispatches per year. Morse invented the concept and machinery, but Wade had brought telegraph service to fruition.

Jeptha confided in his wife, "Susan I'm at the height of my telegraphic business career, but I am still plagued with the effect of cholera contracted as a young man. I hate to do it, but after only one year, I have resigned as president of Western Union. I will remain on the Board of Directors and over time I'll sell my stock. I may be sickly, but we are going to be rich while I convalesce."

"I know how much telegraphy has meant to you. It'll be hard to not participate in its further development," Susan consoled him, "but you can do other things that aren't so demanding, and Randall can help you. Let's have some fun and build a new house, I have had my eye on a lot on Euclid Avenue where many fine homes are being built by the city's business leaders. I would like to be neighbors of your friend Mather and Charles Brush, the founder of General Electric and your business associate, Colonel Stager."

Jeptha Homer Wade

Susan suspected that one reason Jeptha had resigned from Western Union was so that he could invest on his own. Western Union was a mature company and perhaps Jeptha wanted more entrepreneurial challenges rather than more tedious administration. Jeptha wondered if there would be pressure to put the corporation under government control now that its monopoly was nearly complete. Also, the corporate office was moving to New York, and Jeptha wanted to stay in Cleveland.

Upon Jeptha's retirement, the Western Union board held a ceremony to honor him, Samuel L. Mather, and Selah Chamberlain. The board issued a resolution for the occasion: "That to the foresight, perseverance and tact of Mr. J. H. Wade, the former President of the Company, we believe is largely due the fact of the existence of one great Company to-day, with its thousand arms grasping the extremities of the continent, instead of a series of weak unreliable lines unsuited to public wants, and as property, precarious and insecure." Afterward the ceremony, Jeptha and Samuel had a private drink and cigar in a corner of the board room before heading home.

"Sam, I've been thinking about my career. In spite of the accolades, there are things that nag me."

"Like what? You can't be much richer."

"Like the corners I cut early on and the bodies of our competitors fallen along the way. I created a lot of pain for some of them and their families."

"Forget it; it's just business."

"I can't. I think of it every time my wife looks at me with a disapproving eye, no matter the immediate reason for it. And, I know my sister's husband disapproves of me."

"You think too much. Relax. I've got some uncles like that. But you know what, it's a lot easier to be holy when you have little money and little prospect of making any."

"Don't get me wrong. I'm proud of the company we built, and I'm convinced consolidation made sense for the company and the country, but I've never been sure my wife respects me. I disappointed her somewhere along the way."

"Hmm, I've seen her in her jewels at parties while she's telling others about her trips to the West Coast and Europe. I think she enjoys the fruits of your labor."

Jeptha drew on his cigar and blew a smoke ring across the room. "Maybe."

"And surely your contributions to civic causes would make any wife proud."

"Most wives maybe, but I'm not sure of my angel who sees everything as black or white. No grey for her."

"Finish your brandy. Let's not let such thoughts ruin the evening."

But Jeptha would become even richer with his many investments. When the Civil War broke out in 1861, Jeptha had realized that steel would be in great demand. He invested in the Cleveland Rolling Mill Company and became a member of its board in 1863. The company constructed the second Bessemer furnace in the country. In the same year that he resigned from Western Union, Jeptha became a board member of Cleveland Iron Mining Company and Cleveland Shipbuilding. The company had been formed in 1850 by Jeptha's friend, Mather, to exploit what came to be known as Cleveland Mountain, a one thousand-foot wide, mile-long hill of iron ore in the Upper Peninsula of Michigan. One of the ore boats was named the *J.H. Wade*. Wade used the same consolidation strategy he developed at Western Union on the steel business, integrating iron mining with steel making and the use of his own steel in railroads and bridges. In addition to becoming president of Cleveland Rolling Mill Company, he built eight railroads, including the Kalamazoo-Allegan and Grand Rapids in Michigan. He was president of the Citizens' Savings Bank and the National Bank of Commerce and director of the Second National Bank. He built the six-story Wade Building, at 803-805 Superior Avenue, Cleveland, for his own office and that of Rockefeller's Standard Oil.

Cleveland Rolling Mill

Wade Building, Cleveland   **Signature of J.H Wade**

When Randall Wade graduated from the Kentucky Military Institute in 1856 at age twenty-one, he had returned to Cleveland and married Anna McGraw. The wedding was a grand affair even though Anna had no wealth or social schooling, a lack that Jeptha did not count a liability. "The selection of a wife will be the most important event in your life, an event involving all your worldly happiness," he'd cautioned his son. "Mutual worth and moral purity are first in order. Beauty soon fades, and while it lasts may only be a source of jealousy. A beauty is generally a vain and worthless helpmate."

Randall took his father's advice to heart and later told his wife, "You call the lack of wealth a fault, but it is *no* fault, only a circumstance. I think not of it. I have always said that I would never marry for money."

During the Civil War, Randall went to Washington to advise the government on use of telegraphic communication. As chief clerk of the War Department's military telegraph operations, he was one of four men to be entrusted with the Army's secret code. While in Washington, Randall wrote to Anna: *"I don't remember of ever leaving you on the sidewalk but of course the people all know that you were trying to get something that would stick closer to you than I—but I will show you when I get home how close I can stick to you— my muscular system is all in a cramp now to think how I will grab at you, hug you and squeeze you. I am afraid your poor bones will ache when I finally get through ... such sweet thoughts make me home-sick. Oh I wish I was with you even for a little while."*

At the end of the war, Randall returned to Cleveland and was active in the Cuyahoga Mining Company, a concern he later wholly owned. He was also a partner in Hogan and Wade, Cleveland's largest jewelry store. He was a director of the Citizens Savings and Loan Association and of the Kalamazoo-Allegan and Grand Rapids Railroad Company, president of the American Sheet and Boiler Plate Company and secretary-treasurer of his father's Chicago and Atchison Bridge Company.

Jeptha had focused his attention on his only child, grooming him to inherit his business empire. Randall was a dashing swordsman, musician and lover of precious stones and fine art—everything his father wanted him to be, and Jeptha lavished gifts upon him.

Susan was not entirely happy with the amount of time Jeptha spent in his many enterprises and charities. During one of his many absences, she wrote Randall complaining, *"It seems to be my fate to be deprived of sharing my husband's pleasures and enjoyments, or enjoying much of his society. But, I will try to bear it patiently."* She was compensated by the opportunity to meet and host many dignitaries and famous people and a trip to Europe.

After Jeptha's retirement from Western Union, Susan got her wish for a new house on Euclid Avenue built in the Italianate style, with a Tuscan country villa-style house next door for Randall and his family. The complex was completed in 1870, and the grounds contained an array of statuary, shade trees, a pear orchard, a Malaga grape arbor, stone walkways and a front-yard pond with goldfish and a spouting fountain.

Homes of Jeptha Homer Wade and Randall Wade, Euclid Avenue, Cleveland

The family did not have long to enjoy the luxury. In 1876, Randall became ill with pneumonia. It seemed minor at first but soon became worse. Jeptha was consumed with anguish. For days he did not go to the office and instead paced up and down outside Randall's hospital room as the young man lay wheezing his very life away. Randall died at age forty, leaving Jeptha inconsolable. On his rise up the business ladder to build a fortune for his heirs, Jeptha had been driven to cut some corners that earned his wife's scorn. Now, Randall, the object of it all, was dead.

Jeptha then turned his mentoring attention to his namesake grandson, Jeptha Homer, who was only nineteen when his father died. He had had the finest education, including a master's degree from Western Reserve University. "Yes, my son," the elder Jeptha told his heir not long after Randall's death, "the mantle has now shifted to you. You'll command a huge empire of businesses. You will inherit a sizable amount from your father, and when I die, you'll receive an additional fortune."

"I'm very grateful. Just how did you do it?"

"I owe my initial fortune to the late Samuel Morse, but mechanics are only part of it."

"What's the rest of the picture?"

"Morse was not a good businessman. I hope he was pleased that I put together a national system out of all the pieces that had resulted from the indiscriminate way he granted patent rights. An integrated system better served the country and the various companies. I made him richer than he otherwise would've been."

"So what skills do I need?"

"You need a vision, and most of all you need diplomacy and fair dealing to be a good negotiator. Several other telegraphic pioneers had the vision, but they were heavy handed and the other owners didn't trust them."

"I don't know if I can meet your expectations Grandpa, but I'll try my best."

"I know you will. You're not carrying my name for nothing. I came from poverty, and with your fast start, you'll make an even bigger mark."

Always a lover of beautiful things, Jeptha collected fine paintings for his grand home. He loved to race his team of handsome chestnut horses hitched to a Brewster carriage from one end of Euclid Avenue to the other. Jeptha had the finest cutter in the city, a two-horse Russian sleigh mounted with flaming red plumes. On snow-covered winter streets, the racers turned out wrapped in their buffalo robes with charcoal warmers at their feet. Jeptha helped organize the city's social and sporting clubs for men. Remembering the early loss of his own father, he built a home for orphans, even adopting four himself. He organized Lake View Cemetery and donated land for a park, the Cleveland Art Museum and what became Western Reserve University.

One of Jeptha's out-of-state business interests was the Chicago and Atchison Bridge Company's bridge at Atchison, Kansas, and he named two of his sister's sons to positions there. Luther Lindsley Todd became superintendent in 1875, and Civil War veteran, Newell Todd, soon after became toll taker. Newell's wife, Hulda, wrote to her mother-in-law back in Michigan, using the company stationery:

Superintendent's Office, Atchison, Kansas

Feb 28th, 1880

Dear Mother Todd,
  We received your letter this morning. Was very glad to hear from you again. And as I have plenty of time, concluded to answer without delay. We were so sorry to hear Father Todd's trouble. Hope he is better. How hard you have to work. Oh how often I wish you could live differently, that is not being obliged to work to see to everything as you do. I don't see how you can spare Jennie at all. Did Martha receive my long letter? I wrote her some time ago, tell her I am waiting patiently for an answer.
  I heard that Elmore had been down to Buffalo. I know he enjoyed his visit. We occasionally hear from Rosie. Next Saturday Rosie's and my birthdays occur. She is 28, & I am 32. Mercy how old I am getting. I shall have to soon begin to deny my age. The children have been exposed to the measles. Hugh has been complaining for a few days. I think he is coming down. They are having them rather light, so I just as soon they would have them. Lutie reads nicely and asks so many questions. Is trying to find out so much. He carries a lead pencil and paper around with him so to take down the numbers on the cars. You know we live so near the R.R. that he can go out to the back fence and see them as they are passing. Hugh knows all his letters. Is Charlie mischievous any. Jessie goes to school don't she?
  We are having such nice pleasant weather. I don't think it has rained but twice since November. Have had but little mud. and very cold weather. Prospects are that we shall have an early spring. Have you heard that Newell had bought this place, he has and is intending to make different arrangements in the house.
  Charlie Bradley has resigned from the Army and went through to Michigan two weeks ago. Made a short visit of two days here with us. I like him first rate. Hope he will succeed and get a situation soon as he seemed anxious to.
  Sen. Ingalls has a great reception Tuesday eve. A great time is expected I understand. Fireworks, speakers, and a ball in the eve. Delpha is gaining all the time. Luther intends journey to Cleveland Wednesday. Thinks of stopping off in Michigan and making you a short visit. So he will tell all the news better than I can write. Newell and I are both quite well. We send love to all. Hoping to hear from you again.
      (s) From Huldie

  In celebration of his daughter's sixteenth birthday, Bridge Superintendent Luther took Belle on a business trip to Cleveland and on to see her Grandparents Ransom and Sally Ann in Michigan. Years later, she wrote to her son, Luther Todd Hazen, the following notes about her visit to Cleveland:

Jeptha Homer Wade, the man who formed the Western Union Telegraph Co. whose home was on Euclid Ave (Cleveland) was your great grandmother's (Sally Ann Todd) brother. He owned the controlling stock and after making millions sold out to Green and Jay Gould. I used to watch John D. Rockefeller play billiards after dinner almost every night with Uncle Wade. They lived just across the street, but the Wade place was much finer having ten

Luther (Lutie) Anson Todd   **Belle Lutherine Todd**

acres on the corner of Euclid and Case. Strangers were allowed to drive through the grounds any day but Sunday. It was the show place of Cleveland when I was a young lady. A beautiful Art Gallery with an orchestrian and large Turkish baths was in a separate building on the grounds. The orchestrian cost $50,000 and the building about $75,000. Uncle could hear a symphony orchestra any time he wanted with his mechanical wonder.

After Uncle's death, Homer his grandson erected the large receiving vault at a cost of one million in Lake View Cemetery and also where he is buried a very beautiful chapel. The most beautiful marble work and all Tiffany glass. The pews were of white mahogany. In the Wade Art Gallery were magnificent painting, statuary and oriental rugs worth thousands of dollars. The rugs could be taken up and the building converted into a ballroom. A gallery was on all three sides where one could walk or sit viewing the works of art. Hot houses, both for flowers and early vegetables on the grounds and a lovely lake also, but either the head coachman or else the gardener's little child was drowned in the Lake cast a gloom over the place. They never changed servants. Old John the head Coachman was with them 30 years and was pensioned when Autos came in, but remained on while younger men became chauffeurs. The last time I was there they had eight autos but Old John was so fat he could hardly waddle.

But Uncle Wade had to die like the rest leaving one grandchild 30 millions and his granddaughter Alice Wade Everett was enormously wealthy. I do not know how much she inherited.

Your Great grandmother Sally Ann Todd, married Ransom Todd, a poor but honest farmer, a deacon in the Baptist Church in Michigan. One of the best men I ever knew, the father of ten children. He was an honest man, a deacon in the same church, but Uncle had little use for his sister's husband because he was not a man of the world. When a religious man dined in the Wade home he was not even courteous enough to ask them to say grace. But when his only son died, he became interested in Spiritualism and he paid a fool medium $10,000 a year to get messages from the Spirit World. (I am sure at that price I could get messages galore.)

Rev. T.J. Leak a brilliant M.E. Minister of Pittsburgh, married Uncle Wade's niece, Rose Todd. Uncle Wade became very fond of Dr. Leak and although Uncle Wade had been an infidel all his life, he requested that when he passed away he would like to have them send to Pittsburgh for Dr. Leak to preach his funeral sermon.

I often wonder who was the better off, Uncle Wade with his millions that he could not take with him, or his brother-in-law who had devoted his life to charity, good deeds rearing an honest family.

I remember once of Uncle Leak saying, "If you are an infidel, and I am wrong in my belief -- you have nothing to lose if death end all -- but if I am right in my belief, and you are wrong, how are you going to save yourself -- I think I'll be prepared, and be on the safe side, for Eternity is a long time to be absent from those we loved on earth!"

Neighbors Jeptha and John D. Rockefeller had many conversations. Jeptha liked to think that his experience in consolidating telegraph lines had some influence on Rockefeller's business strategy. Those many evenings of pool together must have had some effect. The early days of the oil business, like the telegraph, were marked by too many companies, pumping too much oil and undercutting each other. Rockefeller brought stability to the industry and great wealth to his Standard Oil of Ohio by buying out some competitors and ruining others through schemes such as secret rebates with railroads. The same strategy was employed by Andrew Carnegie who put together the Carnegie Steel Company in 1892 that later became U.S. Steel in Pittsburgh.

Memorial Chapel, Lakeview Cemetery, Cleveland

Jeptha had begun negotiations with his Euclid Avenue neighbor, Samuel Mather, to merge his Iron Cliffs Mining Company with Mather's Cleveland Iron Mining Company, but both men died before completing the deal. Jeptha's grandson and Mather's son completed the formation of the Cleveland Cliffs Iron Company in 1891. Jeptha's grandson had his grandfather's business acumen and advanced the family fortune even further, allowing him to give twenty-five million to charity over his lifetime. Like fathers, like sons.

It was ironic that the steel business of Jeptha and others contributed to air pollution along Millionaires Row on Euclid Avenue. The families, some made wealthy by steel, began to move further out from the city center. Jeptha and his grandson, ever alert to opportunity, accommodated them through their real estate businesses.

Jeptha died in 1890, one year after the death of his wife. His mansion was torn down by his grandson in compliance with a clause in Jeptha's will. The old man had become very superstitious in his spiritualistic beliefs and thought his soul would remain forever wandering in his home, trapped by spirits including that of his first wife, Rebecca. Better to eliminate the dwelling where such haunting spirits might remain.

Randall's house on Euclid was not torn down until 1934. The grandeur of both buildings during their early years was still evident in an article written by a *Cleveland Press* reporter allowed access to the mansion the day before its demolition:

The wrecker's ax will fall tomorrow upon the old Wade mansion in the faded Millionaires Row and soon the northwest corner of Euclid avenue and E. 40th street, once the core of Cleveland's social whirl, will be vacant. Its passing will remove the city's last heritage (save for Wade Park and the Wade art treasures at the Museum of Art) of a family whose name looms large in Cleveland history.

The contract was let today. For $1,000 and other valuable the Globe Wrecking & Lumber Co. of which Samuel H. Tuber is president, was given the privilege of pulling down, its 28 rooms and disposing of their historic contents. It is doubtful if they could be reproduced for $1,000,000.

The conservatory alone cost $100,000. Its fireplace, set apart in a sort of alcove in the mansion's west wing, is a masterpiece of hand carving. Cherubim and intricate designs are worked into oak and teakwood. In the fireplace is a Chinese rope, hammered out of iron, which is pliable as leather. A couch covered in Burmese cloth of gold rests beneath the old Bavarian, water-powered organ which played the arias of the day for the distinguished throngs which danced there. Overhead, massive iron candelabra run the length of the room on each side.

The house was built around 1870 by Jeptha Wade, the portrait painter who became a pioneer in the building of America's telegraph industry, for his son, Randall. Jeptha's house, of which this one is a replica, stood next door and was torn down upon the old man's death. Now his son's will join it in oblivion.

The house hasn't been occupied since about 1920, when Randall's descendants moved to the country. "We thought it best to tear it down," G.G. Wade said today. "We were paying such heavy taxes and it didn't seem to appeal to anyone for them to rent it."

Wrecker Tuber took the writer through the old house today on its last day of inviolability. The front door opens into a court formed by the stairwell. There are three floors, and at each landing the stairs open onto a circular balcony which looks down upon the court below. The circles diminish with their height, and when one looks through them at the colored glass of the dome, it is as though he were peering through a symmetroscope.

To the left of the court is a room, now empty, which contains a gold-bordered mirror, ceiling high and as broad as five men's shoulders. Off this is the music room, with its silk-covered walls now hung with canvas and its carpets rolled on the inlaid floor.

Below, in the labyrinthine cellar, is the swimming pool, one of the first ever built in a private home here, and the bowling alley, and a Turkish bath and steam room. In a store room is an old canopy bed of walnut. In another room is the original map of Wade Park, covering almost a whole wall. Here too, is the record of a meeting of the stockholders of the Cleveland Iron Mining Co., May 27, 1891 because of the (recent) deaths of Samuel Mather (its president) and J.H. Wade and Selah Chamberlain.

Outside, in the carriage house, which will be wrecked too, is a rubber-tired two-wheel buggy, an old battery charger for electric automobiles, and the balloon and basket that Wade sponsored which won one of the first Gordon Bennett Balloon Races at the turn of the century.

The distance between Michigan farmers and balloon racers, between men of faith and those practicing mysticism, seems immeasurable. The deacon and the telegrapher could never understand each other, though Ransom Todd took some pleasure from the two hundred-dollar gift that Sally Ann gave her brother when Jeptha Wade's career was on the rocks. Ransom had died in 1883 and Sally Ann would die in 1893, a few years after her wealthy brother. In the 1880 census, Ransom reported that he was a retired farmer, though he had also been a carpenter and a druggist/grocer. He was the last Todd to work in agriculture. It was the telegrapher/investor who'd brought the modest deacon's sons away from the Michigan farm to Kansas where their progeny would work in the world of commerce and intermarry with other families brought to Atchison during the westward expansion. Ransom never went further west, but he was part of those who did.

Ransom Todd
1805-1883, Bogert (Adrian Center) Cemetery

~13~

The Irish Immigrant

"Don't cry Mum," pleaded John Patrick Brown. "It tears me up."

"I can't help it, son. If you go to America, I'll never see you again."

Mary Daulton Brown was not prone to tears. She had already buried two children, and she knew tears did not bring them back. Even when the potato plants in their little garden at the back of Castlemaine Street turned brown and died, she kept her composure. But now that the lack of food had translated into her son's departure, she broke down and cried. Her husband knew not to intercede. Better to let things work themselves out, he thought.

When emotions had calmed, John, Senior, tried to reason things out with Mary. "The boy is in the prime of his life at nineteen," he told her. "He is old enough to strike out on his own. I would dearly like to dance at his wedding someday, but this famine has turned the world upside down. We are not the only ones. I can almost hear the cries all over town. It's the same all over Ireland."

Later that afternoon when Mary had gone to the High Street to look for anything edible that the greengrocers might have thrown away, John Patrick and his father had time to talk about the details. "Da, I've done my homework," J.P. told him. "I'll walk to Cork and take a sailing ship from the port at Cobb to New Orleans."

"New Orleans? I ne'er heard of New Orleans."

"It's at the mouth of the great Mississippi River in the middle of the country," the son explained. "They say it is a lot bigger than our Shannon. I think I can pay my way by working on the ship because fewer immigrants want to go there. They are like you, never heard of New Orleans."

"Even so, you will need some money. I can only give you a few quid."

"I've saved a tenner in the few jobs I've been able to get during the past year."

"You're a smart boy. You can read and write some and have a strong back. I know you'll make it." The father wished he could say that with greater conviction.

J.P., as friends and family called him, said goodbye to those dear to him. There was one goodbye that he especially dreaded. He had been seeing the red-haired Nuola, who lived in the next block for a few years now. They had made no commitments, but there clearly were feelings between them.

"Nuola, I'm going to America," he finally told her. "You know I hate to leave my folks, and I hate to leave you, but there's no future for me here. I couldn't even consider having a family that I was not sure I could provide for."

Nuola's face turned ashen. The usual sparkle in her eyes disappeared. She could not look directly at him. They said nothing for a few moments. Then she turned and dashed into the house. J.P. thought he had made a mess of it, but soon she came back, pressed something into his hand and gave him a kiss and an embrace he would not forget. Nothing more could be said, and J. P. walked home, never looking back. On the way he opened his hand and found a crumpled tenner. Then he bawled for the first time since he was a child, hiding his face from passersby. She and her family had no money to spare, he thought, I'll never find another like her.

"Mum, I leave tomorrow," the young man announced one fall morning in 1849. "When I've made my fortune, I'll bring you and Da to America to join me. I promise." Neither J.P. nor his mother really believed it, but it eased the pain of leaving a bit. The road along the Shannon was crowded with people, some pulling carts with all of their earthly belongings. For a while, he helped an older couple pull their cart. J.P. knew his few pounds would not last long even if spent only for food, and there was precious little of that to buy anyway. In Limerick, his hunger got the best of him, and as he passed by a bakery, he grabbed a loaf and ran. He promised himself it would be the last time he would ever take advantage of another man.

When J.P. reached Cobb, he enquired if any of the ships at anchor were going to New Orleans. "None that I know of. Maybe latter in the week." J.P.'s confidence dropped, but he found a few hours of work on the dock and bought a loaf of bread and some cheese. A few days later his luck changed. An English ship with a cargo of salt had docked at Cobb, and he learned that it was headed for Louisiana. J.P. had never seen a sailing vessel before, but compared to others at the wharf, it looked tired and shabby, with its paint peeling and sails patched. He inquired about the captain and was directed to a man in a visored cap, whose appearance was not any better than that of the ship. When J.P. asked if any crewmen were needed, he got the answer he was hoping for: "Yes, I could use an extra man in exchange for passage and food."

J.P. looked back to the disappearing green-grey coast as his ship sailed out of Cobb. He tried to put Nuola and his Mum and Da out of his mind. He was put to work on deck doing odd jobs. He had trouble keeping his legs under him, but he was determined to give good value and worked even if his gut was in a knot. After about a month out, he was miserably seasick and wondering if he had made a mistake. Oh well, he thought, I can't get off now. After he'd been sailing three months, often lying in the scuppers soaked in his own vomit, he landed at the Port of New Orleans on New Year's Day 1850. The streets were littered with remainders of a huge party, including quite a few of the celebrants themselves.

J.P. had a gift for making friends and building on acquaintances. Before disembarking in New Orleans, he had already worked out a job with the captain unloading the bags of salt on board. This backbreaking work lasted four days, and J.P. slept among the sacks on the dock, even though it was January. New Orleans, he learned, was the largest cotton market in the world, and slaves were sold to pick it. As J.P. explored the town, he saw seven slave dealers in a single block on Gravier. He asked a fellow Irish dockworker what a slave pen was. "It's a kind of cell where slaves are held for auction," his coworker replied. "Slaves are fattened up and made to look attractive. If they have grey hair, it's plucked or dyed. There are eleven more pens over on Moreau Street."

J.P. was confused because he could see that alongside the slave trade, there was a large population of free colored people holding skilled jobs and working the best jobs on the docks. The French term for them was *gene de couleur libre*. J.P. said his first French words over and over because he liked the sound of them.

J.P. learned that cartage firms were hiring drivers. He had never worked with horses, but he kept that to himself. "How much do you pay?" J.P. asked when he found the master.

"Eight dollars a month," came the gruff reply. "Take it or leave it."

He took the job without complaint. It was enough money to allow him to rent a room with another man, sleeping two to a bed. At least it's dry and out of the wind, he thought.

He ate the cheapest food he could find on the street, saving his money. It took great resolve. As he wandered the streets at night, there were dance halls and brothels everywhere. A skimpily clad woman in a red dress approached him. "Hey there; I've got something for you," she called, emphasizing the word "you." J.P. looked down at his feet, and walked on. He wouldn't mind a dance and a pint or two, but he rationalized it by saying to himself, "They're not playing my kind of music. I did not come to America to work on the docks. I'll never make enough to have a family that way." He learned that New Orleans was known as a port of pestilence and prosperity. The pestilence struck the poor, and the prosperity seemed to be in the hands of a few. J.P. vowed to leave as soon as possible.

He talked to everyone he met, especially the crew of riverboats coming from the north. Depending on their origin and experience, each told of promising work upriver. The one that sounded the best to J.P. was all the way to Pittsburgh. J.P. was not sure how far away this city really was, but he was told they were building railroads in Pennsylvania and there was plenty of work for his kind, meaning Irish immigrants, but J.P. didn't know that yet. When he had saved enough money for the passage, he headed upriver.

When J.P. landed in Pittsburgh, he remained on the dock and engaged the hands there in conversation, asking, "Where can a man find work?"

"Don't know; I'm lucky to have one here," came the answer J.P. didn't want to hear. But he was not discouraged and moved on to another group and asked again, adding, "Do you know anything about where they are building railroads?"

"Nope," one fellow said, "but this be harvest time ya know. I hear there are jobs out in the country." J.P. took the stage to Blairsville west of Pittsburgh on the Conemaugh River and found work on a farm. "Can you drive a team of horses, young man?"

"Indeed I can," J.P. replied with growing confidence in his skills.

In Blairsville, J.P. asked everyone he met about the Pennsylvania Railroad, which he understood had reached Harrisburg from Philadelphia. There were plans to continue the line on to Pittsburgh. "Yep, there are jobs at Greenville, about twenty miles southwest of here."

"That's where I'm headed then." Greenville, named for General Green, one of Washington's trusted men of the Revolutionary War, stood in the middle of rich coal mines, and the new emigrant immediately felt comfortable there. Greenville was the seat of Westmoreland County, the same name as the county where J.P had been born. That was as close to Ireland and home as he could get right now.

In Greenville, J.P. found Wright and Jeffries, civil engineers, who were surveying for the Pennsylvania Railroad between Pittsburgh and Latrobe. He got work driving teams for fifteen dollars a month plus room and board. He resolved, I'll show them that I am the best man they have on their crew. Soon, he was given more responsibility and his pay increased to thirty-five dollars.

J.P. met a fellow worker and struck up a conversation, "Mike, I can tell that you are from the old sod by your accent."

"Yeah, I'm from Galway. No future there. There's lots of us Irish immigrants working to build railroads. We're the grunt workers."

"I'm the same from Athlone, but I won't always earn my pay from hard labor."

"I see you working like a dog all day, and then at night you are studying those books in the bosses' office," Mike told him. "I couldn't do it; I'd fall asleep the next day."

J.P. was studying surveying, math and roadbed-construction engineering. Knowledge gave him confidence, and he kept his ears open for roadbed-building contracts. When he learned that a line was to be constructed between West Newton and Connellsville, he saw his opportunity and went to the engineering department office. "My name is J.P. Brown, and I would like to bid on a section of the roadbed you are planning."

"Mine is William Palmer," the supervisor replied. "Have you any capital and references?"

He doesn't look much older than I am, thought J.P. to himself, but he probably has more education,. "I don't have references," he told the fellow, "but I've saved enough to buy six teams, and I've been studying the engineering books of Wright and Jeffries."

Palmer had heard of J.P. and knew that he had a reputation as a hard worker and was impressed that he had managed to save any money. Most of the Irish workers did not. "I'll vouch for you," he told J.P., "and you can have a contract for one mile. If you do well, I can arrange for a larger section."

J.P. did well. He worked alongside his men, and that got the best from them. The railroad bosses were in a hurry and preferred speed to fine engineering, and that suited J.P.'s skill at the moment. Connellsville was a growing town of fifteen hundred on the Youghiogheny River, in a land that was earlier the home of the Turtle Clan of the Lenape (Delaware) Indians. The town fathers contracted a large debt to bring a railroad line to Connellsville. Service of the debt required a heavy tax, and five hundred residents left town in the next ten years to avoid having to pay it.

J.P. learned all he could from Palmer, who told him of the historic problem of getting cargo and passengers over the Allegheny Mountains at Altoona. It was only four hundred miles from Pittsburgh to Philadelphia, but the mountains were a seemingly insurmountable barrier. In the old days, bulk cargoes in Pittsburgh had to barge down the Ohio and Mississippi Rivers to New Orleans, then around Florida and up the eastern coast to Philadelphia and New York. Canals had then been built from Pittsburgh to the mountains and from Philadelphia to the other side of the mountains. The Allegheny Portage Railroad was built in 1834 to connect the eastern canal to the western canal, reducing the travel time from Philadelphia to Pittsburgh to four days instead of twenty-three. The portage was accomplished by a system of tracks on inclined planes that lifted cars by ropes and cables powered by stationary steam engines. Finally, Pennsylvania could compete with New York's Erie Canal. "You see, J.P., engineering and transportation construction are the keys to economic development," Palmer counseled. "When we complete the Horseshoe Curve and Gallitzin Tunnels in 1854, the railroad can cross the country with no unloading and reloading."

William Jackson Palmer, soon to become private secretary to J. Edgar Thompson, President of the Pennsylvania Railroad, was a good model for the young Brown. He would later command a cavalry unit in the Battle of Antietam and be awarded the Medal of Honor. J.P. could see that success required both technical knowledge and people-management skills. The example would not be lost not on him.

From that point, J.P. knew that construction was going to be his calling and his fortune. His immediate problem was to get a contract for another section of the railroad, which he did with a successful bid for a twenty-five mile stretch of roadbed between West Newton, his headquarters, and Connellsville. He received twenty-five cents a cubic yard for earth excavation and one dollar twenty-five for rock. He worked like a galley slave with his men all day, telling Mike, "I can't expect you to do what I won't do." The job took a year to complete. His next section was only for one mile, but it was through rock and on hillsides, and it also took a year to complete. Once the Pennsylvania Central reached Pittsburgh in 1853, J.P. went into the general-contracting business.

J.P. watched the telegraph lines being erected along the Philadelphia to Pittsburgh line, aware that the telegraph made it possible to better manage the train schedules. He heard about another immigrant, his own age butt Scottish, named Andrew Carnegie who was hired by the railroad to be its telegraph operator. Much later, J.P. learned that Carnegie worked hard and became the private secretary to Tom Scott, the twenty-nine-year-old superintendent of the western branch of the Pennsylvania line. The contractors knew that railroad executives capitalized on insider information and invested in companies soon to be enriched by contracts with the railroad. A private secretary would be privy to the deals cut by his boss and could be made agreeable to keeping it quiet if he were cut in on some deals. J.P. wondered if that was the stuff of fortunes. Whatever that way to wealth might be, he was not interested in pursuing it.

J.P. had become a solid businessman, and his thoughts turned to marriage and family. "Mike, my good fellow," he asked one day as they worked side by side, "how can I go about meeting eligible young women?"

"I think that church is a good place to meet 'em," Mike advised.

"That's a good idea. I was raised a Catholic, but I've not attended for years," J.P. admitted. The next Sunday he attended mass at the Catholic Church in West Newton where there were lots of Irish immigrants like himself, but mostly men. He learned that the local people were more likely to attend the Baptist Church, so the following Sunday, he gave that a look. He had to catch himself to avoid making the sign of the cross at the end of prayers. The Sunday after that, he attended a church social even though that meant he had to be away from his crews. After wandering through the crowd, he introduced himself to a young woman who'd caught his eye. "My name is John Patrick," he said. "What's yours?"

"Sarah Wagner," came the shy reply.

J.P. quickly put her at ease and soon had her laughing at his stories.

Sarah's rather severe Germanic aspect could hardly compare to the red-haired, sparkling Nuola back home, but J.P. had left that behind. This was America, the melting pot, he thought; so be it.

During the week, J.P. confided in Mike, "I think she likes me. Perhaps it's the gift of blarney that sets me apart from the others she knows. It surely is not my good looks. I reminded her that we were both born in a Westmoreland County. I just wish her parents didn't keep calling me Paddy. We are not all named Paddy."

"Be careful of the blarney. A little goes a long way," replied Mike.

Things seemed to be going well between the young couple until one Sunday when Sarah told him, "My parents don't want me to see you anymore."

J.P.'s heart felt like it had dropped to the floor and someone had stepped on it. "You see, we're German, and you're Irish, and they haven't had good experience with the Irish around here."

"In Ireland, we Irish were the subject of discrimination by the English. Now I find prejudice has followed me to America. We are not all fun-loving, irresponsible, drunken leprechauns."

"You're being too hard on my parents."

"And what does your heart say? I hate these stereotypes. I'm a businessman, probably worth as much as your parents. I don't smoke and never touch a drop of spirits. You know that's true."

"My heart says I care for you very much. I will try to explain your prospects and character to my parents. I know I can. I want to spend my life with you."

Sarah did, indeed, convince her parents of her suitor's character. John Patrick Brown, twenty-five, and Sarah Wagner, eighteen, daughter of Henry and Sarah Wagner, were married in West Newton in 1854. Two of their children, Alex and John H., would be born in that western Pennsylvania town.

Railroad contracting was moving steadily westward, and J.P. went with it, taking the stage, railroad, and steamboat to St. Louis via Cincinnati. Fellow Irishman, A.J. McCausland of St. Louis, alerted him to the new opportunity. A Pennsylvania company was building the St. Louis and Iron Mountain Railroad in 1856 designed to carry iron ore from the mine north to the city. The road was completed south to Pilot Knob in 1858. The advertising for the line featured a long-horned steer with the slogan, "Steer For The Iron Mountain Route."

To make an informed bid on the contract, J.P. walked forty miles south from St. Louis along the Mississippi. He returned by steamboat to St. Louis. Still, J.P. was not familiar with pay scales in St. Louis, and he underbid the contract. McCausland helped him revise it. J.P. was grateful for his help and would later take him as a partner. After making a successful bid for preparing two miles of roadbed, he assembled a crew of fifteen men and their teams. While J.P. was in Missouri, his second son was born in Pennsylvania. He knew he should have been there, but he would not be satisfied with an ordinary job in now-settled Pennsylvania. The real opportunities kept moving west, and if he did not keep up, they would leave him behind. I hope Sarah will understand, he thought to himself.

    Sarah did not understand. As her mother and a midwife tended her birthing, she became hysterical with the pain. "Where is my husband? I could die, and he wouldn't even know. I could lose the baby, and he wouldn't even know."

    "Now Sarah, bear down and forget about J.P," her mother told her. "Men are not much good at these times anyway. He might as well be in Missouri."

    A contractor familiar with the terrain he is going through is in a good position to know where the best farmland is. J.P. was also aware that the new railroads would make the surrounding land more valuable. He bought several large tracts at good prices before others knew the lines' location. He was part of the steam, iron and industrial revolution, but being Irish, his heart was in the land. While working on the Iron Mountain, J.P. received a letter from James Coulter, the marshal and unofficial town booster of Atchison, Kansas. J.P. did not know how Coulter had heard of him, but news and reputations seemed to travel in strange ways. Coulter told him about the Atchison & Pikes Peak Line, later to be called the Central Branch of the Union Pacific, that was to be built out of Atchison, partly in response to Pike's Peak gold strike. Atchison boosters expected four rail lines to be constructed to the west coast, and they wanted to be the terminus for one of them. The main line would be out of Omaha. Another out of Kansas City would join the Central Branch somewhere on the Republican River on the hundredth meridian and intersect the main line near Ft. Kearney, Nebraska.

J.P. went to Atchison in March 1859 to check it out. He liked the place so much that he soon brought his teams and grading outfit up the river from St. Louis. He was impressed with its connections to the Hannibal & St. Joseph Railroad and several stage lines and with a Baptist Church and Hetherington's Dry Goods store for Sarah's sake and a common school for the boys. Coulter, his new friend, had become clerk of the school district. J.P. bought some land near Commercial and Second Streets for a stable yard. McCausland joined him as a partner and boarded at the three-story Massasoit House. None of the boarders there knew that the hotel's name came from the chief of the Wampanaogo tribe of Cape Cod, whose greeting of the Pilgrims had been far from friendly.

John Patrick sent for Sarah and the boys to join him. While they were making arrangements for the trip, J.P. built them a house on North Second Street. As he was building the house with his crew, he confided in Mike. "You have been with me since my first contract in Pennsylvania. You know that when I bid on that first mile, I had nothing but confidence in myself. You're the only one here I can talk to. We're kindred spirits from the ol' sod."

"I feel the same way about you."

"I left Ireland to make enough money to support a family. Now, I have some money and a family, but I was not at home when my second son was born. I wonder if I have made the right decision to come here and seek contracts that again will take me away from home and Sarah. I can rationalize it by saying that opportunities are fleeting, but still I have doubts."

"Don't doubt yourself, mate," Mike told his boss. "There is still not much standing between us and poverty. Just one accident or a business depression, and we're back to nothing. To keep working is the best thing we can do for our families."

"There's something else, Mike. Last week I awoke from my sleep in a cold sweat. I dreamed that my parents had died of hunger. It was horrible. I promised them when I left Ireland that when I made enough money, I would send for them to come here. I need to double my efforts."

"Easy, J.P. You already are putting in the hours of two men. Even a bull like you can't do that without hurting your health. These things take time."

J.P. was overwhelmed with emotion when Sarah arrived with their two sons, Alexander and John. He held his eighteen-month-old son for the first time. He spoke softly to his toddler, "You are the third generation to be named John Brown. I want you to be proud of that name. I promise you a better life than the first two had. You will never be hungry." Only Sarah could see a bit of wetness in her husband's eyes as he kissed her and held her in his big arms for the longest time. After they had settled in, Sarah reflected on the early years of their marriage. "J.P., even though I was with my parents, you can't imagine how lonely I felt in Pennsylvania while you were working in Missouri. I hope any babies born here will come into the world and see their papa straight away."

"I deeply regret not being there for John, Jr., but I'm afraid rail-bed construction takes me away for long periods of time. But, I surely will try to arrange to be here when you are close to delivery." Sarah bit her tongue and let the issue rest.

Sarah liked the fledgling town of Atchison immediately. "This afternoon I went downtown and bought lots of clothes for us all at Hetherington's dry goods store," she told her husband "Everything was on sale. Here they call it a 'slaughter' because prices are so low."

"I was hoping you'd like Atchison. It's a fine town and growing every day."

When J.P. had arrived in Atchison, people were impressed with the big, broad-shouldered Irishman with a full beard. He was plainly dressed as a laboring man, but there was something about him that commanded attention. He seemed at the same time to be both unassuming and someone to respect. People just enjoyed talking to him and hearing his stories. The railroad construction was delayed and J.P. looked around for something to utilize his men and equipment. He received a contract to grade streets in Atchison and thus began his long involvement in public improvements and infrastructure in the town. Later he would macadamize those same streets.

J.P. and his crew returned to roadbed construction later that year, working for the Platte Valley line from Weston, Missouri, to a point two miles south of Leavenworth. Eventually the track became part of the Burlington system. He had a crew of one hundred fifty men and finished the work in ten months. Trains from St. Joseph to Atchison were running by April 1861. That same month, the firing on Ft. Sumter, South Carolina, seemed, to the Kansans, so distant as to be in another world. At St. Joe, Missouri, the line connected to the east along the Hannibal and St. Joseph Railroad. That line had brought the first mail to St. Joe to be carried west by the Pony Express in 1860, a year of drought in Kansas.

After completing the Weston project, J.P. took a three-year contract to ferry freight across the Missouri River. This was before Jeptha Wade built the bridge over the Missouri at Atchison and sent the Todds west to superintend it.

News traveled fast among railroaders. J.P. heard that Thomas Scott had become vice president of the Pennsylvania Railroad. Scott made the railroad into a holding company at a time when that was illegal. When the Civil War started, Scott became rail advisor to the Union Army and at one time arranged the movement of twenty-five thousand troops in twenty-four hours, resulting in an important Union victory. After the war, Scott constructed lines in the South using freed Negroes as his labor. He added Ku Klux Klan members to the railroad's board of directors so the Klan would not interfere with his colored work crews. Scott and his protégé, Andrew Carnegie, lobbied the government to award public land to the railroads for building a transcontinental system. J.P. wanted to know where his old Pennsylvania friend fitted into all of this and learned that Palmer oversaw the completion of the Kansas Pacific to Denver, then left the company to found the Denver and Rio Grande Railroad without any government aid. Palmer had taught J.P. a lot about engineering and management, but J.P. was not of a mind to join in the kind of shenanigans that Scott participated in. Jay Gould would buy out Palmer in 1880.

J.P. was an active Republican, though he never ran for office. He subscribed to the *Freedom Champion*, the weekly Republican-oriented newspaper, and voted for Lincoln in 1860. He found slavery an abomination, given his background in Ireland where the British treated the Irish as little more than slaves. He hated all the guerrilla warfare between the pro-slavery groups and the Free Soilers that preceded Kansas's 1861 entrance into the Union as a free state. He had to admit that he enjoyed the story of his countryman, Pat Devlin, who participated in raids across the border in Missouri. Devlin described his forays thusly, "You know, in Ireland we have a bird we call the jayhawk, which makes its living off of other birds. I guess you might say I've been jayhawking."

News of the terrible battle at Antietam reached Atchison. While reading the *Champion*, J.P. commented to Sarah, "I can't imagine men charging and falling back over and over again in a level cornfield in the face of deadly fire. The paper says over twenty thousand are dead or wounded in just one day of fighting. General Lee retreated back to Virginia, but it was no real victory for the Union. The war will go on."

J.P. went beyond mere words in his support for the antislavery cause: The firm of McCausland and Brown made a major contribution to support Atchison men that had enlisted in the Union Army. "Lincoln's Emancipation Proclamation freeing the slaves in the South is impressive," remarked J.P. "This changes the war from simply preserving the Union to the great cause of freedom."

"I agree, but it would be more impressive if Lincoln had freed the slaves in the North as well," Sarah added. "But I understand that he fears the Union would lose the support of border states." Sarah had followed the politics of the war very closely.

Ever alert to opportunities, J.P. recognized the business implications of the discovery of gold in Montana Territory during wartime. By mid-1864, five thousand people were living in an entirely new town named Virginia City, which was soon named the capital of the territory. All these miners would need supplies. McCausland and Brown started freighting from Atchison to Virginia City, which did not yet have rail service. Alder Gulch, one of numerous settlements along a small, alder-lined stream, was known as the route's "Fourteen-Mile City." Lovejoy of St. Joseph contracted with the freighters to ship drugs and other goods, and the partners had rigged thirty-two teams by midsummer of 1865. The shipment was accompanied by McCausland, A.S. Parker, George Howe and a man named McKinney. The shippers were not to be paid until the goods had been sold by merchants Mers and Dinan, who were also traveling with the shipment. Upon arrival in Virginia City, McKinney and McCausland argued over the division of the profits, and in a moment of heat, McCausland drew his pistol and killed the other man. McCausland was subsequently jailed, tried for murder and acquitted after pleading self-defense.

The night before they were to head back to Atchison, McCausland and Parker dined in one of the fine eating establishments in Virginia City. On the hand-written menu was scrawled "Special Tonight, Rocky Mountain Oysters." Parker asked McCausland, " Do you know what kinda oysters could they have clear out here?"

"Derned if I know, but let's have 'em if they're so special."

"Hey, little girl," McCausland called to the waitress. "We'll have two orders of them oysters. What are they anyway?"

"You're strangers here ain't ya? You're in for a treat. Tastes something like chicken. It'll grow hair on your chest."

"I wonder what she means by that?" Parker mused.

When the oysters came they looked good, having been rolled in cornmeal and fried. The taste was a bit wild, but the men hungrily ate them all.

When the waitress returned, Parker declared, "Don't taste like any chicken I ever et. You must have strange chickens out here. Now tell me truly where on an animal do these come from."

"They're the testicles of young calves and sheep," the waitress told them with amusement as the men gulped and tried to maintain their composure. "They say it makes men virile."

"Do you want to find out if it worked?" McCausland asked her.

"No. Shut up and finish your grub," she said without a trace of humor in her voice.

Leaving the drovers to return to Atchison with their teams and wagons, McCausland, Parker, Mers and Dinan started for home on one of Holladay's Overland Stage Line coaches. Knowing their vulnerability to robbers, they kept silent about their departure time and hid some of the sixty thousand they'd been paid in gold dust on their persons and some in a carpetbag under a coach seat. As they mounted the stage, the driver introduced himself. "My name's Frank Williams. I'll try to make good time, but you know the usual trip to St. Joe takes twenty-two days. We get fresh horses at stations twelve to fifteen miles apart, and we eat at stations separated by forty to fifty miles. The grub is nothing special, but it'll keep you from starving."

McCausland asked him about the chance they could be waylaid by robbers. "Well, the most dangerous section of the trip is through Port-Neuf Canyon," the driver explained. "It has high rock walls riddled with side canyons, providing good cover for bandits. We will try to arrive there in mid-afternoon when robbery is less likely."

A.S. Parker rode shotgun beside the driver. As they approached the canyon, each man nervously checked his gun. About halfway through, a burly man who had been hiding in a clump of bushes jumped out and grabbed the bridle of the team and another man yelled, "Halt! Throw down your guns." Nine other armed men appeared at his side.

At the same moment, Parker called out, "Robbers! Fire on them!" But as he raised his gun, he was riddled with lead shot and fell dead. McCausland, Mers and Dinan died in the barrage from ten guns. Another stagecoach passenger was wounded, but he feigned death and avoided the worst. The robbers searched each dead man, took the gold they were carrying and the carpetbag as well.

The driver drove on to the next station with his grisly cargo of dead. A large reward was offered by the stage company for the arrest of those who committed the butchery, and vigilante groups hunted for the desperadoes, but to no avail. Soon after, the driver quit the employ of the stage line and was seen living it up at the saloons of Salt Lake City. This aroused suspicion of those hunting the bandits, and they watched him and surmised that he had not honestly earned the money he was spending. Williams was arrested at Godfrey's Station between Denver and Julesburg, and he confessed that he had been an accomplice in the robbery. "It never occurred to me that the passengers would be killed," he told the men who apprehended him. "I never signed on for no killing. I've had no peace of mind since." Before he was summarily hanged, Williams gave enough information to lead to the apprehension and hanging of some of the robbers, but others were never identified.

Prior to leaving Atchison, Parker had purchased a three thousand-dollar life-insurance policy and made one payment. When J.P. heard the news, he remarked to a friend, "That's a hell of a way to earn three thousand. I thank my lucky stars I didn't make that trip. All I lost was money."

After the death of his partner, J.P. entered into a new partnership with Frank Bier that lasted many years. Frank had come to Atchison the year before J.P. and was engaged in the furniture business until 1860 when he was elected county treasurer.

When construction of the Union Pacific began at Omaha in 1865, J.P. gave some thought to making a bid to construct a section. "I would like to be a part of history when the coasts of this country are linked by rail," he told Sarah, but when he inquired of some his fellow contractors they discouraged him from trying. One who knew about the construction of the Union Pacific said, "I observe that the construction companies for the big lines are not firms like ours.

They seem to be owned by the managers of the railroad. There are rumors that the railroad overpays the construction companies, and the money goes into the managers' own pockets rather than to the stockholders. You'll never get a contract from that system. The big boys play by different rules."

Later in 1872, the Crédit Mobilier scandal broke. Some of the managers had created the company to construct the roadbed and lay the rails. Some seventy-two million dollars in contracts were given to Crédit Mobilier for building six hundred sixty-seven miles of track that should have cost only fifty-three million to build. The construction was paid for with government subsidies. It came out that the company had given stocks to more than thirty representatives of both political parties, including future President Garfield. The Union Pacific (UP) itself was nearly bankrupt, but its executives became rich.

The UP had been undercapitalized for some time. In 1871, it was desperate for cash to build the great bridge over the Missouri at Omaha. Carnegie arranged for a six hundred thousand-dollar loan from the Pennsylvania Railroad. The UP gave the Pennsylvania Railroad its stock to hold as security until the loan was repaid. The apparent rescue of the UP greatly increased the price of its stock, and Carnegie sold it to the profit of himself and the president and vice president of the Pennsylvania Railroad.

When J.P. came to Atchison, city boosters were promoting the Atchison and Pike's Peak Railroad that had just been incorporated by the Kansas Territorial Legislature. Part of the delay in construction was due to negotiation of a treaty with the Kickapoo Indians, who received a dollar twenty-five per acre for their land. This was the tribe of the once infamous Prophet, brother of Tecumseh.

The Atchison & Pikes Peak project transformed into the Central Branch of what became the Union Pacific. J.P. had one hundred men and forty teams at work on section nineteen near Muscotah in October 1865. When he was in town, he told the Atchison *Champion* that he expected to have a crew of two hundred assembled in a week and could grade a mile of road every twenty-five days. Construction was started out of Atchison in the spring of 1866 and continued until December 1867. J.P. and his crew lived in shanties along the route. In the winter, the cold weather would often engulf them before they could reconstruct their shanties along a new section of the line. Snow would cover their bunks before they could get the sides built and the roof on. When J.P. did his bookkeeping at night, the only dry spot was on top of the stove once the embers died down.

If anyone grumbled about the impossible working and living conditions, J.P. would reply, "There is no place to go but forward. There are no towns for miles. There is no turning back. I couldn't turn back when I was seasick for weeks on the ocean coming over from Ireland, and I'm not turning back now." Indeed, "no turning back" had been the story and the motto of J.P. Brown's life.

While J.P. was with his crew on the Kansas plains, Sarah gave birth to son, Frank, and she was sharp with her husband when he hurried home a few days later. "Again, you were not here when I gave you a new son," she told him. "You were not here to support me. This is getting old. Perhaps our last child wouldn't have died aborning if you had been here."

This took J.P. aback. "That's a heavy load to dump on me, Sarah. I apologize, but, I provide for you and our family by constructing railroads on the frontiers of settlement. It takes a while for messages to get to me. I am not a banker, like Hetherington, who can come home every night from work."

Sarah knew that things were not going to change soon. Maybe someday when J.P. was finished with railroads and just managed his construction business in town, he would be home every night.

Congress changed its mind about the railroad routes, and the Kansas City Branch was now to follow the Smoky Hill River directly to Denver via Fort Riley and Abilene, rather than veering northwest and meeting the Central Branch. The Central Branch received one hundred eighty-seven acres of public land and government bonds equaling sixteen thousand dollars per mile for one hundred miles. No further federal subsidies were to be allowed to the Central Branch after it reached one hundred miles. The Central Branch ended at Waterville, Kansas, becoming only a stub serving local traffic. Kansas City was to be the major terminus for the Pacific railroad, partly because a bridge over the Missouri long preceded the bridge at Atchison. The Atchison branch started to the Pacific early but could not finish the job. Still, J.P. and his men were paid for their work.

The Kansas City branch route crossed the reservations of the Delaware and Pottawatomie tribes. The treaties negotiated in 1861 ceded land to the United States, leading to the Delaware's further displacement to Oklahoma. President Lincoln signed the Pacific Railroad and Telegraph Act in 1862 granting to the railroads every alternate section of public land along routes from the Missouri River to the Pacific Ocean. That was five alternate sections per mile on each side of the road.

J.P.'s biggest and most profitable contract was construction of much of the Atchison and Nebraska Railroad. One of the railroad's incorporators was

Atchison businessman Augustus Byram. Atchison County subscribed to one hundred fifty thousand dollars of the capital stock in an effort to stimulate its economic development. Another eighty thousand was subscribed by individuals in the county. Work commenced in 1869, and the roadbed and ties were laid to the northern border of Kansas by 1871, a distance of forty miles. Then it was given to a Boston syndicate who agreed to complete and operate it. Later the road was consolidated with the Atchison, Lincoln, & Columbus Railroad and extended to Falls City and to Lincoln, Nebraska, where it connected to the transnational Union Pacific in 1872. Further consolidation with the Burlington & Missouri River Railroad Company occurred in 1880. Railroad consolidation followed the pattern set by the telegraph companies under the leadership of Jeptha Wade and Western Union. One of the railroad consolidators was the financier Jay Gould.

J.P. was employed to make an assessment of the Atchison, Topeka & Santa Fe line between Parnell and Valley Falls, Kansas in 1872. His report, printed in the Atchison *Daily Champion, included the following*:

The grading is fully as good as any that can be seen on first class Eastern roads. The embankments are very substantial, having a width of fourteen feet at grade; the cuts at grade have a width of twenty feet; the slopes are trimmed and finished to a line; and the entire road bed presents an even, smooth and uniform surface. The masonry of the bridge abutments is 'first class' being composed of an excellent quality of stone, rock face with hammer dressed beds and joints; laid in regular course, and the work throughout all its details bearing the unmistakable imprint of experienced mechanical hands. These abutments are not excelled on any road either East or West. The masonry of the culverts and cattle guards is the very best of its class. Atchison will very soon have another railroad of which her people will be justly proud.

Sarah had a grand time at the Pennsylvania Reunion for Kansans held in February 1878. She told J.P. all about it. "Six-hundred people from all over the state who, like me, originated in Pennsylvania assembled at Leu's Hall for a grand banquet. Women brought typical Keystone State dishes, such as kraut, pumpkin pie, fried cakes, mince pies, apple cakes and cider. I was celebrated as the maker of the largest pound cake."

"You could have come if you had wanted," Sarah told J.P. when he expressed his envy for missing all the good fare. "I had not eaten *schnitzen knep* for a long time. Banker Hetherington made a grand speech about all the contributions of Pennsylvanians to Kansas."

"You are becoming quite the celebrity," J.P told his wife. "I also read in the paper about Atchison's celebration of a baby show. I think it's grand that you provide cash prizes for the cutest baby and the most attractive display of baby clothes."

"You know that I love babies."

Once J.P. had become successful in his construction business, he developed a desire to travel. One night at supper he was bubbling with enthusiasm. "Sarah, I want to take a break and make a trip to Europe before I get too old. I'd like to show you where I was born. And I would like to see the Vienna World Exposition."

"When is the exposition?'

"It runs from May 1 to October 31."

"Can we afford it? I understand we are in the middle of a financial panic. I read where Jay Cooke went bankrupt after borrowing heavily to build his Northern Pacific Railroad."

"That's true. Stocks have fallen drastically in panic selling here and in Europe, but my assets are not subject to the panic. Like I have told you before, the land is always there. Maybe my renters will be slow to pay, but they will come back. The panic is having a major impact on railroad construction, but it will revive. It's a good time to be away, and I want you to meet my parents."

"I'd like to see your birthplace, Paddy."

J.P. had long given up any objection he had to being called Paddy. Now that he was successful, he knew it was a term of endearment and not a stereotypical slur. Just before sailing, news came of an outbreak of cholera that killed thirteen at a Viennese hotel.

"I'm frightened, Paddy," Sarah told him. "Perhaps we shouldn't go."

"I'm not abandoning my plans now."

The Vienna Exposition of 1873 was indeed a splendid event, and Sarah's fear dissipated. J.P. was fascinated by the exhibits of industrial machinery. His favorite was an exhibition and lecture in the Rotunda concerning an electric motor by Professor Pacinotti of the University of Pisa. The professor explained, "Whereas in the magneto-electrical generator we apply mechanical power and take out electrical, in the electro-magnetic engine we apply power and take out mechanical."

"Sarah, this is where I wish I had more education. I only partially understand it, but I can see that someday our horse-drawn streetcars in Atchison will be replaced by electric ones. Here goes creative destruction again."

After attending a concert by the American organist, Clarence Eddy, Sarah remarked, "I wish he would come and play the organ in our church in Atchison." She steered J.P. to the Chinese teahouse where he felt exactly like the proverbial bull in the china shop, but he and the cups survived. She also directed him to the replica of the temple of Kyoto and an Egyptian tent with authentic décor and manikins in costume. When J.P. couldn't hide his fascination with the belly dancers, Sarah hustled him out of the tent.

Later over coffee at the Café Central, Sarah commented, "The grandeur of this city is beyond anything I ever imagined. St. Louis doesn't hold a candle."

"Yes, but the ostentatious display of wealth is too much for my blood."

"I understand that the emperor and his young wife don't get along."

MACHINERY HALL AT THE VIENNA EXPOSITION.

"No amount of wealth and power can compensate for that or for the death of their infant child and the suicide of their son."

"I understand what it is to lose a child," Sarah responded.

J.P. winced at her reminder of a sore spot between them. "When will it ever go away?" he wondered. "Or am I reading something into her comment that she did not intend?"

As J.P. and Sarah passed through London on the way to Ireland, they were very much aware of Queen Victoria's Golden Jubilee. Then the visit to J.P.'s family on Castlemaine Street, Athlone was an emotional one for them both. "Mum, my offer to bring you both to America is still good," J.P. told his mother. "For years as I was trying to get established, I almost gave up hope that I would ever have the money to do it, but today I do."

Castlemaine Street, Athlone Ireland, today

    J.P. thought his dad, who said little as he rocked by the window, looked particularly frail.
    "I'm very proud of you, my son," said his mother. "Our thoughts of you have kept us alive and hopeful all these years after the famine, but I'm afraid your father is not able to travel anymore."
    That brought a lump to J.P.'s throat; he had waited too long. The visit home had been bittersweet, and his leave-taking was no easier than the first time. He was grateful that his aging parents had met Sarah. He did not inquire of Nuola, though her parting kiss years ago played on his mind.
    Back in Atchison, J.P.'s next construction project was on a portion of the Atchison, Topeka and Santa Fe from Atchison to Parnell and later to Trinidad, Colorado. The AT&SF encouraged western settlement to increase traffic on their lines. They had to convince immigrants that Kansas was not a land of drought and grasshoppers. It did not help that a tributary of the Kaw was named Grasshopper. The river's name was changed to the Delaware: Better to honor long-gone Indians than grasshoppers. The railroad distributed a booklet entitled, "How and Where To Get A Living, A Sketch of 'The Garden West'."
    J.P. also did the grading and furnished the ties and rails on the first twelve miles of Jay Gould's Missouri Pacific between Atchison and the Leavenworth County line. Steamboats brought the rails from St. Louis, and some of the ties came all the way from the forests of Wisconsin.
    J.P. joined with the civil engineer Fred Giddings in 1877 to raise the elevation of the bed of the Atchison and Nebraska for sixty miles from Atchison

to Salem, Nebraska. They managed to do it so that no train was delayed, a point of pride for the contractors

While J.P. was engaged in Nebraska, he heard that the Santa Fe wanted to extend its route west from Pueblo, Colorado, along the Arkansas River and through the Royal Gorge. J.P. knew the area well from the days he'd worked on the Santa Fe to Trinidad line. The Denver and Rio Grande Western Railroad also wanted to build on the same route through the narrow gorge which had room for only one line. Two years of armed guerrilla warfare ensued between the two companies and their allies. The federal government forced an out-of-court settlement in 1880 in which the Santa Fe gave up extending its line to Denver and Leadville and the D&RG agreed to pay the Santa Fe for the track already built and to halt plans to build a line to Santa Fe. Thus the West was carved up. J.P. was glad he was not engaged in these high-stakes financial wars.

"Sarah, I think we need a larger house. I have a corner lot at 805 North Fourth Street. Even though some of our children have moved out, it seems we are always sheltering others as well, and we need more room." It was to be a grand two-story brick house in the latest style, with segmented gables, bracketed, wide cornices, decorated porch pediments, polychrome voussoirs in the arches above the windows, color contrasts and stick-style decoration of gable ends. J.P. would use arched lintels, straight stone in a bay window facing the street, while lion heads centered on wrought iron grills would be surrounded with brick and stone to finish the porch. Hood-molds over the windows and wondrously squeezed doorways were designed to attract attention, as were the slender supports for the porch. "Sarah, I will show prospective home builders in town what Brown and Bier contractors can do." J.P. hoped that a new house might make up for all the times he had been gone during critical family moments.

"That sound wonderful, but it does seem that life is a little backwards. When you can afford something grand, most of the children are gone."

"Yes, but they will come for visits, and once Alice is married, she can live here after we're gone. I'm planning some fun details such as a leaf design jigsawed into the wooden trim about the house. There will be a tower with gable finials of orb and fleur-de-lis design."

"I have some ideas for the interior. I would like three fireplaces: one of cherry, one of oak and one of brick. I want a library, living room and foyer with wood paneling and a walnut- spindled stairway. I hope we can use some of the native woods found here in the Missouri valley." Sarah's enthusiasm was growing.

"Great. We can work on the plans together. Sarah, before I start on the house, I am taking a vacation in Colorado with my friends, Web Hetherington and Luther Challis. We will do some fishing and hunt for grizzly."

J.P. Brown house

"I'm telling you right now that I'm not going to have any bearskin on the floor of my house. How long will you be gone?"

"OK; OK. If I bag a grizzly, I'll give it to the other men. We'll be gone three weeks."

After returning from his hunting trip, J.P. regaled Sarah with many stories. She did not know which ones to believe, given his tendency to exaggerate. He casually mentioned that he and George had purchased a Colorado mine. Well, whatever, thought Sarah. After a week, he finally stopped talking about the mountains and turned to other topics. "Sarah, I saw and heard the most marvelous thing at Pandowdy Hall downtown this afternoon. Mr. Sargent demonstrated Edison's phonograph. You speak into it, and it plays back what you have said."

"That's almost unbelievable," Sarah replied. "How does it work?"

"Tinfoil is wrapped around a drum, and a needle tracing on it transfers your voice to the drum. Then the same needle following the grooves will play it back."

"Can anyone speak into it?"

"I think so. After Mr. Sargent listened to it, he said, 'Shut up; go soak your head. G'way,' in a very boisterous manner," J.P. reported gaily. "The playback was so natural that you could smell its breath."

"Are you giving me your blarney again, Paddy?"

"No. I swear it. You can go down tomorrow and hear for yourself."

"I can see it now: Our young people will be dancing to music playing on Mr. Edison's machine, and all of our orchestras will be out of work."

"You can't stop progress."

"I don't want to be a stick in the mud, but sometimes the new fads of our young people alarm me. I rather agree with a former friend of mine who now lives in Boston who wrote the letter to the *Globe*, saying, "Every day I meet in the streets of Boston young ladies who would otherwise look intelligent, reduced to the appearance of idiocy by a peculiar method of combing the hair down over the forehead. This hideous deformity is evidently copied from the patients of lunatic asylums and schools for the feeble-minded."

"Now, Sarah. Don't be too hard on them. If that had been the style when you were a young woman, you would have had bangs instead of wearing your hair in a bun on top of your head as you have done ever since."

"I don't think so!" Sarah replied with a bit of heat.

J.P. knew better than to pursue the subject further. "Sometimes our paper gets a little too personal and free with its comments," he said changing the topic. "Last week, it said. 'Paddy Brown has had a toothache for two weeks.' Now today they printed, 'We regret to tell the autocrat that Paddy Brown's toothache is better.' "

"I guess your quarrel with the Major Downs is now public news. What's it all about, anyway?"

"Downs has let the Central Branch fall into disrepair. He's the superintendent, and I just built the rail bed, so it's not of any direct concern of mine, but I hate to see my work let slide into poor condition. This is Atchison's biggest feeder line, and it will hurt the town's business if shippers stop using it. I'm not the only one who's publicly criticizing Downs, but he now goes out of his way to block anything I try to do for the city."

"Like what?"

"Like when I offered to help the city refinance its debt so they could pay a lower interest rate, he got in the way for reasons I don't understand. Then he delayed the efforts of several of us to secure land for a new union depot for the city. He's just a contrary bastard, excuse my language."

Ed Howe, the *Globe* editor, injected his philosophy about issues larger than the quarrel over local railroad management. The temperance movement had grown steadily toward the end of the century. Kansas had passed prohibition in 1888, but the law was ignored in many towns, including Atchison. Kansas's own native daughter, Carry Nation from nearby Medicine Lodge, had carried the temperance movement to a new level when she entered a saloon in Wichita and destroyed a valuable painting and mirror above the bar.

"Sarah, have you been following the escapades of that Nation woman?" J.P. asked his wife. "She goes too far when she crosses the threshold of a man's world and abandons persuasion for violence. No self-respecting woman would to that."

"Yes, I've read the *Globe's* story. Howe condemns and ridicules her saying 'Mrs. Nation is sixty years old, very fat, and very ugly.' I guess the saloonkeeper in Wichita cowered when confronted with a large, six-foot woman carrying an axe."

"I know for a fact that Howe is a teetotaler as we are, but he argues that prohibition would just make drinking more attractive for many. Do you really think men can be reformed?"

"Only with the help of our savior Jesus Christ," Sarah told him.

"I agree with Howe and you that drunkenness is a matter of personal struggle and can't be legislated. I know it was true for me."

Sarah added, "I feel for women whose men drink up their wages and don't provide for their families, but they should have inquired more deeply into the character of their prospective husbands before marrying them."

"The paper says that Nation is coming to Atchison, and Howe is confident that our officials will not let her try to run things to suit herself. He says she should be whipped and rolled in the dirt and her clothes torn off."

"That seems a bit harsh." Howe had a bad experience with his wife, and Nation suffered from a drunken husband. Perhaps that explains Howe's misogyny and Nation's attack on men.

"A woman's place is in the home as you have demonstrated with our seven children."

"Nation claims to be preaching the word of God, but we Baptists will not let her speak in our church and no one else will either."

Nation did come to Atchison, and for whatever reason, she did no violence, but she did fall prey to some hoodlums who roughed her up. On her way to Atchison, she had entered the train's smoking car and demanded that the men stop smoking and pulled a cigar from the mouth of a very surprised lounging man.

One night, Sarah was all smiles at the supper table. J.P. asked, "What are you bursting to tell me?"

"Alice is going to be married to Warren Peter Byram. I am so excited that she will marry into such a distinguished Atchison family. I know you think a lot of his father, as you both have been in the freighting business and both of you like to invest in farmland."

"Yes, she's our baby and all grown up now. A wedding will be a fitting celebration of the turn of the century." The wedding was a grand affair befitting two of Atchison's leading families.

MISS ALICE BROWN.

One morning several years later, Sarah announced, "I am planning a party to celebrate my birthday seventy years ago."

"What a great idea. Can I come?" J.P. asked slyly.

"You can if you want, but the guests will be mostly women of families that came to Atchison about the time we did."

"OK. I'll make myself scarce."

The day after the party, Sarah was eager to tell J.P. all about it. "It was great fun to reminisce with the old-timers like the Otis, Blair, Challis, Price, McCleary and Ingalls women and, of course, the governor's wife. And Eleanor Holbert was there. Do you remember when she came to town as a bride and used to entertain guests by dancing an Irish jig? I am especially pleased to have had Lilly Hetherington, whom I like a lot. Our daughters and granddaughters helped serve. It was grand. I wore my white dress over a pale pink slip."

"That's one of my favorites. It shows off your figure."

"Oh go on! I'm a conservative old lady. Among the birthday gifts was a stack of seven ten dollar gold coins."

"I wonder what secret admirer gave you that. Should I be jealous?"

"Don't give me any of your blarney. Of course, they were from you, one each for the seven decades of my life. What a sweet, sentimental man you are." She got up and planted a kiss on his balding head. "Thank you."

"Hey, don't you think the birthday girl could give me a bigger kiss?"

She obliged with a warm kiss and hug.

MRS. J. P. BROWN.

Even in her seventies, Sarah loved to hold parties for her friends and made the *Globe* in 1908. "Mrs. J.T. Coplan, formerly of Atchison, who is the guest of Mrs. E.K. Blair, is being entertained most enjoyably by her old friends. Mrs. J.P. Brown invited Mrs. Coplan's old friends to her home on North Fourth Street yesterday afternoon to a very pleasant party, the feature of the afternoon being the elegant refreshments for which Mrs. Brown is noted. .... Mrs. Annie Miller, who is visiting her daughter, Mrs. Lilly Hetherington, was there, and she and Mrs. Coplan were married the same day in Brownsville (PA) over 53 years ago. They took the same boat when they went on their bridal trip. Mrs. Miller was quite the spin for those days, 24 years old."

Community investment was a byword for J.P. He had shares in the gas, electric light, water and streetcar companies of Atchison. He was a major stockholder and director of Hetherington's Exchange National Bank and a major stockholder of the First National Bank as well. He built St. Benedict's Church next to the Benedictine College in 1866.

John Patrick Brown died August 23, 1909, at age seventy-nine. His obituary in the Atchison *Globe* noted that Sarah and John Patrick had six surviving children: John H. and Charles A. of Atchison, Frank of St. Louis and Hattiesburg, Mississippi, Alice who married Warren Peter Byram, Eleanor (Nellie) who married W.F. McDonald of Atchison, and Sarah who married S.F. Stoll of Kansas City. They also adopted an orphan girl, plus they enjoyed eight grandchildren and two great-grandchildren. The *Globe* noted the homes he built for his children in Atchison, Kansas City and St. Joseph, remarking, *"Now isn't that better than denying the children these comforts while their parents live, and then leaving the money for them to wrangle over? Though no one who knows the members of the Brown family, and their love for each other, could imagine them wrangling under any circumstances."*

Upon J.P. Brown's death, the Globe continued with the admiration it had expressed while he was living. "In addition to being a kindly man, he was almost a perfect type of the gentleman. He was also a man of unusual sense: a man of unusual insight into practical affairs. Although compelled to learn to read at night, while sitting around an engineering camp on the Pennsylvania railroad, he accumulated one of the largest fortunes in the West. What would have been his history had he had advantages?"

Some days after the funeral, Sarah was visiting with Lillie Hetherington. "There is only one thing I would do differently in our years of marriage," she confessed. "I gave Paddy a hard time for not being home when some of our children were born. That was unfair."

"I can understand how you felt at the time," her friend replied. "We all do the best we can."

"Still, Paddy was a good man and he provided well for us. I wish I hadn't rebuked him so much."

Sarah survived her husband by six years. Her obituary noted that she had recently completed fifty years of membership in the First Baptist Church as well as years of service in the Atchison Aid Association that helped families in need. The newspaper said, *"Mrs. Brown never could rest if she knew anybody was in want."* The paper also noted that Mrs. Brown had inherited an estate of four hundred fifty thousand dollars from her husband that would now pass to their heirs. One hundred years later, that legacy would be worth ten million dollars.

As he'd often expressed to friends and associates, J.P. believed that land is the only permanent thing on this earth, that it would persist after the railroads and their builders were all gone. So with a careful eye to the surrounding land during his roadbed construction projects, J.P. had acquired a total of four thousand acres in the northeast Kansas counties of Atchison, Jefferson, Jackson, Doniphan and Brown in addition to land he already owned in Missouri. He never sold an acre of farmland during his lifetime, though he bought and sold urban lots. The hungry and penniless Irish immigrant, who could never own a patch of earth in his homeland, finished with enough land to equal quite a few aristocratic English landlords in Ireland. But he had had to leave his first love behind to do it.

As the next generation watched the dirt fall over John Patrick Brown's casket, they were filled with mourning for the old man, but held hope for the future ahead of them. The previous year had brought marvelous wonders. Perhaps the most impressive was Wilbur Wright's flight lasting two hours and twenty minutes. The Wright brothers had first demonstrated that flight was possible in 1903, but the extended flight proved that the invention was more than a toy. That same year, America had shown its might when the Navy's Great White Fleet, including sixteen battleships, had sailed around the globe. It was the time Admiral Peary and Captain Cook both claimed to have reached the North Pole. The new Singer Building in New York had topped out at six hundred twelve feet high, and the Metropolitan Life Building soon followed at seven hundred feet. Sporting excitement was provided by the Chicago Cubs' four-to-one victory over Detroit in the World Series. Americans won fifteen out of twenty-one firsts at the London Olympics that year, and Negro boxer Jack Johnson crushed reigning heavyweight champion, Tommy Burns, who, like previous champs, had refused to fight a black man until Johnson shamed him into a match. Even in defeat, Burns got thirty thousand of the thirty-five thousand-dollar purse, the contracted percentage that had convinced him to cross the racial divide.

President Theodore Roosevelt held the first-ever Governor's Conference on the Conservation of Natural Resources. Just thirty-some years before, the U.S. Government exterminated whole herds of buffalo to deprive Plains Indians of wild food resources and force them onto reservations. At the turn of the century, there were only about a thousand buffalo left in all of North America and past profligacy seemed stupid. In 1902, Roosevelt persuaded Congress to appropriate fifteen thousand dollars for the purchase and feeding of buffalo in Yellowstone National Park.

Few Americans were as well off as the Browns had become. Vast numbers lived in poverty, child labor was common, as were workplace deaths. Ellis Island saw one and a quarter million immigrants pass through in 1907, many of whom never did manage to escape the tenements of the large cities. Violence against African-Americans continued, and there were dozens of lynchings. Anarchists and New York gangs made bombs to avenge their grievances.

At her father's open grave, Alice squeezed Warren Peter's hand and allowed the tears to flow. "Daddy has paved the way for a very hopeful life for our children, Florence and John," she told her husband. "I wonder if they will stay in Atchison and contribute to its growth?"

Warren Peter, himself, never seemed to find the same entrepreneurial success as the previous generation. He tried his hand at several businesses, including making cigars and operating a car dealership and finally seemed to find a promising career with Bailor Plow Company that made a self-propelled cultivator. Use of the modern implement was quite profitable for farmers in the early 1920s when cotton and grain prices were high and labor was in short supply. Yet when farm prices dropped, farmers could not pay the promissory notes they'd gotten to buy the implement, and the company failed. Many of these notes came into the possession of the Exchange Bank that lost money on them. The fortunes of Peter Byram and J.P. Brown provided a comfortable inheritance for Warren Peter and Alice Byram, but over time, it would be eroded.

Alice (Brown) Byram & Children Florence & John

~14~

The Banker and the Gilded Age

William Hetherington went to work at his flour mill in Pottsville, Pennsylvania, one morning only to see black smoke rising from its roof. The fire was already well established by the time the pumping engine arrived, and there was little the firemen could do. William's wife Anna heard the fire bell and went out on the porch of their house and saw the smoke rising above the trees. Her heart skipped a beat, and she called for her three children. They all hurried to the mill with Annie carrying the youngest. Annie frantically looked for her husband in the crowd. It was difficult to maneuver with the children. "Excuse me; excuse me," she called out. "I'm looking for my husband."

"He's over there by the pumper," someone volunteered. But the town constable would not let anyone near the burning building. Anna screamed William's name, and he heard her, turned and came to her. He embraced her and relieved her of the child in her arms. "Annie, I'm afraid the mill will be a total loss." When she started to cry, William tried to comfort her but was near tears himself.

"Was anyone trapped in the building?"

"Thank God, no. The men were just coming to work, and the few already inside got out right away."

Pottsville Pennsylvania, 1845

In a few days when it was clear that the mill was a total loss, William discussed their tragedy. "I think this is a sign that I'm in the wrong business in the wrong place. Pennsylvania in 1858 is filled up, and there does not seem to be great opportunities for new business. Pottsville is just a dirty old coal town. I'm thinking of pulling up stakes and moving west."

"Where would we go?"

"I've heard that Kansas is growing, and that makes for lots of business opportunities."

"But Pottsville is where we started our family and where our parents live. I don't know anything about Kansas. Is it civilized? Are the Indians still on the warpath?"

"Of course not. Those are just wild stories."

"How would we get there? I've never traveled any distance."

"We can take the train to Pittsburgh and then a steamboat down the Ohio. Atchison is right on the Missouri river."

"Sounds exciting," Anna told her husband. "I'll make the best of it."

William Hetherington, his wife, the former Anna Strimpler, and their children, Emma, ten, Webster, nine, and Clifford, two, relocated from Pennsylvania to Atchison in 1859. He arrived with great sympathy for small businessmen who'd had runs of bad luck and could not pay their debts. He knew all about bad luck. He recognized that a businessman had to accept some risk to get ahead. Sometimes it paid off, and sometimes it didn't. Upon his arrival in the growing town, William bought the stock of a bankrupt dry-goods merchant in Leavenworth and shipped it to Atchison.

Soon after their arrival, presidential candidate Abraham Lincoln spoke at the Methodist church in Atchison. After Mayor Samuel C. Pomeroy's introduction, William listened with approval to Lincoln's declaration that the purpose of the Republican Party was to prevent the extension of slavery. The local *Champion* newspaper supported Seward for President and carried no mention of Lincoln's visit.

William opened a store to sell dry goods, boots and shoes on the south side of Commercial between Second and Third. He earned some profit, but it was slow going and he could see other brighter possibilities. In 1865, he moved to a larger space on Third Street and put a desk in the back, asserting that he was the Exchange Bank open for savings and small loans. His oldest son Webster, known to friends as Web, found work in the office of the Champion Steam Printing House that published the newspaper. At its birth, the paper's name was *Freedom's Champion*, an openly anti-slavery voice.

William thought it would be good for business to be visible in the community, so after getting established, he ran for city council and was elected. He soon learned that taking positions on public policy often earned him enemies, as happened when he decried citizens who let their goats munch on their neighbors' shrubbery. His support of an ordinance requiring businesses to obtain city licenses to constrain fly-by-night shysters raised cries from opponents declaring that their freedom had been violated Everyone wants to be free of regulations, but one man's freedom to do as he wants can be another man's pain.

Champion Steam Printing

Methodist Church

When William established his bank in the back of his dry-goods store, he was well aware of the history of early banking in Kansas. The first formal attempt to establish a bank in Atchison was the Kansas Valley Bank chartered by the Territorial Legislature in 1857. The charter provided that half of the capital had to be in gold or silver specie and the remainder in bonds of the subscribers. The volume of loans was limited to two hundred percent of the capital paid in and the maximum interest rate was ten percent. A nationwide financial panic was in progress, and the founders sold the charter to Samuel C. Pomeroy and his associates who later reorganized it as the Bank of the State of Kansas. The bank opened in March 1858, but for lack of business soon had to be reorganized. Pomeroy brought in some heavyweights this time: W.H. Russell and W.B. Waddell of the famed freighting firm of Russell, Majors and Waddell who had made a wagonload of money freighting goods west out of Atchison, Leavenworth and Nebraska City. Russell, Waddell, L.R. Smoot and Pomeroy each subscribed ten thousand dollars. William wished he had that kind of money or knew friends with large purses. He was told that the bank soon had forty-three thousand in circulating notes.

That was the way to quite literally make money: issue your own currency and hope that people would accept it. Annie never understood how it all worked. "Will people accept money other than gold or silver?" she asked.

"They will as long as they believe in the reputation of the banker," William assured her. "With prominent people like Russell and Waddell, it works." Hetherington's banking enterprise followed the same model, only on a much smaller scale. He issued one-dollar notes as loans to merchants and manufacturers who used them to pay employees for their work and farmers for their animals, fruits and vegetables. The small denomination proved popular with ordinary people who could not trade in the larger notes commonly available but who seldom had gold coin. A dollar was a lot of money to a laboring man or farmer.

William advertised in 1862 that he was buying gold, silver and United States demand notes. Pike's Peak gold dust was especially solicited. Demand notes issued in 1861 and '62 were redeemable in gold coin, but redemption was temporarily suspended. The notes were used by the government to pay its employees and military personnel. It was the first government-issued paper money put in wide circulation since the Revolutionary War. The backs of the notes were printed in green, giving rise the popular name "greenbacks." In 1861, the expenditures of the U.S. government were sixty-seven million dollar. The following year with the Civil War raging, they were four hundred seventy-five million, while tax revenues were only fifty-two million. Congress initially authorized the issue of one hundred fifty million dollars in notes to finance the war, with additional authorizations to follow. Jay Gould helped sell government bonds. Prices rose to the delight of farmers, and the paper money encouraged unprecedented production of all kinds.

Hetherington's business was sporadic during the Civil War. The outlaw, Cleveland, rode into town intent on robbing his bank, but his gang was scared away by J.P. Brown's men who were working nearby. Repeated attempts by paramilitary groups to plunder the bank caused William to close his doors for a year. Annie did not say much about it, but she worried about whether her husband could keep solvent and safe.

Between the proslavery Jayhawkers and the abolitionist Bushwackers, the Kansas border was being terrorized. Armed bands from Missouri crossed into Kansas and vice versa. Abolitionist John Brown murdered a group of pro-slavers at Osawatomie in southeast Kansas. William was adamant in his condemnation. "These border ruffians are just using the war as an excuse for thievery," he told Anna "A local vigilance committee is being organized to protect citizens and property."

"We owe a debt of gratitude to these men," she replied, "but I hope you will not carry a gun and patrol the streets."

"Guns scare me," William admitted, "and I'm a little old to join the Union Army. But I want to be a part of the war effort. I don't have much money, as banking and business are at a standstill, but I feel we must make some sacrifices to support the one thousand men who have enlisted from our county. I have donated to the aid of our troops. My friends, McCausland and Brown are also major contributors."

"I want to help by making clothing to be collected by our Ladies Benevolent Society and sent to our soldiers in the field. We also are collecting food and clothing for the families of soldiers during their absence."

"It is little enough we can do."

When the war finally ended, there was a celebration of relief in Atchison. The closest the two armies had come to Atchison was sixty-five miles away at Byram's Ford on the Blue River at Independence, Missouri.

In 1865, the government prohibited the issue of notes by state-chartered banks. These state banks got a bad reputation for frequent excesses, but they made a contribution to the economic growth of the nation since they understood the capacity of local entrepreneurs to turn new ideas into new production. The local entrepreneur could be financed without depending on the limited flow of eastern or foreign capital. With the disappearance of state-banknotes, credit took the form of creating bank loans and thus deposits that the creditor used to write their own checks. The check would come back to the issuing bank for redemption, but if other banks in turn were making loans that were deposited in the first bank, all would be solvent and the overall money supply would grow.

As the war was coming to a close, Hetherington again bought the entire stock of another failing dry-goods merchant and was about to hold a giant "slaughtering sale" when he sold the entire stock to another firm at a good profit. The next year he advertised himself as a real estate agent, available for collecting rents, loaning money and buying and selling real estate. In 1866, the Bank of the State of Kansas was put up for auction, perhaps because of the collapse of the Russell, Majors and Waddell freighting company and its Pony Express. Hetherington bought this once-thriving bank and renamed it the Exchange Bank of William Hetherington and Co, taking as his partners, Augustus and Peter Byram. The Byram brothers had moved from Nebraska City to Atchison in 1859 after acquiring the teams and wagons of Russell, Majors and Waddell when they became overextended. With good management, they had turned the business into a fortune but gave up freighting to the incoming railroads. Businesses rise and fall, and new money replaced old.

William managed to secure the business of R.L. Pease, J. Garside and Co., wholesale grain merchants, George Glick who was later to become governor of Kansas, and William Osborn, who was instrumental in the construction of the Atchison and Pike's Peak Railroad. That railroad became the Central Branch built in part by J.P. Brown and managed by W.F. Downs. Pease had been the cashier and principal officer of the Bank of the State of Kansas and was also running his own fire insurance agency, but he now joined Hetherington's enterprise.

"Annie, look at this July issue of *Harper's Weekly,*" William proudly said to his wife as he waved the publication in front of her face the summer after his purchase of the Bank of the State of Kansas.. "There's a drawing of Commercial Street in front of my bank. The street is full of all kinds of people: a man in a stovepipe hat walking with a finely dressed little girl on the plank sidewalk, men on horseback, men in fur caps returning from the western mines, a discharged Civil War soldier, blacks and whites and of course some dogs and pigs running loose. It makes it look like business is good in our town."

"Wonderful! That should be helpful for business. Too bad they had to include the messy pigs. I'm glad the artist was not here after a big rain when the street is a quagmire."

"The artist was a little free with the buildings portrayed, but that two-story one in the middle with the three arched windows is definitely the façade of my bank."

"It surely is, in every detail."

"The bad news is that when I acquired the bank's assets, they included a note from Samuel Pomeroy who has become our U.S. Senator."

"So, what's the problem?"

"We tried to collect it, but I guess these big politicians think they don't have to pay. Rather, they expect to be paid for political favors."

"That's not fair."

"That's life. I've protested the commercial paper of some of our prominent merchants for nonpayment, and the bank has become the owner of various lots in town through foreclosure sales. But I don't think I want to sue Pomeroy, and he knows it and takes advantage of it."

The bank's customers included Hetherington's brother-in-law, Samuel Hipple, who was a major cattle buyer. Another was G.C. Hixon who operated a large lumberyard. Demand for construction materials was brisk. The Exchange had the accounts of Thomas Murphy when he was in the Indian office, but it was railroad construction that was the big business for the bank. The railroads sold their land grants, and eastern and foreign capitalists funneled money through the bank to pay for supplies and labor. Drafts from the Importers and Traders National Bank of New York City were exchanged. All kinds of money were in circulation, and the bank had to be very alert to ever-changing exchange rates of Canadian notes, English sovereigns and gold drafts, United States bonds and a Dutch money order. There were literally thousands of different kinds of banknotes in circulation across the nation, and Hetherington subscribed to a number of newspapers, a banknote reporter and counterfeit detector to inform and protect himself.

"Annie, I'm going to build a new three-story building with a large iron safe at Commercial and Fourth. The bank will occupy the first floor, various offices will be on the second, and the Masonic Hall will take up the third."

"You seem to have tenants lined up to provide income for the building, but are you sure your business will support it?"

"Indeed, we've been doing very well."

"I have a suggestion for interior decoration. You know, you are always telling me that a bank depends on its reputation so that people will not withdraw their deposits during financial panics. Well, one way to present a solid face to the community would be some art work inside. I know that Theodore Minehart paints very beautiful frescoes. One would be very impressive in your office."

"Great suggestion. I will engage Minehart at once. Everything should be finished by the time our daughter is married next year."

"And one last thing. I think you should hang a picture of President Grant in the lobby. People are in a patriotic mood these days."

"I'm not a big fan of our president, but I think you're right."

At dinner one evening, Anna announced that there was going to be a rally for women's suffrage that evening. "I'm going. It's about time women can vote."

"Dearest, I'm in favor of universal suffrage, but I really wish you would not attend. Men are divided on the issue, and it might not be good for business to have the banker's wife giving public support for it."

"Business? Is that all you can think about? Some matters of principle are more important. I'm going."

William recognized the stridency in her voice. "OK, OK, but please be inconspicuous."

Anna, was not yet ready to let the matter drop. "You really should come and support the movement. Stand up and be counted."

"If I stand up, there will be fewer deposits for the bank to count."

"Coward!" Anna could hardly believe she said that, but she did not withdraw the condemnation.

When Anna came home she told William, "Senator Pomeroy made a speech in favor of female suffrage. Then the leaders of the national movement, Elizabeth Cady Stanton and Susan B. Anthony, spoke. It was thrilling. I got to shake their hands. They are impressive, brave women."

Susan B. Anthony

"Well, I'm glad that old Pomeroy did something right for a change."

"There will be a statewide referendum this fall. You will vote for it," Anna told him, emphasizing the word "will." "I think it's a bitter irony that men get to decide the fate of women."

The 1867 vote failed as would two successive votes before Kansas adopted women's suffrage in 1912.

The Hetheringtons' daughter Emma Louise was twenty when she married twenty-two-year-old Balie Peyton Waggener in May 1869. Balie had recently entered the law office of Otis and Glick but soon he formed a law partnership with Albert H. Horton, then U.S. district attorney. Horton later became chief justice of the Kansas Supreme Court, and Waggener was named general attorney for the Missouri Pacific Railway in 1876 and subsequently became close to financier Jay Gould.

"Annie, you are always reminding me of the work you do in managing the house. I appreciate it more as I have to maintain our new bank building. It seems mundane, but I spent forty dollars digging and walling the privy vault for our staff and customers and another forty-two to finish it. I pay Amanda five dollars a month for cleaning and fifty cents to wash the windows and sprinkle the street to keep the dust down in the summer months. The street lamp on the corner costs five dollars, and then there's the cost of mucilage, pen holders, draft books and passbooks. It all adds up and has to be managed just like a household."

Augustus Byram withdrew from the bank in 1871 after he and William argued over a loan the bank had made to Augustus for the Horn Silver Mine in Utah. Augustus was extremely wealthy now and would soon move to Chicago.

This was the year that seven hundred Texas cattle arrived in Abilene for shipment to the East to meet the postwar demand for meat. Abilene was the most western rail head at the time. "Wild Bill" Hickok had brought some peace to the lawless town that had been plagued by gun-happy cowboys raising hell after long cattle drives. Even though William wished that Atchison had a share of the cattle business, he couldn't change the route the Kansas Pacific Railroad ran to Chicago to accommodate his hometown.

One morning, William was enjoying biscuits served up by his maid when he said, "Annie, I'll be walking to work today. The horses have a kind of influenza."

"I'm sorry the epidemic has spread to Atchison. The papers are calling it the 'Great Epizoötic of 1872.' I read that the U.S. Cavalry has lost so many horses, they are fighting western Indians on foot. Can you believe it?"

"Our town's street railway has almost shut down for lack of able horses. Many trains have stopped running because coal can't be hauled to fuel them."

William checked his tie and adjusted his bowler hat in the big mirror in the front hall, selected a silver-capped walking stick and strolled down the hill toward the commercial district. The next morning's breakfast conversation was no happier. "The banking news is discouraging, Annie. Jay Cooke wanted to build another transcontinental railroad across the northern United States, but now we find that his bonds are no good. Some newfangled railroad bonds that few could understand are now worthless. On top of it all, Jay Gould tried to corner the market on gold. When he was stopped by President Grant's release of government gold, premiums collapsed and highly leveraged speculators went broke. These greedy financiers will be the death of us yet."

"Yes, greed is one of the seven deadly sins you keep warning me about," son Web added. The look on brother Cliff's face said he had oftentimes heard that line as well.

"With unemployment rising, many across the country can't pay their home mortgages after a period of rising prices associated with real estate speculation. Financial failures are spreading, many eastern banks are bankrupt, and now the whole country is in what will go down in history as the Panic of 1873," lectured William

"Has it spread to Kansas?" asked Annie.

"Oh yes. Some Kansas City banks have suspended payments. Work has stopped on the Atchison, Topeka, and the Santa Fe west of the Kansas border. Earlier, the government stopped buying and coining silver, and that has caused a contraction of the money supply, especially here in the West. I read that a bank cashier in El Dorado was killed by a depositor after the bank failed."

"Heavens! Can our bank weather the storm?"

"I'm sure we can, but it's tough on all debtors, especially our farmers." Keeping his thoughts to himself in good banker fashion, William was not really as confident as he sounded. In fact, the depression would drag on for five years, and Hetherington's bank barely survived.

The next year was particularly bad for Kansas as a massive grasshopper invasion resulted in a crippling crop loss. One of the bank's farm borrowers commiserated with William, "I understand that further west, the hoppers are so thick, they crunch underfoot as you walk along. Cornstalks have been stripped to mere sticks as the leaves are all devoured."

"Yes. I know some local governments can't collect enough taxes to service their bonds." William didn't know grasshoppers, but he knew bonds.

"I read in the papers that down in Barber County, settlers are suffering from brutal Indian raids along our southern border. What next? I thought all that was behind us."

"Civilization proceeds slowly and as smart as we are, nature is still to be reckoned with. First, it was equine influenza, now it's grasshoppers. The Indians are just another kind of grasshopper."

While having his lunch with some customers at Stewart's Restaurant on Commercial Street, William overheard a conversation at the next table. "I hear that McClarity's whiskey is not selling well, and he is about to go under." William jumped up, nearly spilling his soup, left his oysters and celery, put a coin on the table, snatched his hat and bolted for the door without a word to his friends. He ran full tilt to his office in a very undignified manner for a banker and grabbed one of his ledger books. He was about out the door again when son, Webster, called after him, "Where you going in such a rush?"

"We made a loan to a whiskey distillery in the next county. I just got word that it's going bankrupt. I'm driving out to see for myself and determine the value of his assets. I'm headed to the livery stable. Go home and tell your mother I may not be back until tomorrow."

"OK, Dad. Drive carefully. Watch those sharp corners."

William did not stop running until he reached the stables on Sixth and Commercial. "Mr. Moulton, I need a light buggy and your fastest horse for the day. Speed is of the essence."

"I've just the steed you need—none faster in the city," said Moulton, repeating a line used with all his customers.

"Thanks! See you later today or tomorrow morning."

On a rough country road William scattered a flock of chickens that had pecked their way out in front of a farm house, and farther on, the buggy nearly clipped an escaped pig. His horse was well lathered when he arrived at the weathered, white building housing McClarity's still. The aroma of the sour mash permeated the air. The owner, tending the fire under his kettle in his shirtsleeves, was surprised to see his banker. Almost immediately, the surprise turned into a frown. "What brings you to my humble establishment?" McClarity asked with suspicion. "Do you need a drink?"

William was sweating from the heat but did not remove his suit coat. He thought he could smell whiskey on McClarity's breath. Foregoing small talk, the banker went straight to the point. "Have you funds to cover your debts? You know your note is coming due, and if you can't pay, I aim to be the first in line to claim enough of your remaining assets to repay the note."

"Don't worry. My equipment is worth enough to cover that claim of yours."

"I'm sorry our relationship has to end this way, but business is business."

This was not the first time that William had acted quickly to conserve bank assets. He had taken products of a meat-packing plant and stocks of a dry-goods and grocery merchant as well. William may have been respected in Atchison, but he was not well loved.

William had minimal education, but he prized it for his children. Web was sent to Gambier College in Ohio. William liked the idea that it was the oldest private college in the state and since it was all-male, there would be fewer distractions for the scholars. After graduating and returning to Atchison to work in his father's bank, Web spoke to his parents one evening after dinner. "I'm going to ask Lillie Miller to be my wife. We've all known her for years. I love her for her free spirit, and she makes me very happy."

"Yes, son. I can believe she is a free spirit. Her father, John, went to the gold fields of California, and later was a surgeon in the Civil War, after which he practiced in several states. I just hope his daughter will want to stay in one place."

"Now, Will, I am sure she will. Her mother, Annie, is a delightful person I admire very much. I was drawn to her initially because my name is Anna and hers in Ruthanna. You know she is descended from a steamboat captain of some renown."

Webster Wirt Hetherington, twenty-five, and Lillie Miller, twenty, were married November 18, 1875. Their first child arrived a year later and was named Ruthanna after her two grandmothers. William made Web a partner in the bank in 1876, and four years later, the young man was elected to the city council, following in his father's footsteps. In the next election he ran for mayor. "Lillie, I had no idea when I entered politics how vicious some opponents can be and how they will lie through their teeth. There is a rumor gong around that I have promised city jobs to certain individuals."

"What are you going to do about it?"

"I'm going to write a statement for the *Globe* and hope that most people will listen to reason. It will go something like this: For the purpose of placing me in a false position before the citizens of this city, a report is being circulated that in the event of my election, I had pledged myself to appoint certain persons to fill the various offices to be filled by the Mayor and Council. In order that such reports may be authoritatively denied, permit me to say that I have made no such promise or pledge."

The electorate must have been reassured, for Web Hetherington was elected mayor of Atchison in 1880.

Banking laws were changing, and more prestige was attached to institutions designated as national banks. As early as 1866, Hetherington had put together the necessary paperwork and wrote to Senator Samuel Pomeroy hoping for his support in gaining that status for his bank: "I enclose a letter of the acting Controller of the Currency which if you endorse, I have no doubt will succeed. Anything I can do at this end of the line command me." But, Pomeroy did not endorse it, perhaps, William thought, because he was still sore about that unpaid promissory note back when he'd taken over the Bank of the State of Kansas. Or perhaps the senator treated awarding of national-bank charters as one of his patronage resources which were going, instead, to David Auld and Henry Kuhn, rival bankers. It did not help that Hetherington was a Democrat and Pomeroy a Republican. Auld's First National Bank soon opened as competitor.

Optimism returned to American investors as the Panic of '73 abated, and the stock market began rising in 1878. The following decade would be a period of prosperity for Atchison and its bankers. Hetherington tried for national-bank designation again in 1882, this time with success. Renamed the Exchange National Bank the business had William as president, James P. Pomeroy as vice president; W.W. Hetherington as cashier; C.S. Hetherington as assistant cashier; Frank Everest and son-in-law Balie Waggener as attorneys; and Balie was also a director along with J.S. Galbreath and Frank Bier, partner in J.P. Brown's contracting business. William had assembled a tightly knit group with his two sons and other relatives in the firm. Bank Vice President Pomeroy, son of a wealthy Boston financier and reputed to be one of the wealthiest men in town, had made a fortune in the coal business. He was by then a big land owner who experimented with large-scale dry farming practices and managed his many real estate and mining interests from his home in Colorado Springs.

Atchison was a commercial hub. One of the major products moving through the town was railroad ties cut from the forests of Wisconsin and Minnesota. With the expansion of rail services to Texas, New Mexico, Colorado and even California rapid growth occurred in agricultural products, grain storage, transportation services, manufacturing, commercial paper and wholesaling in glass, hardware, lumber and coal, The Exchange was often an intermediary between local businesses and correspondent banks in Kansas City, St. Louis, Chicago and New York. Occasionally there were letters of credit from banks as far away as Paris, London and Stockholm. One of the most active wholesale houses in Atchison was Regnier and Shoup who supplied crockery, dishes, Queensware and china. Representatives bought in Europe, and Hetherington's bank exchanged the drafts of retail stores in Nebraska, Illinois and Kansas. The bank paid a dividend of twenty percent to its stockholders in 1882, while at the same time adding to its surplus.

William carefully explained all aspects of the business to Web, who would someday inherit the bank. "Our loans make it possible for commission firms to pay farmers for their produce while these firms wait to sell to processors. If everyone had to wait for payment until the goods reach their final user, our economy would be primitive. Web, you have to be especially careful when loaning money to firms that deal in perishable commodities, such as butter. A carload of butter that arrives in St. Louis or Chicago a few days late has little salvage value. Refrigerator cars are just coming into use, but shippers still rely on natural ice gathered in the winter for cooling. You have a lot less risk with grains and hard goods, such as hardware."

"I know that the competing railroads often erect barriers to trade," Web noted.

"Yes, the Missouri Pacific discriminates between short and long haul and sometimes will not furnish cars for local shipments to Atchison. During peak times, the commission firm may have to arrange for local storage, and that eats into profits and their ability to repay their loans. You need to take this all into account. And it requires a lot of capital. I have about two hundred fifty thousand in assets myself, but I couldn't do it without Pomeroy who is worth four times as much as I. Not to mention J.P. Brown and A.J. Harwi who are now on the board. Always keep them happy, and listen to their advice. The bank has capital of one hundred thousand and a surplus of ten thousand. Always keep an adequate surplus for times of emergency."

"I'm not sure I can handle it."

"If you weren't a little apprehensive, you'd be a fool. You certainly have the character and integrity that this bank is known for. You'll make mistakes; I certainly did. Don't get rattled when a big loan goes bad. It's inevitable. The trick is to be prepared and move on."

805 North Fifth, Atchison Kansas

Even before the national bank designation, Web and Lillie had accumulated sufficient wealth to build a grand home at 805 North Fifth that was finished in 1880. Designed by Alfred Meier, it was a ten-room, three-story brick mansion, topped by a third-floor ballroom. An octagonal tower rose at the rear corner, and the five fireplaces were surrounded with imported glazed tiles and

trimmed with cherry and walnut. Brass gas chandeliers were used throughout. The tall narrow windows were trimmed in limestone. Various styles of dormers graced the slate mansard roof, and a handsome porte-cochere protected guests arriving in their carriages. A two-story carriage house, decorated with a plaster horse head above the double doors, had living space for servants on the second floor and housed the boiler that heated the house.

    Not to be completely outdone by his son, William purchased a large house on North Third in 1882. It belonged to W.F. Downs, J.P. Brown's old nemesis, who was in failing health. Not long after, he decided that the expanding bank business called for a new and bigger building. This one, even grander than the original two blocks away, was erected at Sixth and Commercial at the cost of seventy thousand dollars. When the new building opened in 1886, everyone was awed by the interior decorated with tile, brass and carved mahogany, cherry and oak. Web remarked admiringly to his father about the carved oak mantle in his office, "I hope I can sit there someday."

"You will, son," William replied. I had the counters made by a firm in Chicago, but now I wish I had them all made by O.W. Ulrich, a local man whose craftsmanship exceeds the Chicago workmen. Ulrich did the wood and stone carving at the entrance."

Lillie, I have put together a stag trip to Europe with three of my longtime best friends, Shoup, Everest and Howe. We sail July 9 on the White Star Line's *Germanie*."

"I feel left out. I reserve the right to make a tour with my lady friends in the future. If I weren't pregnant, I would insist on going along."

"Fair enough. We land at Queenstown, Ireland, the homeland of my father's ancestors, and Ed and I plan to visit Scotland, France, Switzerland, Germany and Italy. The others are going in a different direction when we reach Paris."

"How long will you be gone?"
"We return August 27 from Liverpool."
"That's a long time to leave me alone with the children."
"I know I'm asking a lot."
"Are you afraid of being seasick?"
"Ed is taking nine different seasickness remedies in addition to Florida water, brandy, steamer chairs, steamer hats, steamer caps, overcoats, umbrellas, rubber coats, soap, candles and much other stuff which will probably be thrown overboard. You know Ed. He's is always well prepared to a fault."

Howe, ever the trickster, published an anonymous report in his newspaper, the *Globe*, which began as follows:

My roommate, a Mr. Hetherington, from Atchison, Kansas, was not subject to seasickness, and reports came to me occasionally from the smoking room that he was actually enjoying the storm. Indeed, one authority said that when a particularly heavy swell struck the ship, he would say to his companions: 'I love this; it is like the joy of which I have heard European tourists speak; and this action is the poetry of traveling.' Therefore, when two stout stewards presented themselves at my door, carrying Mr. Hetherington between them, I was surprised, though I cannot say I was very sorry for his plight, for I was wretched myself, and longed for company.

When Web and Ed checked into the Langham Hotel on Portland Place in London, Web wrote his first daily letter to Lillie:

London, July 15, 1885
Dearest Lill,
I miss you already and we have only been gone a few days. There is too much ocean between us. I got terribly seasick, tried to walk across the room and crashed and cut open my forehead. Two stewards carried me back to our room. Not to worry, the ship's doctor fixed me up. I will write every day, it makes me feel closer. I have your framed picture beside my bed every night. I'll be glad when we are on the same side of the mailbox and together in the same bed.
Your loving husband,
(s) Web

Another tale of Web, Ed and Frank's excursion to Germany, submitted by Ed, appeared later in the *Kansas City Star*:

They one day took a sort of a plug train and went up to a little town in the mountains to see some ancient ruins. The train was due to return at 8 p.m. and at that hour the two pilgrims were at the station. Pretty soon a fussy little man, wearing a railway uniform and a big mustache, and carrying a lantern rushed into the building and began making signs and talking wildly in German. Howe could not understand the language, but Hetherington professed to. 'Let me handle him,' he said. 'I can't speak Dutch, but I can understand it.' He listened to the little man awhile, and after the official had departed informed Howe that the man had told him that he had a nephew living at Milwaukee and wanted to know if the two travelers had ever met him. This exchange was repeated three times. A fourth time the fussy little man appeared in the station. This time he brought with him a man who could speak English, and who informed the travelers that the man's repeated visits to the station had been to tell them that they might as well go to bed, as the train had been abandoned.

When Web returned to London, he had a stack of mail waiting. The one on top read as follows:

My dearest husband,
I miss you so much it hurts. I'll write every day, but the letters won't be able to find you on the continent. You will have a stack of letters when you return to London. The Come Early and Stay Late Club met last evening. Daisy

Orton and Christine Vogler, two of Mr. Stapper's prize-winning pupils sang. Mary and I also sang. It was a wonderful evening of music, if I do say so myself.

The children are fine, rambunctious as usual. I think they miss playing with their father. I ordered a set of leather-bound Redpath's Encyclopedias from a door to door salesman. They will be instructive for the children, and I think you will enjoy them as well.

All my love, Lill

Howe loved to poke fun at his friends in his newspaper, and sent the following dispatch home to be published:

W.W. Hetherington of Atchison, better known as the Duke of Fifth and Riley, who is in London negotiating with certain lords who are supposed to have money, writes that the lords who have money only devote an hour each day to business. They breakfast at noon, count their money until two o'clock, and then go to business. At three they leave for home again and it is rather difficult to treat with them. We'll bet that when the Duke of Fifth and Riley returns to Atchison he will breakfast at noon, go to business at two o'clock and return home at three.

Homecoming for Web was sweet. After a prolonged hug, Lillie asked for a full report. "Where all did you go?"

"We did the Grand Tour including Scotland, Switzerland, Germany, France and Italy. I especially liked Ireland and the Killarney Lakes, Kerry Mountains and Georgian Dublin. Howe was in charge of getting tickets for musical performances. We heard orchestras in Baden-Baden, Lucerne, Frankfort, Brussels, Cologne, Interlaken and the Royal Siamese Band at London's Albert Hall."

"Now I'm really jealous. Was the eight-day sail home tedious?"

"A bit, but four meals a day helped pass the time. I could get used to oysters, wild game and fish of all kinds."

"Too bad. Now it's time to get back to the reality of carp and catfish from the Missouri.

"At least, when we attend concerts at Price Opera House here and see the painting of Lake Geneva on the drop curtain, I can pretend I'm back in Switzerland."

In later years when Howe recalled the trip in his book, *Plain People*, he wrote, "After I had been in Atchison seven or eight years, I went abroad with three special friends; a banker, a lawyer, and a wholesale merchant, and discovered that friends do not get along when traveling, for we returned on four different ships." It was a good story, but it was not true.

The men of Atchison were a fun-loving lot. Several arranged a "yacht race" on Commercial Street. Sails were rigged on a mast mounted to a buggy. The *Globe* reported it thusly, no doubt with a bit of exaggeration:

At nine o'clock the 'Wiley' turned into Commercial Street from Tenth, and came leisurely down to the starting place, with a big wind at its heels. As she crossed the line at J.T. Hersey's she only had up the mainsail and jib, but once under way, and the great balloon jib was given to the wind by the well-trained crew, and a few minutes later the top-sail and flying jib went up, which attracted a cheer from a crowd in gondolas at the Hetherington corner. The "Petrel" was slow in getting to work, and within five minutes it was known that the drunken captain had no show.

The Bank issued drafts backed by bonds of the United States. These circulated as money, just as did gold and silver. The notes looked impressive and as long as the bank's reputation was good, it had the effect of increasing the money supply.

Sometimes the Bank's reputation was enough without any assertion of specific security. A steel engraving of Web and Lillie's eight-year old Ruthanna started to appear on drafts issued by the Exchange National Bank in 1884.

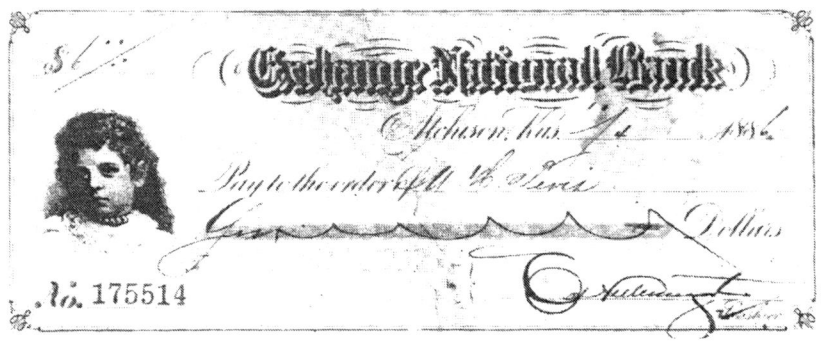

Two years later, on the evening of her tenth birthday, Ruthanna was proved to be one of the most popular children in town, as evidenced by a *Globe* report: "Eighty of her little friends called to congratulate her, bringing with them an orchestra and a full line of refreshments. The surprise was as adroitly managed by the children as the most astute elders could have done."

Atchison's elite loved to party and the *Globe* loved to describe the events in detail:

A Globe man was at S.H. Fullerton's last night when a lot of children appeared at the door and began throwing shelled corn at the house. It was a Halloween surprise party. The children were engaged in playing "clap in and clap out." within two minutes. This is a kissing game. The boys stood behind chairs, and a doorkeeper called for two girls who were in another room. When the girls came in, all the boys tried to coax them to sit down in their chairs. If they sat down in the wrong chair, they were clapped out; if they sat down in the right one, they were kissed. Then they played post office. Jeanette Walcott was door-keeper and announced to the company that there were two letters in the post-office for Wirt Hetherington. Mr. Hetherington went into a little room off the hall, and found a girl there who kissed him twice. These games were kept up for over an hour. Bessie Fletcher was the favorite and was kissed forty-two times. Gail Hetherington was a close second with thirty-eight. The girls openly boasted of the number of times they were kissed. When supper was ready, every boy took a girl on his arm, and marched out, and what he could not eat, he put in his pocket.

Annie Hetherington died at her residence on North Third Street, on March 11, 1887. According to a report in the Atchison Patriot, "In 1855 she came with her husband to the city of Atchison. It was not an inviting place to bring a lady used to the comforts and luxuries of a home in the old Keystone State; but then Mrs. Hetherington had faith in the man with whom she had united her life's fortunes; she believed he knew best—and the result amply justified the trust."

Another paper noted, "She was eminently domestic in her tastes, and while her home was ever the abode of genuine hospitality, and from it flowed countless acts of kindly charity, her purse ever open to relieve the needy and distressed, and her duties to society faithfully discharged, she lived for her husband and her children." Though an active Lutheran all her life, Annie Hetherington was memorialized at a service held at the family residence. In attendance were her husband William, sons Web and Clifford and daughters Emma, wife of Balie P. Waggener, and the not-yet-married Grace. One of the pallbearers was J.P. Brown.

Ruthanna (Annie) Hetherington

In October of that same year, the Hetherington home was the scene of a far happier occasion—the marriage of daughter Grace to William A. Otis. The paper printed the following account:

The bride, a tall, handsome blonde, attracted universal admiration, attired in a cream-colored silk tulle, trimmed in grosgrain ribbon, with a front drapery of crepe de chein, pearl trimmings; no ornaments. After the ceremony an elegant wedding feast was served, the tables profusely decorated with a mirror in the center and pyramids of flowers and ornamental cakes. The groom is engaged in the wholesale grocery trade. His father is the Hon. A.G. Otis, who came to Atchison about the same time as Mr. Hetherington did. He was for a number of years Judge of the District Court and is now president of the Atchison Savings Bank.

In the summer, the family vacationed at the Sea Bright Inn on the New Jersey shore. They entertained several Atchison friends, including Chief Justice Horton of the Kansas Supreme Court, the Reverend Abel Leonard and Frank Howard. Lillie organized entertainment for her guests, including a mock Italian opera with herself, Signora Hetheringtonelli per the program notes, in the lead role. *"The ladies and gentlemen were dressed in costumes, with comic masks on the back of their heads. The ladies wore their hair brushed over their faces, and the gentlemen put their vests on with backs front. This arrangement gave all the appearance of dancing backward and made a very ludicrous scene, creating much laughter."* These trips to the New Jersey shore were fun, but they also allowed Web to develop connections with New York capitalists.

The "Gilded Age" was a term coined by Mark Twain in 1873 to describe the wealth and sometimes excess of the new rich during the last part of the Nineteenth Century. Critics referred to those who grew richest from their business dealings as the "robber barons" because of sometimes excessive financial manipulations. Nationally known exemplars were Rockefeller, Carnegie, Flagler, Vanderbilt and Morgan, but Atchison had its own gilded families, which drew frequent coverage by local newspapers:

"In the splendid procession of society events that has distinguished the history of Atchison within recent years, the GLOBE believes the summit of success was reached last night in the reception given by Mr. and Mrs. W.W. Hetherington in honor of Mrs. Hetherington's sister, Mrs. J. Levin of Omaha. The event served a double purpose,--it afforded Mrs. Levin opportunity to meet her old friends, and also was the formal opening to the social world of Mr. and Mrs. Hetherington's handsome residence since its enlargement. It was in splendid condition to be viewed to advantage,--lighted from parlor to roof, every room thrown open to the use and enjoyment of guests, and decorated with lavish hand by E.C. Schwein, the florist. The invitations numbered several hundreds, and few regrets were received.

The guests began arriving about eight o'clock, and continued until eleven. Mrs. Hetherington was becomingly attired in a rich costume of white surah velvet trimmed in pearls and diamond ornaments. Mrs. Leven wore an empire gown of white Bengalese, flowers. Assisting in dispensing the hospitalities were Mrs. Balie Waggener, costumed of sleeveless black lace, diamonds and flowers; Mrs. W.A. Otis, white silk and velvet, trimmed with pearls, diamonds; Mrs. Frank Howard, superb costume of green silk and velvet, cut steel trimmings, flowers. The costumes of all these ladies were faultless in every detail, and taken as a group, presented a radiant spectacle of beauty and grace. Governor Martin honored the Hetheringtons with his attendance. Young's full orchestra was stationed in the library, with solos by Prof. Stapper.

A bright feature of the programme was a little song by Mary Hetherington accompanied on the piano by her oldest sister, Ruthanna. The little sprite inherits her mother's talent, and her pure tones and modest demeanor last night engaged the undivided attention of the company. Light refreshments were served during the evening in rooms on the second floor, where beautiful tables were spread, and the guests served by a corps of polite young colored men under the direction of Prof. Williams of The Byram Hotel."

Also attending were Mr. and Mrs. N.W. Todd of the Atchison Bridge, C.C. Burnes and wife, the former Francis Byram, and John H. Brown, son of J.P. Brown, and of course Web's European travel buddies, Charlie Shoup and Frank Everest and wives.

William Hetherington

William's name continued to appear as the president of the Exchange Bank, but after 1885, his poor health meant that Web was really in charge. Still, the old man could not let go. "Dad, I know this is your bank built over your lifetime. I have looked over your shoulder to learn the business, but I can't have you looking over my shoulder now and second guessing every transaction I make. You know that bank decisions are not made according to a formula and different people will occasionally made different decisions in the same situation. I need room to make my own decisions and live with them. Rest assured, I will discuss with you and the board any that I feel I don't have the experience to deal with."

"I hear you, son. It is just hard to let go of my creation."

"I can imagine, father, but I want you to be able to take the cure at Hot Springs when you need to and not worry about the bank." The truth was that Web himself was not in the best of health and after contracting malaria earlier, he had sought relief at Hot Springs with its million gallons of one hundred forty-three-degree water flowing each day.

"I stayed at the Arlington Hotel. I think you would enjoy it, Dad."

"I hope you did not visit any of the gambling establishments."

"Not on your life. This banking business is enough of a gamble by itself."

"Just one more thing, son. I want you to take note of the real estate boom that is sweeping the country. It is happening right here in Kansas as well. People are buying lots in Wichita as if it were going to be the next Chicago. There are seven hundred real estate agents, and Dunn and Bradstreet report that Wichita has the third largest number of real estate transfers in the country."

"That's crazy. How do these things get started?"

"They are fed by greed and flimsy paper. Salesmen are selling options on lots allowing people to control property for a short time with a small down payment. Buyers hope to sell quickly at higher prices, but if prices falter, there will be panic."

"I did see an article reprinted in the *Globe* about a man in Indiana who returned from Wichita after earning a big return on his investment and claims the boom there shows no signs of subsiding."

"Don't ever buy into these speculative booms. They're called booms because they always explode with a rush of air."

Nevertheless, at the height of the real estate boom in Wichita, The Guaranty Investment Company, with Albert Horton as president, and W.W. Hetherington as secretary-treasurer, was formed to make new investments for its principals in 1886. Its offices were not just in Atchison but also in New York, Philadelphia and Concord, New Hampshire. Horton was U.S. District Attorney, and Web could not resist the opportunity to be his business associate. By separating the investment company from the bank, real estate failures would not threaten the bank's solvency. This strategy avoided the requirements of the National Bank Act, but only partially adhered to William's admonition about speculative investment.

New capital was obtained from small savers by the creation of the Dime Savings Bank in 1888, with W.W. Hetherington as president. However, not all Hetherington ventures turned to gold. After initial years of prosperity, both the Guaranty Investment Company and the Dime Savings Bank failed in 1890 when locusts and drought set in and destroyed the value of the Kansas farmland and housing lots that had drawn investors from as far away as London and Amsterdam.

Perhaps Web might have paid more attention to his father's advice. The contrast between the white-haired father and his dark-haired, handsome son, could not have been greater. William was usually somber as befitting a serious banker, while Web, dashing with his well-trimmed mustache and fine clothes, was always a focus of *Globe* attention:

"Mr. Web Hetherington had his new carriage out yesterday for an airing. It cost $1,000 in New York, and is unquestionably the handsomest turnout that ever appeared on the streets of Atchison. It has eight springs, and is magnificently upholstered in green broadcloth, so that it is as comfortable on any good road as a parlor chair. It is so arranged that the seat for the coachman and footman may be removed, in case the gentleman desires to handle the reins himself. The top is made of the finest prepared material and the front and shields above the wheels are patent leather. With the carriage came a $300 set of harness, with coin silver mountings and patent leather collars. On the saddle of the harness is the initial "H," in solid silver. Calvin H. Currie, the coachman, now wears light corduroy pantaloons, black broadcloth coat and black silk hat. His new livery, on the way from New York, will include knee pants, with English coachman's boots, yellow tops, turned down."

"Web, did you see the story in the *Globe* today? It makes us sound rather ostentatious. Couldn't you have purchased a carriage from a local manufacturer?"

"It does sound a bit overdone when described in detail that way. But I'm enjoying it immensely, and it adds to the bank's reputation. Besides, I won't live forever to enjoy my hard-earned income."

Web also fitted out a carriage for Lillie's own use. It was an elegant Victoria that, according to the *Globe,* caused quite a stir:

> The first time Mrs. Hetherington used it, she invited her husband's sister, Mrs. B.P. Waggener, to go calling with her. The Victoria was drawn by a handsome team of horses, and chains hung from the silver-mounted harness. The driver was correctly dressed as a coachman, and Mrs. Hetherington and Mrs. Waggener felt quite elegant as they leaned back in the luxurious Victoria, with their feet resting on velvet cushions. But the stunning equipage was too much for the little Atchison boys, and greatly to the dismay of the ladies in the carriage, a perfect crowd of boys followed it. The boys were not rude; did not laugh or make remarks,--they had never seen anything like the Victoria before, and were simply interested in it. Mrs. Waggener and Mrs. Hetherington gave up their calls, and returned home.

When the Rock Island railroad extended its lines in Kansas and Nebraska, it received bonds from the cities along the route. The railroad needed to convert these bonds into cash to pay for construction. Web purchased all of these municipal bonds and resold them to investors in New York and abroad. W.P. Rice, representing a New York bond trader, paid Hetherington ten thousand dollars in cash and the expenses for his wife to take a European tour in 1890. Rice accompanied Hetherington to London to sell the bonds to such firms as Baring Brothers. After going broke with a string of Kansas banks, Rice started over as a bond promoter for eastern capitalists. Rice and Hetherington found that the London investment houses had learned a few things since Andrew Carnegie had pedaled bonds of the Pennsylvania Company there in 1871. Buyers now demanded guarantees that the railroads would finish the lines and that the operating and construction companies would have separate, independent directors. They would not be victims of rail directors who profited from inflated costs of construction while the operating company went broke, leaving its bond holders in the lurch. Carnegie had been sued several times in connection with bond trading.

While Hetherington and Rice were in London, Lillie and her friend, Mrs. Frank Everest, vacationed in Italy. With the assistance of a courier, they toured Spain, France and Switzerland as well. While Web was in London, he received a cable informing him of the death of his father and advising him to stay and finish his business there. I want to honor my father, but I'm going to stay, Web thought. The old man himself would have put business above ceremony.

William Hetherington died January 21, 1890, and again the funeral took place at the residence on North Third Street. "The body rested in the front parlor and was enclosed in a handsome mahogany casket," the paper reported. "The casket plate simply bore the name of the deceased and the years of birth and death. The floral ornamentation was also simple, consisting of only a lily, with trailing arbutus around the edge of the casket. The body was greatly emaciated, but the features, although pinched, were natural."

Reverend Alderman recounted that in a recent conversation, the deceased had said that he was ready and willing to go. The Reverend closed the service with the Lord's Prayer joined by many in attendance. Someone sang "Rock of Ages." Perhaps ironically, one of the pallbearers was David Auld, whose bank beat out the Exchange to be the first national bank in the city. Banknotes printed with William Hetherington's likeness on them continued to circulate for years.

When Web returned from London, he was appointed president of the bank. In celebration, he and Lillie decided to host a grand lawn party for one hundred friends and featuring the music of an orchestra from Kansas City. As the date drew near, thirteen-year-old Mary made her case for attending. She talked of nothing else.

"Mother, Ruth gets to attend. She taught me to dance and said I was pretty good. It's not fair. "

"Ruth is older; your time will come."

The grand house at the top of the hill on North Fourth Street looked even more elevated and imposing because of its location six feet above street level. It occupied a double lot providing a great space for a specially built dance floor on the lawn just south of the residence, plus tables and chairs for one hundred guests. Each table was covered in a white linen cloth with pink napkins. Electric lights were strung from the great trees in the yard. It was like Christmas in June. The weather was perfect: warm enough for the older people to sit outside comfortably but cool enough for the young, vigorous dancers. The arriving carriages were parked for blocks in every direction. Adding to the congestion were the carriages of many uninvited townspeople who heard the music when out for their evening drives and stopped to listen and watch the spectacle.

Mary was still pleading her case as guests began to arrive. "I don't want to stay inside with my nurse. Mother, I have a new summer dress that I have never worn. Please, please," she begged.

Just then her father intervened, saying, "I want to show off my little girl all dressed up for a few minutes at the party."

Wirt, Lillie, Gail, W.W., Mary, baby Hale, Ruthanna, 1885

With that, Lillie relented and instructed Mary's Irish nurse in how she was to be dressed. "Be sure she has a large white ribbon in her hair. She can only stay a few minutes, and then you are to take her back inside."

Her father introduced her to a few of his banking clients and then told her to go back inside. "This is a grown-up party and there are no other children."

"Can I have a piece of cake to take with me?" asked Mary.

"Yes, but then it's inside with you."

The waiter from the Hotel Byram made a great fuss over Mary, telling her, "You are the fairest lady at the party." Mary blushed slightly and took her cake and ate it on the front porch of the mansion while listening to the music. She knew her nurse was watching her through the front window. Before she went inside, Mary watched a plump woman and rotund man each ask the waiter at the refreshment table for two pieces of the white-frosted cake decorated with little pink roses. Two pieces did not fit well on the dainty little plates, but the server managed to balance them, albeit precariously. As the couple turned to walk to one of the little tables distributed over the grounds, the plump lady with her overloaded plate bumped the elbow of her partner, sending both of their double servings onto the lush grass.

The waiter, flustered for a few moments, recovered his aplomb and rushed from behind the table to scoop up the errant cakes so that others would not step in the mess. One piece had fallen face-down on the pointed toe of the lady's shoe. The waiter stooped to wipe it off, and then abruptly stopped, realizing the indelicacy of the situation. From his ground-level position, the waiter couldn't read the expression on the lady's fleshy face. The assurance came with, "It's all right," as she raised her voluminous long skirt a few inches to permit the cleanup. Watching from the porch, Mary doubled up in laughter, but soon muffled her merriment so no one would hear her. She decided to disobey her father further by walking around among the guests for a few minutes more. She managed to get a better look at the elegant dresses as the dancers tripped the fantastic toe before her nurse caught up with her.

The next day the Atchison *Globe* described the sumptuous lawn party in detail. What the *Globe* did not report was the devilry of thirteen-year-old Mary who followed one of the young couples who left the dance floor after the piano player led a group version of Ta-Rah-Rah-Boom-De-Aye. The couple drifted into the shadows toward the carriage house, from which the four Hetherington horses had been removed for the evening. Mary waited outside, hidden by some bushes, and was about to leave when the couple finally came out, disheveled and straw covered. "How come you have straw on your clothes?" she asked. "Shall I brush it off for you?"

But all she got from her impertinent offer was, "Scram, kid, or we'll tell your mother," as the couple hurried back to the lights and the dance.

Never at a loss for a riposte, Mary called after them, "Maybe I'll tell *your* mothers." The young spy couldn't wait to tell her schoolmates all about it the following Monday.

The memorable lawn party was held in 1891, and just one year later, Mary's father died at the age of forty-one. The sting of her disobedience to her beloved father would stay with her for years, but the picture of the fat couple spilling their cake would also stay with her, and it never failed to put a twinkle in her eye. Devilry was never beneath Mary Hetherington.

~15~

Strong Women

W.W. (Web) Hetherington was more prescient than he intended when he expressed his wish to have a fancy carriage before he died. At the time of his death in 1892, Lillie was in Topeka seeking medical attention, and only Web's brother, Cliff, and sisters, Emma and Grace, were with him at the end. His eldest daughter, Ruth, was in school at Knoxville, Illinois, and Mary was boarding at St. Scholastica Academy in town. The three youngest children were in bed asleep while he was dying. When Lillie returned home she was so prostrated that she had to be carried from the Santa Fe train to the waiting carriage.

The paper reported that "The house and yard was filled with sympathizing and mourning friends, while the streets for two blocks were blocked with carriages. The procession on the way to the grave was one of the largest ever seen in this city and covered five blocks."

Many in town were not completely surprised at W.W.'s sudden death. It was widely known that he consulted a liver expert in New York, a pathology probably related to his earlier malaria.

Adding to Lillie's loss, her father John Miller died a few months later on a train somewhere near Yuma, Arizona, as he returned from San Diego. Lillie felt abandoned with the premature deaths of the two most important men in her life. Her father had taken her mother to the dry climate of southern California for her health for the previous several years. Lillie confided to a friend, "My father was a seeker after adventure. I'm not his daughter for nothing. I'm not going to shrivel up and crawl in a hole. I'm much too young, and I can't be a black presence for our children."

"What will you do?" the friend asked.

"I have children to educate and eventually three daughters to see married. I'm going to give parties as before, maybe even grander, and I will travel. Our house on North Fifth is going to be a bright and shiny place. One of the first things I'll do is install a telephone when they finish wiring the town. Got to keep up to date."

"I know you can do it."

"But I am devastated that I was not at Web's side when he died."

"You can't torment yourself over what can't be helped," the friend reminded her. "Life is not like one of your theatrical performances where you can arrange all the characters and their entries and exits."

For a long time after W.W.'s death, when it rained during the night, Lillie remembered his waking her, embracing her, placing his leg over hers and slowly settling between her thighs. They would listen to the rain on the roof until falling into a peaceful sleep again.

Balie Waggener became president of the bank, but because of his many other responsibilities with the railroad, he left much of the management to Web's younger brother Clifford. Cliff was part of the electrification of Atchison, serving as treasurer of the Atchison Railway, Light and Power Company that started operation in 1895 following Edison's 1880 invention of the incandescent light bulb.

The Financial Panic of 1893 spread across the country. Hundreds of banks and one-quarter of the nation's railroads failed, including the Atchison, Topeka and the Santa Fe. Industrial unemployment rose dramatically in many cities to as much as twenty-five percent. Many businesses in Atchison were in trouble. The board of the Exchange National Bank instructed cashier Cliff Hetherington to call all loans in excess of the limit allowed by the National Bank Act and to advertise the sale of certain Atchison Street Railway Company bonds held as collateral for loans made to W.L. Challis unless the overdue loans were paid promptly. It withdrew its loans to some of the bank's largest customers such as the Chicago Lumber Company and withdrew its deposits from the Midland National Bank of Kansas City. For the first time the bank omitted its dividend, yet it kept its doors open.

Things were even tougher for the unemployed. In the winter of 1894, J.P. Brown was concerned that hundreds of temporary workers cutting ice on the Missouri River would have no income come spring. He offered to give one hundred dollars to establish a free restaurant for the hungry unemployed. He knew many had a horror of applying for help at the police station.

Clifford felt very much alone as cashier at the bank. His dashing and worldly-wise brother was dead and he did not feel close to his Uncle Balie, the new bank president. He loved his Aunt Emma, but Balie seemed distant. When Balie made one of his infrequent stops at the bank, Clifford asked, "Balie, you're active in politics. Is there nothing that can be done to stop this recession and alleviate this human suffering? The *New York Times* says there are plenty of things that could be done to create jobs, such as building lines of rapid transit, widening and deepening the Erie Canal and improving the Mississippi."

"Too expensive. Sometimes you just need to let nature take its course."

"That's fine for the rich like you and me to say, but what about the men who can't put bread on the table? I see so many of them despondent and walking aimlessly about town." Clifford couldn't believe what he'd just said so forcefully, but he realized he felt strongly.

"Well, that idiot Congressman from Nebraska, William Jennings Bryan, thinks he has the answer—the coinage of silver. The eloquent windbag claims the money supply is not enough to energize the productivity of our growing population."

"Who are his supporters?"

"Westerners and Southerners who feel constrained by the unavailability of money to invest in business and mines. Always looking to Europe and Wall Street irritates them."

"How would silver coinage work."

"The government already has supplies of silver, and it could buy more at today's low prices. If it made coins with a face value greater than the cost of the metal, it would make a profit. I call it a debasement of the currency."

"But it sounds good to me. It would reduce government debt without raising taxes or selling bonds to J.P. Morgan. When we make a loan and enter the amount as a demand deposit in the borrower's name, we create money. If government coins silver, it likewise creates money. I don't see how they are different."

"They're different; that's all."

"Who opposes silver?"

"J.P. Morgan, I suppose, President Cleveland and me. The world has always run on the gold standard and besides our bank makes a nice profit when wealthy European investors buy our railroad bonds and other businesses. We are not called the Exchange National Bank for nothing."

"Surely we need to consider more than our own narrow self-interest. Grandfather insisted that a good bank must serve all the people of its community. How can we prosper if half the town is unemployed?" Clifford could hardly believe he was lecturing his uncle.

"Can't be helped. And besides, Bryan is a wild man. The damn fool wants to regulate railroads, and you know I represent the Missouri Pacific that is vital to our economy. And he wants an income tax. Ridiculous!"

"Sounds to me like the country and Grover Cleveland cling to the gold standard out of habit more than logic. I've been reading *Coin's Financial School,* and I think I understand how money works."

"That's nothing but socialist propaganda, my son. You don't understand. The country is in the hands of men of property because they know best. They didn't get rich because they were dumb."

Clifford heard a tone of condescension is his uncle's voice. Perhaps the source of great wealth for a tiny minority came from exploiting the little guy, but he dropped the subject. He wanted to be bank president someday, and it would not do to make an enemy of his powerful uncle. Clifford was reflecting the fact that the millionaires who comprised three percent of American families owned twenty percent of its wealth.

A protest march that became known as Coxey's Army went on foot to Washington from Ohio in 1894 to demand that the government create jobs. The five hundred in the ragtag army were greeted by fifteen hundred soldiers. Coxey advocated printing more treasury bills and interest-free municipal bonds to finance the employment of men to build roads. Coxey was arrested for walking on the Capitol grass before he could present his petition to Congress. Ed Howe condemned the marchers for leaving their families

That same year, workers at the Pullman Palace Car Company in Chicago went on strike when the company reduced its wages and continued to insist on sixteen-hour workdays. The strike was broken up by U.S. Marshals and twelve thousand Army troops. Railroad workers joined in, and Cleveland argued the strike interfered with the U.S. mails. Union leader Eugene Debs, defended by Clarence Darrow in the ensuing trial, was sentenced to six months in prison. Through unrest and repression, the depression lasted four years.

Coxey's Army Marches Through A Small Town.

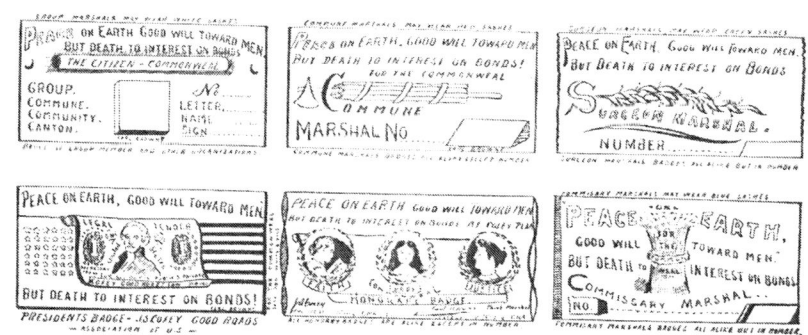

Coxey's Army Name Badges

Bryan, campaigning for silver currency, captured the Democratic Party's nomination for President in 1896. He electrified the convention by declaring, "You shall not press down on the brow of labor this crown of thorns; you shall not crucify mankind upon a cross of gold." Despite drawing huge, enthusiastic crowds in the South and West and even with the continuing depression, Bryan lost the election to William McKinley. The moneyed interests spent lavishly in support of McKinley, and the war of editorial cartoons in Republican papers cleverly made Bryan look the fool. They even showed Bryan in the uniform of Aguinaldo's rebels in the Philippines. Theodore Roosevelt spoke of him as "a mere boy, without intelligence or power." And some employers said they would close their businesses if Bryan won. All in all, McKinley's supporters had mounted an effective scare campaign. While the electoral votes were heavily in favor of McKinley, the margin in the popular vote was seven point one million to six point five, with the narrow majority causing some Bryan supporters to claim vote fraud.

    Bryan carried Kansas, and Clifford derived some pleasure in voting for him. He tried to puzzle out the cause of Bryan's defeat. Why had not labor been more supportive? Wasn't it clear from Bryan's rhetoric that his sympathies were with labor? Why couldn't Bryan release them from the bondage of customary thinking that their jobs, in effect their souls, were owed to the company. Anna Hetherington was the only person who would listen to him without reproach, and he loved his mother for it.

Lillie took her children Ruthanna, eighteen, Mary, sixteen, Wirt, fourteen, Gail, ten, and Hale, eight, to Germany in March 1895. Lillie thought it important to introduce Ruthanna to European culture as she approached marriageable age. Dresden on the Elbe was a center for the arts. Lillie, an accomplished singer, loved the opera, and the Dresden Opera in the Royal Saxon Opera House was known around the world. Lillie enrolled Wirt in an English school there.

    Later, he wrote a report on his European schooling which appeared in the *Globe*:

    The school that I attended in Dresden was not so strict as some English schools are. The building had three stories and was situated in the outer part of the city so as to afford a beautiful view of the surrounding country. I arose at 7 in the morning and was obliged to be at school at fifteen minutes before eight. From 8 till 9 we recited dictation of poetry, and had to learn it by heart. From 9 until 10 we had Latin. I liked my Latin teacher very much. From 10 until 11 we had arithmetic from the same master, and from 11 till 12 we had German. Our German master was very strict indeed. Then we had gymnastics by the same young man. His muscles were like iron. I never saw such a strong man in all my life before. After gymnastics lesson we went home feeling very tired.

    We had to go back at 4 o'clock and from 4 until 5 we had drawing, and from 5 until 6 all the rest of the boys had French, but I did not take French. In that hour I had all my preparation for next day. From 6 until 7, I had German and the other boys had their preparation hour. This finished my school day.

    We took different lessons each morning from 8 until 9. Monday we would recite our Bible lesson. Tuesday we had poetry to recite by heart. Wednesday we had parsing, Thursday we had English history, Friday we had poetry again and Saturday, geography.

We had two half holidays in the week and they were Wednesday and Saturday afternoons. Then the school would go into a park and play football. There were about 30 boys in the school and I liked them all very much.

The family returned home from Europe earlier than planned after just a year abroad because of Lillie's declining health. Wirt continued his schooling back home, first in Atchison public schools, then at Michigan Military Academy in Orchard Lake. Before his graduation in 1900 he'd seen his country's involvement in a brief but disturbing war.

The *USS Maine* had mysteriously exploded in Havana harbor in February 1898. The press stirred Americans into a frenzy demanding retaliation. The U.S. with its imperial-minded President McKinley had been building up its fleet of warships, and the Navy was eager to demonstrate its power. The entire East Coast was frightened and demanded protection against a Spanish fleet that might be hiding at Cuba. But the Spanish did not want war and conceded to all U.S. demands except for the one insisting on Cuban independence. The concessions did nothing to quell the war fever. Mystery ships were claimed to have been sighted off the coast. Fear and panic reigned, and the U.S. declared war, leaving Spain no choice but to defend its Caribbean possessions.

Spain's Admiral Cervera wanted to deploy his fleet to the Canary Islands and wait for the American fleet to engage them there. Instead, he was ordered to sail to Cuba into what he regarded as certain disaster. He anchored in Santiago de Cuba Bay with its narrow entrance protected by shore batteries. At the mouth of the bay the American Navy assembled five battleships with heavy guns and many other smaller craft. The battleship *Oregon*, newly built in Seattle, had sailed around Cape Horn to reach the Carribean in sixty-seven days. The feat inspired a popular song by John James Meehan that contributed to the Americans' enthusiasm for war.

Lights out! And a prow turned toward the South,
And a canvas hiding each cannon's mouth
And a ship like a silent ghost released
Is seeking her sister ships in the East.
When your boys shall ask what the guns are for,
Then tell them the tale of the Spanish war,
And the breathless millions that looked upon
The matchless race of the Oregon.

The Spanish fleet of six heavy cruisers was badly outgunned. It had left Spain so quickly that one of its best ships, the *Cristóbal Colón*, named for the discoverer of America, had not been fitted with its main gun turret. The U.S. Army landed near the bay and marched overland to flush the Spanish fleet out of the protected waters. Admiral Cervera decided to make a run for it into the teeth of the U.S. battleships arranged at the bay's entrance. The entire Spanish fleet was destroyed as the vessels came out in single file, allowing American fire to concentrate on each one in turn. During the battle, private yachts ferrying journalists scurried through the scene.

It was the land maneuvers of the brief war that propelled Teddy Roosevelt to national prominence. As commander of the "Rough Riders" he led their charge up San Juan Hill, providing the name recognition to win him the governorship of New York and on to the presidency.

The Spanish-American War was brought home to Atchison by a visitor to the Hetheringtons. A society note in the *Globe* duly reported the event: *"Ernest Leffingwell, who is visiting in Atchison at the residence of Mrs. Lilly Hetherington, was one of the crew of the famous American battleship Oregon when the Spanish fleet of Admiral Cervera was destroyed off Santiago de Cuba. Mr. Leffingwell is a son of Dr. Leffingwell, president of St. Mary's School at Knoxville, Ill., and is a college graduate. Mrs. Hetherington's daughter, Ruth, attended St. Mary's."*

When Lillie asked Leffingwell what his role had been during the battle, he replied, "I was a common sailor passing ammunition deep inside the *Oregon*. When I did get topside, the smoke was so thick that I could see little."

"It makes these distant wars more palpable when you hear it described by someone you know," Lillie told him. "I'm glad you survived and were not one of those we build a memorial to. I read that the Spanish had four hundred seventy killed or wounded. It all seems so senseless when the Spanish did not want war in the first place."

Later, Ruthanna asked her mother if she could talk to her without the other children being present. "Of course, dear. Let's go into the library."

"Mother, Lute has asked me to marry, but he has to finish medical school first."

"That's wonderful. You've been seeing him since you were children. I recall all of his baseball games that you attended. And he was a big hit singing 'Telephone in de Air' with Haverly's Junior minstrels. You have never paid any attention to another boy. Are you sure there's not somebody out there you might like even better?"

Luther Anson Todd, second row, second from left

"No; he's the one. He's good-looking, intelligent and fun to be with. He tells good stories. He treats me with respect and brings joy to my life."

"I agree, and I'm sure your father would have applauded. The Todds are a fine family, and his father, Newell, is now the bridge superintendent. You know, of course, that when you announce a date, you will be deluged with party invitations from people who'll want to have receptions for you."

Home of Newell Delno and Hulda Todd and son Luther, Atchison

"I understand, but that won't be for a while yet."
"I just want you to be prepared for a hectic schedule."

Lillie's warning to her daughter was most apt, as there were almost continuous parties the two weeks before the wedding. Among the prenuptial affairs was one given by Miss Virge Byram at her country home in Shannon. Another, a tea, was given by Miss Fannie Webb. One luncheon was hosted by Miss Della Brooks and another by Mrs. Norman Barratt. Lucy Hart squeezed in a parcel shower and chocolate at her home one morning.

When Lute told his father that he was going to ask for the hand of Ruthanna, Newell was enthusiastic. But when Lute told him what a hit he was at the Minstrel Show, the smile on his father's face turned sour. "A minstrel show is nothing but an exhibition of racism. It portrays the Negro as a bumbling, simplistic idiot."

"I didn't intend that. Smudging our faces with burnt cork and painting our lips was just good fun."

"Do you think the Negro citizens of Atchison regard it as good fun?"

"I never thought of it that way."

"That's the problem; you're not thinking. I fought a war to free the slaves and restore their human dignity. Now popular culture is portraying them as fun-loving simpletons who are probably not able to govern themselves and surely not worthy of participating in governing us."

"I'll rethink it, Dad. Thanks for the lesson. When Ruth and I have children, I'll pass the lesson on to them."

The headline in the *Champion* of July 13, 1899, read "A Brilliant Affair."

Atchison has had several weddings of prominence, but none has attracted more attention, both from a host of Atchison friends and numerous ones out of town, than the one that took place last evening at Trinity Episcopal Church at 8:30 o'clock when Miss Ruthanna Hetherington and Mr. Luther Anson Todd were united in the holy bonds of matrimony. The church had been beautifully trimmed for the occasion with pink and white carnations on the altar, while feathery asparagus with festoons of white satin ribbon banked the chancel across the front of the church. At 8:30 the Trinity choir boys preceded by the cross bearer, came from the parish house singing the Lohengrin bridal chorus. Miss Gladys Levin and Hale Hetherington preceded the choir boys and carried the broad white ribbons up the center aisle and opened the pretty smilax gates for the bridal party to pass through. Following the choir boys came the ushers and the matron of honor, Mrs. R.K. Smith, a cousin of the bride, followed by Misses Mary and Gail Hetherington as bridesmaids, and then the bride leaning on the arm of her brother, Wirt, who gave her away.

Ruthanna Hetherington wedding

The best man was the groom's brother, Hugh. As the couple went before the altar to take the final vows, the choir boys sang the wedding hymn "O, Perfect Love," without accompaniment.

The bride who is one of Atchison's prettiest young ladies, being tall and graceful with a charm of manner and a sweet personality that has won for her friends by the legion everywhere, never looked more beautiful than in her wedding gown of cream Liberty silk, over white taffeta, with trimmings of real lace. An exquisite pearl girdle and a filmy bridal veil that entirely enveloped her graceful figure, and an immense bouquet of pearl roses, completed a most beautiful costume.

After the ceremony, a reception was given at the handsome Hetherington home on North Fifth Avenue. Here was gathered probably one of the most brilliant assemblies ever seen in Atchison, and hosts of pretty women, exquisitely gowned, the flashing of jewels, the sweet perfume of roses and the music by an orchestra made a most enchanting scene. Mrs. Hetherington, mother of the bride, was beautifully gowned in pale blue silk, embroidered in silver spangles.

The gifts were arranged about the large sitting room upstairs, and were exceedingly elaborate and in great profusion. Everything that money and exquisite taste could furnish were visible everywhere. Cut glass of the most exquisite design, silverware of the most costly and elegant, gems of beauty in rare china and bronze, a cuckoo clock, an elegant brass bed given by the ushers, beautiful hand work in embroidery and filmy lace, pictures and everything that it seemed possible to select, was here in gorgeous array. Mrs. Hetherington presented the bride with a chest of solid silver. Mr. Todd gave the expenses of the bridal trip to Yellowstone Park as his wedding gift.

A few minutes before 11 o'clock the bride came down attired in a handsome traveling suit of blue cloth, tailor made, and amidst a chorus of best wishes, bride and groom were driven to the depot, where they took the Burlington to Omaha. The bride's trousseau was most exquisite and was almost wholly done by the deft fingers of the bride. When the couple returns from their honeymoon, they will reside in New York City while Mr. Todd completes his medical studies at the College of Physicians and Surgeons of Columbia University."

Lute and Ruthanna stayed at the Lake Hotel at the top of the thirty mile-long Yellowstone Lake. The Hotel was built by the Northern Pacific Railroad and had opened just eight years before when the railroad built a branch line to near the northern park entrance. After a stagecoach ride to the hotel, the newlyweds could finally relax. "Lute, the view is stunning. Can you imagine that our Kansas Senator Ingalls in 1883 proposed that the park land be sold to private individuals. He did not want to spend a dime to protect this natural beauty from ruin."

Lake Hotel, Yellowstone

Yellowstone National Park Transportation

"Yes, that would've been a crime. I can just see a big advertising sign on a boat in the lake. Many newlyweds go to Niagara Falls, but I hear it is a tawdry mess. I'm glad my dad gave us this trip."

"This is much more restful after a hectic round of parties prior to the wedding."

Lute, the constant, curious scholar, read to Ruthanna a bit of the park's geologic history. "Six-hundred thousand years ago there was a massive volcanic eruption, and the subsequent collapse of the volcano created a caldera twenty-eight by forty-seven miles across. Yellowstone Lake fills the southwestern portion of the crater."

"Enough, enough! I didn't come here for a history lesson."

"Yes, let's go to bed early tonight so we can get up early in the morning and take a carriage over Craig Pass to Old Faithful."

"I know you, you just want to get me into bed."

"Do you have any objection, Mrs. Todd?"

"None at all. Let's do it."

A year later in New York, Luther was substitute house surgeon at Roosevelt Hospital when one sweltering night in August, his ambulance was called to tend casualties of white attacks on Blacks in the Tenderloin district, one of the few areas of the city where Blacks could live although there was much resentment among the whites over their presence. The driver drove the horses with abandon, causing the ambulance to career around an intersection, hit the curb and nearly tip over. The ambulance itself became a target of bullets and missiles, and Luther narrowly missed being a casualty himself. White mobs attacked Blacks, with the police simply looking on, killing some and causing scores to be hospitalized. The Blacks' homes were sacked and burned, and places that employed Blacks were raided.

When Luther finally returned home the next morning, Ruthanna greeted him with tears in her eyes and a long, warm embrace. Now that he was in her arms again, she didn't want to let him go. Finally, he could breathe again and told Ruthanna of the horror of the night. "Small gangs attacked Negro residents starting in the area of Forty-second Street and Eighth Avenue. By the time I arrived with the ambulance, there were bloody bodies everywhere. Some were already dead."

"Isn't that the area referred to as Satan's Circus?"

"Yes, the streets are lined with brothels, nightclubs, saloons, gambling casinos and dance halls. The corrupt police are paid off to look the other way."

"I was worried sick about you. Couldn't the police stop the violence?"

"They didn't even try. They just stood around and watched."

"Were you in danger?"

"Probably, but I was working so hard, I hardly looked up or thought of myself."

"Why is that area called the Tenderloin?"

"I'm told that a corrupt police captain by the name of 'Clubber' Williams gave it that name when he said that before he was assigned to the area he ate chuck steak, but now I'm going to have tenderloin."

"I won't ask any more questions and let you go to bed. We can talk more when you are rested."

Ruth's next letter to her mother tried to sound reassuring:

Like many riots, things started with an incident. An undercover police officer named Thorpe mistakenly accused a Black woman of being a prostitute, and her husband rose to her defense. The husband was unaware that the white man was a police officer. The officer struck the man with a club and the husband retaliated with a pen knife. Thorpe later died. His funeral erupted into violence with police officers and white gangs running wild in Black neighborhoods. Lute worked feverishly all night trying to save the wounded. Hundreds of Negroes were brought into the hospital, some of them beaten almost beyond recognition. Then the Blacks armed themselves and formed a Citizens' Protective League. The mayor seems unwilling to protect Black civil rights. Things are quite tense now, but we will stay out of the troubled areas. Don't worry about us.

On a happier note, I am pregnant, expecting next February. I hope for a girl, but Lute wants a boy. Both in good time I expect. We will return to Atchison soon for this is no place to raise a family.

Little Ruthanna was born the next year, carrying on into a third generation the name of her Grandmother Bennett. The couple returned to Kansas in 1902. Soon to follow were the births in 1903 of Newell Webster, named for his grandfathers, and in 1908 of Luther Anson, Jr. Both sons were born in St. Joseph, Missouri, where Luther pursued a distinguished career in medicine and also served as president of the city's Board of Health.

Luther Anson Todd's chair while a student at medical school

Back in Atchison, traveling minstrel shows were popular, and local versions were common as the *Globe* reported the role of Ruthanna's brother:

Hale Hetherington's minstrel aggregation of spotted artists, the burnt cork did not appear to go around, who have been starring in North Atchison parlors for two or three seasons, tried the ice at Forest Park last night, and it held them. Two hundred people, mostly relatives of the young comedians and songsters, paid 15 cents each, and have no kick coming, although a great many things had to be overlooked: the substitution of a piano for an orchestra, the absence of bones, and a stump speaker, for instance, but then what can be expected for 15 cents? Hale Hetherington, Heath Frazier, and Jamie Price were the end men, not one of them over twelve years old. Hale Hetherington sang "I'll Make That Black Girl Mine," and Heath Frazier sang "I Don't Care if I Never Come Back." In the second part Hale Hetherington and Dell Small did a tumbling and handspring act.

A bowling alley had opened in Atchison in 1901, and the thoroughly modern, young society girls of the town wasted no time taking advantage of it. In Mary Hetherington's mind, the usual pastimes of tennis, whist and golf were replaced by bowling. With the help of Edith Alice Noble and Muriel Ingalls, she started a bowling club. that included Alice Brown along with a dozen others. The alley accommodated them by closing to all others every morning while the ladies had their game. The newspaper, perhaps to assure the town of the girls' propriety, noted that *"the young ladies wear dark grey golf or walking skirts, averaging in length about four inches from the ground. French flannel, close-fitting waists and Rough Rider hats complete their outfits."* One wonders if there were any higher and lower skirts that made up the average. No matter, no male onlookers were allowed. Mary soon had the local women's bowling record score of one hundred forty-four. Mary was home for the summer after graduating from the Gardner School for Girls in New York City preparatory to completing her musical education in Paris. While in New York, Mary sang at a reception for the philanthropist Mrs. Russell Sage, president of the Emma Willard Association. Emma Willard founded the first women's school of higher learning from which Olivia Sage had graduated.

Each year, Atchison held a Corn Carnival in September. for which many men and women wore costumes made of corn. All the shops had displays made of cornstalks and a grand arch over Commercial Street welcomed people to town. Floats were covered entirely with cornstalks and corn ears. Being short of funds in 1902, the festival managers came up with the idea of having nine young society girls take fares on the streetcars, with all the money going to support the carnival. The *Globe,* never at a loss for hyperbole, reported, *"The pretty and popular girls selected to act as conductors represented Atchison's society circles. . . . .Miss Alice Brown is a daughter and Miss Sarah Brown a granddaughter of Capitalist J.P. Brown. . . .*

Corn Carnival Mementos

Miss Mary Hetherington is the second daughter of the late W.W. Hetherington of the Exchange National Bank. She is regarded as one of the most beautiful young women in the West and it is believed that before many years her voice will make her distinguished."

In the open-pollinated corn grown at the time, an occasional red ear would emerge from crossbreeding. At the first carnival, a young man announced that he would kiss any girl with a red kernel on her costume. The practice caught on, and by nightfall even the homeliest had been kissed repeatedly. In later years, the custom had evolved to the point that if a man held a red ear above the head of a girl, he could kiss her. An enterprising corn dealer brought a whole wagonload of red ears to sell to the eager males. The carnival drew worldwide attention, even meriting an article in London's *Strand Magazine.*

Mary made the acquaintance of Jerome Pillow, the brother of her school friend Jane Pillow at a party given by her Aunt Mary in Atlanta. Jerome was enrolled in the Military Academy at West Point and cut a very dashing figure, indeed.

When the wedding date was announced, a party was held in Mary's honor by Mrs. J.P. Brown, and of course there were many more, including a grand one by Mary's Aunt Waggener. Mrs. Brown's daughter Alice, a good friend of Mary's, had recently married Warren Peter Byram, uniting two of Atchison's leading families who had figured prominently in freighting to the West. The Brown and Byram families were now joined as were the Hetherington and Todd families. Mary and Wirt Hetherington were part of the wedding party. Many in town who understood the history of these families and the social interaction among them wondered if someday the Brown-Byram and the Hetherington-Todd lines might combine.

The *Globe* never missed the opportunity to wax eloquently on society happenings:

The marriage of Miss Mary Louise Hetherington to Lt. Jerome Gray Pillow was celebrated in Trinity Episcopal Church, February 13, 1903. The chancel of the church was beautifully decorated with southern smilax, ascension lilies, and brides' roses. The light of a hundred candles burned on the altar. The matron of honor was the bride's sister, Mrs. L.A. Todd of St. Joseph who wore a dress of pink crepe de chine, with a pleated skirt and décolleté bodice with a bertha of duchess lace, and a tulle veil held in place by a wreath of grape foliage studded with dew drops. The bridesmaids included the bride's sister, Gail, in a pink dress of silk from Liberty's of London, and two sisters of the groom wearing white pineapple tissue dresses over pink silk. The bride was gowned in white Liberty crepe, worn with a bertha of Duchess Lace elaborately open-worked and herring-boned. Her bouquet was of lilies of the valley.

Mary could have been a model for one of Charles Dana Gibson's illustrations with her hair swept up to the top of her head and a cascade of curls dangling down. Under her bridal dress, she wore a swan-bill corset, which she didn't really need.

Both the groom and his groomsman were in full dress uniform of the 14th Cavalry. Ushers included the bride's brothers, Wirt and Hale. After the wedding, a supper was served to one hundred fifty

guests at the Hetherington mansion. As the St. Joseph Daily News reported, "The whole lower floor was thrown open, palms were banked against the stairway and in the windows, ferns were on the mantels, an orchestra played in the reception hall, and in the deep bow window of the drawing room, the bridal party received. Throughout the house the lights were shaded in pink. When the bride's cake was cut, the ring was found by Miss Gail Hetherington." At eleven o'clock the couple left for Denver and nearby Fort Logan where the groom was to be stationed. The bride's mother gave them a chest of silver and the groom's father, a plantation in Tennessee. The groom's great-uncle was General Gideon Pillow, noted for his role in the Mexican War and as commander of a Confederate cavalry unit that had harassed General Sherman's Atlanta campaign during the Civil War. Among the out-of-town guests was Mrs. Annie Miller of Minneapolis, whose husband had been a Union surgeon in the Civil War.

Soon after the wedding, Pillow was ordered to the Philippines. The *Globe* reported that "Mrs. Pillow made much millinery preparation for the life in the tropics, providing forty dresses and twenty pairs of shoes and endless dainties. They had shipped their belongings, including all their bridal presents when along came another order canceling the previous one, and sending Pillow to remain at Fort Logan, Colorado. Their shipped belongings were lost."

The new bride was quite put out. "Can't the Army make up its mind?" she stormed to Jerome in frustration over losing her trousseau and wedding gifts. "How can it fight a war when it can't get its troop movements organized?"

"Mary, you're in the Army now, and that is just the way it is."

Soon enough, Jerome's unit was correctly ordered to the Philippines for two years, and the Pillows shipped out of San Francisco on board the transport *Logan*. Mary insisted on wearing white as they entered the tropics. Her favorite outfit was a white skirt that came down to her white shoes and a white long-sleeved, double-breasted overblouse that came to her knees. The double rows of buttons added a kind of military trim. A black ribbon tie was at her throat, and a flat-topped straw hat with a black ribbon band completed the ensemble.

With the Spanish defeat in the Spanish-American War, the United States purchased the Philippines for twenty million dollars. President William McKinley planned to make the islands an American colony. The reason, explained McKinley, was that, "There was nothing left to do but to take them all, and to educate the Filipinos, and uplift and civilize and Christianize them, and by God's grace do the very best we could for them, as our fellowmen for whom Christ also died."

Indiana Senator Albert Beveridge reflected a similar opinion that God "has made us the master organizers of the world . . . that we may administer . . . among savages and senile peoples."

The Filipinos themselves, who previously had been fighting for their independence from Spain, thought otherwise and had established their own government under President Emilio Aguinaldo. The U.S. sent eleven thousand troops to pacify the rebels who were resisting their new owners. Then in February 1899, a Filipino soldier was shot by an American soldier, and

President McKinley told reporters that "the insurgents had attacked Manila," a deliberate lie aimed at justifying further military action. No declaration of war was made, and, instead, the action was declared necessary to control an insurrection and a rebellion against a legitimate government, which, of course, it was not. An American force of one hundred twenty-six thousand was sent, and heavy fighting commenced. When Manila was subdued, President Aguinaldo ordered his army to engage in guerila warfare that was to persist for years. After McKinley's assassination, President Theodore Roosevelt declared the war's end in 1902 when Aguinaldo was killed, but the guerillas continued their struggle for independence.

It was this struggle that Lieutenant. Pillow entered in 1904. A number of prominent Americans, including Mark Twain, Andrew Carnegie and William Jennings Bryan, opposed the action in which four thousand three hundred twenty-four American soldiers were killed. Pillow, who completed a two-year tour, was fortunate that he was not among them. Civilian deaths exceeded two hundred fifty thousand. The exact number of killed and wounded Filipinos was unknown, as the army did not bother to count them.

During the Pillows' deployment, Alice Roosevelt, the president's twenty-one-year-old daughter was among the eighty-member party that accompanied Secretary of War William Howard Taft to the Philippines. The dignitaries were feted at many parties, feasts and receptions, and Jerome and his wife were invited to one of these. Mary's formal introduction to Alice was in the receiving line, but later Alice sought her out for an extended conversation.

"These affairs, night after night, are beginning to tire me out, and there is so little opportunity to visit with anyone close to my age. So many stuffy diplomats and generals and their boring wives, I could scream," declared Alice.

"Yes, look at that fat, old general dancing with his even fatter wife. They are like two sumo wrestlers rubbing bellies." Alice burst out laughing.

Mary never was at a loss for words, and the two became immediate friends after much girl talk comparing the trunks and clothes they brought with them. When Mary complained about the corset she was wearing, Alice replied, "I try to avoid those painful carapaces with those awful metal stays in front that flatten, but dig into your stomach and ribs and cause your butt to stick out behind like a donkey." Mary was not so sure that Alice's tiny waist was entirely natural, but she did not press the issue.

"Tomorrow I'm going horseback riding in the hills. Oh, do come so I will have someone to talk to. You do ride, don't you?"

Mary had never been on a horse before, but she said, "Of course."

"Great! Riding is my passion. I brought my own sidesaddle. See you later; I am being beckoned."

Anyone who saw the two of them together would think they were perfect Gibson Girls. Alice wore a gown in a pale tint of azure, her favorite color. This was later to inspire a popular song "Alice Blue Gown." Mary was glad she had chosen a gown in white; otherwise, people would have said they were twins.

When Mary and Jerome next danced, Mary told him of her invitation. "I said yes without thinking of what I would wear. I have no boots or riding habit. What am I to do?"

Jerome thought that was just like his tempestuous wife, but he kept it to himself. He was trained to solve problems, not to argue with them. "I will ask some of the other officers if their wives have a riding habit that would fit you."

"You are a sweetheart and a lifesaver."

Jerome beamed. He liked to please his new wife. He hurried off on his mission and soon reported that Mrs. Atkins had the necessary outfit and was willing to loan it.

The next morning, Mary strode across the compound to the Atkins's quarters and tried on the riding clothes. The boots were a bit tight, but she was riding, not walking.

Horses were not a problem in a cavalry unit, but organizing a large party for an overnight ride was a logistical nightmare. Jerome would have preferred to plan a major troop movement. The next day the party went up the trail to Lake Lanao and spent the night at Camp Kemberly.

When Mary rode alongside Alice, she said, "I see you are not riding sidesaddle."

"Yes, the darned girths would not fit these horses so I had to resort to an Army cross-saddle."

Secretary Taft decided he did not want to be left behind, so he came along in an Army wagon. He bounced uncomfortably on the rocky road as sweat soaked through his jacket. His usually upward-pointed mustache hung down limply with beads of perspiration dripping from it. Alice and Mary could not contain their giggles every time they looked on Taft's predicament. Nevertheless, he maintained his good humor all the time his belly rocked from side to side as he held on to the wagon seat for dear life.

On the isle of Jolo, another reception awaited them. The cast of characters and costumes were like something from grand opera. Of course, Alice was the diva in her bright red-linen dress decorated with white shamrocks outlined in black, topped off with a floppy hat and red parasol. Even Taft in his white ducks and Army and Naval officers in formal dress with all of their medals could not outshine the Sultan of Salu and his retinue. The Sultan brought a thousand turbaned Muslim Moros from all of the islands dressed in jackets seeded with pearls, colorful silk shirts and striped trousers belted with heavy silk sashes into which their bolos with elaborately carved handles were inserted. The newspapers reported that the four foot-tall Sultan wanted to add Alice to his harem of six wives.

Later, Alice showed Mary her gifts from the Sultan, including an exquisite pearl ring and a Moro costume called a Bogobo with its girdle hung with bells. "Mary, it is just like Christmas every day. I think the ring is a proposal for marriage." When Alice returned to the States, she came with twenty-seven boxes filled with gifts that was much remarked about in the press. Alice richly earned her moniker of "Princess Alice." Alice loved doggerel, and her friend Willard Straight composed the following lines to commemorate her journey:

When Alice came to Plunderland,
The Crown Prince sought her lily hand,
The emperor had a pipe Dream
That this was where his native land
Could shake the Japs forever and
Secure a friendship ripe with father.

Alice was married a year later to Nicholas Longworth, fifteen years her senior. When Mary read of the grand event, she was sorry she had not been invited. Surely, there was room for one more friend among the one thousand invitees. But then, she realized she had been Alice's friend only for a few days.

The reality of the everyday military life in the islands was quite different from the gay, glittering balls that Alice experienced. When reports of terrorist attacks came in, Jerome saddled up and rode out from Camp Overton with his unit, sometimes for weeks at a time. When he returned to their bamboo house in the officers' section, Mary had a hard time getting him to describe his mission. Finally, he admitted, "We would ride shooting and slashing into a suspect village. Inevitably, women and children were killed. Some were burned in their miserable huts. Children were left crying, clinging to their dead mothers, as the men disappeared into the trees. We ride away not knowing what will become of them. General Wood says this is unfortunate but necessary to pacify the rebels. The general is a bit emotional about it and is offended by Moro blood feuds, slavery and polygamy. At night in my hammock, I couldn't sleep as these images raced through my mind. They never taught us about this kind of war at West Point."

"You poor dear," Mary consoled him. "That's inhuman."

"There were days when I planned to resign my commission when we returned to camp, but then I thought of the shame it would bring to my military family. Gideon Pillow would turn over in his grave. My insides are torn apart."

"I feel your pain and wish there was something I could do to ease it."

"I'll just have to tough it out and look forward to the end of this tour of duty."

Mercifully, Jerome was given a furlough, and he and Mary embarked on a quick tour of Japan and China. They acquired a large twelve by eighteen-foot silk rug with peacocks in the corners, a smaller matching throw rug and several brass candelabras and bowls engraved with Chinese symbols.

Jerome returned to duty, followed orders and was rewarded with a promotion to first lieutenant. After over two years of service, they returned to San Francisco on the *Logan* in the fall of 1905. It was far from an uneventful crossing, being marked by a typhoon, a suicide and a series of thefts from staterooms. They were on board in Manila harbor when the typhoon hit, and the ship rescued many Filipino sailors foundering in the giant waves. One native boat pulled alongside containing a husband, wife, child and pig. To Mary's amazement, the man first sent up the pig, then the baby, then he started up himself, leaving his wife in the boat until the *Logan*'s crew insisted that the woman be next.

Chinese Rug with Phoenix

Once the Pillows were back in the U.S., the Army again issued orders for Jerome's unit to return to the Philippines for one more year. But before that order was carried out, Jerome was told to proceed to Fort Riley, Kansas, instead. This time, the reversal of Army orders met with Mary's full approval.

Immediately after landing, Jerome had been hospitalized with a severe stomach ailment for two weeks. Mary left him in San Francisco and went ahead to Atchison to visit her family. When Jerome was released from the hospital, Mary joined him at Fort Riley. Yet before they could settle in, the 14th Cavalry was ordered to march cross-country to Fort Sheridan just east of Chicago. When Jerome told Mary, he emphasized the word "march," explaining they would ride all the way. "I can't believe it," responded Mary. "Why would they do that?"

"I suppose it is one last hurrah for the cavalry, which is becoming obsolete. I suspect the president had something to do with the decision as we are to be accompanied by his eighteen-year-old son. I guess this is the closest Kermit Roosevelt will ever get to his father's Rough Riders experience."

The following year, the Army's indiscriminate treatment of the Filipino rebels worsened. General Leonard Wood led several bloody campaigns against Muslim Moro natives. Regarding them as irretrievably fanatical, he called for their extermination. The line distinguishing fanatical terrorists from freedom fighters has always been a matter of whose view is taken.

Back in Atchison, Lillie Hetherington maintained the resolve she'd made to stay active after her husband's death. She traveled with Ed Howe and several others to Topeka where an old Atchison friend was entertaining the Hoosier poet James Whitcomb Riley.

Ruthanna and Lute were now living about twenty-five miles upriver from Lillie in St. Joseph, Missouri. One day Lute left an envelope on the dining room table when he set off for his medical office. Inside was a page from his prescription tablet that read as follows:

October 1, 1904
For: Mrs. L.A. Todd
For your health it is recommended that you attend the World's Fair in St. Louis this month. Several days away from the children will be good for you. It is also prescribed that you wear your prettiest lingerie for the health of your husband.
(s) L.A. Todd, M.D.

When Lute returned home for lunch, Ruthanna questioned him, "Isn't the fair just for kids?"

He nodded in agreement and added, "And for people that are young at heart."

When Ruthanna and Lute returned from St. Louis, they stopped to see Lillie and enthusiastically recommended the fair to her. "You stay in the hotel on the fairgrounds so you can spend a few days without having to travel back and forth from the city. The fair is huge and can be exhausting."

"OK, I'm going to do it. I'll call Aunt Mary and ask her to meet me in St. Louis and then come back to Atchison for a stay here.

"Mother, you must ride the Ferris wheel. It's over two hundred fifty feet tall and was brought from the Chicago World's Fair of 1893."

"We'll see about that; I'm not as young and daring as you."

Lillie took the train to St. Louis and checked into one of the Inside Inn's two thousand two hundred fifty-seven rooms, which cost her one dollar fifty per day. She wore a floor-length skirt of brown wool twill decorated with two bands of ribbon at the bottom. Her blouse was a gored white shirtwaist with cummerbund, lace-trimmed cuffs and collar and an embroidered monogram. Her brown wide-brimmed hat had a satin ribbon with tiny satin flowers attached. Lute had said the millinery fashion of the day looked like an upside-down platter whose only merit was to shield her eyes from the sun. She carried a camel-colored suede drawstring bag.

On the first day, Lillie found the fair buildings to be far grander than she had imagined and almost seemed to deserve their designations as palaces. The Palace of Agriculture was the largest, covering twenty-one acres. The Palace of Manufactures covered fourteen acres and the Palace of Machinery, twelve. Because of her son-in-law's being station in the Philippines, Lillie was particularly interested in that country's exhibit, which covered forty-seven acres and housed over one thousand natives. One group of Filipino natives was the Igorots whose feast-day fare was dog meat. After only a short residency at the fair, the Pawnee Indian participants had pulled up stakes and left St. Louis, complaining that the Igorots had eaten all their dogs. Lillie asked the guide, "Is it true that the Bagabos are headhunters?" The guide demurred because he had already turned the group toward the five-thousand seat restaurant at the Tyrolean Alps.

St. Louis World's Fair

After the first day, Lillie and Mary were exhausted, and their feet were aching. "Lillie, we need a different approach. Let's hire a guide and ride from building to building in Cabe-Powers carriages. Inside the buildings, we can hire a couple of boys to push us in those wheeled wicker chairs."

"Good plan; I'm all for it."

The next day they took it a little slower, amazed at each turn by sights like King Cotton in the Mississippi pavilion soaring thirty-five feet high and the cast-iron, one hundred thousand-pound statue of Vulcan towering fifty-six feet over the Alabama exhibit. Superlatives dominated their conversations.

There was one exhibit that Lillie would not go see. "Mary, look here in the catalog. The famed Apache Chief, Geronimo, is selling photographs and autographs."

"Maybe my grandson would like his photo."

"Not me. It is so sad that the man who held off the U.S. Army for months in Arizona is now on exhibit like a prize cow. He is seventy-five years old and still a federal prisoner. They won't let him return to Arizona. I don't condone the lives he took, but we did steal his land."

The ladies particularly enjoyed the Palace of Fine Arts. Lillie paused at Mucha's art nouveau poster advertising the fair in France. "I rather like the art nouveau movement that is sweeping the world," said the adventuresome Lillie.

"Some of it is disturbing," Mary replied, "like that dark figure of the Indian grasping the hand of the white woman. I find the Tiffany glass more to my liking."

On the last day, Lillie said, "Maybe we should try the Ferris wheel today. Ruthanna will razz me forever if I don't ride it."

"OK, but I'm not walking down the crowded mile-long Pike with all its hawkers."

"No problem. We'll get the carriage to take us directly to the wheel on a back road." Lillie was a bit apprehensive when they entered one of the wooden cars, but as the other sixty passengers entered, she felt safer. But when the wheel began to move and the car rocked a bit, Lillie held on tight and felt her stomach trying to catch up even though the wheel moved at the sedate pace of ten minutes for the full circuit. Down below was a line of automobiles that had motored from New York in seventeen days. They looked like toys. The ladies had read in the paper that the Ford Motor Company, in business for less than a year, had a couple of vehicles on display, but the sisters didn't bother to search out those small, inexpensive models. They were interested only in the larger vehicles. Lillie enjoyed the view from the top of the circuit and was glad she had risked the ride. Ruthanna would be proud of her.

On the train home, Lillie reflected on the experience, "I get the distinct impression that electricity, the airplane, and the automobile are going to change our world."

"Yes, I wouldn't mind having an electric oven and refrigerator." But since neither woman did her own cooking, they never updated their kitchens to include the modern marvels.

When Lillie returned home she bored all her friends with descriptions of the Chinese exhibit with a seven foot-long elephant tusk, the Borax twenty-mule team from Death Valley and the sculptures in the Palace of Art. She knew she could not communicate the grandeur of the Festival Hall and Colonnade of the fourteen states that were created from the Louisiana Purchase, especially at night when submerged colored lights illuminated the three cascades leading to the Grand Basin. For her friends, she had purchased vases of ruby flash glass engraved with the name of the fair and the date.

The Globe reported, "Mrs. Lillie Hetherington is entertaining her daughters, Mrs. Jerome Pillow of Fort Riley, and Mrs. L.A. Todd of St. Joe, and her niece Miss Gladys Levin of Atlanta, Georgia. She invited the friends who had known her in her girlhood days to a tea at her home. Mrs. Pillow just returned from an extended stay in the Philippines with her husband. Guests included Mrs. N.D. Todd." Lillie had grown dissatisfied with the looks of her house and had the porch removed and replaced with a wider one with cut-stone pillars. She continued to live her life to the fullest, enjoying a trip to California with her sister-in-law Emma Hetherington Waggener.

Item in the Globe in 1907: "The following ladies will receive New Year's calls on Monday: Mrs. W.W. Hetherington will receive at her residence, corner of Fifth and Riley on New Year's day, assisted by Mrs. Dr. Miller, Mrs. William Hetherington, Mrs. J. Levin, Mrs. B.P. Waggener, and Miss Grace Hetherington."

Little Gail asked her mother, "Why is Uncle Clifford not married? He seems well liked. Surely, there's some woman who would say yes."

"I guess he's just not the marrying kind. He says his mother is the only woman in his life."

"Is he a little strange?"

"No, child. Where did you get that idea? People speculate too much." There was an edge in Lillie's voice, and Gail let it drop.

Years before, among the *Globe*'s many comments on Atchison's notables was the following: "C.S. Hetherington will prove a rare catch for some young lady. He is about twenty-eight years old, holds a responsible position behind the counter of the Exchange National Bank; has a remarkably fine mustache of reddish tint, and a bewitching glance from under a silk plug hat." The rare catch was not to be: Bank cashier Clifford S. Hetherington, bachelor son of William and Annie, died in 1906, the year of the San Francisco earthquake.

The Globe noted, "One of Cliff Hetherington's prevailing characteristics was his intense love and affection for his mother who died in 1887. His room was filled with her pictures, and he had been known to sit and look at them for hours. Since her death, his sister, Mrs. Waggener, has been foremost in his affection."

Prior to Clifford's death, the *Topeka Capital* reported the following:

Six weeks ago there was a run on the Exchange National Bank, at which time a Kansas City financial institution offered to pay all its deposits, and aid amounting to several million dollars was offered. As the run was of short duration, the Exchange National took care of it without help. The run started as a result of Mr. Hetherington's illness. One woman said to another: 'Cliff Hetherington is failing,' meaning his health.

The second woman interpreted her remark as meaning that the bank was failing, and in that way the run had its inception. Mr. Hetherington was a man of splendid nerve, and throughout the run he was the coolest of the bank's officers.

Clifford Hetherington   Wirt Hetherington

    After Clifford's death, his nephew, Wirt Hetherington, son of Web and Lillie, was appointed assistant cashier. The Union Trust Company was organized in 1907 with W.P. Waggener as second vice president and J.P. Brown, third vice president. It later emerged as the Exchange State Bank, emphasizing savings deposits and organized as a state bank to do things not allowed by national banks. The state of Kansas passed a deposit-guarantee law applying only to state-chartered banks. One of the bank's advertising slogans was "It's all right to spend some money on Coca Cola, but you ought to save enough to start a savings account in the Exchange State Bank."

    In the early 1900s, trust companies were booming. They solicited private investors to buy their bonds, then used the bond income to make all kinds of investments. In 1907, Otto Heinze attempted to corner the market for United Copper Stock, and when the scheme failed, the Knickerbocker Trust Company, lenders of the takeover money, went broke. Depositors tried to withdraw their money, and panic ensued. When the New York Stock Exchange closed, it was down fifty percent from its peak in the previous year. J.P. Morgan organized a consortium of New York banks to inject new capital in addition to the funds being deposited by the federal government. Morgan locked the bankers and stockbrokers in his library until they agreed to his plan.

    Out in the provinces, the Exchange Bank was having a run. When the bank failed to obtain currency from equally troubled banks in St. Joseph and Kansas City, it created a clearinghouse with other Atchison banks to issue a local currency, referred to as commercial paper, based on their bills receivable. Morgan was quoted as saying, "If people will keep their money in the banks, everything will be all right." But, of course, when a panic takes over, depositors want their money in hand. At the Exchange Bank, Balie Waggener, Wirt

Hetherington and other officers stayed late into the evening until all depositors who wanted their money were issued the local script, which seemed to satisfy them.

In New York, Morgan's U.S. Steel acquired the Tennessee Coal, Iron & Railroad Company, after persuading President Teddy Roosevelt to suspend his trust-busting efforts temporarily. This stimulated the stock market and the panic ended. In the aftermath, Congress passed the Federal Reserve Act of 1913, creating the Federal Reserve Bank, and later passed legislation to separate banks' commercial and investment functions.

Wirt was visiting with his mother about the latest financial crisis. "From the bank's ledgers I can see the effects of the panics of 1873, 1893 and, now, 1907."

"I've wondered many times if I'm going to have to sell the house and get a job," Lillie replied. "Do you ever feel like you are dodging bullets?"

"Yes, we bankers are like soldiers who see their comrades falling all around them and wonder when bullets bearing their names will find them."

Bachelor Wirt, who was highly educated and could speak German and recite poetry, would later become president of the Exchange National Bank. He allowed himself few luxuries other than a brace of fine hunting rifles and commissioning a huge four-poster bed of walnut, embellished with hand-carved sunflowers, the Kansas state flower.

President Taft came to Atchison in 1912 to attend Balie Waggener's annual Children's Picnic held on Bailie's birthday. Ruthanna brought her children from St. Joe to watch the parade with her mother. Flags and bunting hung everywhere. When Taft's open car passed, nine-year-old Newell called out, "Hi, uncle," to his Uncle Balie but remained completely unimpressed when Ruthanna pointed out the President next to his relative, even after being reminded "We don't often get to see the President of the United States." Newell was eager to get to the children's picnic with all of its games and contests.

When Ruthanna met Taft in the receiving line that evening, she reminded him, "My sister, Mary, met you in the Philippines."

"Oh yes; I recall the beautiful young woman who became friends with Alice Roosevelt."

"Mary is in the Philippines again. I'll write her that I saw you."

**Gail, L.A., Ruthanna, Jerome, N.W., Mary, Lillie, Annie,
Wirt, Ruthanna, 1910**

The brutal World War between 1914 and 1918 was made murderous by the machine gun. Wave after wave of soldiers on both sides were mowed down. Jerome Pillow, a career cavalryman, was ordered to Europe. The war was again a story of a relatively small incident leading, this time, to a world conflagration. The Archduke of Austria was assassinated by a Serbian anarchist. Austria demanded reparations, and then other nations choose up sides, supporting or denying the Austrians. Despite President Wilson's initial effort to keep the United States out of the war, he gave in to the hawks, such as Theodore Roosevelt. This caused Wilson's pacifist Secretary of State to resign. Pillow briefly served in France in the months before the Armistice was signed. In August 1917, he joined the 32nd Division as G-2 intelligence officer in the Second Battle of the Marne near Chateau Thierry, Aisne-Marne and Oise-Aisne when the last German offensive was stopped in its drive toward Paris. Pillow joined in the elation of Finis La Guerre. After the armistice, the division crossed the Rhine at the Coblenz Bridgehead. As G-2, he rode horseback in advance of the main army to gather intelligence, a traditional role of the cavalry. The commanders needed to know what to expect from the German inhabitants and the retreating German Army. Otherwise, the cavalry had been entirely supplanted by the machine guns, trench warfare, mud, barbed wire and artillery of this new kind of war.

Major Pillow was adjutant general for the 89th Division, part of the occupational force in Europe under the command of General Pershing in 1918. In that role he was promoted to colonel. He returned to the States and graduated from the General Staff School at Fort Leavenworth in 1922. After the war, Jerome and Mary returned to Europe where he was military attaché to Italy and Albania from 1933 to 1936. Colonel Pillow represented the U.S. at Mussolini's war games prior to Il Duce's aid to Franco in the Spanish Civil War between 1936 and '39. The Pillows collected a number of paintings and antiques from a dismantled palace that would later decorate their own house. Pillow's last tour of duty was as chief of staff for the 89th Division's Reserve Officers in Philadelphia. He doubted the permanence of the peace and feared the revival of Germany angered and humiliated by harsh reparations. The outbreak of WW II proved him right.

At the end of his career, Colonel Pillow and Mary returned to Atchison and bought a mansion next to the Hetheringtons. He would be a stockholder in Mary's family-owned Exchange Bank when it celebrated its seventy-fifth anniversary in 1934. Jerome never lost his military bearing and sat ramrod straight dressed in coat and tie every night for dinner. The Pillows had no children, and Mary's brother Wirt was a bachelor, thus there would be no fourth generation of Hetheringtons in the bank.

Col. Jerome Pillow

The beautiful and promising world of Ruthanna and Luther in St. Joseph came to a tragic end with his premature death in 1917. The newspaper headline read, "Dies on Inter-Urban Train." Luther Todd had been felled by a heart attack in his early forties, just as his father-in-law Web Hetherington had died prematurely. Lillie was as distraught as her daughter over this cruelly repeated fate. "Why did our good men have to go so soon?" she asked, knowing no answer would come. A memorial fund was collected by Luther's St. Joe friends to go toward the relief of French war orphans. He'd often told his friends that money put into funeral flowers should be spent, instead, to alleviate suffering of the living. Personal tragedy prevented the family from reflecting on the Russian revolution of the same year.

Calamity was not finished with the Hetheringtons. Youngest daughter Gail had been married in 1914, but her husband, Burt Allen, died only five years later. They were living with Lillie at the time of Burt's death, and Gail never moved from her childhood home, always living there with others.

The country's attention was focused on the progress of ratification of the 19th amendment giving women the right to vote in all elections in all states. Lillie was telling Ruthanna something of the history of the movement. "Your Grandmother Anna attended a rally right here in Atchison at which Elizabeth Cady Stanton and Susan B. Anthony spoke. Anna always said it was ironic that women had the right to work in the fields, die in childbirth and nurse the aged but had not the right to vote."

"Since I grew up in Kansas where women have had the right to vote since 1912, I have taken this privilege for granted. It was sad that after working for suffrage so many years, Stanton and Anthony died before Congress passed the 19th amendment."

"Anna told me she had a heated argument with your Grandpa William. He did not want her to attend the rally, but she went anyway."

"Even now, the amendment barely passed. Tennessee was the last state that could provide the necessary two-thirds majority, and legislator Harry Burns cast the decisive vote for ratification."

"Yes, I read in the paper that he had a letter from his mother in his pocket when he cast his vote."

"He was wearing a red rose in his lapel indicating his opposition to ratification, first voted to table the bill, then when that vote ended in a tie, he switched to support it."

"The letter from his mother was sweet. It said, 'Don't forget to be a good boy and help Mrs. Catt with her "Rats." Is she the one that put the rat in ratification. Ha! No more from mama this time. With lots of love, Mama.' "

"And he was quoted as saying, 'I knew that a mother's advice is always safest for a boy to follow.' "

"I wish my sons paid that kind of attention to what I say," said Lillie with a smile.

By the standards of the Gilded Age, the marriage of J.P. Brown's granddaughter, Florence Brown Byram, and Ruthanna's son, Newell Webster Todd, was quite ordinary, but in one respect it was more significant than all the rest. It brought together the family lines that began in colonial Virginia and New York. In Florence's blood flowed the memories of the Byram, Phillips, Brown and Meeker lines; in N.W., the blood of the Todd, Wade and Hetherington lines mingled. The nuptials took place on May 12, 1926, just a few years before the stock market crash and the Great Depression changed everything. Their ancestors had seen many financial panics, but this was to be the big one. At the wedding, the minister commented on the history of these families: "Florence and Newell are here by the grace of the living, but we should say a prayer for those ancestors who died aborning, killed in wars or who died prematurely. We give thanks to those who gave this young couple their future."

Florence's mother gave the couple a honeymoon at the Elms Resort in Excelsior Springs, Missouri, where the mineral springs were famous for their healing powers. "Of what benefit are the springs to us," Florence asked.

"Well, the sign for Sulpho Saline depicts Three Owls, with the verse, 'We're out all night, 'Til broad daylight, But we drink Sulpho Saline in the morning.' I feel more virile already," said Newell with a Cheshire cat grin.

"Oh, you!"

One night, N.W. thought about where they came from.

"It sounds so obvious, Flo, but we seldom reflect on the fact that if we are here now, our ancestors were alive to witness every major event in American history: wars, building of canals, railroads, the telegraph, all of it."

"Hush, Jimmy. Let's snuggle up and let the saga roll on."

Elms Spa, Excelsior Springs, Missouri

Newell Webster Todd and Florence Byram, 1926

Interior of Pillow House, with Jerome and Mary Pillow on far left, circa 1950. Furniture from a palace in Italia. Wirt Hetherington tall man in center. Ruthanna second from right.

Epilogue

These families had been part of the struggle for independence in the Revolutionary War. They had been part of the robbery of the American Indians and part of their salvation. They participated in the enslavement of Blacks and the fight for their freedom in the Civil War. Some survived floods, cholera and financial panics while others perished. Some achieved great wealth and traveled the world, while others had to accept charity at critical moments to survive and some lives were cut short before realizing their promise.

Yet throughout, they prized education and valued the land, whether for agriculture or mining. They participated in the transition from agriculture to the industrial revolution in the form of two revolutionary technologies, the telegraph and the railroad. They were part of a process of creative destruction by which the work and investments of one generation were made obsolete by the next. They enjoyed their extended families, and also relied on them for business purposes. They helped each other thrive, or at least survive. Most took from and gave to their communities where they lived with a strong sense of place—especially a feeling for the land.

Lucy Phillips Byram, born in civilized Virginia in 1752, expressed a family characteristic best when, during an Indian attack in Kentucky, she refused to cower, saying, "I don't want to be a silly girl." Then on her deathbed in 1836, she summed up another family trait that had taken them through all their trials and triumphs: "All my life I have tried to escape from predictability."